Books by

The Eleventh Ring

The Thirteenth Monk

The Seventh Medallion

Orville Mouse and the Puzzle
of the Clockwork Glowbirds

Orville Mouse and the Puzzle
of the Shattered Abacus

Orville Mouse and the Puzzle
of the Capricious Shadows

Orville Mouse and the Puzzle
of the Last Metaphonium

Orville Mouse and the Puzzle
of the Sagacious Sapling

The Translucent Boy and
the Girl Who Saw Him

The Translucent Boy and
the Cat Who Ran Out of Time

Available online at Amazon and Barnes & Noble

THE
TRANSLUCENT
BOY

and the cat who
ran out of time

by Tom Hoffman

Tom Hoffman
Visit my website at thoffmanak.wordpress.com
Email: OrvilleMouse@gmail.com

Printed in the United States of America

First Printing: 2019
ISBN 978-0-9994634-8-2

With lots of love for
Molly, Alex, Sophie, and Oliver

Table of Contents

For all the amazing
translucent kids out there
who spend their days
listening, reading,
and thinking.

"Loneliness and the feeling
of being unwanted is
the most terrible poverty."

– Mother Theresa

**"Walking with a friend
in the dark is better than
walking alone in the light."**

– Helen Keller

THE
TRANSLUCENT
BOY

and the cat who
ran out of time

Chapter 1

Sent by the Gods

They ran on, the girl shielding her eyes from the pounding torrent of rain, the boy's oversized brass goggles casting an eerie green glow in the nebulous shadows of the primeval forest. Her knuckles were white as she gripped his hand, guiding him through the maze of colossal moss covered trees.

"Slug!"

She leaped over the orange mucous covered aberration, the boy thudding into the squirming horror, torn from her grasp, his startled cry lost in the pummeling roar of the deluge, lost in the heavy dark branches swaying above them.

"I dropped it!"

The girl scooped up the burlap sack, pushing it into the boy's arms, pulling him away from the wriggling nightmare.

"Which way?"

The boy wiped the orange slime from his goggles,

3

peering into his unseen world.

"It's all different, everything has changed!"

"Which way?"

"Maybe to the right? I think I recognize one of the buildings, but I'm not sure."

The girl pulled him forward, rivulets of water streaming down her face. She stopped in her tracks, the boy colliding with her, stumbling.

"We can't leave him behind. We can't."

The boy didn't need to see her face to know she was crying. "We have to. We'll get help, we'll come back and get him. He knows we will."

"How much farther?"

"Maybe a mile? It's all different, I don't know why."

"Hurry." She grabbed his hand, squeezing between two titanic trees, the rough bark scraping her arms.

The boy raised the burlap sack to his face, whispering to it.

"It's okay, I'm here. It's okay."

They dashed on, weaving through formless shadows, spattering raindrops dancing wildly on the massive tree limbs.

"Run around the slugs, I can't jump fast enough."

"Okay."

"Why won't they let us go?"

"I don't know. None of it makes sense."

The boy studied the other world as they raced through the forest.

"I see the old church, it's still there. Go straight, about a half mile. You have the sphere he gave you?"

"I have it."

The boy's insides turned to ice. "I hear them, the chattering!"

"Run!"

They sprinted on through the trees, racing across the spongy carpet of thick moss and spiky seedpods, veering wildly around the slugs and the ghastly sightless frogs.

The girl cried out, "Those big frogs are so scary!"

"No time for that, they're getting closer!"

She could hear it now, the high pitched chattering, the song of the chase, the rattle of armor.

"Oh, no. No, no, no!"

"We're almost there! I can see it, another hundred yards!

They dashed onward, the boy pulling the coarse burlap sack close to him. The girl yanked a blue sphere from her coat pocket, gripping it tightly. She glanced behind them, resisting her impulse to scream, not wanting to distract the boy. There were eight of them, armed with deadly spears and arrows.

"Throw it when I tell you!"

The girl twisted the top of the blue sphere, its low vibrating hum drowned out by the roar of the relentless rain. "Ready!"

Ten seconds later the boy cried out, "Now! Throw it now! I see the vortex!"

The girl hurled the sphere just as the dart hit her neck. She grabbed at the feathered projectile, trying to pull it out, but her fingers were already numb, her arms clumsy.

The boy ripped off his glowing goggles, his eyes on the great rippling blue green disc in front of them, black clouds swirling about within it, tiny blue sparks shooting out from the periphery. He turned when he heard the girl's cry, watching in horror as she tumbled to the mossy forest floor with a ragged moan. He called out to her, barely noticing the dart in his neck, his legs suddenly weak, his vision blurry. The burlap sack slipped from his grasp, its contents spilling out onto the soft bed of moss. With a blur of motion it streaked forward, leaping into the vaporous dark roiling disk.

"No! No! Too soon, we still have to set the..." The boy stumbled drunkenly toward the girl, calling her name. He sank slowly to the ground, rolling over like a sinking ship, the rain spattering against his face. He managed to turn his head, watching in disbelief as the swirling black disc and its circle of flashing blue sparks faded to nothingness.

His eyelids drooped, then closed, his body still.

The creatures approached, silent now, the chase over. The tall one prodded the boy with the butt of its spear, then kneeled reverently in the thick moss, studying the two sleeping children with its bright red eyes, gently resting a clawed hand on the boy's shoulder.

"You cannot leave this world, little ones. You are the first of the Chosen Ones, sent by the gods to destroy the Fortress of Rain."

Chapter 2

The Lady in Black

Silas Ward closed his eyes, taking some slight comfort in the rhythmic rocking and swaying of the old school bus. Last night had been bad, worse than most. He'd been alone, his parents out to dinner and a movie. He was on the couch watching a show when he saw her, tried to hide under a blanket, terrified she would turn and look at him, terrified she would speak his name.

Peals of shrieking laughter pulled him back to the moment, back to the raucous rocking school bus. He turned, looking behind him. The tall kid in the purple shirt was pelting his friends with grapes, some of them using their notebooks as shields, batting at them, others shrieking, trying to dodge the splattering wet projectiles.

The bus driver hollered for them to stop. That was part of the fun. A grape hit the window behind Silas with a squishy splat.

Silas spotted Brandon Crouch sitting across the aisle three rows down, currently pulling the shoe off a boy, hurling it to the rear of the bus. A dreadful sick feeling

7

filled Silas as he studied the dark anger on Crouch's face, searching for clues, something to explain how one person could be so cruel. Crouch turned unexpectedly, causing Silas to instantly avert his eyes, his gaze suddenly on the wild grape throwing free-for-all. Crouch scowled.

"What are you looking at, warthog?"

Silas swiveled back around in his seat, his head down.

Crouch hollered, "You need another lesson, wart??"

Silas shook his head, shivering when he heard Crouch's high pitched laugh. "That's what I thought. See you in class, warthog." His laugh was violent and purposeful, two of his friends joining in.

Silas did not turn around again, hugging his back-pack close to him, darting off the bus the moment it squealed to a jarring halt in the school parking lot. He scurried out, running behind the bus, waiting for Crouch and his friends to go inside. The rhythmic coughing of a venerable diesel engine reached his ears. Bus 83 was pulling into the parking lot. Silas squinted through the early morning fog, searching its grimy mud spattered windows, shivering when he saw it. It was always there, always on Bus 83.

He grabbed his pack and ran into the school, keeping his head down as he darted to his locker, groaning silently at the scrawled note taped to his locker door.

BEWARE OF THE WARTHOG!!

He tossed it into his locker with the others, then grabbed his books, hurrying down the hallway.

"Oh, no." Crouch and his two friends were heading his way. Darting over to the lockers, he turned his back, pretending to be reading a book. Something slammed violently into his shoulder, knocking him against the locker, his books tumbling to the floor.

"Watch where you're going, warthog."

"Sorry." Silas had no idea why he said that. He felt sick.

Crouch laughed, high fiving his friends.

Twenty minutes later Silas was in English class. He was glad his last name was at the end of the alphabet, because it meant he sat in the back of the class. They were reading *The Hound of the Baskervilles*, a Sherlock Holmes story written by Sir Arthur Conan Doyle. Silas had read *The Complete Sherlock Holmes* when he was in the sixth grade. He'd read *The Hound of the Baskervilles* three times. He sighed, his thoughts drifting back to the terrifying events of the previous night.

"It's just dinner and a movie. We'll be back by ten-thirty at the latest. There's plenty of food in the fridge, so make whatever you want. Do you have homework?"

"It's all done, I finished it in class."

"Then snuggle up on the couch with a blanket and watch a show. How was school today?"

"It was okay, same old stuff."

"Be good. Don't go anywhere." His dad laughed, but his eyes did not.

"I won't, I promise."

9

When the front door closed, Silas locked it securely, using the bolt and the chain. He flopped down on the couch, flipping on the TV, casting an anxious glance at the stairs leading to the second floor. Maybe it wouldn't happen, maybe it was over. Maybe he'd be normal, just another kid watching TV at home while his parents were out. Maybe.

He was lost in a movie, a caped superhero hurling cars at a titanic rampaging alien gorilla, when the dark motion caught his eye.

"Oh no. Please, no."

He sank down into the couch, trying to make himself invisible, trying to disappear, pulling the blanket up to his eyes, peering up at the stairs.

The woman wore an old fashioned long sleeved black lace dress and black mourning veil. She stepped slowly, purposefully, cautiously down the stairs. Her eyes were dark, sad. In one hand she held a rusty shovel, in the other a wooden box.

The fear Silas felt for Brandon Crouch was a soft summer shower compared to the tempest of terror now raging within him. He was afraid his body would melt, time slowing to an agonizing crawl, the Lady in Black taking a lifetime to descend from the darkness.

When she stepped off the final stair she paused, as she always did, then turned slowly, half walking, half floating down the hallway, her spectral shovel dragging silently behind her. Silas pulled the blanket over his eyes, unable to breathe, terrified she would turn and look at him, terrified her eyes would meet his. This had never happened, but each time he saw her she became more real. When he was very small she had been a pale blue shadow, a barely visible spectral mist. When he was older he gathered up enough courage to tell his parents about her, but they told him there was no such thing as ghosts. It was his imagination, nothing more. Try not to think about it. Even as a child he didn't think his imagination would disguise itself as a woman dressed in black dragging a rusty shovel behind her.

He lowered the blanket, watching the Lady in Black pass through the locked door into the basement. He let out a long, slow breath. She was gone for now. He did not want to know why she was dragging a shovel into the cellar. He did not want to know what she kept in the wooden box.

Chapter 3

The Forest

Odo had the sheet pulled over his head, his small flashlight illuminating the dog-eared pages of *The Hound of the Baskervilles.*

"It came with the wind through the silence of the night, a long, deep mutter, then a rising howl, and then the sad moan in which it died away. Again and again it sounded, the whole air throbbing with it, strident, wild and menacing."

"Whoa, that is one scary supernatural hound. The moorlands of Devonshire are so dark and creepy. I like how Sherlock Holmes uses observation and logic to solve mysteries. Sephie's good at that. His sidekick Dr. Watson is funny. I wonder if Sephie thinks she's the hero and I'm the sidekick? I think we're both heroes, like Superman and Wonder Woman, but with different powers. Being translucent isn't as cool as super strength or super speed, but it does let me shift to other dimensions. Sephie's lucky to be a Fortisian, she can do all kinds of stuff like creating objects with her mind and reading people's brainwaves like an encephalogram. I like our superhero names, Translucent Boy and Encephalo Girl."

Odo froze when he heard his bedroom door creak open.

"Lights out! No flashlights, no reading. Early to bed and early to rise. Everyone knows that."

"Okay, Dad."

Odo rolled his eyes, shutting off his flashlight, setting the book on his bedside table. His bedroom door thumped shut.

"That crazy black hound gives me the shivers. I'm glad I don't live in a spooky mansion in the middle of the foggy moors of Devonshire."

An hour later he woke with a start, sitting up in his bed. "Bad dream. So bad. The black hound was chasing me. Sephie was there, wearing a red cape. Wait, does that mean she's the superhero and I'm the–"

Odo never finished that particular thought, his eyes frozen on something that should not be.

"Why are there giant translucent trees in my bedroom? And why am I hearing rain?"

Odo's eyes locked onto the mysterious moss covered trees.

"I can see through them to the other side of my room. This is definitely something new. Pretty sure I would remember a ghost forest in my bedroom. It's not exactly scary, just extremely weird. And what's with that rain? Maybe it's raining outside."

He pressed his hand against the bedroom wall, the area around it becoming translucent, a trick he had learned when he was little. He peered through the wall, studying the streetlights outside. It was not raining, the ground was dry.

"This is a good mystery. What would Holmes do? He'd probably say, '*Come, Watson, the game is afoot!*' and they'd search for clues. That's what I should do, search for clues."

Odo hopped out of bed, stepping toward one of the ghostly trees. He reached out to touch its coarse trunk, his hand passing through it.

"Spectral trees. Interesting."

He walked through the tree, studying the ghostly forest floor, his eyes coming to rest on a squirming mucous covered creature crawling across the moss.

"Yuck. Wait, maybe I'm still asleep, dreaming there's a ghost forest and a giant slug in my room. I'll walk around the house and see if it looks real. This is probably a dream. That would make more sense." He flicked on his bedroom light.

"ODO! No reading!"

"And... not a dream."

Odo shut off the light and climbed back into bed, closing his eyes. An hour later he opened them again. The ghost forest was gone, the rain had stopped.

The following morning he woke with a grin. It was Saturday, and that meant he was going to the movies with Sephie. It was his week to choose, and he'd picked a good one.

"She's going to love it, I know she will."

He threw on his clothes and dashed downstairs, announcing himself loudly as he approached the kitchen. Two days ago he had walked in on his parents while they were having an argument. They hadn't seen him, even when he sat down at the kitchen table and waved to them. When they did finally notice him, his dad accused him of sneaking around and listening to other people's private conversations.

"It's not polite to eavesdrop. I can't believe you don't know that. Everyone knows that."

Petunia shushed him. "It's not his fault, Albert, he's... *translucent*." She had whispered the word. Whispered it, as though she didn't want the neighbors to hear, as though Odo didn't already know he was translucent.

Odo did not want that to happen again. He called out, "Good morning, everyone! Odo Whitley is in the house."

Albert gave him an irritated look.

"What's wrong with you? Are you sick? Why are you yelling?"

"I just wanted you to know I was here."

"Oh, that." Albert glanced over at Petunia, raising his eyebrows.

Petunia gave her best reassuring smile. "We weren't fighting, Odo, just having a tiny little disagreement. One day you'll be married and you'll have disagreements too. It's just part of marriage."

"Married to his little orange haired girlfriend." Albert grinned at Odo.

"Sephie is not my girlfriend. She's a friend who's a girl."

Albert snorted. "That's what I used to tell my parents about your mom."

"Really? Well, anyway... she's not my girlfriend. We're just friends and we're going to the movies today."

"When I was growing up they called that going on a date with your girlfriend."

Petunia set a plate of toast, bacon, and eggs in front of Odo. "Eat your breakfast. If you say Sephie is just your friend, then she's just your friend, and we'll leave it at that."

"Thanks, Mom."

Albert opened his mouth, stopping when he saw the look on Petunia's face. "Right. Well, I'm off to work, lots to do on the new Silver Chocko CrunchCakes campaign. The photographer is out of town, so I'm handling all the photography. It's a big responsibility. That's what happens when they make you a permanent supervisor, you have to work evenings and weekends."

Three hours later Odo was on his way to Sephie's house, strolling down Asper Street, his face wrapped in a grin.

"This is going to be so much fun. I can't wait to see the movie."

Thoughts of Sephie swirled about in his mind. She

was a lot of firsts in his life; the first friend he'd ever had, the first girl to see him, and the first person to pass him a note in school, a cryptic note which had taken them to the worlds of Plindor and Atroxia by way Girard Station, an interstellar transition gateway. That was another first, the first time Odo had seen alien beings.

"There's the old church, and there's Expergo Street. It's funny that Sephie lives on the same street as Wikerus Praevian. She always says there are no coincidences."

Odo turned down Expergo, stopping abruptly when he caught a flash of motion in his peripheral vision. Something blue had shot across the alleyway.

"Whoa, that was weird. It was going really fast, and definitely too big to be a bird."

He walked down the alley, glancing curiously behind the old wooden buildings, searching for anything which might explain what he had seen.

"Maybe it was sunlight reflecting off a car's windshield."

As he turned to leave, an unexpected and overwhelming sense of dread rolled through him.

"Something's not right, something weird is going on, I can feel it. First there was the ghost forest in my room, and now that blue thing, whatever it was. It's not just my imagination."

He walked twenty feet, stopped, turned around and headed back to the alley. When he peered around the corner he saw it again, a glowing blue object flashing across the alley behind the same two buildings.

"This is definitely not normal. Sephie needs to see this. We're coming back here as soon as the movie is over."

Chapter 4

Popcorn

Odo and Sephie strolled along Expergo Street toward the theatre, basking in the warm afternoon sun.

"Doesn't it sound like an amazing movie? Aren't you glad I picked it?"

"It's about shrieking ghosts who invade our world?"

"Exactly, that's why it's called *Invasion of the Shrieking Ghosts.* I watched the trailer; it's about a brilliant scientist who warns everyone the ghosts are going to invade, but no one believes him. They all think he's a crackpot. That's when the ghosts invade our world, blasting everyone to pieces with their death rays." Odo grinned, rubbing his hands together.

Sephie studied his face. "Did they say what kind of scientist he is, Odo Whitley? If he had impeccable credentials, maybe a doctorate degree in quantum theory relating to paranormal phenomena, people would have listened to him."

"The trailer just said he was a brash young scientist.

Why does that even matter?"

Sephie sighed. "Forget his credentials, let's talk about the ghosts. Their death ray devices are most likely heavy particle beam projectors similar to the Model 14A used during the Anarkkian wars, and we both know it would be impossible for a ghost to carry a particle beam projector because ghosts are beings of conscious energy, lacking physical form. They can't physically interact with the world."

"I think they shoot the death rays out of their eyes."

"That's ridiculous, Odo Whitley. You need to adjust your brain cells, start thinking logically. This is just made up comic book science. Shooting death rays from their eyes? Really?"

"Sephie, the movie isn't about real science, it's about having fun watching ghosts scare everyone and blow stuff up with death rays."

"Cyra said that by law, all the holo shows on Fortisia have to be founded in established scientific principles. Your invading ghosts might be entertaining, but they leave a lot of unanswered questions. For one, why are the ghosts invading our world? What do we have that an army of ghosts would want? They have no use for physical objects, so they're not after our money or our food. And how could a ghost shriek? It would have to create sound waves, which is technically feasible, but highly unlikely. It's possible they could stimulate your auditory nerve so your brain would think it was hearing a sound, but no one else would be able to hear it."

Odo groaned, deciding to steer the conversation in a

different direction. "I saw something really weird on the way here. Something mysterious, a glowing blue object that flashed across the alley between two buildings. I saw it twice. And last night when I woke up there was a ghost forest in my bedroom. I heard rain, but it wasn't raining out."

"This is what I'm talking about, Odo Whitley, real science, not phony made up shrieking ghost comic book science. We should go investigate your glowing blue object. It could be important."

"Can we wait until after the movie?"

"Of course, but while you're watching your shrieking ghost invaders, I'm going to be thinking about the translucent forest in your room. It sounds like you were looking into a parallel dimension. When I think about it, that blue thing could be an alien creature who exists outside of time."

"I'm going to get popcorn."

An hour later Odo and Sephie were huddled together in the movie theatre sharing a tub of popcorn. Sephie's eyes were riveted to the flickering screen.

"Those ghosts are scary, Odo Whitley. I didn't think they'd be this scary. Those people should have listened to the brash young scientist's warning."

"This popcorn is really good. Next time we're at Girard Station I'm going to have the Cerebral Feedback Synthesizer make some."

"Quiet, I'm trying to watch the movie. Oh, no, she shouldn't open that door, I know there's a ghost in there. I know it. What is she thinking?"

Sephie let out a shriek when the ghost popped out, its horrifying face filling the screen.

Odo smiled. Best movie ever.

When the dreaded army of ghost invaders had been soundly defeated, sent back to their own dimension, Odo and Sephie stood up, heading for the exit as the credits rolled.

"What did you think?"

"It was entertaining, even though the science was nonsensical. Ghosts can't pick up furniture and throw it at people. It showed them picking up chairs with their hands."

"You screamed when the ghost popped out of the closet."

Sephie ignored Odo's pointed observation. "Tell me about the glowing blue object. Where did you see it? I'm getting a strange feeling from my deeper self. I think the blue object is connected to your ghost forest. We'll have to be careful."

"Even though you're a brash young scientist, I will heed your warning."

"Do you remember what the brash young scientist did to the ghost after it threw the chair at him?"

Odo gave her a sideways glance. "I saw it about a block down from Asper Street."

"Let's go, Odo Whitley. It's time for Translucent Boy and Encephalo Girl to save the universe."

"Sounds like fun."

The pair of friends headed down Expergo Street, Sephie admitting that she had enjoyed the ghost movie.

"It was fun, Odo Whitley, even if it wasn't scientifically accurate. It made me want to go on another adventure with you."

"That's what I was just thinking, a wild adventure to some weird and cool dimension. How fun would that be? Here we are. It was down that alley between the gray building and the blue one. When I looked around the corner, I saw something blue flash across the alley."

"Interesting."

The pair of friends crept forward.

Odo whispered, "Okay, when I say three we both look."

"Wait here." Sephie stepped around the corner, catching a quick glimpse of the mysterious blue object flashing across the alley.

"I saw it, Odo Whitley. Now you look. I think I know what's happening."

Odo peered around the corner and the object flashed past again. "How many of those things are there?"

"There's only one, but it's out of time."

"Out of time? What does that mean?"

"It means no matter where we are in the time stream, we can see it."

"I have no idea what that means."

"Imagine a giant building with a thousand windows. If something is outside the building, you can see it through any of the windows. We're looking through our little window of time at an object that's out of time, so we can see it through all the little windows of time, just like the people in the giant building."

23

"Oh, that sort of makes sense, but why does it only fly past when we look around the corner?"

"It's complicated, but Fortisian scientists have known for centuries that by observing the world, we're changing it. Our looking at it transforms it from an infinite probability to a solid reality."

"I read something about that in a physics book, but I didn't quite understand it."

"Cyra taught me all about it. It's not spooky, just science. Imagine I have a closed box, but I won't tell you what's inside it. For you, the box could have anything in it; a spoon, an apple, a little mouse, or a gold coin. It could be a million different things, but once you open the box and look inside, you turn that infinite possibility into a solid reality, you know exactly what's in the box. It becomes real, part of your world."

"That's a weird way to look at it, but it does explain why we see it every time we look around the corner. What do you think it is?"

"I know how we can find out, but it could be dangerous. More dangerous than an army of shrieking ghosts throwing chairs at us and blasting us with death rays."

"I will ignore your dire warning, brash young Sephie Crumb. Let's do it. What's your plan?"

"It's simple. We walk down the alley with our eyes closed, so we're not observing it, so it's still a probability. When we're close to where it crosses, we open our eyes and watch it become a reality. We'll be close enough to see exactly what it is. Whatever you do, don't let it hit you, Odo Whitley. That could be very dangerous."

"I won't. Let's go."

The two friends stepped back around the corner.

"Ready?"

"I was born ready."

"Never say that again, Odo Whitley."

"Why not? The more I say it, the funnier it gets."

"Let's compromise. You can say it, but not every time I ask if you're ready."

"How often can I say it, exactly?"

"How about every fourth time I ask? Would that be acceptable?"

"It's a deal, every fourth time. Ready?"

"I was born ready, Odo Whitley."

"Sephie, that's my line, we can't both say it. We each have to have our own line. You have to pick something else to say."

"Done. I know what I'm going to say."

"Hey, Sephie, it's time to find out what that blue thing is. Are you ready?"

"Let's rock and roll."

Odo blinked. "That's way cooler than my line."

Sephie laughed. "Close your eyes."

Sephie and Odo felt their way around the corner of the building.

"Okay, it's about thirty feet away, so if we take nine giant steps we should be close to where it crosses the alley."

Odo counted their steps out loud. Everything was

going according to plan until the ninth step, when Odo's foot landed in a pothole and he tumbled forward. Unfortunately, he also made the critical mistake of opening his eyes as he was falling, instantly converting the streaking blue object from a probability into a reality. He gave a piercing shriek when the blue form collided with him, its claws sinking into his chest.

Chapter 5

Watson

Odo flailed wildly at the ghostly blue creature, trying to push it away.

"Get it off me! It has claws!"

"It's a cat, Odo Whitley."

Odo stopped, eyeing the creature standing on his chest. "You're right, it is a cat, a ghost cat. Wait, are you thinking what I'm thinking? *Invasion of the Shrieking Ghost Cats*?"

Sephie ignored Odo's hilarious comment.

Odo jumped to his feet, the ghostly blue feline sauntering around him, rubbing against his legs. It sat down and began licking its paw. Odo reached down, gently rubbing its head.

The cat purred softly.

"I can touch it. It's not a ghost, it's translucent. How weird is that?"

"It's not weird at all, Odo Whitley. The cat was a probability while it was running out of time, but when it collided with you, it matched itself to your physical form, becoming a reality, a translucent cat."

"It's kind of cute. Where do you think it came from?"

Sephie shook her head. "That's the big scrumbly mystery, but I have a feeling it has something to do with your ghost forest. We should talk to Wikerus Praevian."

"I think the cat likes me. He keeps rubbing against my leg."

"He's marking you with its scent, letting other cats know you're part of its territory."

"Eww. He's still cute though. I always wanted a pet, but my parents wouldn't let me get one. This is perfect, they won't see him. A translucent cat for a translucent boy."

"Are you sure that's a good idea?"

"Are you kidding? It's the best idea ever. He can be my sidekick. He'll need a name though."

"How about Sylvester? Or Garfield?"

"I'm not naming my sidekick after a cartoon, but you did give me a good idea. I'm going to call him Watson, after Sherlock Holmes' sidekick."

"We just read *The Hound of the Baskervilles* in English class."

"We read it too. So spooky. I had a nightmare the hound was chasing me. That's when I woke up and saw the ghost forest."

Sephie's eyes narrowed.

Odo frowned. "What? Why are you looking at me

like that?"

"I think we should talk to Wikerus Praevian."

"Okay."

Odo walked down the alleyway, his eyes on Watson.

"He's following me. I think he likes me, Sephie."

Sephie studied Odo's brain waves, a smile appearing on her face.

"I think you like him too, Odo Whitley."

With their newfound friend Watson trailing behind them, they headed to the home of Wikerus Praevian, their boss and the owner of the Serendipity Salvage Company. Wikerus was an orange haired Fortisian who had arrived on Earth right after Sephie was born, formshifting himself into the grandfatherly figure Odo had once called 'the man in the gray hat'.

"There it is, his spooky old Victorian mansion."

"I remember when you discovered Wikerus was the man in the gray hat."

"I was so surprised. I thought he was loopy at first, telling us that translucents could shift to other dimensions using waystones."

"I had the best time on Plindor, especially sailing across the desert with those pirates. That was so much fun."

"Have you heard anything from Cyra?"

"She's sent me a few thought clouds. She made it safely back to Fortisia and they shut down the spectral planetary moat. She said she's busy working on her powers, training with a mentor. She's so amazing."

"Really amazing. She was so scary when she

formshifted into the Magician. Even when I knew it was her she still scared me."

They headed up the steps, the door swinging open as Odo raised his hand to knock, a pleasant looking older woman wearing an ill fitting gray dress smiling at them.

"Hi, Mrs. Preke. We're here to see Wikerus. We had a few questions for him. I woke up in the night and saw a ghost forest in my room."

"Were you wearing your work ring?"

"No, but I was having a nightmare that a giant hound was chasing me through a bog."

"Wonderful. That reminds me, I have your monthly retainer and paycheck at the Nox Avenue office."

"Thanks, I'll stop by tomorrow."

"Are you aware there is a translucent cat standing behind you?"

"His name is Watson. We just met him."

Mrs. Preke nodded to the cat.

"Good afternoon, Watson. It is a great pleasure to meet you. Is this your first time on Earth?"

Watson let out a dreadful hiss, arching his back, baring his teeth.

Mrs. Preke took a step back. "Oh dear, it's a real cat, not a formshifter. I'm afraid cats are not very fond of me. I believe they can sense I am a Plindorian, something which has a less than desirable effect on them.

"Sorry." Odo was remembering how surprised he was when Mrs. Preke had formshifted back to her true form, an enormous yellow octopus from Plindor. He scooped up Watson, stroking his fur.

"It's okay, little one, it's just Mrs. Preke. She won't hurt you."

Watson rested his head on Odo's shoulder, purring softly.

Odo and Sephie turned when they heard Wikerus Praevian's voice coming from the hallway.

"Odo and Sephie, what a wonderful surprise. Mrs. Preke said you had questions about a rather intriguing ghost forest in Odo's bedroom?"

"We just got here, how did you–" Odo turned to Mrs. Preke, but she was gone.

Sephie nudged Odo. "I think we still have a lot to learn about Mrs. Preke."

Wikerus motioned for them to follow him. "This is not the first time I've encountered such visions. I believe I shall be able to shed some light on your mysterious ghost forest."

"That would be great. It wasn't scary, just kind of weird. There was a big orange slug, though."

Odo and Sephie took a seat on an exquisitely em-broidered blue couch, Wikerus sliding into his comfort-able stuffed armchair. He drummed his fingers slowly, studying Watson with some curiosity.

"A translucent cat named Watson."

"Named after Sherlock Holmes' sidekick."

"Of course. The game is afoot. Tell me about your ghost forest."

"It started with a nightmare about a scary supernatu-ral hound chasing me. When I woke up I saw the ghost forest in my room. The trees were huge and went up through the ceiling, and it was raining really hard. When I tried to touch one of the trees my hand went right through it. I could hear the rain. I checked to make sure it wasn't raining outside."

"Where did you find the cat?"

Odo told Wikerus the story of how they had found Watson, and Sephie's theory that he had been traveling outside of time.

"Describe his collar."

"I don't know if he has one, his fur is really long. I called him Watson because he's my sidekick."

Wikerus smile politely. "His collar?"

Odo felt for a collar. "You're right, he does have one. It's made out of leather and has a design carved into it."

Odo examined the collar. "Four leaf clovers, it has a row of four leaf clovers on it."

"And what does that tell you?"

"Um…Watson is from Earth?"

"Very good. The concept of a four leaf clover as a conveyor of good fortune is a creation unique to this world."

"Why would a cat from our world be traveling outside of time?"

"A mystery for the moment. Your ghost forest is less of a mystery, however. Are you familiar with a practice known as the Traveling Eye?"

Sephie nodded. "Cyra and I used it when we healed Sensus on Atroxia. Our center of awareness, our consciousness, traveled outside our physical body."

Wikerus nodded his agreement. "Quite so, but leaving your body and viewing the world around you is just one small aspect of the Traveling Eye. Odo unwittingly used the Traveling Eye to view a parallel world, his ghost forest."

"That place really exists? How could I visit another dimension without a waystone to take me there?"

"You cannot travel physically to another dimension without a waystone, but you can use the Traveling Eye to view the dimension. With practice, you would be able to view your ghost forest almost as though you were there. It would look solid, but of course you would not be able to physically interact with that world."

"You're saying I could lie in bed and fly around other dimensions?"

"In time, and with practice, that will indeed be possible. What I don't know is why you were spontaneously viewing this particular world, this particular forest. I can assure you it was not accidental, however. The forest you saw holds some deep significance for you."

"Do you think it's connected to Watson?"

"Of course, a connection which will become clear as events unfold. Make sure you wear your work ring, the ring Mrs. Preke gave you when you were hired by Serendipity Salvage."

"How does the ring work exactly? It caused a lot of weird coincidences."

"The ring increases the power of attraction between the unseen connections of our world. As an example, you would have eventually become friends with Sephie, but your work ring sped up the process by slightly altering events, drawing you together sooner."

"It made that scary dog appear so I'd cross the street and meet Sephie?"

"Precisely."

"But how does it work exactly? How does the ring alter events?"

"I'm afraid I have no answer for you. It is an unfathomably ancient technology from the time of the Primorians, the first beings to inhabit our universe. We don't understand how the rings work, only that they do."

"What should we do now?"

"I will tell you it was no accident that you found Watson, or that Watson found you. He holds a deep and profound secret, one which you must discover on your own. Come back when you have found it. The game is afoot, my young friends."

Chapter 6

Bus 83

Odo woke the following morning to find Watson stretched out across his legs, giving a complaining meow when Odo tried to move.

"You're so funny. I like having a cat." Odo slipped out of bed, doing his best not to disturb Watson. He pulled on his clothes and headed downstairs. His mom was at the kitchen table drinking her morning coffee.

"Odo Whitley is in the house!"

"Good heavens, Odo, you don't need to holler that every time you walk into the kitchen."

"Where's Dad?"

"At work. He's very busy with the new ad campaign. He has a lot more responsibility now that he's a permanent supervisor. He's been bringing work home almost every night."

"Does he like the new job? It sounds like he has a lot to do."

"He does like it. He's in a much better mood these

35

days. It makes him feel good to have an important job."

"I'm glad he likes it. I'll make my own breakfast."

Odo stepped over to the counter, humming as he dropped two slices of bread into the toaster. He had just poured a glass of orange juice when he glanced up to see Watson strolling across the kitchen table. "Oh no, this is bad. Mom can't know about Watson. I have to do something."

He attempted to sound casual. "Could you make me some pancakes?"

Petunia set her coffee down. "I thought you were making your own breakfast? You want toast and pancakes? You must be hungry."

Odo could feel his heart pounding. Watson was next to Petunia's coffee cup, tapping it gently with one paw. He knew enough about cats to know they loved to knock things off tables. "Right, I'm really–"

Before Odo could finish his sentence, Watson swatted Petunia's coffee cup, batting it off the table in front of her startled eyes, the cup smashing into a thousand pieces, coffee spattering onto the wall. Watson turned and ran, leaping off the table and dashing out of the room.

Petunia gaped at the shattered coffee cup, pressing her hand to her chest.

"It's Daddy!"

"What?" Odo had no idea what Petunia was talking about.

She turned to him, her eyes wide.

"You saw it, didn't you? The cup flew off the table

by itself?"

"Um, it was kind of close to the edge. Maybe it just sort of fell off?"

"It was Daddy. He's back, watching over me. He was the one who sent me the perfume that made you translucent. He knew I was pregnant, he knew I loved peach scented perfume."

"But your dad is… um… he died before I was born?"

"Yes, that's the miracle, he's watching over me from the other side, from the great beyond."

Odo knew two things that Petunia did not. He knew it had been Wikerus Praevian and Mrs. Preke who sent the tainted perfume that caused Odo to be born translucent, and he knew that Watson had knocked the coffee cup off the table.

Petunia stood up, her eyes bright. "Daddy wants me to stop drinking coffee. That's the message he's sending me. He wants me to take better care of myself. I'm going to go for a walk every day and make your dad go with me. We're going to get healthy. No more sitting on the couch and eating crackers. It's a sign."

Odo thought for a moment, then said, "I think your dad really is watching over you from the other side. I've read about stuff like that."

"It's a miracle, that's what it is. Albert won't believe it, but I don't care. I know it's true. Sometimes I feel like Daddy is standing right next to me."

Odo gave his mom a hug. "He probably is. I have to go, the bus is here."

He ran to the front door, grabbing his coat and backpack, dashing outside just as the rattling orange bus squealed to a halt in front of their house. Odo pounded on the door, hollering to the driver.

"I'm here!"

The white haired bus driver squinted through the grimy glass. The door squealed open.

"Sorry, kid, didn't see you there."

As was his routine, Odo hopped onto the bus and headed down the aisle, grabbing an overhead rail at the back. No one ever noticed him, no one called out his name, no one saved him a seat. He had told Sephie that being translucent was like being a tree that people walk past while they're reading a book, barely noticed and instantly forgotten. His life had been an achingly lonely one until he met Sephie.

He studied the other kids on the bus, watching them call out to each other, hollering, laughing, making faces. He saw one boy who was reading, lost in his book.

"I used to sit and read on the bus until Bruno Leski sat on me. That was the last time I ever did that."

The claws dug into Odo's neck, his painful yelp drowned out by the raucous shouting of the students. He whipped around but saw nothing, no clawed alien creature behind him. It only took him a moment to realize the culprit was Watson, a surprise stowaway in his backpack.

Odo slipped off his pack, smiling at the paw waving out from under the flap.

"What are you doing in there, you crazy cat? You'd better not get me into trouble at school."

He opened the flap and Watson leaped out, hopping onto his lap, Odo gently scratching the top of his head. "You're in trouble, mister. Big, big trouble." Watson curled up, licking his fur.

Ten minutes later the bus squealed to a halt in the school parking lot, the doors rattling open. Odo waited until everyone had gotten off, then exited the bus, listening to the familiar chugging of the ancient diesel engine. He set Watson gently back into his pack. "Hey, Watson, how was your first ride on old Bus 83?"

Chapter 7

Leave Me Alone

Odo strolled down the empty hallway to science class, Watson curled up in his backpack. Odo's daily routine was unique, but one born of necessity. As a result of numerous painful collisions with unseeing students in crowded corridors, he had been forced to wait until everyone else was seated in their next class before stepping into the hallway. He was a few minutes late to every class, but the teachers never noticed, never looked up when he walked in and took his seat. He was frosted glass, eyes looking through him, never at him.

Science was Odo's fourth class of the day, with Mr. Gnaritas. It was his favorite class, partly because he liked science, but mostly because he sat next to Sephie. It was here that she had passed him his first note.

Sephie gave him a quick wave and a smile when she saw him step into the room. Her parents had died when she was a baby, murdered by Stirpians. Her mother was human, her father Fortisian, born of a race holding remarkable powers. The source of the Fortisians' astonishing abilities was something unique to their world which they called the Glow, sometimes a barely visible blue dust in the atmosphere, sometimes pure energy, the life force found within all living things. The Glow was responsible for the startling evolution of their remarkable powers.

One of Sephie's powers was the ability to see the electromagnetic energy fields that surround all living creatures. She had also spent a great deal of time studying brain mapping, learning which areas of the brain are active when people experience specific thoughts or emotions. She could tell a great deal about someone by watching their brainwaves. She couldn't read their specific thoughts, but she could read their emotions.

She studied Odo's brainwaves as he slid into his chair. He was excited about something. She laughed when she noticed a second set of brainwaves in his backpack. She scrawled a quick note and passed it to him.

"Is Watson hiding in your backpack??"

Odo nodded, grinning.

Sephie sent another note.

"Don't let him get loose. No pets allowed in school, you could get in trouble."

"He's translucent, no one can see him."

"What book are you reading today?"

Odo was about to send his answer when he heard a low whisper coming from behind Sephie. It was

Brandon Crouch.

"Everyone hates your freaky orange hair, Creepy Crumb."

Odo watched a wave of anger wash over Sephie's face, vanishing as quickly as it had come. It had taken a long time, but with the help of Odo and their Fortisian friend Cyra, Sephie had come to accept herself for what she was, a Fortisian with flaming orange hair and astonishing powers. A year ago, being called Creepy Crumb would have wounded her deeply, but those days were over. Now she was Encephalo Girl, a superhero.

She smiled, turning to face Crouch.

"Sorry, I was reading, did you say something?"

Brandon Crouch was a bully and a coward, and as such, was completely unnerved by the look on Sephie's face. There was not the slightest inkling of fear, her piercing green eyes staring directly into his. She was daring him to say something. He shifted uncomfortably in his seat.

"Mind your own business, I got work to do."

Sephie turned around, smiling at Odo. She tossed him a note. "I didn't even have to alter his thoughts. He won't bother me again."

Odo gave a thumbs up to Sephie. If Crouch knew the truth about her powers he would run screaming from the room. Odo pulled a book from his backpack, trying not to disturb Watson.

Every morning he chose a book from his library at home to read during his classes. Because Odo was never called on by his teachers, he had as much time as he needed to read as many books as he wished. The unintended consequence of his voracious reading was that Odo's knowledge in most areas far surpassed what was being taught in his classes. Most of his science books were at college or graduate school levels. He also had an undeniable fondness for early visionary writers such as H.G. Wells, Jules Verne, and Sir Arthur Conan Doyle.

Sephie watched him pull a tattered old book from his pack. He gave a toothy grin when he showed her the title, *The Invisible Man* by H.G. Wells. She laughed, giving him a thumbs up sign.

When the bell rang he waved goodbye to Sephie, waiting until the hallway was empty before exiting the room.

As he walked down the hall to his next class he spotted two students, one with his hand on the other boy's neck, pushing him against the lockers. Odo recognized them both.

"It's Brandon Crouch and Silas Ward. What is wrong with Crouch? Why does he pick on kids like Silas?"

Silas reached into his pocket and took out some money, giving it to Crouch. Crouch stuffed it into his pocket, giving Silas a violent shove into the lockers. He turned and left, leaving Silas standing alone.

Odo decided to check on him, make sure he hadn't been hurt. As he stepped toward him, Watson began thrashing wildly inside his backpack. Odo panicked, pulling the flap open.

"What's wrong? Are you okay?"

Watson leaped out, streaking down the hallway, coming to a stop in front of Silas.

Silas backed away, his eyes wide.

Odo stopped. "He can see Watson. How is that possible?"

Silas was shaking, his eyes on the cat. "Go away."

Odo ran toward him, calling out, "Silas!"

Silas turned at the sound of Odo's voice. He took two steps backwards, then covered his eyes with his hands, his voice a strangled whisper. "Go away, go away. Leave me alone. You're not real." He turned, wrapping his arms around himself, pressing against the lockers.

Odo had no idea what to say or do.

"Silas?"

"Please. Leave me alone. You're not real."

Odo grabbed Watson and darted down the hallway. He spent most of the day trying to understand what had happened. How could Silas see him, and what had scared him so badly? After school he told Sephie about Silas and Crouch.

"Crouch was taking money from him?"

"I've seen him take money from other kids. He's a bully and a coward."

"You're right about that, Odo Whitley, all bullies are cowards, but it doesn't explain how Silas could see you and Watson."

"Maybe Silas is an alien. Maybe he's a formshifter."

"I would have noticed his alien brainwaves."

"That's true. Let's think about this. He could see us and he was terrified. What would explain that? We weren't trying to hurt him or scare him."

"Even more curious is why Watson ran to him. That's very odd. Has Watson ever done anything like that before?"

"Never. Maybe Silas had a tuna sandwich in his backpack."

Sephie stared at Odo.

"What's that weird look for? Cats like tuna. Everyone knows that."

"Everyone knows that? Never say that again, Odo Whitley. You know you hate it when your dad says it."

"Oh, right. Fine, forget the tuna sandwich. I don't know why he was so scared. He was pale, like he'd just seen–"

"Like he'd just seen a ghost! That's it, Odo Whitley! Silas Ward thought you and Watson were ghosts."

"Do you think he can see ghosts? Really? Is that possible?"

"Of course it is, but it doesn't explain why Watson ran to him."

"Wikerus said Watson has a secret we have to discover. I think his secret has something to do with Silas Ward."

"And something to do with ghosts."

Odo shivered.

45

Chapter 8

The Vase

Sephie and Odo decided to walk home instead of taking the bus, giving them time to discuss Watson's puzzling attraction to Silas Ward.

"Watson was in my backpack, but he knew Silas was there, somehow sensing his presence. He started wriggling around, trying to get out."

"Maybe he recognized Silas' scent. A cat's sense of smell is far more sensitive than ours. They have twice as many receptors in their olfactory epithelium as we do."

"But why run to him?"

"Maybe Watson already knew him."

Watson yowled, reaching one arm out of the backpack, batting at Odo's head.

"What are you doing, you crazy cat? What's wrong with you?"

"He wants out. Let's let him loose and we'll see where he goes. We can follow him."

"Did your inner voice tell you that?"

"Not exactly, but I'm getting a good feeling about it. I think he'll lead us somewhere."

"I'm pretty sure he'll just walk behind me. I guess we could try it though."

Odo opened his pack and lifted Watson out, setting him on the ground.

"Okay, Watson, Sephie wants you to–"

Before he could finish, Watson bolted down the sidewalk, streaking into a side alley.

"Whoa! We have to catch him! Run!"

Sephie and Odo took off after Watson, sprinting down the narrow lane.

"Hurry!"

They darted out onto Larua Street.

"There he is! That way!"

The two friends raced after him.

"He's so fast!"

"He ran into that yard and jumped the fence!"

"Crazy cat! Where is he going?"

Sephie sprinted ahead, reaching the fence before Odo did, leaping up and pulling herself over it.

"Whoa, how did you do that?"

"Hurry! I don't want to lose him!"

Sephie pushed through a tall hedge into the next yard, racing across the lawn onto Umbra Avenue. She stopped when she saw Watson sitting in front of an old house.

"Odo is not going to like this."

She turned at the sound of Odo's footsteps.

"Do you see him?"

Sephie pointed to the ramshackle house.

Odo's chest tightened. "It looks haunted, and I definitely don't like the looks of that iron fence with all the spikes on top."

"Don't tell me you're still afraid of ghosts."

"Of course I am. Ghosts are scary. Everyone knows–"

"Don't say it."

"I was going to say, most people, but not everyone, think ghosts are scary."

"Do you even know what a ghost is?"

"Of course I do. They're… you know… blue, and you can see through them. They float around and moan and wave their arms. They love to scare people, that's their favorite thing."

"Seriously, Odo Whitley, they moan a lot and wave their arms? They love to scare people?"

"Just like in *Invasion of the Shrieking Ghosts*."

"Snap to it, Odo Whitley, this is about physics and science. A ghost is an energy field, a consciousness, a life force without a physical body. We talked about this before. Your body is like a car. Your true self gets into the car when you're born and drives it around until you die. Then you get out and–"

"And moan and scare people." Odo waved his arms at Sephie. "Woooooooooo! Wooooooooo!"

"Something is wrong with you, Odo Whitley. Let's find out who lives in that house."

They stepped across the street next to Watson, studying the dilapidated old mansion.

"Someone needs to paint this place."

Sephie's eyes were locked on the front window.

"There's someone standing by the curtain, but I can't see their face."

The figure turned.

"It's Silas Ward! Watson led us to his house."

"This is officially very creepy. How could Watson know where Silas lives?"

Sephie shook her head. "I don't know, but we need to talk to him."

"He'll get scared if he sees me. He thinks I'm a ghost."

"Do you have your Sinarian ring?"

Odo hesitated. "I've only used it once, at Wikerus' house when the Sinarian gave it to me."

"Put it on, Odo Whitley. You need to be solid if we're going to talk to Silas."

"Right, solid." Odo took the ring from his inner coat pocket, studying it.

"Do it."

Odo slipped the ring on, watching his hands become solid.

Sephie studied his face. "All the girls would say you're cute."

"I'm so used to being translucent it feels really weird being solid. I don't exactly like it." He scooped up Watson and put him in the backpack.

The iron gate squealed as Odo and Sephie pushed it open. They walked up the front steps, Odo ringing the doorbell.

Silas peered through the glass. The door swung open a moment later.

Sephie smiled at Silas. "Hi, I'm Sephie Crumb."

"I know who you are, I've seen you at school."

"This is my friend, Odo Whitley."

"Hi."

"Odo goes to our school."

"What do you want? Are you selling something?"

"No, it's not that. We need to talk to you about ghosts."

Silas shut the door.

Sephie whispered, "He's scared. You should see his brainwaves."

Odo called out, "We have to talk to you, it's really important. It's about what you saw at school today, right after Brandon Crouch took your money."

The door creaked open.

"What did I see?"

"A ghost boy and a ghost cat."

The door opened a few more inches. "What do you want?"

Odo twisted the ring on his finger. "Can we talk?"

Silas motioned for them to enter. "Our house is old. I don't know why my dad won't remodel it. We can sit in the living room. How do you know what I saw at school?"

Odo sat down on an antique flowered couch.

"You can see ghosts?"

"You need to tell me why you're here."

"It's kind of a long story. I want to show you something first though. It might be a little scary."

"You don't know what scary is."

Odo pulled his ring off.

Silas skittered backwards. "You're a ghost!" He looked at Sephie with wide eyes. "Did you know about this?"

"I'm not a ghost, Silas, I'm translucent. I was born this way. Touch my arm."

Sephie gave Silas a reassuring smile. "It's okay. Odo is my best friend. He's just translucent, that's all. He's not a ghost."

"I'm your best friend?"

"Stay on track, Odo Whitley."

Silas touched Odo's arm.

"You're solid, not a ghost."

Odo slipped the ring back on. "This ring makes me solid. It was given to me by–"

Sephie jabbed him with her elbow.

"It was given to me by someone we know, a scientist."

"You're hiding something. Either tell me everything or leave."

Sephie stood up. "That's a lovely vase you have over there. Do you mind if I look at it?"

Silas did not reply.

Sephie raised her hand, a pale blue light shooting over to the vase. Silas' jaw dropped when the vase floated up, drifting across the room. Sephie plucked it from the air, examining it.

"It's pretty. My mom has one kind of like it, but hers has blue flowers, not pink ones."

Silas took a step back. "Who are you? What are you?"

"You should probably sit down. This could take a while."

Chapter 9

The Shovel

Sephie and Odo told Silas about the blue flash and how Watson had been pulled into this world when he collided with Odo. They revealed Odo's ability to shift between dimensions, but did not mention Fortisia, Girard Station, Wikerus Praevian, the Serendipity Salvage Company, or their previous otherworldly adventures.

"We think Watson recognized you, but we don't know how or why. He jumped out of my pack and ran to you in school. When we let him loose he led us right to your house."

"I don't know why he would do that. We've never had a pet."

"Would you mind if we let Watson loose in here? Maybe he wasn't being drawn to you, maybe he was being drawn to something in your house."

"I guess." Silas looked less than enthusiastic about Sephie's plan.

Odo flipped open his pack and Watson jumped out, sniffing the air. He walked around the furniture, rubbing against it, then turned abruptly, racing up the stairs.

"Can we follow him?"

"Okay."

Odo and Sephie ran up the stairs, stepping into a long hallway.

"Whoa, your house is big. I don't see Watson. Any idea where he might have gone?"

Silas pointed to a partially opened door at the end of the hall. "Probably in there. You can look if you want, but I'm not going in."

A chill washed through Odo. "What's in there?"

"An old rocking chair."

They walked down the hallway, peering into the shadowy room, empty except for a tall black rocking chair sitting in a dark corner. Watson was curled up on the seat.

Odo shivered. "This is seriously creepy. Why is he in that chair, and why is the room empty?"

"Silas, do you know where the rocking chair came from?"

"It's always been here. The house is old, built in 1910."

"No one uses this room?"

"Never."

"Why?"

"My dad says he's going to turn it into an office, but he never does, and he never goes in there. He's been saying that since I was little."

Sephie was studying Silas' brainwaves. It was very clear that the room terrified him. Her face softened. "Silas, Odo and I have seen some frightening things, but no matter what we see, it can always be explained by science. I know you see ghosts, but you don't need to be afraid of them. They can't interact with this world because they don't have a physical body, and that means they can't hurt you. If you try to understand the science behind things like this, it makes it less scary."

Watson hopped down from the chair, strolling out of the room to Odo.

Silas looked away from Sephie, his voice barely audible.

"I call her the Lady in Black. She wears a black dress and a black veil. She sits in the rocking chair."

"She's a ghost?"

Silas nodded.

"Tell us more about her. Does she look at you, talk to you?"

"No, but I'm afraid she will."

"Does she do the same thing over and over?"

Silas looked up, studying Sephie's face. "Why does that matter?"

"Not all apparitions are the same. Some have consciousness and awareness, some are singular events that echo across time."

"She does the same thing over and over. I've seen her since I was little. When I was small she was pale blue, hard to see. I wasn't even sure she was there. The older I got, the more real she became. She's changing, and I'm afraid she's going to get so real that she won't be a ghost, that she'll come into my room while I'm sleeping."

"Silas, it's not The Lady in Black who is changing, it's you. Your ability to see ghosts is getting stronger as you get older. The Lady in Black is an echo of something that happened a long time ago. Whatever she's doing only happened once, but you can see it across time. It only looks like she's doing it over and over."

Silas rubbed his eyes. "You can't even imagine how scary she is."

"What does she do? Why is she scary? This is a mystery to be solved, not something to be afraid of. Forget your fear for a moment and think about it using logic. Watson was traveling outside of time. How did that happen? How did he get there? Did he used to live in this house? Why did he run to the rocking chair? Why did he lead us to you?"

"You think Watson used to live here?"

"I think he knew the Lady in Black. I think he used to sit on her lap in that chair. What does she do exactly?"

"No one else in the house sees her, just me. Sometimes at night I hear her in the rocking chair. When I'm on the couch watching TV in the evening she walks down the stairs and goes into the basement. She walks right through the door."

"Is there anything else? Any other clues about what she's doing?"

Silas' voice was shaky. "She carries a wooden box and drags a shovel behind her."

Odo's eyes widened. "A shovel? She's going into the basement with a shovel?"

Silas nodded. "It's so scary. I don't want to know what she's doing down there."

"Odo Whitley, have you already forgotten about the demons we saw in the old Atroxian military base?"

"I know what you're going to say, they weren't really demons, they were just big insects. This is different though, it's a ghost dragging a shovel. She's dragging a shovel, Sephie."

"We need to find out what she's doing down there. It's important. Watson led us here and we need to find out why."

Silas shook his head. "I can't go down there by myself."

"You don't have to, Odo and I will go with you. Nothing can hurt us down there, I promise."

"I see her in the evening, usually after dinner. No one else knows about her."

"You're not alone now, Silas. We'll find out what's going on here."

"I could tell my parents you were coming over to study. They wouldn't mind, they're always telling me to make friends."

Odo nodded sympathetically. "I know what that feels like. It was really lonely growing up translucent. I didn't have any friends."

Sephie smiled at Silas. "We'll see you at school

tomorrow? We can sit together at lunch."

"Okay." Silas paused. "Odo, I was wondering, do you ride on Bus 83?"

"How did you know that?"

"I've seen you. I thought the bus was haunted."

Sephie nodded. "One less thing to be scared about."

Odo attempted a smile, but was imagining the scraping sound of a shovel being dragged down the cellar stairs by the Lady in Black.

Chapter 10

Into the Basement

They met Silas the next day in the school cafeteria, planning their ghostly nocturnal adventure.

"My parents said you could have dinner with us and we could study after. I think my dad wants to meet you, make sure you're okay. He's afraid I'll make friends with the wrong people. I don't know why he worries so much. He's way worse than my mom."

"Dinner sounds great. I'll wear my Sinarian ring, so I'll be solid."

"I told them you're both really smart and get good grades. My dad liked that."

"If we can get a giant brain with five thousand legs to like us, your parents shouldn't be a problem."

Silas gaped at Odo. "What?"

"Just someone we met on Atroxia. I'll tell you about it sometime."

"Odo was so scared he almost barfed on me."

"I wasn't scared at all. I laughed in the face of danger."

Silas snorted. "Even I don't believe that."

"This is going to be fun, Odo Whitley. I can't wait to meet the Lady in Black."

"I'll try not to barf on you."

* * * *

Odo stopped as they were approaching Silas' house. "Do you really think there's a ghost?"

"Of course there is, Odo Whitley. I didn't tell you this before, but Silas said his mom is an evil witch and his dad practices dark magic."

"What?? Are you serious?"

Sephie laughed. "Let's rock and roll."

"Is that a gargoyle over the front door?"

Sephie rapped on the heavy wooden door, greeted moments later by Silas' mom.

"You must be Odo and Sephie. Silas has told us so much about you. It's lovely to meet you both."

"Thanks for having us over for dinner. You have a lovely home."

"If by lovely you mean old and spooky, then I would agree with you. I keep trying to get Silas' dad to renovate it, but he likes it the way it is. He grew up here. Maybe one day I'll convince him."

Sephie was studying her brainwaves. She was deeply worried about something.

"Dinner's ready, come have a seat at the table."

Silas waved when he saw them.

"Hi, Odo. Hi, Sephie. Welcome to the biggest dining room in the world."

Odo laughed. "That chandelier is amazing. I could probably swing from it, like in the movies when they have sword fights."

Silas' dad sat at the end of the long mahogany table.

"It's been here since I was little. I think my parents brought it back from Italy. They traveled a lot before I was born."

Sephie nodded, reading his brainwaves. He was sincere, but there was an intense sadness about him. She took a deep breath and sat down at the table. Something bad had happened in this house, something that had changed his life.

After a lovely dinner with lots of talk about school, classes, and teachers, Silas' mom said, "You can study in the sitting room. There's lots of snacks in the kitchen if you get hungry."

"Thanks, dinner was delicious."

The three friends headed to the other room, taking a seat on the couch facing the stairs.

Sephie whispered, "What time does the Lady in Black show up?"

"Any time now. I never know exactly when."

Four minutes later Silas gave a start.

"It's her. She's coming down."

Sephie scanned the stairway. "I can see her energy field, but it's faint."

"You can see her? That's a big relief. I was worried that maybe I was loopy, that she didn't really exist."

"You're not loopy, you're amazing. I can see her energy field, but you can see all the details. Tell us

61

exactly what she looks like."

"She's wearing a long black lace dress and a black veil."

"It sounds like she's in mourning. People used to dress in black for a year after someone they love died. Some people wore black for the rest of their lives."

"It's hard to see her face clearly through the veil, but I don't think she's old, maybe about my mom's age. I never noticed this before, but she's wearing a gold ring on her left hand."

"These are all good clues. We know she lost someone dear to her, and we know she's wearing a wedding ring."

"What does the box look like?"

"It's made out of dark wood with ivory inlays on it."

They watched the Lady in Black half walk and half float down the hallway, disappearing through the cellar door.

"I've never seen her this close before. I always tried to hide from her."

"Let's go." Sephie stepped down the hallway to the basement door, unlocking it and swinging it open.

"The light switch is on the right."

She flicked on the light and the three friends crept down the rickety wooden stairs.

Sephie checked Silas' brainwaves. His fear was spiking severely.

"Silas, remember the Lady in Black doesn't exist here, she's only a shadow of something that happened a long time ago."

Silas gave a weak smile. "Thanks, I'm okay, better than I thought I'd be."

Odo stepped onto the gritty basement floor, eyeing the massive wooden beams overhead, brushing aside cobwebs.

"This place is really old. Look at those iron pipes and the old fashioned wiring. That's not safe, your dad should probably rewire all the–"

"Focus, Odo Whitley."

Silas pointed. "She went to the far corner in the back. It's dark, I can't see what she's doing."

He stepped closer, giving a low groan. "She's digging a hole."

"Creepy. Wait, how could she be digging in concrete?"

"Good question, Odo Whitley. She must have lived here before there was a concrete floor."

Silas whispered, "She's burying the wooden box. That's what she was doing down here. I was afraid she was burying a body."

"She's gone." Sephie stared at the empty space where the Lady in Black had been.

"What do you think was in the box?"

"We'll know soon enough, Odo Whitley. We're going to dig it up and find out."

Chapter 11

Odo's Surprise

The three friends hurried over to the spot where the Lady in Black had buried the wooden box.

Odo scraped his shoe across the rough concrete floor.

"There's no way we can dig through that. Hey, Silas, would your dad mind if we used a big jackhammer and a bulldozer to break up the cellar floor?"

Silas laughed. "Not at all. He'd love that."

"Sephie, can you use your purple light to vaporize the concrete?"

Silas looked at Sephie in surprise. "What purple light?"

"It's really cool. Sephie can blast out this purple light that–"

"Zip it, Odo Whitley. We have to get it without destroying the floor, or the box."

"That's not possible. Unless we tunnel under the floor."

"A tunnel? Really?"

"I guess that would be worse than vaporizing the concrete."

Sephie grabbed his arm. "You can make the concrete translucent, just like you made the wall translucent on Pacalia."

"Good idea. At least we'd know exactly where the box is, and maybe we'll be able to see what's inside it."

"Do it."

Odo kneeled down, pressing one hand against the concrete floor.

"What's he doing?"

"Odo can make things translucent by touching them, making them become part of his body."

"Really?" Silas looked dubious.

Odo nodded. "Here goes. The concrete is over a foot thick, so I have to really concentrate." He closed his eyes, pressing both hands against the cold cement floor.

Sephie gave a start when she saw a blue aura forming around Odo. This was new. His brainwaves were flaring brightly, also something she'd never seen before. "Odo, be careful please. Don't hurt yourself."

Odo did not reply, his breathing slow and steady.

Silas' eyes widened when the concrete turned translucent. "I can't believe I'm seeing this."

Odo was bathed in a bright blue light. Sephie gave a shriek when his hands pushed into the concrete.

"Odo, your hands! What's happening?"

"Quiet, I can do this."

Sephie and Silas could see the box now, buried

under eighteen inches of solid concrete. Odo was lying on his stomach, his eyes closed, reaching into the floor as though it was a pool of rippling water.

Silas whispered, "This is unbelievable."

Odo's fingers touched the dark mahogany box, pushing against it. The box moved slightly, his hands grasping it. In a single fluid motion he pulled the box up through the concrete.

"Got it." He gave a triumphant grin, holding the box up for Sephie to see.

"Odo Whitley, how did you do that?"

"I'm not sure. I need to ask Wikerus about it. He told me there was a lot more to being translucent than just dimensional shifting."

"You can reach through solid objects."

Silas gaped at Odo. "You're like a wizard."

Sephie said, "It's not magic, it's just science we don't understand, no different than you seeing the Lady in Black. I did notice there's a section of your brain that's a lot brighter than in most people. I think you see ghosts because you're sensitive to certain unusual frequencies of the electromagnetic energy spectrum."

"I've always been able to see them."

"You can see other ghosts? Not just the Lady in Black?"

Silas nodded. "She was the scariest because she was in my house, and she terrified me when I was little. I've never told anyone except my parents, and they didn't believe me."

Sephie eyed the wooden box gripped tightly in

Odo's hands.

"Odo, I hate to say this, but we can't open the box now. I'm getting a bad feeling about it. Really bad."

Odo set the box on the floor, stepping away from it. "What kind of really bad feeling?"

"The Lady in Black buried it for a reason. She didn't want anyone to find it. I think whatever is in the box killed someone she knew, and she didn't want it to happen again."

"We should take it to Wikerus."

"Who's Wikerus?"

Odo glanced at Sephie.

She answered, "He's a friend of ours, a mentor. I can't tell you anything else right now."

"That's okay. I can't believe we figured out what the Lady in Black was doing down here. I'm not even scared of her now, I'm curious about what's in the box. I want to know more about her, who she was, who died, and how they died."

Sephie smiled, picking up the wooden box.

"Now you're thinking like a scientist, Silas Ward."

Chapter 12

The Photograph

Odo hopped out of bed when his alarm sounded, a grin on his face.

"Saturday, my favorite day of the week. It's off to the movies with Sephie, and then we show Wikerus the spooky wooden box. I can't imagine what's in it. Maybe it's something super creepy, like an old dried up mummy hand with a curse on it. That would make a good scary movie."

He pulled on his clothes and ran downstairs to the kitchen.

"Odo Whitley is in the house!"

"Odo, you don't need to say that. We heard you running down the stairs."

"Sorry, I forgot. Whoa, is that a camera? It's huge."

Albert nodded. "I brought it home from work to take pictures for the ad campaign. Don't eat the Silver Chocko CrunchCakes on the counter. I need them for the photoshoot."

Odo nodded. "I won't." The first time he had tried a Chocko CrunchCake he'd spit it out. His mom had made him promise not to tell his dad.

"Fancy camera. Why is it so big? It looks really expensive."

"It's a large format Glickensdorf Model 3000 AXC, and you're right, it's very expensive. It uses four by five inch film. The AXC model costs over seven thousand dollars."

"Whoa, don't drop it."

Albert glared at Odo. "Don't even joke about it."

He gingerly set the camera on the kitchen table, using a soft brush to clean the lens. "You can't be too careful with something like this. Trust me, they don't just let anyone take these home." He looked over at Odo, raising his eyebrows.

Odo was about to reply when he saw something more terrifying than the Lady in Black. Watson had leaped onto the kitchen table and was strolling curious-ly toward Albert's seven thousand dollar Glickensdorf Model 3000 AXC large format 4x5 camera.

Odo's heart was pounding, remembering what Wat-son had done to Petunia's coffee cup.

Albert was dusting the lens when Watson tapped the camera gently with one paw.

Odo panicked. He had to do something and he had to do it now. He lunged across the table to grab the camera. Unfortunately for Odo, Watson got to it first, batting it with his paw, Odo's hand grabbing at empty air. The horrific sound of the Glickensdorf Model 3000 AXC hitting the kitchen floor was a sound Odo would remember for the rest of his life.

Albert turned white, looking in disbelief at the camera on the floor. He turned to Odo in stunned surprise. Odo was stretched across the table.

"WHAT DID YOU DO??"

"I… I…was just… I didn't… I thought it was going to–"

"SEVEN THOUSAND DOLLARS!"

Watson leaped off the table and streaked out of the room.

"I'll get it fixed, I'll pay for everything. I'll take it to the camera shop and have them fix it today. I'll use the money I earned from Serendipity Salvage. I've been saving all my money."

Albert's face was now bright red. "You'll take it there and pay for all the repairs?"

"Yes, I promise. I promise I'll pay for everything. I'll get it fixed, it will be just like new."

Albert eyed Odo. "All right. Get it fixed and I'll forget about this." He shook his head. "I can't figure you out, Odo. Why did you grab at it?"

"It looked like it was going to fall off the table."

"I know you're young, but you can't be so impulsive, you have to think before you act. You did volunteer to pay for it, so that's in your favor. You didn't try to say it wasn't your fault."

Petunia gave Albert a look.

"Your mom says you're saving up for college?"

"I'm saving everything I can. Except for spending money, like when I go to the movies with Sephie."

Albert studied Odo. "I'm glad you met Sephie, glad you have a friend. When the time comes, we can probably help you a little with tuition. We have some money put away, and I'm making more with my new job. College is important. Everyone knows that. I regret not getting my degree."

Odo wasn't sure what to say. This was the first time his dad hadn't treated him like a little kid. "You did great, even without finishing school. You're the Silver Chocko CrunchCake permanent supervisor."

"Thanks. Don't worry too much about money. You have such good grades you'll probably get a scholarship."

"I forgot about scholarships."

Albert picked up the camera, examining it. "It doesn't look as bad as I thought it would. Maybe it won't cost too much."

Twenty minutes later Odo was walking down Asper Street, the heavy camera case slung over his shoulder.

"Okay, Beasley's Camera Shop is at 62957 Forster Street. I hope they're open on Saturdays."

He put on his Sinarian ring, smiling when he saw the OPEN FOR BUSINESS sign hanging in the window. He stepped inside, waving to the gray haired man behind the counter.

"You repair cameras, right?"

"For the last forty-two years. What do you have there, son?"

"It's kind of an emergency. It fell off the kitchen table and my dad needs it today. It's a Glickensdorf Model 3000 AXC. I don't know how badly damaged it is."

"That's a pricey one. Well made, though. Solid. Bring it here and I'll give a look. Ten minutes and I'll have your estimate."

Odo set the camera on the counter, gazing around the shop. "Where did you get all the old photos?"

"I bought a big collection from Jonathan Morse, the antique dealer. Most go way back, but some are from the 1920s."

"I've been to his shop. He has a lot of stuff."

"He does know his antiques. Bit on the cranky side, but nice once you get to know him. We've been to dinner a couple of times with him and his wife. Take a look at the photographs while I check out your camera. Days gone, but not forgotten."

Odo strolled around the shop, studying the old sepia tone images.

"Look at these crazy old cars. I bet my grandpa drove one like that. There's one of horses pulling carts and some kind of trolley thing. This must have been before they had subways and cars. The men are all wearing suits and ties and funny hats. The ladies are wearing those crazy long dresses. How did girls even walk around wearing all that stuff? He snorted, trying to imagine Sephie in a long old fashioned dress. Here's two pictures of a family sitting on their–" Odo's jaw dropped when he realized what he was looking at. He could hardly breathe.

"No. Way."

He turned to the old man at the counter.

"Um… is there any chance I could buy these two photos? I really like them a lot."

"Ten dollars and they're yours. Good news on the camera. Nothing broken, just needs to be aligned and adjusted, one small part replaced. Told you these were solid. Fifty smackers and she'll be like new. Take about an hour."

"That's great news, thanks so much. Wait, a smacker is a dollar, right?"

The old man gave a wry smile. "I'd charge you fifty clams, but that was way before your time."

"My dad calls them that sometimes. Would you happen to have a magnifying glass I could borrow?"

"How about this?" The old man reached into a drawer and pulled out a six inch wide magnifying glass.

"Whoa, that will definitely work."

"I'll take your Glickensdorf into the back and work on it. You're going to wait?"

"Yes, I promised my dad I'd get it back to him as soon as I could."

Odo stepped over to a wooden bench and took a seat, setting the two old photographs on his lap, studying the first one closely.

"These are definitely pictures of Silas Ward's house taken in the 1920s. There are five people sitting on the front steps; a man, a woman, and three kids. Two boys and a girl."

Odo gulped when he saw the cat sitting on the woman's lap.

"No way. It can't be."

He studied the cat using the magnifying glass, letting out a low gasp.

"Four leaf clovers on his collar. I don't believe it. It's Watson. This is the Lady in Black."

Odo was filled with a sudden overwhelming sadness when he studied the faces of the three children in the photo.

"What happened to you? Did you all die? Is that why she wears black? And what did she bury in the box? Is it what killed you?"

Chapter 13

Forgotten Memories

"I bet your dad was glad to get his camera back."

"Really glad. He said he was proud of me for being responsible, for volunteering to get it repaired. He even said he'd teach me how to use it. It's the first time he's ever said he was proud of me."

"I told you one day he'd see you the way I do."

"Thanks, Sephie. What movie did you choose?"

"It's supposed to be really good, Odo Whitley. It's called *Forgotten Memories,* about a woman who loses her family in a tragic car accident. She almost dies, and she's in a coma for three years. When she finally wakes up she can't remember anything about her past or her family."

Odo attempted a smile. "Sounds good."

"That's the same face you made when you had to go to the dentist."

"No, really, it sounds like a good movie, it's just…"

"There aren't enough shrieking ghosts in it? No car

chases, no scary monsters? It's a movie about real people, and it's won a lot of awards."

"I said it sounds great, really good. Definitely award winning."

"I can read your brainwaves, Odo Whitley, and they don't look award winning."

"Oh, right, I forgot. Do you want popcorn?"

"It wouldn't be the movies without popcorn. Get a box of those sour candies too."

"Speaking of boxes, you have the wooden box?"

"It's in my backpack. We'll take it to Wikerus after the movie."

"I have the photos of the Lady in Black and her family. Wikerus said we should come back when we discover Watson's secret. This has to be it."

An hour later Odo leaned over to Sephie, whispering, "She's going to recognize the photo, remember her family. I know she is. I hope she marries the doctor. He's secretly in love with her."

"Shhh. Wait, you think he's in love with her?"

"I know he is, he's just afraid to tell her. Guys are like that."

Sephie studied Odo's brainwaves.

The two friends stood up when the credits began to roll.

"That was really good, and you were right about the doctor. He was in love with her, but it was hard for him to show his feelings because his dad never did." She gave Odo a curious smile.

"Why are you smiling like that?"

Sephie grabbed his arm. "Let's go see Wikerus and find out what's in the box."

The two friends stepped out of the theatre, turning left on Expergo Street.

"Isn't it weird how I found the photos of the Lady in Black at the camera shop? If Watson hadn't knocked the camera off the table, I never would have found them. Do you think he was leading me there on purpose? I've been wearing my work ring."

"That's not exactly how it works, Odo Whitley. If you drop a marble, does the marble decide whether or not to fall?"

"Of course not, it falls because of gravity."

"It falls because that's what has to happen at this time and in this place. Finding the photos in the camera shop is the same thing. You were pulled there because that's what had to happen. You were a marble falling to the ground."

"I just remembered, Wikerus said the same thing about us. He said that's why we met, that I was a marble falling to the ground. Wait, suppose I'd decided not to go to the camera shop? Suppose I'd told my dad I wasn't going to fix it because it was Watson's fault?"

"Then that would be what had to happen, and you wouldn't have found the photos."

"It's not really logical that everything that happens is what has to happen."

"It's perfectly logical. Whatever you choose to do is exactly what has to happen. It can be no other way."

"You're giving me a headache."

"Maybe Wikerus will have a box of those imported chocolates."

"Yum, those are so good."

"Here we are."

Sephie swung open the front gate and they ran up the steps.

The door swung open before she could knock.

"You're back. Have you discovered Watson's secret?"

Odo nodded. "I think so. He belonged to the Lady in Black, a ghost at Silas Ward's house who buried a wooden box in their basement back in the 1920s. I had to reach through the concrete floor to get it. I've never done that before."

"You did that on your own? I'm impressed, Odo."

"I was trying to make it translucent so I could see the box, but my hand went right through the concrete like it was water."

"Marvelous. It won't be long until you'll be doing this." Wikerus turned and walked through a wall into the sitting room.

Sephie and Odo gaped at each other. "Whoa! He walked right through the wall like a ghost."

They ran down the hallway into the sitting room, a smiling Wikerus Praevian seated in his favorite chair.

"How did you do that?"

"You already know how. You put your arm through concrete, I went a little further and put my entire body through a wall, all thanks to the laws of quantum tunneling. The good news is, you don't need a degree in

78

quantum mechanics to walk through walls."

"Can Sephie learn how to do it?"

"Of course, she's half Fortisian. It will take practice, but she'll be strolling through walls in no time. It's quite remarkable that you were able to do it without instruction."

Sephie pulled the wooden box from her backpack, setting it on the table in front of Wikerus.

"This is the box the Lady in Black buried in her basement. We think whatever is inside it may have killed someone she loved, and that's why she wears black."

"Have you opened it?"

"No, we thought it could be dangerous."

"Maybe a dried up old mummy hand with a curse on it. Or a mummy brain."

Wikerus smiled. "Open it."

Sephie ran her fingers across the top of the box.

"Here goes."

Odo took a step back.

Sephie pulled on the lid.

"It won't open. It's locked."

"It can't be, there's no keyhole."

"Oh dear, it would appear you haven't discovered Watson's secret after all. Perhaps next time."

Odo grabbed the box, trying to force the lid open.

"It won't open. It's locked."

"I just said that, Odo Whitley."

"I know, I was just thinking…"

"You were thinking I was wrong, thinking you could

open it even though I couldn't?"

"I wasn't thinking you were wrong, just maybe… slightly, I don't know, I just wanted to try it. I knew it was locked, but…"

Wikerus interrupted. "Odo, show me the photographs of the Lady in Black."

Odo pulled the photos from his pack, handing them to Wikerus. "They're really interesting photos, but kind of sad once you know that something bad happened to them."

Wikerus studied the sepia images. "This one will do nicely, sharp and clear. I see our old friend Watson."

"What do you think we should do?"

"Odo, I want you to tell me what I'm holding."

"You mean the photograph?"

"We see photographs every day, but what exactly are they?"

"Well, the camera has light sensitive film inside it, and a lens focuses an image on the film when you click the–"

"Not that, something else. What is a photograph? Go deeper."

"Um… it captures a moment in time so we can remember all the details of something that happened?"

"Much better. It is a four dimensional record of an event, portraying a particular location at a particular time, three spacial dimensions plus a temporal one." Wikerus gave Odo a questioning look.

"I'm sort of confused. I don't really understand what you're asking."

Wikerus looked away for a moment.

"I fear I shall irreparably alter this chain of events if I say too much. I'm afraid the puzzle of Watson and the Lady in Black is one you and Sephie must solve on your own. I will tell you this much, however. The Sinarians would call the photograph I am holding a four dimensional waystone."

"What does that mean?"

"That's all I can tell you. The rest is up to you. Come back when you have discovered Watson's deep secret. That's when things will get very interesting."

Wikerus smiled as he watched Odo and Sephie walk down the hallway toward the front door.

"I believe I am growing quite fond of those two."

Chapter 14

Click!

"Did you guys find out what was in the box?"

Silas slid into a chair across from Odo and Sephie, setting his tray on the cafeteria table.

Odo shook his head. "We showed it to Wikerus and tried to open it, but it was locked. We still don't know what's in it."

"What are you going to do?"

"I don't know. I'd take it to a locksmith, but there's no locking mechanism."

"You could bash it open with a hammer."

Sephie shook her head. "That could damage whatever is in it. It's also possible the box itself is what killed someone. We don't want to destroy it before we understand what it is and how it works."

"You're right. Odo, could you make it translucent with your hand? Look inside it?"

"I tried, but it didn't work. It's all black, but I don't know why."

"Odo Whitley, if you were Sherlock Holmes and had to solve *The Case of the Mysterious Locked Box,* what would you do first?"

"Well, I'd definitely look for clues, and I'd have reference books in my study about antique boxes. I'd read them and find a secret way to unlock it, something that would surprise Watson. I guess we should find someone who knows about antique wooden boxes."

"Someone like Jonathan Morse the antique dealer. He's sure to know about them."

"Great idea. Silas, want to come with us?"

"I wish I could, but I have to go straight home after school. My dad worries a lot. He's always afraid something will happen to me."

"Like what? You'd be with us."

"I know I'd be fine, but my dad… I can't…"

"That's okay, I understand. We'll tell you what we find out. It might be nothing, maybe the Lady in Black buried it because she thought it had a curse on it or something. The box might have nothing to do with what happened to her family."

Silas stood up, scanning the cafeteria. He groaned when he saw Brandon Crouch. "I have to go." He grabbed his backpack and ran for the door.

Sephie felt a dark anger growing inside her. Silas should not have to live in fear of someone like Crouch.

"Why does he do it, Odo Whitley? Why does Brandon Crouch bully kids like me and Silas?"

"I thought he stopped bothering you."

"He did, and that's my answer. He bullies kids who

are afraid of him. I should knock him through the wall with a force beam. That would teach him a lesson, teach him not to bully kids."

"You don't mean that."

Sephie gave a sigh, her anger fading. "You're right, Odo Whitley. If I did that, I'd be the bully. I'd be just like him, full of anger."

"You stood up to him, so maybe Silas will do the same thing when he's not so afraid. He already said he's not scared of the Lady in Black."

"Maybe we can help him the way Cyra helped me."

When school was over, Odo and Sephie set off for Jonathan Morse's antique shop.

"Too bad Silas couldn't come with us. I wonder why his dad worries so much?"

"I think something happened to him, something that still scares him."

"That has to be it. I read a psychology book that said there's always a logical reason why people do the things they do, but most of the time we don't know what that reason is. Once you know the reason, their weird behavior makes perfect sense."

"Which would also mean something happened that made Brandon Crouch become a bully."

"Exactly. And something happened to make Silas afraid of people like Brandon Crouch. Maybe it's because he sees ghosts. That would be a scary life, being so different from everyone else. It's a little bit like being translucent."

"What could have happened to make Brandon

Crouch become a bully?"

"Maybe his mom or his dad is really mean to him, or makes fun of him, even hits him. He'd be angry all the time and take it out on anyone he could."

"You're making me feel a little sorry for him."

"Don't feel sorry for him, he could stop if he wanted to."

"You're right, he's old enough to know exactly what he's doing."

"Here's Debra Avenue. I wonder why Jonathan has his shop here? It's kind of a run down area."

"Maybe it was nice when he first moved here."

Odo knocked on the weathered black door, the shop's interior concealed by ancient yellowing newspapers taped to the inside of the window.

Someone pulled back a corner of the newspaper and peered out.

"Looks like he's here."

The door creaked open, Jonathan Morse eyeing them, one hand in the pocket of his brown tweed jacket.

"You again. What is it this time? Still looking for that missing doll?"

"No, we found it, thanks to you. We tracked down Advenus Bandiir and he told us where the doll was. He'd given it to his daughter." Odo did not mention that Advenus Bandiir lived on Plindor, was a formshifting alien, and his daughter Addy was being held captive by murderous Stirpians.

"All's well that ends well. How can I help you?"

Sephie pulled the wooden box from her backpack.

"We can't open this."

Jonathan's eyes lit up. "Marvelous, I haven't seen one of those in ages. Where did you find it?"

"It was in a friend's basement. It belonged to the people who used to live there."

Jonathan motioned them into the shop.

"You have a real treasure there."

"What is it?"

"It's an antique puzzle box from the late nineteenth century. I'm guessing it was made in London around 1895."

"That's amazing. How do you know all that?"

"Lots of reading and forty-five years in the antique business."

"Do you know how to open it?"

"Let's find out."

Jonathan strolled over to an old roll top desk, flicking on a brass reading lamp. He pulled his hand out of his coat pocket, setting a heavy antique percussion derringer on the desk.

Odo glanced at Sephie, raising his eyebrows.

Jonathan slid open a drawer, pulling out a magnifying glass, examining the box.

"Some puzzle boxes are simple, some are very complex. There's always a key piece, the first one you move. These ivory inlays aren't just decorative, they serve a purpose, they're part of its hidden locking mechanism."

Jonathan used the eraser end of a pencil to gently push against the ivory pieces running across the top of the box.

"Here we go." One of the ivory bars slid over an inch. He pushed two more, a small side panel sliding open.

"Now we're getting somewhere."

Odo eyed the four small brass knobs hidden behind the panel. "It looks like a combination lock."

"Exactly. We have to position them correctly to unlock it. There are four knobs, each with two possible positions. First we'll try one up, and three down. Nope. Now two up and two down. Nope…"

Five minutes later Odo heard a sharp click.

"That's it. I'll let you open it. Maybe it's filled with gold coins. It's heavy, far heavier than it should be."

"You do it, Odo Whitley. You found it, you should open it."

Odo grasped the lid of the puzzle box, raising it slowly.

"It's empty."

Jonathan Morse laughed. "You wouldn't make a very good detective. Look at it and tell me what's wrong."

Odo picked up the box, turning it slowly, running his fingers across it.

"The top section of the box is too shallow. It has a false bottom. There's something hidden under it."

"I stand corrected, you would make an excellent detective. Most people wouldn't have noticed that. Let's try those brass knobs again." Two minutes later there was a second click.

"Grab that little ring and lift it."

Odo gently removed the false bottom, eyeing the dull gray box beneath it.

Jonathan tapped it with one finger. "It's lead, that's why it's so heavy. No gold coins, I'm afraid."

Odo gingerly unlatched the lead box. He hesitated, glancing at Sephie.

"Do it, Odo Whitley. Let's see what's in it."

Odo raised the lid.

A wave of pulsating energy blasted out, sparks flying from Odo's fingertips. "Agghh!!"

"Close it! Close the box!"

Odo slammed the lid shut, his hand still tingling.

Jonathan Morse looked at them in stunned surprise.

"What was that thing?"

Chapter 15

Sarah

"I don't think we should tell Silas what we found. Maybe later."

"I agree, Odo Whitley. It would be too much for him now. Let's tell him we found a painted blue wooden figure with four arms."

"And most likely the Lady in Black thought it was cursed."

"Good idea. That was quick thinking to tell Jonathan the box was acting like a lead-acid battery."

"It was the first thing that popped into my head. I've never seen a waystone that powerful. Ever. We need to talk to Wikerus about it. This is taking a strange turn."

"It's a lot more complicated than we thought. We know the Lady in Black buried a powerful waystone, but we don't know where it came from or why she buried it. Did it kill someone she loved, one of the people in the photo? Did it kill all of them? It gave off a powerful shock."

"Or did it send them to another world?"

"That could be it, Odo Whitley. The waystone could

be so powerful that it transitions anyone who touches it, not just shifters, sending them to the carved figure's original dimension. Maybe Wikerus will know where the waystone is from. A blue figure with four arms should be a good clue. In the meantime, the box stays closed."

"I agree. Let's go see Wikerus after school. I was also thinking Silas could show one of the photographs from the camera shop to his parents. His dad grew up in the house, so he might know something, maybe recognize someone in the photo. Maybe he even knows the original owners."

"Good idea. Silas won't have to mention anything about the Lady in Black or Watson. He can tell his dad we just happened to find an old photograph of their house. Nothing spooky about it."

"I'll give it to him at lunch. It would help if we could track down the original owners, or at least find out what happened to them."

Odo and Sephie met up with Silas at lunch, telling him about the carved wooden figure they had found in the lead box.

"Well, it's a clue, but it doesn't help a lot. You're probably right about the Lady in Black thinking the figure was cursed. People used to believe a lot of strange things back then. I'll show the photo to my dad and tell him you found it at Beasley's Camera Shop. Maybe he'll know who the people are."

"Perfect. How are things going with Brandon Crouch? Is he still bothering you?"

"He can't bother me if he never sees me. I keep out of his way."

"Don't forget you have two friends now. You don't need to be afraid of a bully like Crouch."

"I know you're my friends, but I'm not a superhero like you are. I'll let you know what my dad says about the photo."

* * * *

"Silas! Dinner!"

Silas grabbed the photograph from his backpack and ran downstairs. His parents were sitting at the dining room table.

"How was school today?"

"Okay. Same old stuff."

"You're still friends with Odo and Sephie?"

"We eat lunch together. It's nice not to sit alone."

"I'm glad you found some friends. You're a wonderful boy and people like you once they get to know you. You'd probably have a lot more friends if you weren't so quiet."

"I know. Oh, Odo gave me this photo. He found it at Beasley's Camera Shop and recognized our house. Do you know who these people are?"

Silas slid the photo across the table.

His dad's fork clattered to the floor.

"Where did you get this?"

"Odo found it at Beasley's Camera Shop. Mr. Beasley said it was taken in the 1920s. What's wrong?"

The color had drained from his dad's face, his finger tracing the image of the Lady in Black.

Silas felt a chill run through him. "What is it? Who are those people?"

Silas' mom squeezed his dad's hand.

"Joseph, you should tell him. He's old enough. He should hear it from you."

Silas' dad nodded slowly. He pointed to the younger of the two boys in the photo.

"That's me when I was seven years old. Mother hired a photographer to take this photo."

"That's you? Who are the other kids?"

"I… can't…"

"You need to tell him."

"This is my brother Arthur, and this is my sister Clara. Something happened the day after this photo was taken. Something bad. My father, my brother, and my sister all disappeared. Two weeks later the police arrested my mother. They said she murdered them."

Silas' jaw dropped.

His dad continued. "There was a trial and she was found not guilty. There was no proof they had been murdered, and no motive. One witness said she thought my father might have run off with another woman and taken my brother and sister with him. They said he didn't take me because I was the youngest. My mother raised me. It was dreadful, some of her friends wouldn't talk to her after that, they thought she was guilty, thought she'd killed her family. She wore black for the rest of her life. She almost never smiled."

"She always wore black?"

"She was in mourning until the day she died. She wore a black dress and veil, almost never left the house. I know she didn't kill them, she loved them more than life."

"You never found out what happened?"

"No, they just vanished."

"Oh."

"Silas, you remind me a lot of my father, you always have. He was quiet like you, and smart, a brilliant inventor. He had a lot of patents, and did very well, never ran out of ideas. Like most brilliant people he could be a little eccentric at times. I remember my mom laughing about some of the funny things he did when we were little. He once told me ghosts were real, but said I shouldn't be afraid of them. I didn't sleep for a month after that. My mother told me he was just joking."

It took almost a minute before Silas could speak, his mind spinning wildly.

"I didn't know any of that."

"It's why I worry so much about you. I'm scared of losing you, afraid you'll disappear like they did. I know it's silly, but I still worry."

"What was your dad's name?"

"His name was Mirus, my mom was Sarah. I have some old photos I can show you."

"Do you think your dad saw ghosts?"

"I don't know. He never said he saw them, but he did say they were real."

"Thanks for telling me all that. Now I know why you worry so much. I always thought it was because you didn't trust me."

"Didn't trust you? Silas, I trust you completely. I'm the one with the problem, I can't let go of what happened and I don't know why. Part of me just keeps holding on to it, even today. Your mom says it's not healthy, and I know she's right."

He paused, looking at Silas. "If you want to hang out with Odo and Sephie after school, that's fine with me. Just let us know where you'll be."

"I will, I promise. Thanks, Dad."

Chapter 16

Odo's Discovery

Odo lay on his bed staring at the photograph of the Lady in Black.

"I'm missing something, I know I am. Wikerus said the photo was sharp and clear, that it should do nicely. Do nicely for what? And what did he mean about the Sinarians calling it a four dimensional waystone? Why does he always talk in riddles?"

Watson hopped up on the bed, stretching out next to Odo.

"Hello, sidekick. Are you here to help me solve *The Case of the Four Dimensional Waystone*?"

Watson yawned, batting at Odo's chin with his paw.

"Cats are weird, especially ones who pop out of time."

Odo studied the photo, the germ of an idea forming in his mind. "Time is the fourth dimension, and Wikerus called this a four dimensional waystone. A regular waystone takes me to another dimension, another place, but not to another time. Is he saying I can travel back in time using an old photograph as a waystone? That can't be possible. On the other hand, I used to think dimensional shifting wasn't possible."

Odo sat up in his bed. "If I use this like a waystone and align my inner vibrations to the deeper vibrations of the photograph, would I travel back in time to the moment the photo was taken? This is kind of scary, I should probably talk to Sephie about it. Maybe to Wikerus."

He looked at Watson, sprawled on his back, eyes closed, purring softly.

"You didn't ask anyone, you just jumped out of time all by yourself. I'll do it. It probably won't work anyway."

By now the process of shifting was second nature to Odo. He would focus on the photo, imagining an old radio dial in his mind, visualizing the dial slowly rotating, adjusting it until his hands began to turn solid. When he was completely solid he would instantly transition to the original dimension of the waystone. To get back, he used the registered homestone medallion tucked under his shirt.

"Here goes nothing." Odo concentrated on the photo, turning the radio dial in his mind.

"Whoa, my fingers are starting to turn solid. This is crazy, I think this might actually be–"

With a flash of blue light Odo was gone. Watson rolled over with a yawn, resting his head on Odo's pillow.

From Odo's perspective, he had not vanished, but his room had been replaced by another world, in this case, a glorious summer day in 1921.

"Whoa, no way, it's Silas' house. Everything looks new, the house looks like it was just built. That must be the photographer who took the picture."

Odo gazed at the man in the tweed suit and matching flat cap, standing behind a large box camera.

Odo strolled across the lawn, his eyes on the camera and its heavy wooden tripod. He attempted to sound casual, mildly curious, as though he was completely at home in 1921.

"Nice camera you have there. What kind is it?"

The photographer did not reply, pulling a black cloth over his head, peering through the camera's viewfinder.

"Hello? Nice camera?"

The photographer raised one arm, calling out, "When I drop my arm everyone hold still for ten seconds. Try to keep the cat from moving. We want a nice sharp picture, no blurred faces. On my mark!" He lowered his arm, clicking the shutter, counting to himself.

"One Mississippi, two Mississippi, three Mississippi..."

Odo turned to look at the family on the front steps. It was far different seeing them in person, not just as an old photograph in a camera shop. They were real now, they were living their lives, just like him, just like Sephie.

"The Lady in Black is wearing a bright yellow dress

97

and she doesn't look sad. The man in the gray suit must be her husband. They sure dressed funny back then. I guess I should say they dress funny now, not then. Even the boys are wearing little suits with short pants, and the girl is in that frilly dress. They probably got dressed up for the family portrait."

The photographer clicked the shutter a second time.

"We're on the trolley, folks!"

"They talk funny, too."

The three children laughed, jumping to their feet and clapping.

The man in the gray suit stepped down onto the front lawn, strolling over to the photographer.

"Swell rig you've got there. I'm afraid those old Master Views have seen their day though. I'm working on a camera so small you can tuck it in your pocket, and she'll make prints as big as the moon."

The photographer laughed. "You on the level? You did that, you'd be rolling in mazuma like a Rockefeller."

"If only. Sarah said you'll have prints for us sometime next week?"

"Next Thursday afternoon. I'll drop them by. We Jake?"

"We are. I look forward to seeing them."

It hadn't taken Odo long to realize that no one could see him or hear him. He had also learned the Lady in Black's name was Sarah.

"This is just like being translucent, no one sees me. Whoa, maybe I'm like a ghost. That's a scary thought.

It must have something to do with traveling back in time. I'm going to take a look inside the house, search for clues."

Odo walked up the front steps, stopping to look at Sarah. She was watching the children play, a gentle smile on her face. A wave of sadness rolled through Odo.

"What happens to you? Why do you dress in black?"

With a long sigh, Odo stepped into the house.

"It's Silas' house, but with different furniture. Not so drab, lots of colorful rugs and nice paintings, bright wallpaper. Looks like a happy home." He scanned the front hallway. "There's my first clue, that pile of mail on the side table. Let's see who lives here."

He strolled over and picked up a few letters, letting out a low gasp when he read them.

"They're addressed to Mirus and Sarah Ward. These must be Silas' grandparents. That means one of the boys in the photo is Joseph, Silas' dad. This is incredible, I can't wait to tell Sephie the Lady in Black is Silas' grandma."

Odo continued searching the first floor of the house, finding nothing else of interest. He stopped abruptly. "What am I thinking? The room at the end of the hall on the second floor, the one with the rocking chair!"

He raced up the stairs and down the hallway, pushing the door open, staring in surprise at the interior of the room.

"Whoa. What is this stuff? All kinds of weird tools and electrical equipment. It must be a laboratory or a workshop. Wait, Mirus told the photographer he was working on a new kind of camera. He must be an inventor, and this is his workshop. Look at those big brass goggles."

Odo stepped over to the long cluttered workbench, picking up the heavy goggles, examining them. He flicked a small lever on one side and the lenses glowed green.

"These are definitely not welding goggles. Maybe Mirus was inventing night vision goggles."

Odo slipped them on, giving a yelp.

"No way! It's the forest I saw in my bedroom, but it looks real." He reached out to touch one of the trees, his hand passing through it.

"Not real. It's so clear, I can see the pouring rain and the moss on the ground, weird seedpods all over. Eww, there's one of those giant slugs. So gross. I wish Sephie was here, this is all really confusing. I'm back in 1921 looking through weird goggles invented by Silas' grandpa at the same forest I saw in my bedroom."

Odo slipped off the goggles and set them back on the bench. He froze when he saw the lead box.

"That's the box Sarah buried."

He held his breath, gingerly raising the lid.

"It's the blue figure with four arms, the waystone. No electric shock though, maybe because I'm a ghost from the future."

Odo jumped when the workshop door creaked open, one of the boys peering in, his sister right behind him, looking over his shoulder.

"Do you see it?"

"It's on the bench."

"Go get it. I want to look at it, it's blue and has four arms."

"What if Papa catches us?"

"Quit being a scaredy cat, little baby Arthur."

"I'm not a baby, so quit calling me that. I'm almost as old as you are."

Arthur glared at the girl, then crept forward, his eyes on the lead box. He reached up to open it.

"Arthur Ward! What are you doing? You're not allowed in here! It's very dangerous. Both of you, go to your rooms. I want you to take an hour to think very carefully about what you just did."

Arthur ran out of the room, scowling at his sister.

"It was Clara's idea. She made me do it."

"Not another word! To your rooms, both of you. One hour."

The workshop door slammed shut.

Odo snorted. "Brothers and sisters. Some things never change." He scanned the workshop.

"What were you doing here, Mirus Ward? You're definitely up to something. Sounds like you're an eccentric genius. Not a lot of people inventing interdimensional goggles back in 1921. Well, look what we have here."

Odo walked over to the heavy iron safe in the back corner of the room. He rubbed his hands together.

"Let's see what you're hiding, Grandpa Mirus."

He kneeled down next to the safe, pressing his hand

against the cold metal, watching the stout iron door become transparent, the contents of the safe visible.

"Not much in there, just a book, but it must be important if he keeps it locked up."

Odo closed his eyes, concentrating deeply, his hand pushing slowly through the iron door. A moment later he was holding the cloth bound volume.

"Looks like a journal."

He read the word written in black ink on the cover.

Ghostwatchers

"Whoa." Odo flipped the book open and began to read. Twenty minutes later he closed the journal, putting it back in the safe.

"This changes everything. I have to go back and tell Sephie and Silas."

Odo eased the workshop door open and stepped into the hallway. He stopped when he saw the black cat walking toward him.

"Watson?"

The cat gave a soft meow, walking around Odo, rubbing against his legs.

"You're wearing your four leaf clover collar. It is you! Wait, you can see me? Cats can see ghosts from the future?" Odo reached down and scratched Watson's head.

Watson purred, heading back down the hallway, strolling into one of the bedrooms.

"Hi, Fluffy, what are you doing here? Did Papa send

you to your room for an hour to think about what you did?"

Odo grimaced. "Fluffy? Really?"

He heard the children whispering.

"We'll try again tomorrow, when Papa goes to the post office. It's not dangerous, it's just a little wooden doll."

Chapter 17

Ghostwatchers

Odo ran all the way to the cafeteria. Silas and Sephie were setting their lunch trays down when he darted up to them, out of breath.

"You're not going to believe what happened last night. It's unbelievable, that's what it is. Unbelievable. I solved the mystery of the Lady in Black." He paused for effect, raising one eyebrow.

"If you're going to tell us the Lady in Black is Silas' grandma, we already know that."

Odo's grin vanished. "What? How could you know that? You ruined my big surprise." He slumped into a seat.

Silas smiled sympathetically. "Sorry, my dad told me last night when I showed him the photo. He said when he was seven years old, his dad, brother and sister vanished. The police accused my grandma of murdering them, but a jury found her not guilty. There were witnesses who said he may have run off with another woman and taken my brother and sister with him."

Odo perked up. "Would you be referring to Mirus,

Arthur, and Clara?"

"How could you possibly know their names, Odo Whitley?"

"Child's play for a time traveling superhero like me."

"Spill it, Odo Whitley, or I'll vaporize you where you stand."

Odo laughed. "It was incredible. Remember how Wikerus said the photograph was a four dimensional waystone?"

Twenty minutes later Silas and Sephie sat wide eyed in front of Odo.

"I take it all back, you're amazing, Odo Whitley. You traveled back in time using a photograph! I've never even heard of that before."

"You're saying my grandpa was inventing goggles that would let people see ghosts?"

"Exactly, he was going to call them *Ghostwatchers*. He was like you, he could see ghosts, but his parents told him they didn't exist. They also told him not to tell anyone about it or people would think he was crazy. He was a brilliant inventor and he wanted to prove to the world not only that ghosts were real, but also that they weren't scary, they were just normal people existing in a different dimension. The problem was, the goggles didn't do what they were supposed to do. They wouldn't let you see ghosts, but you could see other dimensions, sometimes even visit them. That's where the blue carved figure in the lead box came from. He brought it back from another world."

"So what happened to him? What happened to Arthur and Clara?"

"I don't know for certain, but I have an idea. First, we know the blue carved figure in the lead box is an incredibly powerful raw waystone."

"What's a waystone?"

"It's any object from another dimension, another world. When Sephie and I align our deeper vibrations with those of a particular waystone, we transition to that other dimension. It's called shifting. Wikerus Praevian taught us how to do it. He's a Fortisian, like Sephie. A raw waystone means we don't know where it's from, what kind of world it will take us to. Those are dangerous."

"You can both really travel to other dimensions?"

"Yes, both of us. Silas, your grandma didn't murder anyone. I could tell from the way she was looking at Arthur and Clara that she loved them more than anything else in the world. She never would have hurt them, or Mirus."

"What do you think happened?"

"While I was there I heard Arthur and Clara talking about the carved figure in the lead box. They were going to sneak into Mirus' workshop and get it the day after the photograph was taken."

"My dad said they vanished the day after the photo was taken. I still don't understand what happened to them."

"We think the blue figure is such a powerful waystone that anyone who touches it will transition to its

106

original world. I think Arthur, Clara, and Fluffy touched the waystone, transitioned to another world, and your grandpa went after them when he realized what had happened."

"And they never came back. Who's Fluffy?"

"Fluffy is Watson. Somehow he managed to find his way back to Earth."

"But in the future."

"His timing was a bit off. You know how cats are, they show up whenever they feel like it."

Sephie snorted.

Silas was clearly confused. "What does this mean? Why is all this happening?"

"The universe wants us to find Mirus, Arthur, and Clara, and bring them home."

"We need to go see Wikerus. This time I know we've discovered Watson's secret."

"Maybe he can tell us where the blue figure is from. We have to find out what kind of world it is before we shift there."

Sephie looked at Odo. "Why does it always feel like Wikerus knows exactly what's happening, but won't tell us?"

"Because he knows exactly what's happening, and won't tell us."

"I'm going to vaporize you, Odo Whitley."

* * * *

The next day Odo and Sephie ran all the way to

107

Wikerus' house after school. Odo knocked on the front door, Sephie pulling the lead box out of her backpack.

The door swung open.

"Hi, Mrs. Preke, is Wikerus in?"

"He's waiting for you."

"He's waiting for us?"

"He is."

The two friends ran down the hallway into the sitting room. Wikerus was seated in his chair.

"There they are, my two favorite detectives. You have discovered Watson's secret?"

"He accidentally shifted to another world with Arthur and Clara when they touched the blue figure we found in the wooden box."

"The box that was buried by Silas' grandmother. Her name was Sarah and her kids were named Arthur, Clara, and Joseph."

"After they shifted, their dad went after them."

"His name was Mirus Ward, Silas' grandpa."

"Excellent, I am most impressed. What will you do now?"

"Find them and bring them home, but first we have to find out where the blue figure is from. Do you know?"

"I do not. I do, however, know someone who will be able to help you. An old retired friend of mine named Bakis Merriweather."

"Where does he live? Is it far from here?"

"Quite a distance, I'm afraid. He lives in Palusia."

"Where is that? Wait, is it one of those little islands

in the Pacific Ocean?"

"It's a little farther away than that. You'll need to buy a ticket at Girard Station. Don't forget your travel rings."

Odo looked at Sephie, then back at Wikerus.

"What kind of world is Palusia?"

Wikerus paused, drumming his fingers on the arm of his chair.

"It's… a very interesting world. Very interesting indeed."

Sephie's eyes narrowed when she saw the wave of energy roll through Wikerus' cerebral cortex. Something had struck him as enormously funny.

Wikerus smiled.

"You are quite correct, something did strike me as humorous. I was remembering an especially comical story Mrs. Preke told me the other day about three Sinarians ordering pizza in a restaurant. How soon can you leave for Palusia?"

Chapter 18

Girard Station

Odo and Sephie stepped off the city bus in front of the massive triangular shaped Proto's Taste-E Kakes building.

"Taste-E Kakes is Chocko CrunchCakes biggest competitor. My dad is always telling me how awful they are, but I think they're delicious."

"You have your travel ring?"

"In my backpack. How much do you think tickets to Palusia will cost? I brought two hundred dollars, but they could be way more than that."

"No idea. Wikerus said Serendipity Salvage will reimburse us, so keep your receipt."

"Suppose tickets are ten thousand dollars? How much money did you bring? I only have the two hundred dollars."

"Odo Whitley, stop worrying about things that haven't happened yet. Do you think Sherlock Holmes sat around worrying about how much train tickets to

Devonshire were going to cost?"

"It's clearly not the same thing. Sherlock Holmes was a fictional character, Sephie. He didn't actually exist, so he didn't have to worry about how much tickets cost."

"You need to adjust your neuronal synapses. We'll ask Captain Freddie how much the tickets are, and if they're ten thousand dollars we'll go talk to Wikerus and ask him what we should do. Stop worrying."

"Fine, I am no longer worried about the price of tickets. Ten thousand dollars, a hundred thousand dollars, a million dollars, no problem."

"There's Captain Freddie's Fish n' Chips food truck. We're in luck, there's no line."

"I don't think Captain Freddie likes Fortisians. Remember the snarky comments he made about your orange hair?"

"Captain Freddie is not what he seems to be. I scanned his brainwaves last time we were here and he's not human. I think he's like Mrs. Preke, a formshifting Plindorian, which would explain why he doesn't like Fortisians."

"He's probably still mad about the Fortisians not helping Plindor when the Stirpians invaded."

Odo and Sephie strolled up to the food truck and dinged the little silver bell.

"Be there in a second, just getting things ready for the lunch crowd."

Captain Freddie stepped over to the window, dressed in his signature yellow rain slicker and matching floppy yellow rain hat.

What'll it be today, folks? Fish and chips, or chips and fish?" He gave a booming laugh, stopping abruptly.

"Oh, it's you again. Knock knock."

"What?"

"Knock knock."

Sephie gritted her teeth, glaring at Captain Freddie.

"Who's there?"

"Orange."

Sephie grimaced.

"Orange who?"

"Orange you glad I didn't say anything about your hair?"

Captain Freddie roared with laughter, slapping the counter.

Sephie's hands glowed with a brilliant purple light.

Captain Freddie's smile vanished. "Take it easy, Forty, just making a little joke. Don't be so sensitive."

"What did you call me?"

"Forty. It's short for Fortisian."

"My name is Sephie Crumb, not Forty, and this is my friend Odo Whitley. I've never been to Fortisia, but my dad was Fortisian and my mom was from Earth. They both died trying to protect our planet from the Stirpians. I know you're a Plindorian, but you need to get over what happened between Plindor and Fortisia. That was a long time ago, before either of us was born."

"And just so you know, young Sephie Crumb, I had relatives on Plindor when the Stirpians attacked. Most of them were killed. Plindor thought the Fortisians were our friends, right up until they walked away and left the Plindorians to be massacred."

"Those were dark times, we all know that. I don't know why the Fortisians did what they did, but it was a long time ago. It's time to move on, start fresh."

"If only it were that easy. I'll tell you what, you seem okay, so I'll take you off my snarky list and we'll start over. What can I get you guys today?"

Odo said, "How much is a ticket to Palusia?"

"Palusia? Why would you want to go there?"

"We just have to. How much are they? Are they really expensive?"

"Don't even get me started on the price of transition tickets. Did you know they've raised prices over twelve hundred percent in the last five years? It's an outrage. Who can afford that? I've complained, but nobody listens, nobody cares. I heard they're raising prices again next month. It's unbelievable. They don't care a whit about their customers, all they care about is money."

Odo gulped, glancing over at Sephie. "So, how much is a ticket to Palusia?"

"Hold on to your adventuring hat, my young friend. These days a ticket to Palusia will set you back eleven dollars, and that's one way, not round trip. One. Way."

Odo blinked. "What?"

"Yes, you heard me right, eleven dollars. When I was growing up we used to transition from Plindor to Earth for thirty-five cents, and that was a round trip ticket. Makes me mad every time I think about it."

113

"Right. It's an outrage, but I guess we don't have a choice. We'll take two one way tickets to Palusia."

Odo didn't mention they would be shifting back to Earth using their homestone medallions.

Captain Freddie turned and hollered, "Two Palusian specials, no onions!"

Moments later he slid two styrofoam boxes across the counter. "The data's been uploaded to your travel rings. Safe journeys, Sephie Crumb and Odo Whitley."

"Thanks, Captain Freddie."

Sephie grabbed the boxes and they stepped to the rear of the truck. Odo opened his, taking the silver card out.

"We pop it into that little slot on the truck?"

"Easy peasy. Next stop, Girard Station. Ready?"

"Can I say the thing I say when you ask if I'm ready?"

"Not yet. That was only the second time since we made our agreement."

"In that case, yes, I am ready to go to Girard Station."

Sephie laughed, pushing her silver card into the slot on the back of Captain Freddie's food truck, vanishing in a blink of light. Seconds later Odo was gone, his world instantly replaced by a massive white corridor. He turned around to look at the huge mural behind him, an artful rendering of Captain Freddie's Fish n' Chips truck.

"We're here. There's the painting of Captain Freddie's food truck."

Sephie pointed to the towering windows on the other side of the hallway. "Look at that view, Odo Whitley."

"Two suns in a violet sky, and we're sitting in the middle of a gigantic blue green ocean. It's just as amazing as the first time we saw it."

"At least now the guards won't make fun of us for not having travel rings. Remember what he asked us?"

"That was actually kind of funny. 'Have you guys invented fire yet?'"

The two friends strolled along the gleaming white corridor, watching a stream of extraordinary creatures passing them by.

"There's two of those praying mantis creatures like the one you sat next to on the *Canthus*."

"Volu was nice, I liked him a lot. Oh, I brought the universal translator discs they gave us last time we were here." Odo stuck one of the small gold disks on his left temple, handing the other to Sephie.

Sephie whispered, "Look, there's a group of those talking ants in the brown robes. The one in front is carrying a yellow flag. Maybe it's a tour group."

Odo eyed an enormous yellow octopus wheeling an orange travel bag in front of him. "I hope we run into Juvo again. That would be fun. He was really nice, a big help. Speaking of Juvo, we should get lunch at one of those Cerebral Feedback Synthesizers that read your memories. I'm hungry."

"We're almost there."

The two friends reached the end of the great curving corridor, six massive cylindrical guard stations marking the entrance to Girard Station.

"Same guards as last time, the big blue mice."

Sephie stepped up to the guard, smiling brightly. "Hello, lovely day, isn't it?"

The guard wore a maroon uniform with a single row of gold buttons running down the front. He gave her a stern look, then turned to a flickering holoscreen. He pointed to a green pad on the counter.

"Tap."

"Tap my travel ring? Don't you need to know my world of origin? Last time we were here you asked us that."

"You are Sephie Crumb and Odo Whitley from Earth. On your last visit Odo Whitley had a grilled cheese sandwich, Sephie Crumb had a tuna sandwich, and you transitioned to Plindor. Your destination today is Palusia." He squinted, reading the holoscreen again. "Wait, is that correct? You're really going to Palusia?"

"Yes, Palusia."

"Why would you want to do that?"

Odo was getting a bad feeling.

"We work for the Serendipity Salvage Company. Our boss is sending us there."

The guard gave a loud guffaw. "And I thought my boss was loopy."

Odo's smile vanished. "What's wrong with Palusia? Is it dangerous? Are there weird creatures there?"

A second blue mouse stepped out of the cylindrical guard station, this one with two rows of gold buttons on his uniform jacket. He eyed the first mouse with a severe frown.

"Is there a problem here, Smithers?"

"No, sir, no problem at all." He gave an excessively polite smile, gesturing grandly toward the green pad.

"If you would be so kind as to tap your travel rings, my good friends. Do enjoy your trip to Palusia. It's supposed to be quite lovely this time of year. Have a marvelous day, and welcome to Girard Station. We thank you for your patronage."

Sephie tapped her ring to the pad, the silver doors to Girard Station whirring open.

"Here we are, Odo Whitley. Are you ready?"

"Yes, I am ready to walk through the door into Girard Station. Okay, next time I get to say it."

Odo rubbed his hands together, grinning at Sephie.

Chapter 19

Dr. Livingstone

Odo and Sephie stood spellbound, gazing at the teeming throng of strange lifeforms crowding the sprawling floor of Girard Station.

"This is so amazing. I'd forgotten how big Girard Station is, how many transition cylinders it has. I don't know how they could build a dome this big."

"There's one of those worm creatures. Is that its suitcase?"

"I don't think so, it has legs."

"You're right. There's a group of Plindorians. Odo, look, over by the far wall, one of those giant black beetles."

"I definitely remember those guys. He was nice."

"What are those? The things that look like floating balloons with eyes."

"They're cool, but sort of creepy. That light inside them keeps changing colors."

"This place is so amazing. Let's walk around for a

while before we transition to Palusia."

"Why do you think everyone is so surprised we're going there? That guard sounded like he thought we were crazy."

"He said it was supposed to be lovely this time of year."

"He only said that after his boss came out and yelled at him. It seems weird that everyone would be so surprised, and not a good kind of surprised."

"Let's find those Cerebral Feedback Synthesizers and have lunch. You can get your favorite giant cinnamon roll like the ones at Madam Beffy's Diner."

"I know you're trying to distract me, but a cinnamon roll does sound really good. Let's go. They put melted butter on them."

The two best friends pushed through the horde of alien travelers, stopping to look at any they didn't recognize.

"Whoa, it looks like a little basketball with wings."

"And long green legs. Do you think it can fly?"

Odo froze, whispering, "Giant spider. Giant creepy spider wearing a blue scarf."

Sephie gave a start when she saw the six foot tall hairy spider scurrying toward them. She tried to stay calm, remembering what Cyra had taught her about the true nature of fear. "There is no fear in the box, the box is empty. Not a real spider, just a friendly alien who resembles a spider. Not a real spider."

The spider stopped, gazing curiously at Sephie and Odo, its three red eyes blinking rapidly. "I can't decide which of you to eat first. Maybe the cute one with the orange hair."

Sephie's legs turned to rubber.

The spider burst out laughing, spraying green saliva across the floor. "You guys kill me. What is it with humans and spiders?"

The enormous furry arachnid chuckled as he stepped past them. "Safe travels, humans."

Sephie managed a weak smile. "Thank you, large furry spider."

"That was definitely scary. I need something to eat. Let's find the food machines."

"They're over there. I'm going to get the tuna sandwich like my grandma made when we went to visit."

"It's so weird how the machines can read our memories. Sort of creepy how much they know about us. The guard even knew what we ordered for lunch the last time we were here."

"It's just science, Odo Whitley. The machines read the information stored in your brain. It's a little more complicated than that though, since your brain stores different parts of a memory in different places. What I don't understand is how the food machines can gather all the pieces and put them together into one coherent memory."

The two friends stepped up to the long wall of food machines, a cheery voice greeting them.

"Hi, Odo! It's great to see you again. How's everything going with you and Sephie?"

"Great, thanks. We're off on another adventure."

"Sounds wonderful, hope you have a marvelous time. What do you feel like having for lunch today? Last time you had a grilled cheese sandwich like you get at Madam Beffy's Diner. Would you like that again?"

"I think I'd like a big cinnamon roll from Madam Beffy's Diner this time. With melted butter on it."

"Can I do a quick scan of your memories?"

"Sure, go ahead."

"Got it. Would you like anything for Watson? Maybe a bowl of fish?"

Sephie's head whipped around, her eyes staring daggers.

"What is the machine talking about, Odo Whitley?"

"Um... did I forget to mention Watson is in my backpack?"

"What's wrong with you? You brought Watson? What were you thinking?"

"He's my sidekick. You know, like Sherlock Holmes and Watson."

The food machine spoke again.

"Hey guys, sorry to interrupt, but pets are more than welcome at Girard Station. In fact, we encourage them. Odo, you probably should have told Sephie you were going to bring Watson on your adventure. She's your best friend and deserves your complete honesty and your respect. You could have explained to her why you felt the need to have Watson with you, told her about your lonely childhood and how you never had a pet. Sephie loves you, and you love Sephie, and that's all that really matters. Love conquers all. You both know that."

Odo's jaw dropped. Sephie's eyes were wide.

The machine added, "Did you still want that cinnamon roll, Odo?"

"Uhh… sure."

"Sephie, would you like your favorite tuna sandwich?"

"Yes, please. And a bowl of fish for Watson."

"Coming right up. It was great to see you both again. Enjoy your meal, guys."

Three minutes later Odo and Sephie set their trays down on a table.

"That cinnamon roll smells really good, Odo Whitley."

"You can have half if you want. It's really big. I'm sorry I didn't tell you about bringing Watson. The food machine was right about why I brought him."

"It's okay, I don't mind at all."

"Your tuna sandwich looks yummy."

"We can share it if you want."

Odo nodded, glancing at Sephie, trying to gauge her reaction to the other things the food machine had said.

Sephie was studying Odo's brainwaves, a smile creeping across her face.

Their pleasant lunch was interrupted by a strangely familiar voice. "Good afternoon, my old friends Odo Whitley and Sephie Crumb. It's a great pleasure to see you again. You're looking quite well."

The two friends looked up in surprise.

"Dr. Livingstone?"

Odo studied the six foot tall blue snake like creature with two scaly arms, recalling when Dr. Livingstone had knocked him unconscious and dragged him into a cave on Atroxia.

Dr. Livingstone glanced down at a rectangular piece of paper in his hand.

"I'm touched that you remembered me, Odo. Tell me, what brings you to Girard Station on this fine day?"

"Are you reading that from a card?"

Dr. Livingstone studied the card in his hand. "Reading what from a card?"

"It looks like you're reading everything you're saying from that card in your hand."

"Fine. You caught me. Congratulations. At least I didn't whack you on the head and drag you into a cave. You got that going for you."

"I was just curious, that's all. It's great to see you again."

"Cyra gave me the card. She said I need to work on my social skills. The card tells me what to say. It's supposed to help me learn how to get along with people. Seems like a big waste of time. Who cares what they think?"

"It actually sounds like a really good idea. How is Cyra doing? Sephie's gotten a few thought clouds from her."

Dr. Livingstone glanced down at the card. "She's doing quite well. Her mentor is very pleased with her progress, saying she's a quick learner. Her powers have become quite remarkable. She said she misses you both."

"Her powers were already incredible, I can't imagine what they're like now."

Dr. Livingstone scanned the card. "She says thanks, she can't wait to visit you on Earth."

"You're talking to her now?"

"The card is linked directly to her thoughts."

"Hi, Cyra! How's everything going?"

"It's going great. I love my mentor, he's brilliant. You can't believe the stuff I can do now. We should go on another adventure when I'm done with my classes."

"That would be great. Odo and I are on our way to Palusia."

"I know. Dr. Livingstone has a present for Odo."

Dr. Livingstone reached into his pocket and pulled out a small silver flashlight, handing it to Odo.

"Whoa, it's just like the one I lost on Plindor."

"It's the same one. Sort of. I thought it might come in handy on your trip to Palusia. I love your cat, Odo. He's really cute. I wish I had a cat."

"Thanks. We're trying to find out where he came from. That's why we're going to Palusia. Wikerus Praevian told us to talk to someone there named Bakis Merriweather."

"Sounds great, but I have to go. Have fun on Palusia. Don't get too scared, Odo! Ha ha! Bye, Sephie!"

"What do you mean don't get too scared?"

Dr. Livingstone looked up from his card. "She's gone. Can I have a bite of your cinnamon roll?"

"I guess so, I was going to share it with–"

"Thanks." Dr. Livingstone grabbed the cinnamon roll, stuffing it into his mouth. "Tasty. Well, gotta go. Cyra says I need to practice my social skills for two hours a day."

"Right. Thanks for the flashlight. It was great to–"

Dr. Livingstone turned abruptly, disappearing into the crowd.

"Better make that three hours a day."

Sephie snickered. "You can get another cinnamon roll."

"Good idea, I'll run grab one."

Odo jumped up and ran back to the food machine. Ten minutes later he was still chatting with it, glancing over his shoulder at Sephie.

"Odo! What are you doing?"

He darted back to the table. "Nothing, just chatting."

Sephie studied his brainwaves. "You know what, I have a sudden craving for an oatmeal cookie just like my grandma used to make. I think I'll go get one."

"An oatmeal cookie like your grandma used to make."

Sephie smiled, heading to the food machine. Fifteen minutes later she came back with a large oatmeal cookie.

Odo pursed his lips. "That took a while. Was there something wrong with the machine?"

"No, we were just chatting. You know, about stuff."

"Right, about stuff."

"Those food machines are amazing, aren't they?"

"They do seem to understand people."

"They do indeed, Odo Whitley.

Chapter 20

Mike the Mechanic

Odo and Sephie strolled around Girard Station for two more hours. Finally Sephie gave a long sigh and said, "I guess we should go. This has been really fun, Odo Whitley. I love coming here."

"So much fun. I can't believe how many different kinds of creatures are here. They all seem to get along pretty well."

The two friends stepped into one of the thousands of towering purple transition cylinders that filled Girard Station.

"Okay, Odo Whitley. One tap of our travel rings on the gold sphere and we'll be in Palusia."

"Just like when we transitioned to Plindor, except this time we know what we're doing."

"Are you ready? Don't forget, this is the fourth time I asked you."

Odo did his best impression of a rugged intrepid adventurer. "I was born ready."

"Let's rock and roll!"

The two friends tapped their rings on the glowing gold sphere, vanishing in a blink of white light.

Sephie arrived a split second after Odo, just in time to hear him shriek, "We're in dark space!"

She scanned the inky blackness that surrounded them, the veil of darkness broken by a sea of tiny glowing lights. "We're not in dark space, Odo Whitley. I can hear your voice, and I can breathe. There's no sound in space because there's no air to carry the sound waves."

"We're floating, though, that's pretty weird. Now that I look at them, those lights aren't stars, they're more like little glowing bubbles, like we're inside a giant fizzy drink."

"Have you looked at your hands?"

Odo gave a start when he looked down. "Whoa! My whole body looks like liquid flowing colored light. This is so weird, but it's also kind of cool." He looked over at Sephie. "You look like liquid light too. What is this place?"

"I have no idea."

"How do we find Bakis Merriweather? There aren't any houses, just these bubbles."

"I like floating, this is fun."

"How do we move around?"

"Probably by using our mind. I'll imagine I'm floating over toward–"

Before Sephie could finish her sentence, she shot forward, crashing into Odo, the two of them spinning head over heels toward one of the bubbles.

Odo was screaming and laughing at the same time.

That was when they heard the voice.

"You don't belong here. What do you think you're doing? Stay away from that bubble."

Odo grabbed Sephie's hand, trying to stop spinning. "Who is that?"

"Odo, look! That little bubble is getting bigger!"

Odo watched as the rapidly expanding bubble flashed toward them, transforming first to a vaporous glowing form, then to a solid living person wearing a pair of grease stained coveralls and a ratty old San Diego Padres baseball cap, his name embroidered in red letters on his breast pocket. He was carrying a large silver crescent wrench.

Odo and Sephie gaped at him. "Who are you?"

He pointed to his embroidered pocket.

"Like it says, I'm Mike the Mechanic. You don't belong here. You need to leave."

"It's sort of complicated. Wikerus Praevian sent us here to find someone named Bakis Merriweather. Have you heard of him? Where do people live here? I don't see any buildings."

"I know Bakis. You said Wikerus Praevian sent you?"

"Yes, Wikerus sent us here. Do you know him?"

"Special offer, one time only, I'll grant you a three question challenge. If you can answer just one of the three questions correctly, I'll take you to Bakis. If you miss all three, you die horribly, devoured by starving rabid weasels. Agreed?"

"What? We die? No, that's not okay at all. Why would we agree to that?"

"Fair enough, if you miss all three questions, you stay here for twenty years and work as my underpaid assistants, sorting nuts and bolts from dawn to dusk, putting them in little paper bags."

"That's almost worse. Who are you, anyway? What do you do here?"

"I'm Mike the Mechanic. I fix broken stuff."

"There's nothing here to break, just all these little bubbles."

"Seriously? There's tons of stuff to fix. You can't even imagine all the things that break here. My phone rings fifty times a day with calls about this or that not working."

"This or that?"

"All right, here's my final offer. Miss all three questions and you go home, never come back."

"That's a little better, but it still doesn't exactly sound fair. Wikerus sent us here to find Bakis. Wikerus is our boss."

"Don't you dare use that tone with me, young man. I know precisely who Wikerus Praevian is. I'll thank you to mind your manners and remember who you're talking to."

"What tone? I wasn't using a tone." Odo looked helplessly at Sephie.

She shrugged. "Okay, we'll do it. Ask your three questions."

Mike the Mechanic slipped the crescent wrench into his back pocket. "You got it. First question is for you, sonny boy. Should I call you Odo or sonny boy?"

"Odo, please. Wait, how do you know my name?"

"I'm Mike the Mechanic, that's how I know. Here we go, question number one is for Odo Whitley. Who is your favorite author?"

"What?"

"Your favorite author? A simple enough question, just tell me the name of your favorite author. Do you need me to ask the question again? I could write it in block letters on a slip of paper if you'd like, read it to you slowly, enunciating each syllable."

"I heard the question, it's just not the kind of question I was expecting. Whatever I say has to be the right answer. I can't really get it wrong."

"Confidence, I like that. What's your answer, sonny boy?"

"Well, I guess it's a toss up between Sir Arthur Conan Doyle and H.G. Wells. They both wrote amazing stories, but I'd have to say my favorite is Sir Arthur Conan Doyle because I like Sherlock Holmes so much."

"So sorry, I'm afraid that answer is incorrect. I'm surprised you missed that one, given how confident you were. It's kind of sad, not even knowing who your favorite author is."

"It's not the wrong answer! Sir Arthur Conan Doyle is my favorite author."

"No, he's definitely not. Your favorite author is the

one who wrote this book."

"What book?"

"This one, the one you're in."

Odo looked over at Sephie. She was shaking her head.

Odo glared at Mike the Mechanic. "I'm not in a book, and my favorite author is Sir Arthur Conan Doyle. I think you've been floating around here so long your brain turned to–"

Mike the Mechanic held up one hand. "Let's not get carried away, sonny boy, we'll just agree to disagree. Don't forget what I said about being rude. Relax, calm down, deep breaths. In. Out. In. Out. Okay, second question is also for you. Ready?"

"I guess so. No trick questions though."

"Of course not. Clear cut, black and white, no gray areas. Question number two centers on Marcel Proust's seven volume, four thousand three hundred and thirteen page novel, *À la Recherche du Temps Perdu.* More than likely you know it as *In Search of Lost Time,* translated from the French by C. K. Scott Moncrieff between 1922 and 1931."

Odo's shoulders sagged. "I haven't actually read it, but I've heard of Marcel Proust."

"Excellent, just do the best you can. Just wing it, as the kids say." Mike the Mechanic gave Odo a reassuring smile.

"Okay."

"Odo Whitley, name all the characters in Marcel Proust's epic novel, *À la Recherche du Temps Perdu.*

Please use the original names, not their English translations. You have one minute to name all two thousand and nine characters. Go."

Odo gave a screech.

"What kind of question is that? That's crazy! Even if I knew them all, I couldn't name them in one minute."

"Sorry, that's two down, one to go. Bad luck, Odo. I have to say, I'm a little disappointed. I was expecting more of you. Let's hope Sephie can do better."

Mike the Mechanic turned to Sephie, deep concern etched on his face.

"All right, Sephie Crumb, it's all up to you. If you miss this question, you both go home, never to return. I can only imagine the look of disappointment on Wikerus Praevian's face when you tell him what happened. Have you ever seen him when he's angry? It's truly mind boggling, a sight to behold. I also know for a fact he holds a grudge forever. Let that sink in for a minute."

Sephie gulped.

"Very well, the third and final question is for Sephie Crumb. It's all or nothing, stay or go, hit or miss, do or die. Are you ready?"

"Yes."

Mike the Mechanic let out a yelp. "You got it! The correct answer was YES! Congratulations, Sephie Crumb, well done, indeed."

Odo's eyes bugged out. "What?? Why did I get those crazy hard questions, and Sephie gets a ridiculously easy one? That's not fair at all."

Sephie gave Odo a smirky smile. "My question wasn't exactly easy, Odo Whitley. I really had to think about whether I was ready or not. I wasn't quite sure if I was, but then at the last second I decided to say yes."

"It's not fair."

Mike the Mechanic put his hand on Odo's shoulder.

"You did the best you could, young man, and that's what counts in life. You've learned a valuable lesson, and one day we'll all look back at this over a delicious cinnamon roll covered in melted butter and have a hearty laugh. Would you like an oatmeal cookie as a consolation prize? They're yummy for the tummy. So tasty. You're not going to cry, are you? You look like you might cry."

"I should have listened to that blue mouse."

Mike the Mechanic roared with laughter. "Well said, sir. Sephie and Odo, it's time to meet Bakis Merri-weather. Follow me!"

Chapter 21

The Hound

Odo and Sephie floated behind Mike the Mechanic for what seemed like hours, flashing past swirling clouds of the curious glowing bubbles.

Finally Mike the Mechanic held up one hand, slowing down.

"Here we are, that's Bakis." He pointed to one of the bubbles.

"What do you mean?"

"I mean that's Bakis. I mean here we are. Done deal. Finito. Full stop. Whoop whoop. End of the line. Hop off the trolley. There's no other way to say it, sonny boy."

"What are we supposed to do? Do we talk to it?"

Mike the Mechanic stared at Odo, his eyes blinking. "You don't have the slightest idea where you are, do you?" He gave a great guffaw, slapping his leg.

"Of course we do, we're in Palusia."

"But your old friend Wikerus didn't tell you anything about Palusia, did he? He shoots, he scores, a three pointer. Okay, sonny boy, I'll give you a clue, no extra charge. Run into that bubble like it's Pennsylvania Station, Track 29."

"I have no idea what that means. What will happen?"

"Whoops, gotta go, broken dihydrogen monoxide pipe at 221B Baker Street, big mess. Say hello to Wikerus for me."

Mike the Mechanic gave another rousing laugh, vanishing in a blaze of green light.

Odo and Sephie stared at the glowing bubble.

"I don't really get what's happening here."

"I don't either, but there's only one way to find out."

"Let's do it."

The pair of adventurers held hands and shot toward the little bubble. A split second later they were rolling across a quagmire of wet moss and putrid slimy mud.

Odo staggered to his feet, looking down at his pants. "This is great, my pants are ruined. I just bought them, they have the big pockets in front. I'll never get these stains out. Why is it so gray and dismal here? What is this place?"

"It looks like we're in the middle of a boggy marshland. Look at all the spongy moss."

"I don't have to look at it, I'm up to my ankles in it. Is that a worm? It looks like a worm crawling around in the muck."

"I'm confused, Odo Whitley, and I never get confused. I have no idea where we are, or what that bubble was."

"Mike the Mechanic said this is where Bakis Merriweather lives, but I don't see any houses. Do you think he was tricking us? I don't exactly trust him, especially after his phony three question challenge."

"It's getting lighter out." Sephie squinted, peering across the marshland. "I see a silhouette in the distance. It could be a house, it's hard to tell."

"I see it too. It does look like a house."

Odo yanked his foot out of the muck with a glurpy noise. "Yuck, this is bad."

"I have an idea." Sephie drew a symbol in the air.

"Are you shaping something?"

"I was trying to shape snowshoes so we could walk across the bog, but it's not working. I don't know why."

She flicked her wrist three times. "Nothing. I can't even shape a light orb. My powers don't work here."

Odo put his hand on the ground, concentrating deeply.

"I can't make the ground translucent."

"Interesting. I guess we slog through the muck to that house, knock on the door and see who answers."

The pair of friends set off across the marshland toward the mysterious structure. Two hundred feet later Odo was hopping around on one foot, trying to retrieve his shoe from the foul smelling bog. That was when they heard the eerie howl roll across the marsh. Odo gave a yelp, grabbing his shoe and slipping it back on his foot.

"My socks are ruined. Did you hear that sound?

What was it?"

"I don't know, but we should head for the house. I don't have any powers here, and that means I can't shape an energy shield to protect us from whatever was howling. I'm getting a bad feeling, Odo Whitley."

"Let's go."

Odo and Sephie took off running across the soggy marshland, splashing through shallow ponds, pushing through the spongy moss and thick stagnant mud.

An unearthly howl floated across the shadowy land, transforming into a low agonizing moan, filling the adventurers with an overwhelming sense of dread.

"It's getting closer! What is that thing? Can you see it?"

"Hurry! Another half mile to the house!"

On they ran, Odo crying out, "I lost my shoe again! It's stuck in the mud!" He turned, glancing behind them, giving a shriek. "I saw something! It's black, but I couldn't tell what it was."

"Leave your shoe! Run!"

The deep moans from the creature transformed to a long strident pulsing wail. Odo tried to cover his ears as they raced toward the house.

"Aggh! I stepped on something weird and squishy! It's all over my foot! I think it's green!"

"Faster! It's getting closer!"

Watson let out an irritated yowl from inside Odo's backpack.

"Sorry, Watson! Something is chasing us! Hold on!"

Six minutes later Odo and Sephie came to a halt in

front of a dilapidated three story Victorian mansion, its ancient wrought iron fence perched at odd angles, sections of it sunken into the oozing quagmire.

They leaped over the derelict fence, racing up the cracked uneven walkway to the covered porch with its rotting moss covered wicker furniture, decaying floorboards sagging precariously.

Odo whipped around when he heard the low guttural growl behind them, skittering backwards when he saw the monstrous snarling hound, its blood red eyes piercing the dark haze that clung to the old mansion like a cloud of angry black flies.

"Sephie!!"

Sephie looked in horror at the unearthly green glow forming around the hound. It raised its head, letting loose a horrific moaning wail that slammed through Odo and Sephie, turning their insides to slivers of ice. The hideous beast crept forward, its piercing gaze fixed on Odo, its gold flecked red eyes mesmerizing him, his mind a dark swirling miasma, his thoughts drifting back to his first day at school.

"Odo Whitley! Snap out of it!" Sephie grabbed his arm, yanking him toward the door. She pulled it open, dragging him inside, slamming the door shut just as the unearthly beast thudded violently against it.

Odo sank to the floor. "Whoa, that was close. That thing was controlling my thoughts, I couldn't move. I've never seen anything like it. So scary. What was it?"

Sephie's eyes locked onto Odo. "You know exactly what it is. We've both seen that creature before, but only in our imagination."

"It's the hound of the Baskervilles! How is that possible? Wait, if that's the hound, this must be the mansion in the lonely moorlands of Devonshire. We're in the middle of a Sherlock Holmes story. I'm so confused. How can this be happening?"

"It's pitch black in here, and I can't shape a light orb."

Odo reached into his pack, pulling out the silver flashlight Dr. Livingstone had given him. He flicked it on, moving its narrow beam across the room. Watson leaped out of the backpack, landing on the floor with a yowl, rubbing against Odo's legs.

"We were lucky Cyra gave us this flashlight."

"I don't think luck had anything to do with it. She gave us the flashlight because she knew we'd need it."

"How could she know that?"

"I don't know, maybe it's one of her new powers. Remember how she laughed and told you not to get too scared on Palusia? She must have known about this."

"This house is beyond creepy, way scarier than the mansion in the book. All the furniture is covered with white sheets, and there are cobwebs and dust everywhere." Odo ran his finger across a table top. "So much dust, I don't think anyone has been here in a hundred years."

"So where is Bakis Merriweather?"

"I almost forgot about him. I don't know, Mike the Mechanic said he lived here. Wait, where *is* here? Is all this inside that little bubble?"

"That's a good question. We're either inside the bubble, or it sent us somewhere else through a spectral doorway. Either way, we have to explore the house. There's something here we need to find. I can feel it."

Odo leaned down and scratched Watson's head, then looked up, grinning at Sephie.

"I get to say it."

"Say what?"

"Come, Watson, the game is afoot!"

Chapter 22

Bakis Merriweather

Odo and Sephie crept around the ancient dust filled derelict mansion for almost an hour, poking through drawers, peering into closets and under beds, checking under the moldy sheets that covered the moth eaten furniture. They even braved the attic, brushing away cobwebs and stepping over decaying mouse nests.

"GHOST!!"

Odo skittered backwards with a shriek, his head whipping around. Sephie was grinning at him.

"Just wanted to make sure you were paying attention, Odo Whitley."

"Very funny. Ha ha. I don't see anything here, just more dusty old furniture. Bakis Merriweather doesn't live here, the house is totally deserted."

"There's one place we haven't checked, and I think you know where it is."

"The basement. The thing is, Bakis Merriweather is clearly not going to live in some dank creepy cellar full of spiders and poisonous lizards. There's no point even going down there to check."

"Poisonous lizards? Where did that come from? I don't even need to read your brainwaves to know how scared you are, Odo Whitley."

"I will freely admit I have some slight trepidation about going into the basement, but it also seems like a complete waste of time, like looking for fish in the desert. There's no way he's there."

"One quick look and then we'll leave. Or, if you'd prefer, we could go outside now and deal with that supernatural mind controlling hound."

"Good point. We should check the basement."

The two friends crept down three flights of creaky stairs, reaching the first floor.

"Try the door at the end, the green one."

Odo moved his flashlight from side to side as they made their way down the long hallway. He studied the dark green door.

"I think you might be right about someone being in the cellar."

"Why?"

"The padlock is open, it has a key in it, and there's no dust on either of them."

"I'm impressed, Odo Whitley. Jonathan Morse was right, you'd make an excellent detective."

Sephie twisted the tarnished brass knob, the door hinges squealing painfully as she pulled it open.

"That door could use a little oil, maybe I should look around and see if I can find some."

"Focus, Odo Whitley, we're not here to fix doors."

Odo shone his light on the narrow stairway, the two friends creeping down into the musty cellar. They stopped at the bottom, listening.

"Do you hear that?"

"It sounds like tapping."

"This is not good, not good at all. It's very bad when you hear weird tapping in a creepy basement. Remember how the creatures in *Killer Mole People from the Deep* were always tapping on stuff in basements? Remember what happened to everyone who went down to check on the noise?"

"Odo Whitley, I don't want to hurt your feelings, but that was probably the silliest movie I've ever seen. None of it made sense."

"That's not the point, I'm just saying that tapping sounds in a creepy basement are not a good sign." Odo flicked off his light and pointed. "Way down there, light coming from under that door."

Sephie tilted her head slowly, listening closely. "It's also where the tapping sounds are coming from."

"Maybe it's a tap dancing hermit, a friendly one."

Sephie burst out laughing.

Odo liked it when Sephie laughed at his jokes.

"Okay, let's go see what's making the creepy noises."

They made their way through the cluttered shadowy basement, Odo moving his light across tangled piles of old chairs and rows of inky black doorways.

"This place is ridiculously creepy. It's like we're in a

scary movie. Yuck, more spider webs!"

The tapping was louder now, Odo listening carefully. "Is it just me, or does that sound like an old fashioned typewriter?"

"It does sound like one, Odo Whitley. Should we knock, or barge in?"

"In this case, I think we should knock. You know how killer mole people get when you barge in."

Sephie rolled her eyes, rapping on the door.

The tapping stopped.

Odo could not breathe.

They heard shuffling footsteps from the other side of the door.

"So scary. So scary." Odo's hands were clenched, his knuckles white.

The brass door knob squeaked, turning slowly, the heavy door creaking open half an inch, light flooding into the shadowy basement.

"Yes?"

"Um... we're looking for someone named Bakis Merriweather?"

"Odo and Sephie?"

"What?"

"Odo Whitley and Sephie Crumb? Is that you?"

"Are you Bakis Merriweather?"

The door swung open to reveal an old man in a plaid bathrobe wearing round black rimmed glasses, his face unshaven, his gray hair unkempt, a half eaten candy bar in one hand.

"Come in, come in, Wikerus said you might be

145

coming, but I was unclear about the timing. How was your trip to Palusia? I hope you didn't have too much trouble finding me. I apologize for my ghastly appearance, I've been working on my book all morning. Still on the first draft, I'm afraid."

"Um... Mike the Mechanic showed us where you live. We had to answer three questions though."

The old man gave an exasperated groan. "That man is so peculiar, tormenting everyone he meets with his ridiculous three question challenges. I have no idea why he does that. He should spend more time repairing things and less time asking those infernal questions. So peculiar. So peculiar. I've called him at least a dozen times about my leaky dihydrogen monoxide pipe and I'm still waiting for him to call back."

"You're Bakis Merriweather?"

"Yes, of course. Please have a seat."

Bakis shuffled over to a small couch, clearing off a stack of papers and books, setting them on the floor, motioning for the two friends to sit. He slid into a creaky wooden office chair on metal rollers and spun around, facing the two friends.

"What do you think? Is it scary enough?"

Odo and Sophie glanced at each other.

"Is what scary enough? You mean... the...."

"My book, yes, of course, is it scary enough? Too scary? I don't want it too scary, just scary enough so it's enjoyable, entertaining."

"When you say your book... you mean..."

Bakis furrowed his brow. "My book, the one I'm

working on. What do you think of it?"

"We haven't actually had time to read it. At all."

Bakis studied the two friends with a new curiosity.

"You don't have the slightest idea where you are, do you?"

Odo glanced at Sephie, then at Bakis. "That's what Mike the Mechanic said. We know we're in Palusia, and we flew into a little bubble. After that it's… a bit foggy."

"Ah, all is clear where once all was clouded." Bakis gave a sympathetic smile. "Would you care for a cookie? I have oatmeal or chocolate chip, and I assure you the chips are pure milk chocolate, not those dreadful semi-sweet travesties. Ghastly stuff, simply ghastly. They should be outlawed, the inventor flogged."

"Um, we're fine, thanks. Where are we, exactly?"

"Of course, forgive me. You're inside my mind. That bubble you flew into was my mind, my true essence, my infinite eternal self. I'm currently without physical form, my mind residing here in Palusia until further notice, as they say."

Odo and Sephie stared silently at Bakis.

"Ah, I see what's happened. Wikerus thought it would be amusing to let you figure this all out on your own. Wikerus Praevian, up to his old tricks. Some people never change, that's what I always say. It's quite simple really. As you know, we have a true self, a deeper self. Yours are currently inhabiting your physical forms. When your physical form wears out, your true self leaves, in my case, transitioning to Palusia. It's no different than stepping out of a carriage into a lovely hotel."

"Right. But we can see you. You have a physical form."

"This? A rumply old man in a bathrobe? That's not real, it's a mental construct I use to help me feel like a crusty old jaded writer, helps get me in the mood. I'm retired of course, but writing is my new vocation. I'm working round the clock on the first draft of my first book."

"So you're not really you? You're not an old man in a bathrobe?"

"Oh, dear, no, that would be quite dreadful, quite dreadful indeed. You're still confused. Odo, imagine you're having a dream, walking into the kitchen to get a tasty snack. Is your body in that dream really you? Is the tasty snack really a tasty snack?"

"No, it's just a dream body, a thought. And a dream snack. My real body is sleeping in my bed."

"Exactly. That's more or less what this is. Everything you see around us is a sort of dream world my deeper self is creating. I suppose you could call it a waking dream."

"So everything we saw, the moors and the big scary glowing hound, is all your imagination?"

"Of course, it's me working on my book, it's what I'm thinking about. That's why I was asking if you thought it was scary enough. Or if it was too scary. I don't want it to be too scary."

148

"We're inside your mind while you're writing a book?"

"Bingo, now you've got it. My first novel is about a derelict old mansion in the middle of the desolate foggy moors. There's a ghastly supernatural hound that howls in the night, terrorizing everyone who visits the spooky old home. I haven't gotten to the chapter where the brilliant detective arrives and finds the dead body in the marsh, but it will be lying a few hundred feet from the porch, torn to pieces by that wretched hound."

Odo hesitated. "Well, it was super scary, especially the spooky moors and the part where the hound was chasing us. And the mansion is really scary too, but not too scary. No ghosts, so that's good. I don't like ghosts. The thing is, though, your story sounds an awful lot like one that–"

Sephie jabbed Odo sharply with her elbow.

"I think Odo is saying it sounds like one that would make an amazing movie. We go to the movies every Saturday, and we'd definitely go see one about a scary supernatural hound who lives in the foggy marshlands. I think people would love it."

"Great heavens, do you really? That would be marvelous. I've never even considered the possibility of a movie adaptation. Very interesting. I might have to rewrite several sections with that in mind, make them more visually appealing."

"Sounds great. So, um… did Wikerus happen to mention why we were coming?"

"He said you were trying to find out where your

waystone came from. It's from Emerus, a dreadful place I'm afraid. Very hot, mostly desert, sparsely inhabited by those curious blue Emerusians. They're friendly enough in their way, I suppose, but some of the wild creatures there are simply awful."

"How could you know where the waystone is from? We haven't shown it to you."

"Wikerus faxed me a picture of it and I recognized it instantly. I've been to Emerus several times. It's been a while, of course, at least a thousand years. I suppose things could have changed since then."

"Wikerus faxed you a picture? He faxed it?"

Bakis pointed to a large boxy machine standing in the corner of the room.

"My Excelsior 9000 Fax-o-matic. They were just coming out with these when I died and transitioned to Palusia. Quite a marvelous device. I use it almost every day."

"Are you saying we didn't have to come here, that you could have just told Wikerus where the waystone was from?"

"I did tell him, that's why I was confused by your arrival."

Odo gave a dark look. "Wikerus was not laughing about three Sinarians ordering pizza, he was laughing about sending us to Palusia when he knew we didn't have to go."

"It doesn't matter, Odo Whitley. I wouldn't have missed this for anything. I had so much fun, especially when the hound was chasing us across the moors and you lost your shoe. I wanted to stop and laugh, but the hound would have caught us. Think about it, we got to see Dr. Livingstone and we got to talk to Cyra."

"I guess you're right. Mike the Mechanic was sort of funny, I actually kind of liked him. Plus we got to talk to those crazy food machines. That was… intcresting."

"It was interesting, Odo Whitley. Those machines are amazing."

Odo turned to Bakis. "Thanks so much for your help, and good luck with your book. It sounds really great. Super scary. But not too scary. I've never met a real author before."

"Thank you, Odo, that's very kind of you to say. I'll let you in on a little secret, something I learned long ago, and something which might explain why Wikerus sent you here. Becoming is far more interesting than being. In my particular case, it's much more fun becoming a good writer than it is to actually be one. Do you understand?"

Odo nodded. "I think so. Learning to be a good writer is the fun part because it's so challenging."

"Bingo. Come back and visit any time. Who knows, maybe by then I'll be working on my next book. I've decided to turn it into a series. Who doesn't love thrilling detective stories?"

"It would be cool if your detective had a sidekick, someone kind of funny he could talk to."

"An intriguing idea, a humorous sidekick."

Odo flipped open his pack. "Okay, Watson, my old sidekick Watson, it's time for us to head home, Watson."

Chapter 23

Ordinary Superheroes

Odo and Sephie shifted back home to Wikerus Praevian's sitting room using their registered homestone medallions.

"Why is it so dark? Where's Wikerus?"

"That's odd, he's usually here." Odo flicked on the overhead light. "So what's our plan?"

"I've been thinking about it. I think Silas and Watson should come with us to Emerus."

"I was thinking the same thing. Silas definitely has a big part in this, and Watson might lead us to Mirus, Clara, and Arthur, just like he led us to Silas."

"And it would be good for Silas to go on an adventure. Our trip to Plindor and Atroxia changed my life, made me see the world in a different light. When I came back I could see Brandon Crouch for the coward he is, and he didn't scare me anymore. Odo Whitley, the food machine said your friendship changed me. It said one of the reasons I don't feel like Creepy Crumb anymore is because of you, because of the nice things you say to me."

"That's what you were chatting about?"

Sephie nodded.

"I was chatting with it too. It said you changed my life more than I would ever know, that meeting you was not an accident. That you're my best friend."

"Did it say anything else?"

Odo turned at the sound of footsteps. Wikerus was standing in the doorway, a grin on his face.

"Ah, there you are, back from Palusia already? It all went well, I hope?"

Odo nodded. "It was great, I'm glad we went. Even if we didn't really have to go."

Wikerus made no attempt to hide his amusement. "I have always found the journey to be far more enlightening than the destination."

"We did learn a lot. We're going to take Silas with us to Emerus."

"Excellent. I have no doubt he will prove to be a most invaluable and trustworthy companion."

The following day Odo and Sephie met Silas in the school cafeteria, telling him about their adventure in Palusia.

"We want you to come with us to Emerus, help us find your grandpa."

"How do we get there?"

"The same way your grandpa did. We touch the carving of the blue creature."

"How do we get back?"

"We hold hands and use our registered homestone medallions to shift home."

"You're sure it's safe?"

"Getting there and back is safe, but there's no way of knowing what will happen once we're on Emerus. Bakis said it's a sparsely populated desert planet. He mentioned something about dangerous creatures, but Sephie's powers can protect us from anything like that."

"It does sound fun. I've never been on a real adventure. Do you really think my grandpa and Arthur and Clara are still alive after all this time?"

Sephie nodded. "I'm certain they are. My inner voice said we should look for them."

"I'll do it, I'll go. Wait, what about my parents? My dad will worry."

"Time doesn't work the same when we shift to another dimension. In our world we're gone for less than an hour. And don't forget, if things get too scary there we can always shift back home."

Odo added, "Bring extra clothes, hiking boots, and a hat to protect you from the desert sun."

"We leave tomorrow afternoon. We'll meet at the theater and be back before the movie is over."

Sephie studied Silas' brainwaves. His anxiety was rising. "Silas, I was nervous the first time I shifted, but it turned out to be fun, not scary at all."

"It's not that, it's something else. We're sort of friends now, right?"

"Of course we are."

"So if I told you something… disturbing, we'd still be friends?"

"What kind of something disturbing?"

"It's about Odo."

"About me? What is it? What's disturbing about me?"

"You know I can see ghosts, right?"

"Right, you can see the Lady in Black."

"There are others."

"What kind of others?" Odo's hands were suddenly clammy.

"There's a ghost standing behind you, Odo. I've seen him watching you before but I didn't say anything. He's wearing an old fashioned sailor's uniform from World War Two."

"A ghost is watching me? Why would a ghost be watching me? You're serious? There's a ghost standing behind me right now? He's watching me?"

Sephie touched Odo's arm. "Stop. Ghosts can't hurt you, Odo Whitley. They're just people without physical bodies."

"I know that, but it's still creepy. Why is a ghost watching me?"

"He's gone now. He's not scary. I've only seen a few scary ghosts, angry about something that happened when they were alive. They were angry then, and now they're angry ghosts. Almost all the ghosts I see are nice, they stay behind to watch over people they love. I don't really know why I was so scared of the Lady in Black. I guess because she was in my house and I didn't know who she was."

"The Ghost Sailor isn't scary?"

"Not even a little. I think he's protecting you. I think he cares about you. It sounds weird, but I think he's kind of funny. I felt like laughing when I saw him."

"Oh. That's not so bad, I guess. You don't know who he is?"

"I don't. I can't talk to ghosts, I just get feelings about them."

"You've seen ghosts since you were little and never told anyone except your parents?"

"My dad told me not to tell anyone. He said people would think I was crazy. They said the same thing to my Grandpa Mirus."

"Seeing things other people can't see doesn't mean you're crazy. It's a cool power. The Ghost Sailor freaked me out a little, but mostly because I was surprised. You can't even imagine the creatures Sephie and I have seen. They used to scare me, but now I don't think twice when I see a weird alien. It's just life in a different physical form. The universe is filled with billions of different life forms, but it's all just life."

"I always thought there was something wrong with me."

Sephie nodded sympathetically. "And I thought there was something wrong with me because I could see people's brainwaves. Odo thought there was something wrong with him because he was translucent."

"It turns out we were superheroes and didn't know it."

"Maybe one day I'll feel like a superhero. Mostly I

just feel different and wish I wasn't. I wish I fit in more with the other kids."

"You'd probably feel more like a superhero if you had a superhero name. Sephie and I were talking about it, and we think your name should be Ghostwatcher. That's what your Grandpa Mirus called the goggles he was inventing."

A grin crept across Silas' face. "Ghostwatcher. That's kind of a cool name. Mysterious."

"That's it then, you're Ghostwatcher. Tomorrow afternoon we leave for Emerus, just three ordinary superheroes on a routine adventure to another world."

Chapter 24

Emerus

Odo and Sephie left for the theatre on Saturday afternoon, arriving twenty minutes early.

"So, Sephie, I was thinking, this is my week to choose the movie, but since we're not going to actually see it, I should probably get to choose next week instead."

"Sorry, Odo Whitley, that's not the agreement we made. We take turns choosing, every other week, no exceptions, no loopholes. I'm sad to say it looks like we're going to miss out on *Radioactive Death Worms from the Ninth Dimension.*"

"It's supposed to be really good. These giant atomic fire breathing worms come up through the storm drains and it turns out–"

"Did you remember to bring a hat? Don't forget, Bakis Merriweather said it's a scorching hot desert planet."

"Of course I remembered, I haven't forgotten how brutal the sun was on Plindor. I also brought sun screen and two flashlights, in case your powers don't work.

But back to the movies, since we'll be missing *Radioactive Death Worms from the Ninth Dimension,* maybe next week you could pick one that–"

"Hi, Odo! Hi, Sephie!"

Odo turned to see Silas approaching.

"Hi, Silas. Are you ready for Emerus?"

"I was born ready."

Sephie groaned.

"What?"

"Nothing, it's just that Odo and I agreed never to say we were born ready."

"I believe you said I could say it every fourth time."

"I changed the rules. You never get to say it."

"Fine."

"Let's go behind the theater so no one will see us shift. I have the waystone in my pack."

The three friends made their way to the rear of the building, stepping into a small alcove. Sephie pulled the lead box from her pack.

"Are we ready?"

Odo and Silas glanced at each other.

"Yes, we're ready, Sephie."

"Silas, when I open the box you're going to feel a powerful electric shock. We'll touch the blue carved figure on three."

Sephie flipped the lid open.

Silas let out a yelp, sparks flying off his fingertips.

"One, two, THREE!"

Three hands simultaneously touched the blue carved figure.

The movie theater vanished, replaced by a long shadowy room filled with dusty glass display cases.

Silas' jaw dropped. "I can't believe it. It worked! This is incredible. Hey, Odo, did you know you're solid?"

"I'm only translucent on Earth. When we transition to another world I turn solid. It was weird at first, but now I'm kind of used to it."

Sephie pointed to one of the display cases. "See anything familiar, Odo Whitley?"

"Carved blue figures. I think this is a museum. Lots of artifacts. That case is full of stone knives and beads."

"This all makes sense. Mirus found the carved blue figure here and brought it back to Earth. You said those brass goggles let him transition to other dimensions?"

"His journal said he could enter some dimensions, but not all of them. He didn't understand why, though."

"The good news is we know where they arrived. Now we have to figure out where they went."

The look of astonishment had not left Silas' face. "I can't believe we're on an alien world. It feels like a dream."

Odo laughed. "That's what I said when we shifted to Pacalia. Sephie pinched me, but I didn't wake up."

Sephie stepped around the display cases to a tall window, pulling back a heavy curtain, looking outside.

"Odo Whitley, you need to see this. I don't think you're going to need that sunscreen."

"What is it?" Odo darted over to the window. "Whoa, it's all flooded, a big flooded city. The water

160

looks deep."

"The first two or three floors of the buildings are underwater."

Silas yelped when he peered through the dusty window. "Blue creatures in the wooden boats! They're aliens! I'm looking at aliens."

"I guess Bakis was wrong about Emerus being a desert planet."

"He did say he hadn't been here in a thousand years."

"How could a desert world flood like this?"

Sephie shook her head. "Maybe it's just this one area. Or maybe Emerus had ice caps that melted."

"It seems like a lot of water for melting icecaps."

"Maybe there was an earthquake and the ground sank."

"You brought your translator disk?"

"Got it. We should have gotten one for Silas at Girard Station."

"I did get one, Odo Whitley." Sephie handed the small gold disk to Silas.

"What's this?"

"It's a universal translator disk so you can talk to other creatures. The guard at Girard Station laughed at us because we didn't know about them. He said they've been around for millennia. You stick it on your left temple."

"Done."

Sephie looked around the room. "Stairs are over there. Let's head down."

161

"We'll need a boat."

"First things first, Odo Whitley." The three friends walked cautiously down the steps.

"This floor is flooded. Let's climb across the display cases to that big window."

Ten minutes later Odo was standing on a wide ledge outside the building.

"There's a boat floating next to that building. It's not tied up, I can swim over and get it."

"No need for that, Odo Whitley." Sephie climbed onto the ledge. She held out both hands, concentrating deeply, a pale green light shooting across the water to the boat.

"What are you doing?"

"It's moving!" Silas watched in stunned surprise as the wooden craft turned, drifting across the water toward them. "Are you doing that?"

Odo grinned. "Of course she is. Encephalo Girl has amazing powers."

Silas grabbed the boat when it bumped up against the ledge. "You can move objects with your mind?"

Sephie nodded. "Learning how to control it was the hardest part. Cyra taught me. She said Fortisians start training when they're little kids. She's incredible."

"All aboard!"

They hopped into the boat, Odo flipping his pack open, letting Watson out. He sniffed the air, curling up next to Sephie.

"He seems pretty relaxed for being on another world."

162

Odo grabbed the oars. "Where to, Captain Sephie?"

Sephie scanned their watery surroundings. "This looks like Venice, beautiful old stone buildings and lots of water. See all the boats over that way? It looks like a market. Let's head over there and see if anyone remembers humans passing through here. I don't think that's something they would forget."

"I'll sing a sea shanty while I'm rowing."

"No sea shanties."

"I know a good one about a drunken sailor. It's really funny."

"Start rowing, Odo Whitley. Put your shoulders into it. No time for drunken sailor songs."

Silas' grin faded when he looked back at the museum. A lone figure was standing on the ledge, a sailor dressed in a crisp white uniform and cap, his eyes on their little boat.

Chapter 25

The Lighthouse

"Let's ask these guys." Odo pointed to a small boat being paddled by two of the blue creatures.

Odo waved to them as they approached. "Hello, there! Could you help us?"

The creatures paddled faster, passing without a glance or a nod.

"That was rude. Maybe they can't see us."

"That's not it, Odo Whitley. I was studying their brainwaves. They were afraid to look at us. Think about it, if you were paddling a boat past a red eyed scaly demon and it called out to you, would you stop to chat?"

"We're not exactly red eyed demons, Sephie. There's really no excuse for rude behavior like that."

"Maybe they're shy, have a hard time talking to people they don't know."

Odo and Sephie glanced at each other.

"That's possible, but when I studied their brain-waves I definitely saw a lot of fear. They were afraid of us."

"Let's try the market, there's bound to be someone there who will talk to us. They can't all be afraid."

Ten minutes later their little craft approached the flotilla of small boats, a cacophony of sounds filling the air, dozens of exuberant vendors loudly proclaiming the wondrous virtues of their wares.

"Whoa, this place is busy."

Silas studied two of the blue creatures in a nearby boat. "I just realized something. They have two arms, not four. The blue carved figure had four arms. And these creatures have bright green eyes, not red ones like the carving."

"Interesting. Maybe the carved figure is a mythological creature, like a dragon or a unicorn."

"Maybe."

Odo rowed their boat into the bustling market.

This was followed by a sudden and profound silence, the only sounds being the lapping of small waves against the boats.

"Uh oh, this can't be good. No one is talking, and no one is looking at us."

Sephie called out, "We're trying to find our friends who came here a long time ago. They're lost, and we want to bring them home."

Silence.

Silas took a deep breath and cried out, "It's my grandpa and his two children. We just want to find them, we're not here to hurt anyone."

Silence.

He called out again, "Please help us! Please!"

A single whispered word floated across the water.

"Augur."

Other voices rang out.

"Augur! Augur!"

Odo waved to them. "Thank you! Is Augur a place? A person?"

Silence.

Silas saw the white uniformed Ghost Sailor on top of a low building. He was pointing to the east.

"So, anyway, I was thinking we should head east, that way. I'm getting a really strong feeling that's where we should go."

"Really? Did your inner voice tell you?"

"Not exactly, but I'm certain we should go east."

"Okay, east it is."

Odo turned the little boat, leaving the bustling market behind them. It wasn't long until they heard the boisterous vendors once again hawking their wares.

The three companions headed through the maze of magnificent stone buildings. Watson was now curled up on Sephie's lap.

"I like Watson. I wasn't sure how I felt about cats, but he's nice. I like that he has a mind of his own, does what he wants, doesn't just obey commands. I can't imagine how he got back to Earth from Emerus."

"That is a mystery. These buildings are really cool. They remind me of ancient Rome. They had some amazing architecture and engineering back then. It's interesting that the creatures in the market weren't using any advanced technology. They had wooden boats and crude paddles, but that's it. Their clothes looked hand made."

"The old civilization must have collapsed when the planet flooded. Remember what happened to the Atroxians?"

"I wish I knew what caused the floods. Bakis Merriweather said it was a scorching hot desert planet, and now it's covered in water. How is that possible?"

"A giant ice comet could have hit it, then melted and flooded everything."

Sephie shook her head. "A comet that big would have been an extinction event, destroying everything on the planet, wiping out most of the lifeforms. It's something else."

"Silas, any idea how far we have to go? We're at the outer edge of the city, no more buildings, just open water."

Silas glanced around them. The Ghost Sailor was floating above the sparkling sea less than twenty feet away. He was still pointing to the east.

"We go east, that's all I know."

Sephie let out a yelp. "What was I thinking?" She reached into her pack, pulling out a pair of dark green glasses. "I brought the long distance glasses Cyra gave me."

She slipped them on, adjusting a small silver dial on the side, giving a triumphant shout. "Got it! I know where we're going."

She handed the glasses to Odo. He put them on, looking to the east. "What is that?"

167

"I think it's a lighthouse."

"That must have been the shoreline before it flooded. That would explain why there's a lighthouse way out there."

Silas nodded. "The oceans rose and flooded everything. I read if the ice caps on Earth melted, the ocean would rise two hundred feet and flood all the coastal cities."

"But if Emerus used to be a scorching hot desert planet, wouldn't the ice have already melted?"

"Good point, Odo Whitley. This is definitely a scrumbly mystery."

"And we have to unscrumble it?"

"Precisely. We need to get to that lighthouse. Get cracking, Odo Whitley. Time is money."

"In case you hadn't noticed, this isn't a Roman galley ship, Sephie. But it does remind me of when we got captured by the *Canthus* on Plindor and I had to pedal all day long. I wish we had a sail."

"There's no wind here, a sail wouldn't help us."

Silas said, "Let's trade places and I'll row for a while. We'll take turns."

"Sounds great. Hey, Sephie, how about shaping us some lunch? I'm starving."

Sephie drew four symbols and a tray filled with sandwiches, drinks, and Proto's Taste-E Kakes appeared next to her.

"You remembered the Taste-E Kakes."

"Of course I did, they're your favorite. We'll be having a big salad for dinner, in case you were wondering."

"Great, who doesn't love a big leafy green salad?"

An hour later Silas was still rowing.

"You're sure you don't want me to row?"

"No, this is really good exercise. My dad always says I should exercise more instead of doing my other stuff."

"What other stuff?"

"I play around with electronics, build things. I know, big surprise, the kid who sees ghosts and gets bullied by Brandon Crouch is a geeky nerd."

"That's not what I was thinking at all. I was thinking you sound like your grandpa, and he was an amazing inventor. Seriously, he made goggles in 1921 that let you see into other dimensions."

"I guess he was pretty cool. He must have been really smart."

Odo slipped on the long distance glasses, studying the lighthouse. "Do you want the good news or the bad news?"

"The good news."

"Someone in the lighthouse is watching us."

"What's the bad news?"

"He's blue, has four arms and red eyes."

Chapter 26

Augur

"Let's land on that little beach."

"I don't see the blue guy anywhere. Do you think he might be dangerous?"

"He lives in a lighthouse, Odo Whitley. He's not a howling supernatural mind controlling hound. I wonder why no one in the market would look at us?"

"Maybe my grandpa did something that scared them."

"That seems unlikely. Help me drag the boat onto the sand."

The three friends pulled the wooden craft ashore, gazing up at the towering lighthouse.

"It's way taller than it looked."

Sephie climbed the rocky slope to the arched silver doors of the monolithic structure. She was raising her hand to knock when the doors whirred open.

"Whoever lives here is generating their own power."

Sephie peered inside. "It's packed with crates and

boxes and all kinds of equipment."

Odo entered, scanning the room. "Circular stairway. The blue guy was watching us from the top floor. Let's go find out why they sent us here."

Fifteen floors later Odo stopped to rest, his legs burning. He took a seat on a wooden crate, Watson hopping onto his lap.

"That's a lot of stairs."

"Fifteen floors, all jam packed with wooden crates and strange looking machines."

"Our Mr. Blue could be the world's biggest pack rat."

"Odo Whitley, you should probably turn around."

"He's standing behind me, isn't he?"

Sephie nodded.

Odo turned to see the eight foot tall, four armed blue creature looking down at him with unblinking red eyes.

"Chosen Ones. You were exiled?"

"Chosen Ones?"

"Why are you here?"

"Are you Augur?"

"Why are you here?"

"We're looking for three of our friends who came to Emerus a long time ago, a man and two children. We want to bring them home."

The creature paused for a moment, then said, "Follow me."

After four more flights of stairs they reached the top of the lighthouse.

"Whoa, the view up here is incredible. That water

goes on forever. There's another city way over there. I can just barely see it."

Silas was eyeing stacks of gleaming glass panels on the floor.

"Are those solar panels?"

The blue creature turned to him in surprise. "What would you know about solar panels?"

"I know a lot about them. They convert solar energy into electrical energy." He kneeled down and examined one of the panels. "These are far more advanced than ours. It looks like they capture light from the full solar spectrum. Very efficient."

"They convert ninety-four percent of solar energy to electrical energy, all the power I need."

"Do you know how they capture the whole solar spectrum?"

"I will show you. I am Augur. I am here because I was banished, first by my own people, then by the Flatlanders."

"Why were you banished?"

"I disagreed with a decision made by the Council of Three, was betrayed by an old friend, then exiled to the Flatlands. The Flatlanders decided I was a demon, their conclusion based on the number of arms I possess. They banished me to this old lighthouse. Oddly enough, I have grown quite fond of it, spending most of my time studying the technologies of Those Who Came Before."

"Those who came before what?"

Augur did not answer.

Sephie took a seat on a wooden crate. "Augur, you

called us Chosen Ones. Were there others like us?"

"Your friends, a man and two children. My people took them captive."

"Why did they take them?"

"Because the Altusians have become lost in a morass of superstition and childlike magical thinking. A fraudulent seer declared your friends to be Chosen Ones, sent by the gods to save our world. The Council of Three believed him, and now they sit and wait for a day which will never come."

"What are they supposed to be saving your world from?"

"Why are you really here? Why would you come so far to save three strangers?"

"They're not strangers, they're my family. My grandpa Mirus, my uncle Arthur, and my aunt Clara. I never got to meet them. They came here when my dad was a boy."

"Family. A worthy enough cause for such a perilous venture. I can tell you where they are, but any attempt you make to reach them could well cost you your lives."

"Where are they?"

"Across the Great Sea, deep in the Mountains of Altus. You will find them in the Forest of Dark Creations near the Fortress of Rain."

Odo was remembering the forest in his bedroom.

"Does it rain a lot in that forest? Are the trees really big, lots of moss? Creepy slime covered orange slugs crawling around?"

"You have described the Forest of Dark Creations. You have been there?"

"It's complicated."

Augur leaned back against a wall, eyeing the three adventurers, his gaze turning to Sephie.

"What about you? You are far more than you appear to be. Who are you?"

Sephie held out one hand, a beam of pale blue light shooting out. A heavy crate floated up, drifting across the room, landing with a thump next to Augur.

"I'm a Fortisian."

"A wizard. I thought as much."

"Not a wizard. A girl who can use the energy of her mind to move objects. It's science, not magic. The Flatlanders would say your solar panels are dark magic, something to be feared."

Augur laughed. "I have been bested by your logic."

"How wide is the Great Sea? Can we row across it?"

Augur shook his head. "Unlikely. It is a four thousand mile journey across the sea to the Mountains of Altus. You'll pass a number of cities on the way, but it's mostly open water."

"How did you get here when they banished you?"

"I was carried on the back of a Gnorli bird."

"Right, a Gnorli bird. Well, our little rowboat is clearly not going to work, so we have to find a bigger boat, one we can sleep in."

"How will that help us, Odo Whitley? A bigger boat is harder to row. It's just physics, the acceleration of an object as produced by a net force is directly proportional to the magnitude of–."

"Follow me, please." Augur stepped over to a gray metallic panel, tapping a violet disc next to it. The panel slid open, revealing a small room.

"What's in there?"

"The elevator."

"You have an elevator? Seriously?"

Chapter 27

Let's Light this Candle

The adventurers followed Augur outside, heading to the rear of the lighthouse.

"This island is bigger than I thought. What's in those two buildings?"

"One contains something which may aid in your passage to the Mountains of Altus."

Augur approached the long dark blue metallic structure, tapping on a grid of gray squares. A twenty foot wide door rolled up with a low rumble.

"Whoa, is that a boat?" Odo peered into the darkened building, his eyes on the gleaming hull of a sleek thirty foot long silver craft. "So cool."

Augur entered the building, running a hand along the smooth surface of the boat. "I've spent a great deal of time trying to understand what powers this ship, but its secrets have eluded me, its technology beyond my understanding."

"Let's have a look." Silas clambered up a short

ladder, hopping onto the deck. "Wow. Seriously, wow."

He climbed up to the bridge, finding a curved console holding only a single black disk. He tapped it. "Nothing. Where's the engine?"

Augur pointed to a green deck panel near the stern of the ship. "That lifts up."

Silas raised the hinged panel, studying the rows of clear glass tubes circling a dull golden sphere. "I have no idea what this is. Odo, does the ship have a propeller?"

Odo ran to the stern of the ship. "No propeller, just two big silver tube things poking out. It looks like they can move around."

"Look under the hull. Is it smooth?"

Odo crouched down, studying the underside of the ship. "It has some kind of big open grid on it, about six feet long and three feet wide."

"It's a water jet. Water is sucked in through the grid under the ship and shoots out the two jets at the stern. You steer it by moving the jets. What I don't understand is what powers it. There's no gas engine, no batteries, and no controls besides the black disk on the bridge console."

Silas froze when the Ghost Sailor appeared on the bow of the ship, kneeling down, pressing one hand against the hull, his head tilted as though he was listening to something.

Odo called up to Silas. "What do you think?"

"I'll let you know in a minute. I'm just checking on something."

177

The Ghost Sailor stood up, motioning for Silas to follow him.

Silas hopped down from the boat. "Just need to check on something. Be right back."

Odo glanced over to Sephie. She shrugged.

Silas trailed behind the Ghost Sailor, watching him drift through the door into the lighthouse.

"Guess I go inside."

The doors slid open and he entered, the Ghost Sailor waiting for him on the circular stairway.

"I hope you're not going all the way to the top."

Nine floors later the ghost stopped, Silas trying to catch his breath. "You're in pretty good shape for a ghost."

The Ghost Sailor floated behind a stack of wooden crates. Silas clambered over the boxes, the ghost pointing to a long black metallic case.

"What's in there?"

The ghost vanished.

"Okay, let's find out what our friendly ghost wants me to see."

He looked up when he heard Odo and Sephie coming up the stairs.

Odo peered between the crates. "What are you looking for?"

"Just checking on a few things."

Silas unlatched the metal box and flipped it open. "This is incredible, so incredible."

"What are those things?" Odo eyed the row of eight glowing golden spheres.

"These are our tickets to the Mountains of Altus. Help me carry this down to the boat."

"What do they do? How did you know they were here?"

"You know, just a hunch."

Odo snorted. "Seriously? You're going with that? A hunch?"

"I'll tell you later. We need to get these to the ship, then we have to figure out how to launch it."

"We have to lug this box down nine flights of stairs?"

Silas pointed to the elevator.

"Oh, right, I forgot."

The three friends carried the box of gold spheres back to the ship, setting it gently on the deck.

Silas raised the green engine panel, pointing to the dark gold sphere. "Needs a new battery, that's all."

"That gold sphere is a battery?"

"It's a power source, but not like anything I've ever seen. I don't have the slightest idea how it works."

He reached down, gently pulling on the gold sphere. "It feels like it's being held in place by a magnetic force." He lifted the sphere out of the engine compartment, replacing it with one from the black box.

"That's it?"

"Let's find out." They ran up to the bridge, Silas holding his finger over the black disk. "Ready?"

Odo looked at Sephie.

She groaned. "Fine, go ahead and say it."

"Let's light this candle."

179

"Odo Whitley, you stole that line from *Invasion of the Shrieking Ghosts*. That's what the brash young scientist said when he turned on his ghost vaporizing blaster."

"It's still cool, almost as cool as let's rock and roll."

"Don't say it again. It hurts my ears."

Silas cleared his throat loudly.

"Oh, right. Yes, we're ready."

Silas tapped the black disk, giving a triumphant cry when he heard the humming from below deck, the black disk turning bright green. A colorful holoscreen blinked on above the console.

"It worked!"

Sephie studied the images on the holoscreen. "It's a map, and controls. Right there, this is where we arrived, and this is the island we're on. That's the lighthouse."

"That blinking red dot on the island is the boat's location."

Silas pointed to the base of the map. "Those are the ship's controls; speed, direction, and coordinates. It looks like we can enter the coordinates of the Mountains of Altus and the ship will take us there using an autonomous guidance system."

"We don't have to steer it?"

"We tell it where we want to go and it takes us there."

Augur had been standing silently behind the three friends. "You are all quite remarkable."

"We just had to replace the ship's power source, the gold spheres."

Odo looked down to the shoreline. "The good news is, the boat has power. The bad news is, it's not in the water."

"And we have no way to launch it. No ramp, no trailer."

"I could try to move it with my mind."

"It's too big. You've never moved anything this big before. It sounds dangerous. You could hurt yourself. "

"If Cyra can shape giant lighting storms, I should be able to move a boat."

"Are you sure? Do you promise to stop if you start feeling lightheaded, like you might faint?"

"Knock it off, Odo Whitley. Let's rock and roll."

Chapter 28

The Phoenix

Sephie drew four quick symbols in the air, then held out both hands, a rippling sheet of blue light enveloping the gleaming silver craft.

She closed her eyes, concentrating deeply, the blue light intensifying, pulsing rapidly.

Odo whispered, "It's moving!"

"Quiet."

"Sorry."

The boat rocked gently, as though floating in water. It took all of Odo's self control not to shout out when the thirty foot long craft lifted gently up from the floor, floating toward the open door.

Silas' mouth was hanging open.

Sephie opened her eyes, both arms extended in front of her, the ship drifting out of the building.

"I think I've got it. It's not as hard as I thought it would be. The mass of the object isn't important, it doesn't really matter. It's not about physical mass."

She walked behind the immense craft, following it down the rocky slope to the shoreline.

Odo let out a cheer when the boat dropped into the sea with a great splash. "You did it! Three cheers for Encephalo Girl!"

Sephie gave Odo a smug look. "I told you I could."

Her eyes rolled back in her head and she collapsed, Augur grabbing her before she hit the ground.

"Sephie!" Odo ran to her, kneeling down beside her. "Is she all right?"

"I don't know. She's breathing."

Odo shook her arm. "Sephie? Are you okay?"

She moved her head slightly, her eyes still closed. "…that dumb shrieking ghost movie last time…"

"Dumb shrieking ghost movie? Why is she saying that?"

"I think she's talking in her sleep. It must have taken all her energy to move the boat, much more than she realized. She needs to rest."

Augur picked Sephie up and carried her inside, setting her on the couch. Her eyes flickered open for a split second, then closed. "Thanks, Mom. Big test tomorrow." Watson hopped onto the couch, curling up next to her.

Later that afternoon Silas was showing Odo how to link solar panels to an electric motor when they heard Sephie call out.

"Odo Whitley!"

He leaped up and ran inside. Sephie was sitting up, rubbing her eyes.

"Are you okay?"

"Why am I sleeping on the couch? What time is it?

We need to launch the boat."

"What?"

"The boat, we have to get it in the water. Why was I sleeping?"

"You don't remember fainting?"

"I don't faint, Odo Whitley. No time for jokes."

"Sephie, the boat is in the water. You moved it with your mind, then you fainted. You've been sleeping for six hours. You don't remember any of that?"

Sephie jumped up and looked through the murky glass. She turned in surprise when she saw the long silver craft tied up at the dock.

"I did that?"

Odo nodded. "It was incredible. When you were moving it, you said it was a lot easier than you thought it would be, that the mass of the object isn't important, that it didn't matter."

"I don't remember any of that. I wonder what I meant by the mass isn't important?"

"You're not doing anything like that again until we talk to Wikerus. Seriously, Sephie, you could have damaged your brain or something."

"I don't use my physical brain to move objects, but you're right, I should talk to Wikerus. It's a little scary that I fainted and can't remember anything."

"There's something else. Right after you fainted you were talking in your sleep and said something really weird, something that didn't sound like you at all."

"Was it my voice? Did I explain why the mass of the object doesn't matter?"

"It was your voice, and you said *Invasion of the Shrieking Ghosts* was a dumb movie."

Sephie froze. "I must have been delirious, Odo Whitley. You know, from moving the boat. I'm still feeling a little dizzy." She held out both arms, weaving back and forth.

"You don't look dizzy."

"Snap out of it, Odo Whitley. The movie was entertaining, but it was dumb. Being friends doesn't mean we have to like the same movies."

"I just wanted you to like it as much as I did. I understand what you're saying though. *Forgotten Memories* was sort of silly, so predictable."

"What? So predictable? For your information, that movie won more awards than any other–"

The front door swung open, Silas and Augur stepping inside.

"How are you feeling?"

"Much better, still a little tired."

"I packed everything we'll need for the trip. Augur and I took the boat out for a test run and it functions perfectly. It's really fast, cruises at about fifty miles an hour. If we run it non-stop, it should take us five or six days to get there. Augur helped me enter the coordinates for the Mountains of Altus, so we're good to go."

"That's great, Silas. We'd still be stuck here if you hadn't found those gold spheres. That was amazing. Let's leave first thing in the morning, I need a little more rest. Augur, you're sure you don't want to come with us?"

185

"As tempting as it sounds, I must decline. I have a great deal of work to do now that Silas has discovered the gold power spheres. I found two more boxes of them on the eleventh floor, and there are a number of curious machines in the second storage building which are powered by them. I am quite anxious to discover the nature of those devices."

"Sounds fun."

The following morning the three adventurers rose with the sun, had breakfast, and headed down to the dock, the silver ship rocking gently in the blue green waters of the Great Sea.

Odo was climbing aboard when Sephie held up her hand.

"Stop! We forgot something!"

"I'm sure I packed everything we need."

"Not that, we forgot to name the ship."

Odo's eyes brightened. "Good idea. We should name it something cool like... *The Screaming Tiger.* Maybe not that, but something sort of like it."

"I want to call it *The Phoenix.*"

"*The Phoenix?* That's kind of boring. If you want to name it after a bird it should be an eagle or a hawk, maybe a vulture. Maybe *The Screaming Clawed Eagle.*"

"Don't you remember, Odo Whitley? *Ex cineribus resurgam?*"

"Of course I remember, that's Latin for *Out of the ashes I shall rise.* I know the Phoenix is a bird that dies in a fire and rises up again from the ashes. But a name like *The Screaming Tiger* is way cooler."

"Odo Whitley, think about it. Each of us has risen up from the ashes in our own way. You were born translucent, I never knew my parents, and Silas grew up seeing ghosts. It hasn't been easy for any of us. It was hard to overcome all those obstacles. We were all lonely, but now here we are, three friends exploring a distant world. Could you ever have imagined you'd be doing this?"

"Odo, Sephie's right. It's a really good name."

"You've convinced me, Sephie Crumb. *The Phoenix* it is.

Sephie drew a quick symbol, the new name appearing in large black letters on the side of the ship. A bottle of champagne blinked into her hand.

"Bless *The Phoenix* and all who sail on her. May we find happiness and friendship on all our voyages."

The bottle shot forward, shattering against the prow of the ship, the glass vanishing before it hit the ground.

"Whoo hoo! All aboard!"

Odo clambered onto *The Phoenix,* followed by Sephie and Silas. The three adventurers bid their farewells to Augur, taking their places on the bridge.

"Here we go!" Silas touched a blue circle on the holoscreen and *The Phoenix* slipped silently away from the shore, turning to the east.

"The engine is quiet, I can hardly hear it."

Silas tapped the blue circle a second time and the ship shot forward, skimming across the sparkling waters of the Great Sea.

Chapter 29

Ribbit

Odo stood on the bow of *The Phoenix*, the wind blowing through his hair. He called out to Sephie, "We're crossing a mysterious ocean on a silver alien speed boat. What could be more amazing than this?"

Sephie was lying on the cushioned seats that lined the bow of the craft, her eyes closed. "Sit down, you're blocking the sun. See anything new?"

"Looks like another city ahead of us. I can't tell where the old shoreline is though."

Silas slid open the bridge window. "Big city up ahead! The autonomous guidance system is sending us right past it, but if we get too close I'm taking over. We don't know who lives there, it could be bandits or pirates or something worse."

Odo turned to Sephie. "Remember the pirates on Plindor? That was so much fun."

"Only because Cyra was there to protect us."

"That's true. The pirate captain was scary, but not as scary as Cyra."

Odo studied the skyline of the approaching city. "A

lot of it is on dry ground."

Sephie sat up, slipping on her long distance glasses.

"You're right, it was built on a big hill. There's something flying above the city." She twisted the silver dial on her glasses. "This is not good, Odo Whitley. Flatlanders on giant birds are heading this way, and it looks like they're carrying weapons."

"Silas!" Odo pointed to the black dots in the sky. "Flatlanders with weapons!"

Silas tapped the holo controls and the ship shot forward, veering away from the city, planing across the smooth sea at sixty miles an hour.

"They're gaining on us! How is that possible?"

"Those birds are gigantic."

"Augur said a Gnorli bird carried him across the Great Sea."

"They must be Gnorli birds. I can't believe how fast they can fly!"

Silas glanced back at the birds, tapping the controls again. The ship sped up, ripping across the water at eighty miles an hour.

"They're catching up to us!"

Odo saw a puff of smoke come from one of the Gnorli birds. A second later the sea around them erupted with a thunderous explosion, their craft rocking wildly.

Odo screamed, "Faster!"

Sephie drew three symbols in the air, an enormous rippling blue energy field blinked into existence above them. A second puff of smoke billowed out, the

Flatlander's deadly projectile hitting Sephie's energy field, exploding harmlessly overhead.

"They're turning back! I think you scared them off."

Silas slowed the ship down and flipped the guidance system back on. "That was amazing! You can project defensive energy fields?"

Sephie nodded. " Cyra taught me while we were on the *Canthus*."

Odo rubbed his hands together. "I'm starving. How about shaping us lunch? I'm thinking grilled cheese sandwiches, fries, chocolate shakes, and a box of Proto's Taste-E Kakes."

"Mmm, that does sound yummy." Sephie drew a quick symbol and a large bowl of salad appeared on Odo's lap. "Bon appetit, Odo Whitley."

"What's this?"

"It's called salad. You need to eat more fruits and vegetables, not just Taste-E Kakes."

Odo grimaced. "I guess." He was poking at the salad with his fork when he felt *The Phoenix* decelerate rapidly. "What's wrong? Why are we slowing down?"

"I'm not sure." Silas ran to the bridge. "The power level is way down, and there's a blinking gold circle on the holo screen."

"Maybe it needs a new power sphere."

"That must be it. I wasn't sure how long they'd last. Lucky for us I brought all seven of them. They're in the hold."

Odo nodded, peering over the side of the ship. "We're officially dead in the water." He dipped his hand into the sea. "Nice and warm. Perfect for swimming."

Sephie leaned over the side. "If you don't mind swimming with a little frog."

"What?"

Sephie pointed to a cute orange frog face poking up from the water.

"I love frogs. They don't give you warts, you know." Odo reached down for the little amphibious creature.

"Don't touch it, Odo Whitley. It could be poisonous."

"It doesn't look poisonous, it looks friendly." Odo plucked the wriggling creature from the water, holding it up for Sephie to see. "Not scary at all. Hey, Watson, look at my new froggy friend. I should call him Hoppy."

Watson looked up at Odo, leaping straight up when he saw the frog. His back arched, his ears flattening against his head, his jaw chattering wildly. He bared his teeth, hissing at the frog.

Much to Odo's surprise, the frog let out an ear splitting shriek, spraying a clear fluid across the deck toward Watson.

Odo gave a yelp, tossing the frog back into the water.

"What is that stuff? What did it spray?"

Sephie sniffed the air. "It smells familiar."

Silas touched his finger to the deck, sniffing the clear iridescent fluid. "I think it's gasoline."

Odo peered over the side of the boat. "Gasoline?

How could a cute little–" He stopped when he saw the hundreds of little frog faces popping up from the water. "There's a zillion of them!"

Sephie darted over next to him, a chill passing through her when she saw the army of frogs bobbing in the water.

"What are they doing? What do they want?"

Odo screamed when the gigantic frog surfaced, a massive surge of water cascading off its back. A second enormous frog rose up, its bulbous purple eyes looking directly at them.

"Silas! We need to get out of here! Now!"

"I have to put the new sphere in! Hold on!"

He wrenched the black case open, grabbing one of the gold spheres.

"Sephie, what's that antenna thing on the big frog's head?"

"It's sparking, like an electric eel. That must be how they protect themselves. Don't get near it!"

A light blinked on in Odo's head. "The little frog sprayed gasoline, and the big frogs can make sparks."

"Silas! Now! We need to go now!!"

Silas yanked out the old sphere and dropped in the new one, racing to the bridge. The holoscreen popped up and he tapped the blue circle, the ship leaping forward just as the gargantuan frog spewed out a massive stream of gasoline across the stern of the ship. His antenna sparked violently, a sea of flames erupting around them. The small frogs went wild, spraying streams of the flammable liquid into the air, a churning ball of fire exploding behind the ship.

"We're on fire!" Odo pointed to the raging wind whipped flames on the stern of the ship.

Sephie drew two quick symbols, a dense white fog enveloping the flames. Moments later the fire was out, the deadly inferno behind them.

"What did you do?"

"Shaped a cloud of carbon dioxide. The fire can't get oxygen and it goes out."

"Quick thinking."

Sephie slumped down on a padded seat, eyeing Odo.

"Weren't those frogs cute, Odo Whitley?"

Chapter 30

Old Salt

Learning a valuable lesson from their near deadly encounter with the fire breathing frogs, Silas kept a spare power sphere next to him on the bridge, Sephie and Odo watching for any potential threats lurking beneath the surface of the Great Sea.

It was Odo who spotted the titanic silver cube on the fourth day of their journey.

"What is that? Sephie, use your long distance glasses."

Sephie put on the dark green spectacles and twisted the silver dial, studying the titanic structure.

"Just what it looks like, a gigantic silver cube sitting in the middle of the Great Sea."

Silas called out, "Nothing on the holomap. We're crossing flooded land, but no cities in this area. It could be a building, or maybe a vessel. It's an odd shape for a ship though."

"I'm being drawn to it, let's take a look."

"Do you think there's someone there we're supposed to meet?"

"I don't know, Odo Whitley, but there's definitely something there."

Silas flipped off the guidance system, sending their ship toward the mysterious cube.

Sephie studied the great silver structure as they sped across the water. "It's emitting a soft energy glow, but I'm not sure why."

"You mean like brainwaves? Is it alive?"

"No, not like that, but there is an electrical field surrounding it."

The titanic size of the structure became startlingly apparent as they drew closer.

"Whoa, it must be a half mile across."

Sephie put on her long distance glasses. "I don't see any entrances. Let's circle around and see what's on the other side."

Odo studied the gleaming walls of the astonishing structure. "No windows."

Silas sent *The Phoenix* around the cube.

"Look!" He pointed to a long loading dock, currently occupied by a black cargo ship listing hard to port side, its stern under water.

"That ship's about to tip over."

Sephie pointed to a ragged gaping hole in the side of the cube.

"Whatever caused that hole happened inside the cube. The walls are pushed out, not in. There was probably an explosion, which would also explain the damaged cargo ship."

"Let's go see what their cargo was."

"Good idea. We can dock over there."

Odo and Sephie secured the ship's hawser lines to the loading dock, the three friends heading toward the partially submerged cargo ship.

"There's a gangplank going up to the cargo hold."

Sephie motioned for them to stop. "We don't need to board the ship. They were unloading it with that crane when the explosion happened. Look at all the green cylinders scattered across the dock."

Odo ran over to one of the twelve foot long cylinders. "There's writing on it, but I have no idea what it says."

"That one is smashed open."

The three friends stepped over to the shattered cylinder, studying the mound of white crystalline granules which had spilled out onto the dock.

"What is it?"

Silas grabbed a handful of the unknown substance, sniffing it. He touched one finger to it, then tasted it.

"What are you doing? It could be poisonous."

Silas shook his head. "It's not poisonous, it's salt. Sodium chloride, NaCl, the stuff the makes potato chips so yummy."

"It must be a desalinization plant, converting salt water to fresh water. That would explain all the salt."

"That can't be it. They were unloading salt from the cargo ship, not loading it. They were delivering salt to the cube. Besides, when we were being attacked by the fire breathing frogs, water splashed onto me. It was fresh water, not salt."

"This doesn't make sense. What were they using the salt for?"

"I don't know, but whatever they were doing used a lot of it."

"Let's go inside."

Silas turned, stopping short when he saw the Ghost Sailor standing next to the gaping aperture in the cube, waving them in. "We should definitely go inside and check."

Odo grabbed a heavy wooden crate. "Help me stack these boxes so we can climb up."

Sephie drew three symbols and a wooden ladder appeared. "Or we could use a ladder."

"Nice." Odo stopped halfway up, running his hand across the cube's outer wall. "Hey, Silas, check out the surface of the cube. Look familiar?"

Silas nodded. "It's a solar panel, just like the ones Augur showed us. Whatever they were doing uses massive amounts of electricity. We'd better be careful."

Odo scampered up the ladder, entering the cube's interior.

"Whoa."

Sephie jumped down next to him, gazing at the two hundred foot wide glass cylinders extending from the floor to the top of the cube, a series of wide vertical gold pipes running up the center of each cylinder.

"They're filled with some kind of liquid, probably water, skillions of bubbles coming from the gold pipes.

197

Are they pumping some kind of gas into the water?"

"It's a mystery, Odo Whitley."

Silas gave a start when the Ghost Sailor appeared next to Odo, pointing to his backpack. A thought from the ghost popped into his head, the first time this had ever happened.

"We should let Watson run around, get a little exercise. He's been cooped up in *The Phoenix* for five days."

"Good idea." Odo flipped open his pack, lifting Watson out and setting him on the floor. "Okay, Watson, run wild, run free."

Watson sat down and began licking his paw.

"Cats are so weird."

"Let's see if we can figure out what these giant cylinders are for."

A cluster of brilliant lights shot out from Sephie's hands, spreading out across the interior of the cube.

"Now we can see. There are more of the giant glass cylinders down that way."

Odo and Sephie meandered through the maze of pipes and glass cylinders, stepping over mounds of rubble left from the explosion.

"That looks like a control center." Odo pointed to a two story glass structure halfway up the far wall.

"Let's go check it out."

The three friends continued on, Watson strolling behind them.

"Everything is so big here." Odo stopped in his tracks, pointing to a pair of legs sticking out from behind a large silver pipe. "Is that what I think it is?"

Sephie darted around the pipe. "It's not what you think it is, Odo Whitley."

Odo and Silas stepped over to Sephie, staring down at the creature.

"What is it?"

"An automaton."

"A robot?"

Sephie nodded. "Exactly, but it doesn't look anything like the Flatlanders or Augur."

"Its head looks like a big yellow egg with almond shaped green eyes. Creepy."

"And a dark green body with two legs and two arms. Only three fingers though. Definitely doesn't look like Augur."

"It's dead, right?"

"Deactivated. It was probably damaged in the explosion, its torso ripped open."

"If this was a movie, its eyes would pop open and it would grab one of us."

Sephie let out a terrified shriek.

Odo screeched, jumping back. "What is it??"

"Just wanted to make sure you were paying attention, Odo Whitley." Sephie burst out laughing.

"Something is wrong with you, Sephie Crumb. Why do you do that? What's Watson doing?"

"He's poking at something inside the robot."

"Yuck."

"It's a machine, Odo Whitley, not a dead body."

"It's still creepy. He's batting at something."

Watson swatted his paw and a green glass ball flew out from inside the robot, rolling across the gleaming Morsennium floor. He chased after the sparkling sphere, pouncing on it, throwing it, then pouncing again, grabbing it and rolling over on his back.

"He's just playing."

Odo ran over to Watson, taking the glass ball. "This could be dangerous. It doesn't look like glass, it's more like..." His eyes widened. "...it's more like a giant emerald worth about a jillion dollars." He glanced over at Sephie, remembering her scorn for treasure hunters. He slipped the sparkling spherical gem into his coat pocket.

Sephie called out, "What was it?"

"Just a glass ball. Let's go check out that control center."

Chapter 31

Thanks

Odo clambered up the wide metal ladder, stepping into the fifty foot wide glass enclosed room.

"Definitely high tech. Look at all the buttons and screens. I wish I knew what they were doing here."

Silas scanned the sprawling floor of the mysterious facility.

"There are ten giant glass cylinders, the big pipes on top connecting the five cylinders on the left. Same thing with the five cylinders on the right. The top section of that one cylinder was damaged, probably in the explosion. Or maybe that's what exploded."

Sephie gazed silently at the ten cylinders. After a few moments she said, "Why does this look so familiar, Odo Whitley? I feel like I've seen it all before."

"I was just thinking the same thing. Is it something from school? Maybe in our chemistry class?"

Sephie grabbed Odo's arm. "Electrolysis! It was one of our experiments. They're breaking down water molecules into hydrogen and oxygen using electricity. I didn't recognize it because it's so gigantic, the enormous scale of it threw me off."

"That's why they needed the salt. You add salt to the water, then put the two electrodes in. Oxygen bubbles off the anode, hydrogen off the cathode."

"What were they doing with all the gas? It doesn't look like they were storing it in cylinders or putting it on the cargo ship."

Silas gave a triumphant laugh. "I know exactly what they were doing. They were trying to get rid of the floodwater. They were breaking it down into hydrogen and oxygen, sending the gas up through those giant overhead pipes and out the top of the cube. The hydrogen gas would float straight up to the top layer of the atmosphere."

Sephie nodded her agreement. "Yes, and once it reaches the top of the atmosphere it will eventually escape the planet's gravitational pull, drifting off into dark space. That happens on Earth every day."

"Their planet was flooding, and they were trying to get rid of the water."

Sephie pointed to a map on the wall. "Each of those little red lights must be a water separation plant. There are dozens of them scattered across the planet."

Odo eyed the map, a puzzled expression on his face. "So we know what they were trying to do, and how they were doing it, but we still don't know..."

"Where the water is coming from, why their world was flooding, and why they couldn't stop it. If you have a leaky pipe, you fix the pipe, you don't just keep mopping up the water."

"Exactly."

"My guess is we'll find answers when we reach the Mountains of Altus. We should get there in a day or two."

Odo glanced across the floor of the cube, a jolt of fear shooting through him. "They followed us." He pointed to the gaping hole in the wall.

Silas gulped when he saw the monstrous orange frogs hopping around the entrance. "There must be twenty of them, even bigger than the ones we saw."

"More of them are coming in. We're safe up here, but we need to get back to the boat."

Sephie whispered, "We have to be really quiet. The last thing we want is a fire in here. Hydrogen, oxygen, and fire are a very bad mix. The damaged cylinder is releasing hydrogen and oxygen into the cube, and if a flame ignites it, we're in big trouble. I don't know if my energy shield could protect us from a blast like that. We have to sneak out of here without the frogs seeing us, and the only way out is the way we came in."

"Can you see the frogs' brainwaves?"

"Yes. Why?"

"Remember when Cyra distracted the pirates by making them see those imaginary flying bat creatures? Could you do something like that? We could sneak out while they were busy fighting them."

"Not a good idea, Odo Whitley, the frogs would shoot gasoline at them and start a fire."

"Oh, right. Good point."

"But I could make them think we were giant frogs.

When they looked at us they wouldn't see humans, they'd see frogs."

"You can do that?"

"Cyra taught me how to project a mass illusion. She said it would come in handy one day. She was right."

"Let's do it then." Odo tucked Watson into his backpack. "Okay, Watson, no meowing, just frog noises. Ribbit!"

Sephie drew a series of symbols, then closed her eyes. A vaporous yellow cloud drifted across the floor, enveloping the army of fire breathing frogs.

"Okay, everyone down the ladder. Walk slowly, don't make any sounds, no talking. If they hear us speak, the illusion will be broken."

"No problem for the Translucent Boy."

"Odo Whitley, you need to stay focused. No talking, I mean it."

"I get it, no talking."

The three adventurers crept silently down the ladder, their eyes on the congregation of frogs near the exit.

"They're not looking at us."

Sephie glared at Odo, putting a finger over her lips.

"Sorry."

Sephie stared daggers at him.

They stepped slowly across the floor of the huge plant, weaving their way past massive gas pipes and towering cylinders, climbing over piles of shattered stone and glass.

Odo froze when a huge orange speckled frog hopped out from behind a row of vertical green pipes, landing with a squishy glopping noise next to them, its bulbous purple eyes looking right at Odo. It turned and hopped away.

Sephie gave the thumbs up sign and they continued on.

Odo's fear was diminishing rapidly. This might work. The exit was only a hundred feet ahead of them.

Sephie motioned for them to stop when she saw the squirming mass of orange frogs, at least fifty of them now, all clustered around the hole in the wall. She watched them, studying their behavior. When a frog wanted to leave the pile, it climbed over the others.

She grabbed Odo's arm, pointing to a frog who was wriggling across the pile.

Odo shook his head. There was no way he was going to climb over a pile of fifty giant frogs.

Sephie glared at him, pointing to the slimy amphibians. She strode over to a gargantuan frog, leaping onto its back, waving for Odo and Silas to follow her.

Odo took a deep breath and approached a ten foot long warty slime covered amphibian. The smell was horrific, a vile mix of gasoline and burbling decaying muck from the depths of a putrid swamp. He took a running jump onto the creature, scrambling onto its back, then stood up, extending his arms for balance. The frog moved abruptly, Odo leaping to the next one.

"So bad. Squishy. That smell, I might barf." Silas was two frogs over, scrambling toward the exit. Much to Odo's surprise he realized he did not want Silas to reach the exit before he did. He was imagining Sephie clapping Silas on the back, telling him how brave he was, what a great job he'd done. "No way is that going to happen." Odo jumped to the next frog, held captive by this dreadful feeling of jealousy.

Sephie scampered across the last frog, leaping to the hole in the wall, pulling herself up. She waved for Odo and Silas to follow her.

Odo groaned. He was going to need twenty showers to get rid of the gasoline slime smell. He watched Silas leap across a large frog, heading toward Sephie.

"He's not going to beat me."

Odo scrambled over two smaller frogs. "Slippery. So gross. Only three frogs to go."

Silas was almost to the wall.

Odo's eyes narrowed. Do or die. He ran across the frog and leaped. Unfortunately, in his haste to beat Silas he miscalculated the distance, jumping over the first frog, but not far enough to land on the second one. With a dreadful squooshy sound he slid down between the two mucous covered creatures.

"Unghh...getting squished." He tried to grab the side of the frog and pull himself up, but there was nothing to grab. The two huge frogs were pressed tightly together. "Not good... can't breathe."

A hand reached down and grabbed his, pulling him up. It was Silas.

Odo took a deep gasping breath, putting his hand on Silas' shoulder to steady himself. It was then that Odo made a critical, although quite understandable mistake.

"Thanks! I thought I was–"

Every frog in the building stopped, their heads whipping around, their bulging purple eyes on Odo and Silas.

"Oh, no."

Sephie screamed, "RUN!"

Odo and Silas leaped across the last frog, grabbing the wall and pulling themselves up next to Sephie.

"To the ship! Now!"

The frogs went wild, their piercing shrieks filling the air, massive streams of gasoline spewing up toward the three friends.

They leaped down from the wall and hit the ground running, racing toward *The Phoenix.*

A massive ball of fire rolled out of the cube, followed by a dozen of the monstrous shrieking frogs.

"Hurry!! Faster!"

They sprinted across the loading dock to *The Phoenix*, Odo arriving first, followed seconds later by Sephie and Silas. Silas raced to the bridge and hit the holomap, tapping the blue circle.

"We're tied up! Hawser lines!"

Two brilliant purple beams shot out from Sephie's hands, the ropes vaporizing. The sleek silver craft was pulling away from the dock when the frogs arrived, dousing the ship with great streams of gasoline.

"No!"

Silas hit the blue circle again, *The Phoenix* leaping forward. Sephie drew a quick symbol, a shimmering wall of energy blinking up between the ship and the frogs, blocking them from the raging inferno of flames

207

that exploded on the dock. They could still hear the frogs' horrific shrieking when they were a half mile away, the dock engulfed in a massive wall of fire, the frogs still spewing out streams of gasoline.

Odo slumped down into a seat, his clothes drenched in frog slime and gasoline. He looked at Sephie. Her face was pale, her hands shaking. He slid over next to her.

"I'm sorry, it was my fault, I don't know why I said thanks. I was just so glad to get out from between the frogs, I couldn't breathe. Are you mad at me? It's okay if you're mad at me. I understand."

Sephie put her arms around him.

"I'm just glad you're safe, Odo Whitley. That was really scary."

The cube was a black silhouette on the horizon when they saw the blinding flash, like a small sun, the thundering boom of the cataclysmic explosion reaching them a minute later.

Chapter 32

Land Ho!

Odo sniffed his sleeve. "Do I smell like gasoline? I think I can smell it. Maybe it's the frog smell, kind of like sulfur and barf mixed together."

Odo Whitley, you've washed those clothes five times with the laundry detergent I shaped, and I have vaporized every frog related molecule on this ship. There's no smell, it's all in your head."

"Maybe it's from the explosion, it could still be in the air."

"The cube is two hundred miles away. Why don't you go help Silas on the bridge, I'm trying to read."

"Fine, enjoy your book." Odo stood up and walked to the bridge, taking a seat next to Silas.

"Thanks again for pulling me out of the frog pile. You saved my life."

Silas shrugged. "Oh, it was nothing, just a another day in the life of an ordinary superhero."

Odo snorted, his dreadful feeling of jealousy vanishing. It was silly of him to worry about Silas and Sephie.

"So... Odo... I was just wondering... is Sephie your

girlfriend?"

Odo felt like a thousand angry snakes were wriggling around inside his stomach.

"We're just friends. We like each other, but not like that."

"Does she have a boyfriend?"

"I don't know. Why, do you like her?"

"She's kind of cute." Silas stopped short, his eyes on the Ghost Sailor glaring at him through the ship's windshield. The ghost was slowly pulling a finger across his throat, his message unmistakably clear.

"I mean, cute in a different way... not in a way that I think is cute... I don't like her or anything, I was just curious, just idle chit chat. She's not my kind of cute."

"She is kind of cute, I guess. She's really funny, too. And she doesn't like it when people look at her. I'm not exactly sure why, I guess she doesn't realize how... well, that's she's sort of cute. She says the best things, like once she said a flock of sheep looked like sheep clouds floating in a green sky. I even wrote it down so I wouldn't forget."

The light of realization blinked on in Silas' eyes. "You're in love with her."

"What? No, I'm not. We're just friends."

"If you say so." Silas snorted.

Odo changed the topic. "Are there any girls at school you like?"

"There's one I kind of like, but I'm afraid to ask her out. She'd probably laugh at me."

"Who is it? You should ask her."

"It's Nia, she sits behind me in math class."

"She's cute, seems nice. I bet she'd go out with you."

Silas glanced through the windshield. The Ghost Sailor was gone, but something in the distance had caught his attention. He pointed to the horizon.

"What does that look like to you?"

Odo peered through the glass. "Maybe a big storm? It looks like black clouds running across the horizon."

"Whatever it is, the Mountains of Altus are right in the middle of it."

Odo groaned. "Of course they are. Where else would they be? It does makes sense that a giant storm would be over the mountains, though. Augur said it's always raining in the Forest of Dark Creations."

Sephie stepped onto the bridge, stopping when she saw the odd smile on Silas' face. "What is it? Why are you smiling?"

"No reason, Odo and I were just talking. There's a big storm ahead."

Sephie studied Silas' brainwaves. He was hiding something. Something he thought was funny. Sephie was not fond of secrets.

"I guess I should shape some rain gear."

"The forest in my room had giant slugs in it."

"So… rain gear and a bottle of slug repellant?"

"I'm not being funny, Sephie. I saw a giant orange slug crawling around in my room."

"Was it worse than the fire breathing gasoline frogs?"

Odo glared at her. "Maybe the slugs spray acid, or control your thoughts and make you murder each other, like Sensus did on Atroxia."

"An orange slug is going to make us murder each other? Really?"

Silas interrupted. "We should hit the outer edge of the storm in about an hour. We'll be safe on the bridge. The door is watertight, and fresh air is pumped in through these two vents. The boat is unsinkable, and I put a new power sphere in this morning. We're good to go."

"Augur said we'll find Mirus in the Forest of Dark Creations, near the Fortress of Rain. Are there any fortresses on the holomap?"

"I couldn't find anything that looked like a fortress. The mountain range is four hundred miles long and a hundred miles across. See how it curves along this arc? We're here, about fifty miles from the eastern end of the range."

"Okay, Sephie, we're going to need rain gear, a bottle of slug repellant, and a magic carpet."

Silas pointed to the darkening sky.

"We're getting close. I'll seal the bridge and switch on the ventilation pumps."

Ten minutes later large raindrops were spattering against the windshield.

"Whoa, it's really coming down."

"Look up ahead."

"It looks like a black wall."

"Except it's rain, not a wall."

"This is definitely not a scorching hot desert planet."

The Phoenix shuddered when it collided with the wall of pounding rain, the sound deafening.

"Whoa, I can't see where we're going. Are you sure the ship can take it?"

"Absolutely. This is highly advanced technology created by Those Who Came Before. We'll be fine. There's no wind, so there's no big waves, just this incredible rain. You said you can't see where we're going? Check this out." Silas tapped a green square on the holomap, the bridge window taking on a green hue.

"I can see everything again! What is that?"

"The windshield sees through the rain using a wavelength of the electromagnetic spectrum not normally visible to us."

"Amazing. I wish we could take this boat home with us. Is that land?"

Sephie slipped on her long distance glasses. "It's land. Watch out for the treetops in the water."

"It's about fifty feet deep here. Do you think this rain is causing all the flooding?"

"I don't see how it could be. Rain is part of the water cycle. Water evaporates from the oceans, rises up, hits the cold air over the mountains, condenses, then falls and flows back into the ocean in streams and rivers. Rain isn't new water, it's existing water being recycled."

Odo did not look convinced. "There's something very weird about this storm though. I don't think the normal rules apply."

"You might be right, Odo Whitley. I'm getting a strange feeling about this place."

Silas flipped off the ship's auto guidance system, taking control of *The Phoenix*. "I'll bring us in next to that big rock. We can use it for a landmark if we need to find the boat. It looks kind of like a bird's head."

Silas guided the ship between the trees, stopping when the bow scraped onto the shoreline.

Sephie drew a quick symbol and a hundred feet of stout rope appeared on the deck. "We can tie up to one of the trees."

"Okay, put your rain gear on. We're going to need it."

Sephie flipped up her rain hood, pulling it tight. "Let's light this candle, boys."

Silas hid his smile when he saw the unmistakable look Sephie had given Odo. It was clear to him why the Ghost Sailor didn't want him to interfere.

Sephie swung open the bridge door, stepping into the torrential downpour. She staggered back a step. "This is incredible! I've never seen anything like it!"

The three adventurers clambered down from the ship, Silas tying it securely to one of the massive trees.

Odo was shielding his eyes from the pounding sheets of rain. "This is really bad! I can't see!"

Sephie drew a symbol and three pairs of glass goggles appeared in her hand. "Put these on, they should help."

Odo slipped on the goggles. "Nice. Much better. Which way?"

"Up."

An hour later the three friends had traveled less than a half mile up the side of the mountain. Odo was out of breath.

"It's steeper than it looks, hard to climb with all this water. Can we rest for a minute? This rain is crazy."

Sephie shaped an energy shield above them, blocking the rain.

"Thanks. So what's our plan? We look for the Fortress of Rain? I was thinking it might not be an actual fortress, it could be a natural formation, like a mountain or a big cave or something."

"Let's keep climbing for a few more hours. Maybe we'll see something. We'll camp for the night when it gets dark."

"Good idea. Let's go."

When it was almost dark, they stopped in a small clearing, Sephie shaping an energy dome and tents.

"The dome will protect us from the rain."

"And the giant slugs."

"I'm pretty sure you can outrun a slug, Odo Whitley. I just hope it doesn't wake me in the middle of the night and make me murder you."

"Very funny. I'd laugh, but I'm too tired. I'm exhausted, time for bed. Odo crawled into his tent and curled up in his sleeping bag, soon lost in the world of dreams.

Odo was normally a sound sleeper, but he woke with a start in the middle of the night, Watson batting his face.

"Crazy cat, what are you doing? I'm trying to sleep, we have a long day tomorrow. Wait, did you hear something out there?" Odo slipped on his clothes and crept out of his tent, peering into the darkness.

"I can't see a thing, there could be a full moon and I wouldn't know it with all these clouds. Not a star in sight. At least the dome will keep weird creatures out. Like those creepy slugs."

He was stumbling back to his tent when he spotted three small flickering lights in the distance.

"Whoa, those look like lanterns, maybe windows. They're down the mountain a few hundred feet, directly to the west. Good thing Watson woke me."

Odo crawled back into his tent. Watson was sound asleep, curled up next to the Ghost Sailor.

Chapter 33

Sherlock

"You're certain you saw them?"

"Yes, three lights, down the mountain, directly west. Watson woke me in the middle of the night, whapping my face with his paw."

"Let's go check it out."

The three adventurers packed up their gear, Silas watching with interest as Sephie converted the tents and sleeping bags back into energy fields, blinking off the energy dome.

"I don't understand what happens to the tents and sleeping bags. Where did they go?"

Sephie held out one hand and an oatmeal cookie blinked into existence. "Shaping is compressing energy into physical objects, using the power of your mind, also known as your deeper self. The first step is visualizing the oatmeal cookie clearly in my mind, which creates a dense thought cloud. The second step is asking your deeper self to compress that thought cloud, or energy field, into a physical object. I can't create the cookie on my own, my deeper self has to do it. It's infinitely more powerful than my normal conscious self. Making objects vanish is just the reverse of that, your deeper self converting the physical object back into a thought cloud."

Odo added, "Every time you have a thought it creates a thought cloud. Wikerus can pull them in like a magnet and hear your thoughts."

"That's a little creepy."

"He wouldn't do it without telling you. He says that would be like reading someone's diary, it's just not done."

"I can't believe there are so many things I don't know."

"Just wait until you see Girard Station. It's incredible, so many different kinds of aliens. They all seem pretty nice and mostly they get along. Some are really strange, like the Sinarians. They don't have faces and they float above the ground when they walk."

Sephie whispered, "Buildings ahead. It looks like a village. Be careful, this could be who took Mirus, Arthur, and Clara."

The adventurers crept forward through the gigantic trees, the endless deluge of pounding rain spattering on the forest floor.

Odo peered out from behind a massive tree trunk at a dozen low wooden buildings in a large clearing.

"Pretty rustic, definitely not high tech. The door on that one house is wide open. This place looks deserted, but I saw lights."

"Looks like it used to be a nice little mountain village. Let's check out that big building first."

They walked down the muddy street, cautiously approaching the long dark building. Odo stopped, pointing to one of the windows. "A lantern."

"Let's see who's home." Sephie walked up to the front door and knocked.

They waited for almost a minute, but the door did not open.

"Maybe nobody's home. Maybe they just left a lantern burning."

Sephie unlatched the door, pushing it open.

"Hello? Anyone here?"

Odo peered inside, his voice a sharp whisper. "In the back, sitting in a chair."

Sephie studied the creature. "It looks like the automaton we found in the silver cube; egg shaped head, big green eyes."

"What's it doing?"

"I think it's reading a book."

"They can read? It doesn't have ears, maybe it didn't hear your knock. It could be deaf."

The creature's head flickered with a pale yellow light.

"I am not deaf, I am reading. Are you here to destroy me?"

"Destroy you? No, of course not. We're looking for our lost friends."

"Am I one of them?"

219

"Um… no, they look like us, humans from Earth."

"Carry on, then." The automaton went back to his book.

"Excuse me, would you mind if we asked you a few questions? We're kind of lost."

"I would be of little assistance. I am also lost."

Odo studied the interior of the old building. One wall was lined with crude wooden bookshelves, a half dozen hand crafted tables and chairs scattered about in front of a massive stone fireplace, three iron cauldrons hanging from heavy chains.

"What is this place? Does anyone else live here?"

"I have not seen anyone since I arrived. This would appear to have been a central meeting house for the villagers."

"Why are you here?"

"I woke up at the bottom of a deep ravine with no memory of how I had gotten there or who I was. My head was severely damaged." The automaton turned, displaying a jagged hole in the back of his egg shaped head, hundreds of tiny blinking lights inside. "My thoughts become disorganized when I leave the building. I believe the rain is adversely affecting my neuronal synapses and associated networks."

"Your head does look pretty bad. You don't remember anything about where you're from? We found an automaton who looks exactly like you inside a giant cube in the Great Sea. It was an electrolysis plant, converting water into hydrogen and oxygen."

"Did he state his purpose?"

"We didn't actually talk to him. He was... um... deactivated. What do you mean by his purpose?"

"The purpose for his existence, his function in this world. I used to have one, but when I woke up it was gone. I could not remember who I was, what I was supposed to be doing, or where I should go. I wandered through the forest until I found this place. Once I was out of the rain my thoughts became clearer, but I can remember nothing of what happened before. I have been searching these books, hoping they will hold some clue to my past."

Sephie stepped over to the automaton, sitting down next to him. "You don't remember your name?"

"I am uncertain if I ever possessed one."

"We could give you one, if you'd like. Odo is good at names."

"If you wish."

Odo thought for a moment.

"We could call you Sherlock. He was a famous detective in our world, really good at solving mysteries. That's sort of what you're doing, trying to uncover the mystery of your past, trying to find your lost purpose. You're a detective."

"This is logical, and suits me well. You may call me Sherlock."

Sephie said, "It takes time to find your purpose."

"Did you also fall and injure your head?"

"No, it's a little different with humans. We are not born knowing our purpose, we have to discover it on our own. Mine is to help people. We're trying to find

221

Silas' family, they're lost in this world."

Odo flipped open his pack and Watson hopped out, rubbing against Odo's legs. "Sherlock, I'd like you to meet my sidekick Watson." He grinned at Sephie.

Sephie glared at him. "Sherlock, I can repair the back of your head if you'd like. You'd be able to walk in the rain again."

"And by helping me, you would be fulfilling your purpose?"

"Yes."

"Very well." Sherlock turned the back of his head toward Sephie. She gently examined the jagged hole, running her fingers across it. She drew four symbols, the spider web of cracks slowly filling in, the hole growing smaller. Three minutes later it was gone.

"All done, good as new."

Sherlock's head glowed brightly.

"Excellent. I shall wander the forest, searching for my lost purpose."

"Sherlock, have you ever heard of a place called the Fortress of Rain?"

"I have not, but it is located forty-two miles due west of our current location."

Odo looked puzzled. "You've never heard of it, but you know where it is?"

"Correct."

"How is that possible?"

"Different elements of my memories are stored in different sections of my brain. The accident must have erased my memory of the name, but not the location.

Hearing the name created a new neural connection."

Sherlock's head was flickering brightly.

"I believe your presence is affecting my neural pathways. They are being altered, rerouted. Perhaps my forgotten purpose shall be restored."

Sephie nodded. "Don't get discouraged, it will take time. You'll remember it, I know you will. We have to leave now, but thank you for helping us find the Fortress of Rain."

Sephie slung her pack onto her shoulder, heading for the front door.

Odo leaned over and whispered, "This is just like *Forgotten Memories.* Maybe he'll find an old photograph and recognize his family."

"Focus, Odo Whitley. We're off to the Fortress of Rain."

Chapter 34

Barnacles

An arduous five day trek took the adventurers westward through the dense rainforest, their feet sinking into the wet moss, streams of water pouring down from the branches onto their heads.

Odo let out a screech, shaking his fist at the roiling black sky. "Stop raining! Seriously, you need to stop!"

"I don't think that's going to help, Odo Whitley."

"It helps me. This rain is driving me loopy. There's another one of those giant slug things. I don't even like looking at them. At least it's not a creepy blue frog."

Silas studied the slug. "They're herbivores, they eat moss. They can't hurt you. Their thick layer of mucous acts like a natural raincoat."

"I'd rather drown than wear a mucous raincoat. Besides, you never know with alien creatures. They could sprout legs and claws and start chasing us. Or spray us with some weird deadly poison like the gasoline frogs."

Silas laughed. "Not every creature is out to get you, Odo. Some just wander around in their mucous raincoats and eat moss."

Sephie gave an exasperated groan. "Will you both please stop saying mucous raincoats!"

"Hey, I think the rain stopped!"

Odo's grin vanished when he looked up. A forty foot wide black pancake shaped craft was jammed between the trees a hundred feet above them.

"What is that thing?"

"It has to be some kind of flying machine, there's no other way it could have gotten up there. We should check it out, maybe we'll find something."

"It's a hundred feet up. How do we get up there?"

"There is one way, but you might not like it."

Odo's eyes narrowed. "What is it?"

"The same way I launched *The Phoenix*. I'll float you up to the ship, then you drop a rope down so we can climb up."

"Are you crazy? Suppose you sneeze or something when I'm ninety feet in the air? What happens if I fall?"

Silas shrugged. "I'll do it, I'm not afraid of heights."

The dreadful feeling of jealousy roared through Odo. He did not want Silas to be the first one to the ship, the brave one, the one not afraid of heights.

"I was just kidding, I'm not afraid of heights. Let's do it, Sephie Crumb. Float me up to the top of the tree. This will be fun."

Sephie studied Odo's brainwaves, but said nothing. It did not look at all like he thought it would be fun.

"Are you sure?"

"Nothing scares the Translucent Boy."

"Okay." Sephie drew two symbols and a long coil of knotted rope appeared. "I'll float you up to the ship. Tie the rope and drop it down."

Odo grabbed the rope and slung it over his shoulder.

Sephie concentrated deeply, a pale blue light enveloping Odo. "Here we go." She extended both arms, palms facing outward.

Odo gave a yelp when his feet left the ground.

"Are you okay?"

"I'm fine, it just feels a little weird, like I'm swimming in the air."

Silas watched Odo drift upward, weaving his way around the gigantic tree limbs.

Two minutes later Odo was a hundred feet up. He hollered down to Sephie, "There's a big hole in the bottom of the ship just to my right!"

"I see it!" Sephie floated Odo over to the ragged tear in the craft.

"I'm good! I'm inside! I'll tie the rope and toss it down."

Silas and Sephie scrambled up the long rope, Odo helping them into the mysterious vehicle.

Four orbs of light shot out from Sephie's hands.

Odo groaned. "Skeletons. I hate skeletons."

Silas studied the bones on the floor. "It looks like three fish and one of those giant frogs."

"There's something else." Sephie pointed to the small jagged conical formations on the bulkheads.

"Barnacles. I saw them on the outside of the ship too. I think this was a sunken ship. The hole in the hull was probably caused by an explosion."

"The ship crashed and sank in the ocean?"

"That would explain the barnacles."

"How did it wind up in the trees?"

Silas was examining the controls of the large disc shaped craft. "Very high tech. I don't understand what I'm looking at, but it could be a gravitational drive. It doesn't have any propellers or jets or wings."

He tapped a few of the small cubes on the control panel.

"Nothing. No power."

"They had gravity ships on Atroxia, glass spheres you could ride in. They looked really fun."

Sephie stepped over to the control panel. "It's not an interstellar ship, but it is a very advanced flying machine."

"A flying machine that crashed in the ocean and wound up in the treetops?"

"It's another mystery, Odo Whitley. Maybe a giant waterspout sucked it up out of the ocean and tossed it in the trees."

"Except there's almost no wind here. Let's look around and see if we find anything useful."

"You mean treasure you can take home and sell?"

"Don't be ridiculous. I'm a superhero, not a treasure hunter." Odo's hand was gripping the three inch wide sparkling green emerald he'd taken from the deactivated robot.

227

Sephie snorted. "You're so transparent, Odo Whitley."

"Excuse me? That's kind of rude. I'm transparent?"

Sephie burst out laughing. "I didn't mean it that way, but it is kind of funny."

"Maybe a little."

Silas called out from the other side of the ship. "Check this out, a vehicle with eight legs. There's a glass dome on top with controls inside it, but it's much too small for Altusians. Whoever built this ship was small."

"We haven't seen any creatures like that. They could be from another part of the planet, but Bakis never mentioned anything about little creatures with flying machines."

Sephie nodded. "I don't see anything here we can use. Let's go find the Fortress of Rain." She took a deep breath and grabbed the rope, climbing down, her eyes closed. Silas followed her.

Odo stood alone in the ship, staring at the rope.

"No problem for a superhero like the Translucent Boy. No problem at all. Grab it, climb down. Easy enough. Just climb down the old rope."

"Odo! What are you doing?"

Odo's insides turned to ice when he heard Sephie's scream. He grabbed the rope, half falling and half climbing down, landing on the forest floor with a thump.

"Sephie! Sephie? Are you all right?"

Sephie and Silas were nowhere to be seen.

"Sephie! Silas! Where are you?"

Odo never saw the dart that hit his neck, his vision suddenly blurry, his arms and legs refusing to obey his commands.

"Something stung me… have to find Sephie… " He stumbled forward, taking three steps before he sank to his knees and collapsed on the spongy forest floor.

Chapter 35

Odo's Plan

Odo's eyes fluttered open, his vision still blurry, his thoughts vague and confused. "Why am I so tired? Why am I lying in the rain? Watson, you crazy cat, quit batting my face! Wait, something happened, I was in that black ship in the trees. Something stung my neck. I have to focus. What is that?"

He reached over and pulled a small feathered projectile from the moss. "It's a dart. I didn't get stung by an insect, I got hit with a dart. Sephie! I remember now, Sephie and Silas!" He leaped to his feet, or more precisely, attempted to leap to his feet. He staggered back, falling to his knees.

"Unhhh... my head. I have to find them. Whoever knocked me out with that dart must have taken them. But why take them and not me? Why leave me here? This is not good. I have to think. Tracks, I'll look for tracks."

He turned, screeching at the sight of the giant orange

slug sitting behind him. Grabbing Watson, he jumped away from the mucous covered monstrosity.

"So creepy."

Odo studied the ground, spotting a trail of indentations in the moss. "This whole area is trampled down. There must have been a lot of them." He followed the trail for several hundred feet, then stopped.

"It's going uphill. Maybe they're taking Sephie and Silas to the Fortress of Rain. Fortresses are usually high up, so that would make sense. Augur said the Altusians thought Mirus and his children were Chosen Ones, sent to save their world. Maybe they think Sephie and Silas are Chosen Ones. But why take them and leave me here?"

He pushed on through the dense forest, stopping to tighten his hood and adjust his goggles.

"This rain is bad. Thank goodness Sephie shaped these goggles." A dark oppressive feeling crept through him. He leaned over, still slightly dizzy. "Why did they take Sephie? Why did they leave me behind? I don't know what I'm doing, I have no idea where she is. She has her powers though, so that's something. Once she wakes up she can clobber them. She'll be okay, I know she will." He realized he didn't know that at all. "Okay, I'm going to stop thinking about it. Sephie says don't worry about things that haven't happened yet."

He pressed on through the forest.

"Those little plants are mashed down, I'm still on the trail. This mountain is steep. I wonder how tall it is? The Fortress of Rain must be at the top. I wonder why they call it the Fortress of Rain? Probably because it's in the middle of this giant crazy rainstorm. Why else would they call it that? Why are the clouds so low? I can almost touch them."

Fifty feet later Odo was lost in the dense black clouds.

"Not good, I can't even see the ground." He kneeled down, studying the forest floor.

"Broken branches, someone stepped on them. I'll keep going up the mountainside. They must be heading for the Fortress of Rain. They probably think Sephie and Silas are Chosen Ones, unless they think... okay, stop imagining things and keep going. Think about something else."

An hour later Odo sank to the ground, his legs burning.

"I don't even know if these are the right tracks. They could belong to anyone, a bunch of hunters or a pack of wild animals. Is it me, or are the clouds getting lighter? Maybe I'm near the top of the cloud layer."

He staggered to his feet. "The trees are smaller here, farther apart, some of the moss replaced by rocky ground. This is better, not so dark, but I've lost their trail without the moss. I'll just keep going up. I think I'm getting close."

He ran forward, stopping when he heard the strange noises ahead of him. "What is that? Maybe it's them. Wait, what do I do if I find them? There could be twenty Altusians armed to the teeth with swords and spears. I'd better sneak up and see what it is before I go barging in. I wish I had powers like Sephie."

He crept forward, inching around a tree, peering through the gray mist, eyes alert for movement.

He let out a groan when the swirling mist revealed the creatures ahead of him. It was not Sephie and Silas, it was a large group of two foot long blue frogs.

"I've been trailing a bunch of stupid frogs. They're not the fire breathing ones, they're the weird blue ones. How can they see without eyes? Maybe they use sonar, like bats."

Odo picked up a small stone, hurling it past the frogs. They scattered when the stone ripped through the leaves of a small tree.

"They scare easily, so that's good. Not like those crazy gasoline frogs. I didn't find Sephie and Silas, but at least I won't be frog food. I'll keep heading up. Once I'm above the clouds maybe I'll spot the Fortress of Rain. Maybe Sephie left a message or marked their trail."

Odo clambered up the side of the mountain, the trees gone now, replaced by scraggly bushes.

"This is a good sign, the rain is barely a drizzle. I must be close."

Half an hour later Odo stopped.

"Whoa. That has to be the Fortress of Rain."

His eyes were on a monolithic black structure perched on top of the mountain, silhouetted against a brilliant blue sky.

Odo studied the titanic building as he scrambled up the rocky slope.

"Look at the walls on that thing, two hundred feet tall. I don't know what those big towers are. There are six of them, glowing blue spheres running all the way up to the top. The spheres are pulsating from bright blue to dark blue. They look a little like radio towers, but I have no idea what those blue spheres are. I do know one thing, this has to be the Fortress of Rain. It's not actually located in the rain, but how many weird giant fortresses can there be?"

He stopped, looking down the mountain at the dense black cloud layer spanning the horizon, then took a seat on a flat boulder, setting his pack down. Watson crawled out, stretched, meowed, and lay down in the warm sun.

"You look comfy. This is nice, no rain. Warm. My clothes should dry out pretty fast."

Odo took off his boots and socks, setting them out to dry in the sun.

"What do you think, Watson? Are Sephie and Silas in there? Is that where the Altusians took them? Augur said the Chosen Ones were sent to save their world, but we don't know from what. Maybe what they're afraid of is inside the Fortress of Rain."

Odo knit his brows, oblivious to the Ghost Sailor standing next to him. "This is going to drive me crazy. It's a little thing, but why would they call it the Fortress of Rain when it's not in the rain? Why didn't they call it the Fortress of Sun? Or the Fortress on the Mountain-top? That would make more sense."

He lay back on the boulder, staring up at the brilliant

blue sky. "What am I missing?"

The Ghost Sailor whispered silent words.

The image of an apple pie in a bright blue box appeared in Odo's thoughts.

"Why am I thinking about apple pie? I must be hungry. Yum, it wouldn't be Thanksgiving without a tasty apple pie from Molly's House of Pies. I wish I had one now."

Odo gave a yelp, sitting upright.

"Molly's House of Pies! That's my answer! Molly's House of Pies is where they make the pies, and the Fortress of Rain is where they make the rain. It's the source of the flooding, and it's destroying Emerus. The Altusians must think the Chosen Ones were sent by the gods to shut down the Fortress of Rain and bring an end to the flooding."

Odo eyed the ominous black structure. He pulled on his socks. "Nothing better than dry socks. Okay, time to find out what's inside this big mysterious fortress."

The Ghost Sailor vanished.

Making his way up the rocky mountainside, Odo approached the imposing structure.

"No windows, no doors. No sign of life except for the weird pulsating blue spheres on the towers. Outer walls are smooth, two hundred feet tall. This is definitely high tech, not some moldy old medieval stone castle. If Sephie was here, she could float me up to the top. If I can get inside I can probably figure out how to shut off whatever is making the rain."

He stepped up to the wall, running his hand across

its smooth surface.

"It's a synthetic material like Morsennium, the same stuff the Atroxians used to build their interstellar ships."

Hiking along the rocky perimeter of the structure, Odo searched for a way in, finding nothing on the east wall. He peered around the corner to the north side of the fortress.

"Whoa, it's an automaton just like Sherlock. He's walking toward that black dome."

The robot was carrying a dark blue sphere the size of a basketball toward the gleaming dome. A circular doorway slid open, the creature stepping inside. Odo could hear clanking and grinding noises, see colored lights flashing through the open doorway. Twenty minutes later the automaton stepped out, walking back to the fortress without the blue sphere. It entered the fortress, swinging the door shut behind it.

Odo darted over to the entrance, but could find no trace of the door.

"I know he went in here. There was a door, but now the wall is completely smooth."

He slid down to the ground, leaning back against the fortress.

"At least the sun is nice and warm. What do you think, Watson? How are we going to get inside?"

Watson hopped onto Odo's legs, stretching out and falling asleep.

"You like that sun, don't you?" Odo gently scratched Watson's head. "Let's use logic, just like Sephie does.

The automaton has to be the one who opens the door, and I don't want him to see me go inside. That means I have to hide somewhere when he comes out, then create a distraction that will give me time to sneak inside."

Five minutes later Odo grabbed Watson and jumped to his feet.

"Back into my pack, sidekick. The Translucent Boy has a plan."

He reached into his coat pocket and pulled out the large spherical emerald he had found in the cube.

"Good bye, incredibly valuable gem, you're going to be my distraction. You came from a deactivated automaton, and if that doesn't get his attention, I don't know what will. I'll set it in front of the dome so the sun hits it just right. This could work. Or it could get me killed."

Odo closed his eyes, feeling the warmth of the sun on his face. "I'm certain we're here to stop the flooding. I can feel it. Maybe it's my deeper self. I don't know where Sephie and Silas are, but if I can stop the rain, maybe whoever captured them will let them go. I might be saving their lives. I have to do this."

Odo perched the emerald on a rock in front the black dome, the gem sparkling brilliantly in the sunlight.

"He can't miss that. Okay, now to figure out exactly where the door is."

He walked back to the fortress, studying the rocky ground. "The ground is smooth here, no pebbles. This is the path he takes when he brings those blue spheres out. This is where the door is. Let's rock and roll." He wished Sephie was there to laugh at his joke.

"Okay, here we go." Odo picked up a rock and bashed it against the fortress wall three times.

Two minutes later the door swung open, Odo concealing himself behind it.

The creature stepped outside, scanning the area. It stopped when it saw the sparkling green emerald, walking silently toward it.

Odo crept out from behind the door and into the fortress. He peered out, his eyes on the automaton. With a blood curdling shriek the creature grabbed the emerald and hurled it at a boulder, smashing it to pieces.

Chapter 36

The Council of Three

Sephie let out a yelp when she woke to find herself being carried by a seven foot tall red eyed Altusian.

"You have awakened, Chosen One." He set her gently on the ground. She looked around, spotting Silas standing between two of the enormous four armed creatures. He called out to her, "They don't want to hurt us. They say we're Chosen Ones, whatever that means."

The Altusian who had been carrying Sephie nodded his agreement. "There is no need to fear, little one, no harm shall come to you."

"Where's Odo?"

The Altusian look puzzled.

"Our other friend, there were three of us. Where is he?"

"Only two of you shall stand before the Council of Three, so it has been written by Kalumnia."

"He was in the black ship, up in the trees."

"You should not have entered a house of demons, little one. You were lucky to escape with your lives."

Silas said, "There was no one in the ship, no demons, just a few old skeletons."

The Altusian backed away from Silas. "You did not touch them?"

"Why would I touch old skeletons?"

"Only a demon can survive the touch of another demon. This is well known."

"I didn't touch them, and they weren't demons, just some fish and a big frog. They're just animals, not demons."

"Demons from the Black Sky, Chosen One."

"What's the Black Sky?"

"You must stand before the Council of Three. They shall decide your fate."

"Augur told us about the Council of Three. Were there others like us, other Chosen Ones? Brought here to save your world? A man and two children?"

"Do not speak the traitor's name. He is dead to us. Walk in silence."

Silas and Sephie trudged through the maze of titanic trees, the unceasing rain cascading down from above.

Silas whispered to Sephie, "Use your powers to get us out of here."

"No, this is where we're supposed to be. This is how we bring Mirus and Arthur and Clara home. Odo has his part to play, but he has to do it on his own."

"How do you know that?"

"My deeper self just told me."

"Odo was telling me about that deeper self thing." Silas did not look convinced.

240

"I've been studying the Altusians' brain waves. They don't want to hurt us, but they're afraid of something and think we can help them."

"Help them do what?"

"I don't know."

The grueling trek through the unrelenting deluge took six long hours. Sephie did not use her powers to create an energy umbrella, afraid it would terrify the Altusians. The last thing she wanted was for them to think she was a demon.

The Altusians stopped. "We have arrived."

"Where are your houses?"

"Do not fear, little one." He picked Sephie up, stepping through the trees to the edge of a staggeringly deep gorge. Sephie's legs turned to rubber. The gorge was a mile deep, a thousand feet across. On the far wall she could see hundreds of caves connected by a network of wooden ladders and rope bridges.

Her voice was a whisper. "I don't like heights." She tried to push through her fear as Cyra had taught her, but this was too much. There was a raging silver river at the bottom of the gorge. She calculated the fall would last twenty seconds. Twenty seconds, then… Her breathing was fast and shallow.

"I will keep you safe, little one." Sephie screamed when he stepped off the edge of the gorge, falling twenty feet before grabbing a heavy rope with his two free arms. "We are safe here, this is our home. No harm shall come to you."

She closed her eyes, doing her best to imagine herself standing on solid ground.

Silas was not happy about being carried by an Altusian.

"You don't need to carry me, I'm not afraid of heights. I can climb down a rope."

"A fall kills both the fearful and the brave. You are not strong enough to climb, your arms are puny and weak, your hands small."

"I'm not puny and weak. My dad said I should lift weights, but in gym class I can–"

The Altusian stepped off the ledge, falling fifty feet before grabbing one of the ropes.

"I think I'm going to throw up."

"You are safe, little Chosen One. We will soon reach the Council of Three. We cross there." He pointed to a long rope bridge spanning the gorge.

"You should probably hold the rope with two hands."

The Altusian laughed. "Two hands."

Silas had no idea why that was funny.

The Altusian let go of the rope and they fell a hundred feet before he grabbed it with one hand, sliding to a stop a few feet above the rope bridge.

"We cross here. Do you wish to walk, or should I carry you?"

"It's really windy in the gorge, the bridge looks kind of slippery from all the rain. Does it always sway like that?"

The Altusian gave a snort, dropping down to a wooden platform near the bridge. Sephie was halfway across, her eyes closed.

Silas looked down as they were crossing.

"Good view of the river from here. It's big."

"If I slip, you shall have a far better view."

"Good one. Funny."

The bridge ended at the entrance to a large tunnel, a dozen Altusians standing guard, armed with deadly spears and silver swords.

Their captors set Silas and Sephie down.

"You may enter now, Chosen Ones."

Sephie and Silas stepped forward through the long dark tunnel, emerging in a massive cavern illuminated by torches, a crowd of several hundred Altusians sitting cross legged on the stone floor. At the far end of the cave were three ornately carved wooden chairs perched on a raised platform, a colorful symbol painted on the wall behind each one.

"I guess we're going to meet the Council of Three."

The cave grew silent when the gong echoed through the cave, the Altusians bowing their heads.

Dressed in long pale green robes, the Council of Three stepped out of the shadows, walking with deliberate ceremony to their chairs. They turned toward the crowd at precisely the same moment, taking their seats. This was followed by a long silence, ending when the gong sounded three times.

A voice cried out, "Let the Chosen Ones approach the Council of Three!"

The Altusian next to Sephie and Silas pushed them forward, whispering, "Do not speak unless commanded.

Answer all questions truthfully under penalty of death."

The two friends stepped forward, approaching the Council. Sephie was studying their brainwaves. She could see no anger, no fear.

The Council member in the center chair said, "One of you is not here, as it should be. The prophecy states we shall be visited on this day by two of the three Chosen Ones."

Sephie raised her hand.

"You may speak."

"Do you know where our friend is? His name is Odo."

"So it is written in the prophecy of the great Kalumnia. First shall arrive the Three, then shall arrive the Two, the One never to be seen by the Council of Three. These six Chosen Ones from beyond the veil shall save our world. So it was written by Kalumnia."

Sephie whispered to Silas, "I think that means Odo is okay."

Any fear Silas had was gone, replaced by curiosity. How could the seer Kalumnia have known they were coming? Augur had said he was a fraud, a self serving charlatan. Why were they here, and what were they supposed to save the world from?

"Chosen Two, you may ask what questions you wish at this time."

Sephie raised her hand again.

"Speak, child."

"What do you wish us to do? What is the threat to your world?"

"You have been sent by the gods to destroy the Fortress of Rain, to end the floods, to heal our land. You are the spark that shall transform our world to its former magnificence, as it was during the reign of Those Who Came Before."

"What can you tell us about the Fortress of Rain? Who built it? What does it do?"

The Council member seated in the left chair nodded, holding up one hand.

"We anticipated your question. Auctor the Storyteller, approach the Council of Three!"

An elderly Altusian rose to his feet with the help of a heavy wooden staff. He hobbled across the cavern, standing before the Council.

"Bring forth the Storyteller's chair!"

A young Altusian darted out of the shadows with a wooden chair, setting it in front of Auctor. The storyteller nodded his thanks, seating himself with an audible sigh, his sunken eyes on Sephie and Silas. "Much better, thank you."

The only sound to be heard was the distant whistling of the wind in the gorge.

"We shall hear from Auctor the Storyteller how the Fortress of Rain came to be, how the demons arrived from the Black Sky, how the rivers widened, the oceans rose, the cataclysmic floods bringing to an end the world of Those Who Came Before."

The Storyteller rested his staff across his legs. He leaned back in his chair with a long sigh, beginning his story.

245

Chapter 37

The Black Sky

In the time of Those Who Came Before there lived a child named Videns, a child born of rare promise, a child of singular vision, a child of significant ability. It was Videns who saw the darkening sky long before it grew visible to others, but as is the way of this mortal world, his dire warnings went unheeded, his words lost to the four winds.

On the third moon of his tenth year, young Videns was visited by a being of white, a being who could see without eyes, a being who could hear without ears, a being who could speak without a mouth, a being whose feet did not tread upon the ground. This mystical messenger from the great beyond spoke to Videns of a coming apocalypse, a cataclysmic flood caused by creatures from a distant realm, creatures unlike Those Who Came Before. The Black Sky would signal their arrival, a harbinger of the final days of Those Who Came Before.

The glorious being of white instructed Videns to

travel alone across the scorching sands of Furens to the sacred Mountains of Altus, a lone child sent to bear witness to the arrival of demons from within the Black Sky. For one year Videns trekked across the blazing sands of Furens, for one year Videns braved the fiery breath of the Rana, the wintry snows and frigid winds of Collis.

Videns sat in silence for a second year, living without food or water, his gaze never veering from the ever darkening circle above the sacred mountains, great bolts of lightning flashing wildly along the outer edges. The mountain people fled in terror, but the being of white had instructed Videns to stay, to bear witness to the arrival of demons. Videns was without fear, the comforting words of the glorious being of white ever in his thoughts.

First came a pale shadow, a great circle of unknown substance and purpose, a circle which transformed over two passes of the moon to a gleaming silver sphere of such monstrous proportion that it darkened the sky, dwarfed the Mountains of Altus.

Three great black disks emerged from the sphere, circling the world of Emerus for one pass of the moon, vanishing without trace into the Great Sea.

Videns watched in silence as the Fortress of Rain began to form, great beams of blinding light shooting down from the silver sphere, the walls of the Fortress growing taller with each sunrise, the six deadly towers sprouting up like wild Morelias in the springtime.

247

Spheres of blue light blossomed on the towers, the Fortress reaching completion after a single pass of the moon.

There was a great and dreadful silence when the silver sphere faded to nothingness, when the Black Sky vanished, leaving in its wake the terrible Fortress of Rain. Those Who Came Before celebrated when the Black Sky was gone, celebrated when the three black disks vanished into the ocean, celebrated when the great silver sphere faded to nothingness. They celebrated when the rains began to fall above the Mountains of Altus.

Grass grew in the sands of Furens, farms appeared, crops flourished, great swaths of brilliant wildflowers blossomed for the first time in memory. Those Who Came Before celebrated the arrival of the Black Sky, the great Silver Sphere with its gift of rain.

Videns saw the verdant grasslands, the farms, the flowers, the trees, but he did not celebrate, warning the people a second time, telling them the rains would not stop, telling them of the approaching cataclysmic flood. Again they did not listen, their eyes only on the bountiful harvests of the present, no thought for the future of their world, of their land.

Videns retreated deep into the Mountains of Altus, watching alone from on high as the rivers widened, as the Great Sea rose, creeping across the green fields of Furens, watching as the great black clouds above the Fortress of Rain grew to cataclysmic proportion, blotting out the sun and the stars and the moon. Those Who Came Before now wept, cursing the Black Sky and the great Silver Sphere with its unseen demons from a distant realm.

It was with a heavy heart that Videns retreated from the world of Those Who Came Before, moving to the very cave in which we now sit, living in solitude until he was once again visited by the glorious being of white, telling him his work was done, that one day his story would save the world of Altus. The being of white offered to carry him to a distant paradise, but Videns chose to live out the remainder of his days on his beloved world of Emerus.

So is the story of Videns, as it has been told for over three hundred years.

The crowd of Altusians murmured, "So is the story of Videns, as it has been told for over three hundred years."

Auctor the Storyteller rose from his chair, bowing to the Council of Three, returning to his seat on the floor.

Sephie whispered to Silas, "This is incredible, Videns was visited by a Sinarian, the being of white. Those are the beings who visited us in Wikerus' house when we got back from Atroxia. Their feet never touch the floor, they walk six inches above the ground. The Sinarians wanted Videns' story to be told, they wanted us to hear it, they wanted us to stop the rain."

Sephie raised her hand.

"You may speak, Chosen One."

"Auctor's story has given us much needed knowledge, but to stop the rain we must first speak with the Chosen Ones named Mirus, Arthur, and Clara."

The Council of Three huddled together, their whispered voices inaudible. After several minutes they turned to Sephie.

"So it is written, the Two shall become Five, and those Five shall become Six, the Six who shall restore the world of Emerus, the Six Chosen Ones who are named Mirus, Arthur, Clara, Sephie, Silas, and Odo."

Sephie did not attempt to conceal her surprise. "You know our names?"

"The great seer Kalumnia wrote these names one year ago. He foresaw your coming, he foretold your names."

"He is a powerful seer indeed." Sephie gave Silas a sideways glance. She didn't know how Kalumnia had gotten their names, but she knew he was a fraud.

The Council of Three rose as one from their chairs.

"All but the Chosen Ones shall leave."

Ten minutes later Silas and Sephie were alone in the cave with the Council of Three.

"The first three Chosen Ones are being kept in a secure location for their own safety. The two named Arthur and Clara attempted a return to their world through a small Black Sky, but were stopped, brought back to the Mountain of Altus to fulfill the prophecy as written by the seer Kalumnia. We will take you to them, allow you to speak with them. Kalumnia will be present, using his formidable mystical powers to make certain there are no further attempts at escape."

Sephie shook her head. "We won't try to escape, our purpose is clear. We are here to destroy the Fortress of Rain."

"So it shall be. Follow us, Chosen Ones."

Chapter 38

Kalumnia's Secret

Sephie and Silas followed the Council of Three into a long low tunnel hidden at the rear of the cave, emerging into a luxuriously appointed hall filled with exquisitely carved wooden furniture and stunningly beautiful art, the massive room brightly illuminated by dozens of carved crystal oil lamps.

Sephie's face darkened. The Council of Three clearly had a far different lifestyle than the rest of the Altusians. She eyed the silver trays scattered about the room, filled with delicate pastries and sugary confections, carved glass decanters filled with sparkling beverages.

One of the council members tossed a rough blanket across a beautifully embroidered couch.

"Sit there. Don't move, don't touch anything. This is a sacred place and must not be defiled. Kalumnia will be here shortly."

As if on cue, a tall Altusian clad in a long purple

robe festooned with yellow stars and moons made an overtly theatrical entrance from the shadows. On his head he wore a pointed red felt hat covered with incomprehensible silver symbols. He stopped, feigning surprise at the sight of Sephie and Silas, gesturing grandly with one arm.

"It is I, the great Kalumnia, holder of infinite wisdom from the great unseen realms, the most powerful seer to ever grace the world of Emerus. It was I who foresaw your coming many years ago. Welcome to Altusia, small Chosen Ones. You may speak to me now, if you wish. Do not be afraid, I will not use my astonishing powers to harm you."

Silas tried to convert his laugh to a cough.

Sephie had to bite her lip. Kalumnia was clearly a pompous fraud, just as Augur had said.

"It is a great honor to meet such a powerful seer. Thank you for seeing us. Will you be taking us to see the Chosen Ones named Mirus, Arthur, and Clara?"

"Of course. I also foresaw their coming many years ago, in case you were curious as to the extent of my fantastic mystical abilities."

"You are truly incredible." Sephie bit her lip again. "We can't wait to see them."

One of the council members gave a dismissive wave, motioning for Kalumnia to leave.

Kalumnia bowed deeply. "As is your wish, Council of Three."

He turned to Silas and Sephie. "I will take you to see the others now. Do not be afraid, I will not harm you with my wondrous powers."

Sephie tried not to roll her eyes. There was no one in the world she was less afraid of than Kalumnia.

They followed the purple robed fraud down a narrow darkened tunnel.

"Your fellow Chosen Ones are safe in their chambers at the end of this tunnel. They were moved here after two of them mistakenly attempted to return to their world, clearly unaware of my deeply prophetic writings."

"Did they have a small furry animal with them?"

"Yes, a ridiculous little creature named Fluffy. I allowed it to escape through the small black sky. I foresaw many years ago that he would lure the final three Chosen Ones to Emerus."

Silas looked puzzled. "When did the first three Chosen Ones arrive here?"

"Less than a year ago, as I wrote long ago in my prophecy."

"How is that possible? They disappeared from our world almost fifty years ago."

Kalumnia attempted to conceal his surprise. "Of course, the altered time, just as I had said... the time... between various worlds is... unstable, always changing, dependent on many mystical factors far beyond your paltry comprehension."

Sephie gave a silent laugh. Kalumnia did not have the slightest understanding of how the passage of time was related to the warping of space by a planet's mass and its relative velocity.

"It must be wonderful to understand such complex things."

"It can be a heavy burden to carry such deep wisdom and understanding of the universe when those around you know so little."

Silas stopped, eyeing the heavy iron door in front of them.

"What's this?"

"This is where your friends are staying, all thanks to the kindness and generosity of the Council of Three."

"It looks like a prison cell."

"Quite the opposite, I assure you, it is meant to keep them safe, that they may fulfill my glorious prophecy, bringing an end to the cataclysmic rains of Emerus."

Kalumnia pulled a heavy key from his cloak, unlocking the stout iron door.

"This way, please. Follow me, no need to be afraid, I shall protect you from all harm using all the full array of marvelous mystical forces at my disposal."

They followed the pompous seer into a sparsely furnished twenty foot square room. Silas stopped in stunned surprise when he saw Mirus, Arthur, and Clara.

Mirus spoke first. "Who are you? Where did you come from?"

"Grandpa?"

"Who is Grandpa?"

"I'm Silas Ward, and you're my grandpa. And you're Uncle Arthur, and Aunt Clara. You disappeared from Earth over fifty years ago."

"Good heavens, child, are you mad? I have no

grandchildren, and we have been here for less than a year."

Sephie interrupted. "Only one year has passed in this world, but fifty years have passed on Earth. Silas is the son of Joseph, your oldest boy."

Mirus sank down onto a hard wooden bench. "Is this true? Fifty years have passed? What about Sarah? Where is my Sarah?"

Silas' expression told Mirus everything he needed to know.

"Sarah is…?"

Silas nodded.

Mirus covered his face with his hands.

Arthur and Clara were clearly confused. "Why is Papa crying? Who are you?"

Silas sat down next to them. "I am from the future, and my name is Silas. I am the son of your brother Joseph."

Arthur burst out laughing. "Joseph is a boy, he doesn't have children, that's silly."

"He doesn't have them now, but he will grow up and have a son named Silas. I am Silas. We came here to find you."

Mirus put his arms around Arthur and Clara, holding them close to him. "It's all right, dear children, they have come to take us home."

"Is Mama worried about us? Does she know we're safe?"

Mirus hesitated. "She's not worried, she knows we're safe." He turned to Silas. "When do we leave?"

"It's a little more complicated than that. Do you know anything about the Fortress of Rain?"

"Only what Kalumnia has told me, that it was–"

Kalumnia sharply interrupted him. "Enough about my incredible abilities, we shall speak of other things." He glared at Mirus, slowly sidling over to Sephie, leaning down next to her, pretending to adjust his boots. His whisper was a low hiss.

"Listen, and listen carefully. I know you have spoken with Augur, the Sinarians have told me everything. They told me you would be coming. I did not betray Augur, I saved his life. I convinced the Council of Three to banish him instead of throwing him into the gorge. The Council of Three is going to kill you. They do not want the Fortress of Rain destroyed, they like things as they are. You've seen how they live. There will be warriors armed with arrows and spears waiting for you at the Fortress. The Council will tell everyone you failed in your mission, that you were not the true Chosen Ones. Do not speak, they are watching and listening."

Sephie's jaw dropped.

Kalumnia stood up, extending his arms. "I am sensing something, a profound revelation. Some of you are related, I'm seeing uncles and aunts, perhaps a grandfather. I am correct, am I not?"

Silas nodded, "Right, um… that's kind of what we were just talking about." Sephie kicked his leg sharply.

"You're incredible, Kalumnia, truly incredible. Your words have had a powerful effect on me."

Mirus looked confused. "What is happening here?"

Sephie answered, "We are the Chosen Ones, sent here to destroy the Fortress of Rain, sent here to end the floods and return this world to the glorious days of Those Who Came Before. So it was written by the great and powerful Kalumnia."

Kalumnia nodded, resting his hand on Sephie's shoulder. "Well said, Chosen One."

Mirus turned to the Ghost Sailor standing next to him, listening attentively to his silent voice. An imperceptible smile appeared on Mirus' face. He took Arthur and Clara's hands in his. "Come children, let us restore the world of Emerus to its former glory. Lead the way, great and powerful Kalumnia."

Chapter 39

Section 14B, Paragraph 2.7

When Odo saw the automaton's violent reaction to the emerald sphere, he turned and ran, searching for a place to hide inside the fortress. He was also having second thoughts about his plan to shut down the Fortress of Rain on his own.

"What was I thinking? That thing is going to kill me, seeing the emerald made him go crazy. There's a ladder, I can hide up there."

He scrambled wildly up the wide ladder to a metallic walkway running around the interior of the gargantuan fortress, squeezing behind a row of orange cylinders that extended up through a second overhead walkway.

The sound of a door slamming echoed through the vast facility. Odo slumped down, leaning against one of the cylinders.

"He's back. What am I going to do? There's no way I can fight him, he's a million times stronger than I am. I have to use stealth, shut this place down without him seeing me."

He crawled silently to the edge of the walkway,

peering through the heavy wire mesh.

"Okay, six giant cylinders going straight up through the roof. Those are the towers I saw outside with the blue spheres on them. That has to be what's causing the rain, but I have no idea how they work. They look like they're made of Morsennium, one of the strongest synthetic materials known. There's a big glowing cube in the center of the building, maybe a power supply. It's pulsing like the blue spheres on the towers."

Odo spotted the automaton at the far end of the fortress, seated in front of a long curving control panel.

"This is good, a control panel. Maybe I can use it to shut the rain machine off. I wonder if automatons sleep? Probably not."

Two hours passed and Odo's eyes were drooping, the automaton still seated at the console.

"So tired."

His eyes popped open when the blaring alarm sounded, a jolt of fear shooting through him. He flattened himself against the walkway. "I must have fallen asleep, maybe I set off that alarm." He peered through the wire mesh rail, watching the automaton stride over to one of the six cylinders, the deafening alarm silenced when he tapped a glowing violet disk. With a soft whirring noise a curved panel opened, a heavy tray holding a dark blue sphere sliding out.

"That's the same kind of sphere I saw him carrying to the black dome outside. Perfect, last time he was gone for twenty minutes, plenty of time for me to check out the control panel and figure out how to shut off the rain."

Odo crept over to the ladder, waiting until he heard the side door open, the automaton stepping outside. He slid down the ladder, racing across the gritty floor to the long console.

"Whoa, this is huge, there's a zillion little dials and buttons on it. How do I shut it off? I guess I could push every button and turn every dial." Odo stopped when he noticed three curious portraits on the wall facing the control panel.

"Portraits of fish? How weird is that?" He was re-membering his dad's painting of the dogs playing cards. "What am I doing? I have to focus." He turned his attention back to the control console. "I'll press every button and turn every dial, then run for it. Hopefully the place will explode after I get out."

As he reached for the first dial he heard the side door slam shut, the automaton's heavy footsteps heading in his direction.

"Yikes!" Odo darted behind the console, ducking down and peering over the top. The automaton was standing in front of the glowing cube in the center of the sprawling fortress. Odo watched a tray slide out holding a glowing blue sphere.

"That's where he gets the new spheres. It's just like the gold power spheres on *The Phoenix*. This is great, I can shut the place down by taking out all six of the blue power spheres."

He slipped over to the side wall and crept back to the ladder, climbing silently to the walkway above while the automaton was walking back to the control panel.

"Whew, that was close. Okay, what do I know? I know he takes the old spheres outside, but I don't know how often. If I could lock him out, that might give me time to take out all the blue power spheres." Odo stopped, his thoughts flashing back to the curious fish portraits on the wall.

"Maybe those aren't just goofy paintings, maybe those are real portraits. Maybe they're alien creatures. Alien creatures who built the Fortress of Rain."

He sank to the floor, realizing the implications of this unexpected idea.

"I think I know what's going on here. The aliens are aquatic creatures and they're flooding this world so they can live here. It's probably how they expand their civilization, they build rain machines on worlds and come back when the planet is flooded. The fish skeletons in the black ship weren't just fish, they were the ones flying the ship. One of those fire breathing frogs must have gotten inside and they crashed into the trees. This is incredible."

Odo gave a long sigh, studying the six massive cylinders. "I've been fooling myself, I can't do this alone. No way can I beat that automaton. Even if I take out all six power spheres, he would just put them back in again. I need to get out of here and find Sephie and Silas."

Odo waited until the automaton was seated at the control panel, then crept down the ladder.

"Okay, Watson, no yowling. We have to sneak out

the door without the crazy robot seeing us."

He inched his way along the outer wall, ducking under the massive pipes that led to the six towers, stopping when the automaton turned suddenly, looking in his direction.

"Yikes."

Odo stood motionless for a full minute.

"Okay, he turned away, he's working again. That was close. Another twenty feet and I'm home free. The Translucent Boy makes his daring escape."

He stepped silently across the floor, his eyes on the violet disk next to the door. "One tap and I am history. See you later, crazy robot."

When Odo touched the violet disk, three things happened. An earsplitting alarm sounded, the door did not open, and the automaton gave a shriek, leaping to its feet.

"I knew it! I knew there was someone in here! Prepare to die, intruder!" It raised one arm, a powerful beam of purple light blasting across the room, exploding six feet from Odo. He staggered backwards, stunned by the explosion, managing to turn and run toward the ladder.

"Can't use the ladder, he'll see me!" He searched frantically for a place to hide, ducking under an enormous gray pipe and slipping behind a stack of large crates piled against the wall. Squeezing between them, he found a hiding spot next to the outer wall.

"I don't think he can see me here."

Odo held his breath when he heard the approaching

footsteps.

"Intruder! You have entered a Highly Restricted Piscorian Water Production Facility. Section 14B, Paragraph 2.7 of my programming code states all unauthorized intruders shall be instantly vaporized."

Odo groaned. "This is bad. I have to think of something."

"I know you're in here, intruder! There is no escape for you! I will find you!"

Odo took slow breaths, trying to calm himself. He turned, studying the outer wall, an idea popping into his head.

"Whoa, this could work. Wikerus did it, maybe I can."

He pressed his hand against the thick Morsennium wall, closing his eyes, concentrating deeply. A circular section of the wall became translucent, spreading out in all directions. At first it felt as though he was pushing his hand through thick pudding, then water, his arm moving easily through it. A strange calmness filled him, he knew exactly what to do. Odo Whitley stood up and stepped through the fortress wall into the brilliant Emerusian sunshine.

Chapter 40

Double Time

Odo scrambled behind a large boulder on the west side of the fortress, keeping a wary eye out for the automaton.

"That was amazing, I can't wait to tell Sephie I walked through a wall. I need to find her and Silas so we can clobber that automaton and take out the blue power spheres. Sephie can stop him with her powers."

His ears perked up at the sound of voices. He peeked out from behind the boulder. "Whoa, Altusian warriors armed with spears and arrows. I wonder what they're doing here? Maybe they're looking for me. Maybe they're going to attack the fortress. They must not know about the automaton. He could vaporize them in a heartbeat."

Odo watched the soldiers spread out, concealing themselves behind rocks. The leader of the group shouted out, "Stay hidden until they attempt to gain entrance, then kill them all."

"Whoa, kill them all? I don't like the sound of that. I wonder who they're planning to kill?"

Odo was so focused on the Altusian warriors that he didn't notice the footsteps behind him. A hand clapped over his mouth, muffling his scream.

"Quiet! It's us!"

He turned to see Sephie, Silas, Mirus, Arthur, and Clara.

"You found them! Where have you been? Who took you? I know how to shut down the fortress!"

The adventurers huddled together behind the gigantic boulder, whispering their stories, Sephie telling Odo about Kalumnia and the Council of Three, Odo telling them about the automaton inside the fortress and the Piscorians' scheme to flood the planet.

Odo couldn't take his eyes off Clara, Arthur, and Mirus. "I can't believe we found you. I don't know if Sephie told you, but I traveled back in time to the day they took the photograph of you on the front porch, the day you guys sneaked into your dad's workshop and got sent to your rooms. I even tried on the Ghostwatcher brass goggles you invented. Hey, I almost forgot!" Odo flipped open his pack and Watson leaped out, darting over to Clara and Arthur.

"Fluffy! You're okay!" Clara hugged him while Arthur rubbed his head. "He jumped through the spectral gateway when we were trying to escape. Kalumnia gave us a blue sphere that opens a doorway to our world, but the Altusians stopped us before we could adjust the settings and go through it."

Silas added, "Fluffy led Odo and Sephie to my house. It took us a while to figure out what had happened to you." He did not mention the Lady in Black or the fact that she had been accused of murdering them.

Mirus pulled the heavy brass goggles from his coat pocket. "I still have the Ghostwatchers if you need them to get home."

"We don't need them. Sephie and I are dimensional shifters, we can transition between worlds and bring you with us."

Sephie nodded. "But first we have to shut down the Fortress of Rain."

"We'll have to be careful, there's a bunch of armed soldiers hiding in the rocks. They're waiting for someone, and they're going to kill them. I heard them talking."

"They're waiting for us, Odo Whitley."

"What? They want to kill us? Why?"

"Kalumnia told us the Council of Three doesn't want us to destroy the Fortress of Rain, they like things the way they are. You should see how they live compared to everyone else."

"Can you use your powers to stop the warriors?"

Arthur and Clara turned to Sephie. "What kind of powers?"

"Sephie is a superhero, she can do lots of amazing stuff."

"What's a superhero?"

"Um… it's a hero, but with weird powers. You'll

learn all about them once we get home. Silas is a superhero too. He can do… other stuff."

"Odo Whitley, you come with me. Everyone else stay here. I'm going to send these assassins on a little trip."

"Are you going to kill them with your super powers, Sephie?"

"No, of course not, I would never take the life of a living creature. I have other plans for our big blue friends. Let's get cracking, Odo Whitley. Time is money."

Odo grinned. Sephie Crumb was back.

The pair of best friends strolled out from behind the boulder, stepping around the corner to the front of the fortress. Sephie scanned the area for brainwaves.

"Sixteen of them hiding up there, I can see their energy fields." She waved to the soldiers. "Hello! Here we are!"

The blue warriors popped up from behind the rocks.

Odo eyed their spears and bows and swords. "They have a lot of weapons."

Sephie drew four rapid symbols in the air, a shimmering wall of energy appearing in front of the two friends.

Twelve warriors raised their bows, a salvo of deadly razor sharp arrows hissing through the air toward Odo and Sephie. Much to the soldiers' surprise, the arrows bounced off the rippling wall of energy, falling harmlessly to the ground.

"Look sharp, they're wizards!"

A blue cloud shot out from Sephie, enveloping the sixteen warriors.

A shrill whistle sounded and the soldiers leaped forward, charging toward them. Sephie raised both arms, drawing the final symbol.

As one, the soldiers stopped, a look of confusion on their faces. The whistle blasted again and they formed two columns. Their commander raised his sword.

"March! Double time!"

Three minutes later the soldiers were gone.

"Where did you send them?"

"They suddenly remembered they were supposed to march fifty miles to the east, hide in the forest for a week, then report back to the Council of Three that we had all been killed."

"You're amazing, Sephie Crumb."

"I was worried about you, but I knew you'd be okay, Odo Whitley."

"I walked through a wall to escape from the automaton."

"No way!"

"I did, I figured out how to do it. It's not that hard."

The other adventurers ran out from behind the huge boulder. "You sent them away!"

"I told you Sephie was a superhero."

Mirus turned to Sephie. "Astonishing. How did you do it?"

"It's complicated. I'll tell you about it when we get home. Right now we need to shut down the Fortress of Rain."

"I can walk through the wall and open the door."

Clara's eyes were wide. "You can walk through walls? You are also a superhero, Odo?"

Odo laughed, "Well, I don't want to brag or anything, but I can–"

Sephie realized she did not like the way Clara's gaze was lingering on Odo. She did not like it at all. "Snap to it, Odo Whitley. What's your plan?"

"It's brilliant and it's foolproof. We go in through the wall, you defeat the automaton, we shut down the fortress and all go home."

Sephie stared silently at Odo.

Chapter 41

Doppel

"Tell me how you walk through a wall."

"It's pretty easy once you know how. I put my hand on the wall and imagine it's part of my body. Once the wall becomes translucent, I imagine my atoms passing through the atoms of the wall. It feels a little like walking through water. Wikerus said it's called quantum tunneling."

"I can walk through it?"

"I think so, as long as I keep my hand on the wall."

"That's our plan then. You and I will go in through the back wall. Everyone else stays here, it's too dangerous."

"The automaton tried to blast me with some kind of particle disruptor beam."

Silas said, "You're sure you don't need any help?"

"We'll use stealth to defeat the automaton. You stay out here and keep everyone safe."

Silas eyed the Ghost Sailor standing next to Odo. He was giving the thumbs up sign. "Okay, be careful though."

"We will. Let's go, Odo Whitley."

The pair of friends walked around to the west wall.

"I came out right there. We'll be hidden behind a big stack of crates. How are you going to defeat the automaton? Can you make him see stuff that's not there? Maybe we could scare him, make him leave."

"I have a better idea. Where are the portraits of the Piscorians?"

"On the far end of the building in front of the control panel, past all the towers."

"I'll use my long distance glasses. I need to see them."

"Why?"

"Because when the automaton sees us, he's going to see the Piscorians from those paintings. Then I'll order him to shut down the plant."

"Clever." Odo pressed his hand against the fortress, a six foot tall section of the wall rippling like water. "Okay, you go first."

Sephie cautiously poked her hand into the shimmering wall. "It works." She stepped into the fortress, followed by Odo.

Odo peered between the huge crates. "I can see him, he's at the control panel. The portraits are on the wall in front of him."

Sephie slipped on her long distance glasses and studied the Piscorian images. "They look like big

272

catfish."

"Big catfish wearing uniforms."

Sephie laughed. "Okay, I've got it." She drew four symbols in the air and closed her eyes, visualizing the Piscorian portraits. A pale blue light flashed across the fortress floor, enveloping the automaton.

"Do you think it will work?"

"We're about to find out. If anything happens, run for the nearest wall and use your powers to get us out of here."

Sephie squeezed between the crates, stepping out onto the open floor. Odo joined her moments later, his eyes on the automaton.

Sephie hollered, "ATTENTION, SOLDIER!"

The automaton leaped to its feet, turning to face them, its hands glowing with a brilliant purple light. It stopped, taking a step back, the purple light fading.

Sephie strode across the floor, a fearsome scowl on her face.

The automaton was standing at attention.

Odo laughed to himself. Sephie was amazing.

She approached the automaton, giving a dismissive wave. "What have you been doing here? Why is this plant still operational?"

"Sir?"

"You were ordered to shut the plant down. We sent the transmission two weeks ago. Why isn't it done?"

"Transmission, sir?"

"Are you deaf? Did you not hear my words?"

"I don't recall receiving a transmission, sir."

"We're shutting down the facility. Piscorians have evolved and no longer need to live in an aquatic environment."

"You don't need to live in the water?"

"DO I LOOK LIKE I NEED TO LIVE IN THE WATER? ARE YOUR EYES MALFUNCTIONING?"

"No, sir, you're walking... not in the water, or swimming... on the land... um..."

"DO YOU HAVE MARBLES IN YOUR MOUTH?" Sephie was shrieking at the automaton. Odo was trying not to laugh.

"No, sir! No marbles in my mouth, sir. I will shut down the water production facility immediately, sir."

"That's more like it. Get to it, time is money."

"Of course, sir. I'll just need the emergency shut-down code."

Sephie froze. This was not part of her plan, she needed time to think. She turned to Odo. "You heard him, he needs the emergency shut down code. Give it to him."

"Yes, sir, the emergency code, coming right up." Odo pretended to check his pockets for the code. "Not here, I may have left it in my wallet."

The automaton looked sharply at Odo. "Your wallet? When did Piscorians start carrying wallets?"

"Oh... you know, since we evolved. They're great for keeping stuff in, like important emergency codes."

The automaton held up one hand, a pale yellow light washing over Odo and Sephie. It let out a screech, its green eyes bulging out.

"IMPOSTERS! You're not Piscorians, you're unauthorized intruders! Prepare to be destroyed!"

Sephie shrieked, "RUN!"

The two friends turned, bolting toward the nearest wall.

Odo slapped his hand against it, trying to concentrate.

"I WILL OBLITERATE YOU, IMPOSTERS!"

The automaton stood ten feet away from them, its hands glowing brightly with a terrifying purple light.

A blazing blue beam shot out from Sephie, striking the automaton's egg shaped head. It made a strange gurgling noise and sank to its knees, its eyes closing.

Odo whispered, "What happened? What did you do? Did you kill it?"

Sephie shook her head. "No, but I don't think you're going to like what I did, Odo Whitley."

"Are you kidding? You saved our lives. What's not to like about that?"

The automaton's eyes popped open, a familiar voice filling the air.

"I'm starving. Hey, Sephie, can you shape me a box of Proto's Taste-E Kakes? And a cinnamon roll from Madam Beffy's Diner?"

Odo blinked. "Why does he sound like me? What did you do?"

It was the first time Odo had ever seen Sephie look embarrassed. "I... replaced his personality with yours. I only had a split second to do it, and you were the first person I thought of."

The automaton stood up, stretching its arms.

"It's my week to pick the movie. No way are we seeing *Forgotten Memories* again. So predictable."

Odo glared at Sephie. "What were you thinking? Wait, do I really sound like that?"

"Maybe a little?"

Odo turned to the automaton. "What's your name?"

"That's weird, I can't remember. I don't think I have a name. Oh, well, names are dumb. Sephie, what's up with the Taste-E Kakes? Still starving. How's that cinnamon roll coming along?"

Odo hesitated. "I don't talk to you like that, do I? Am I rude like that?"

"Of course not."

Odo turned to the automaton. "I guess we have to call you something, but it's not going to be Odo Whitley. Let me think. I know, I'll call you Doppel, that's short for doppelganger, someone's double."

"Love it. Speaking of short, how come you're so short?"

"What?? I'm not short. How come you're so rude?"

"I'm not rude, just making an unbiased observation. Quit being so sensitive. Compared to me, you're short. Height is relative. Ever hear of the theory of relativity? I can't believe you don't know that. Everyone knows that. You should try opening a book once in a while."

Odo's eyes widened, his face turning bright red.

Sephie interrupted the rapidly deteriorating conversation. "Doppel, we need to shut down the Fortress of Rain. What's the best way to do that?"

"Give me the emergency shut down code, the one Odo has in his wallet. Let's have it, Odo. You do have it in your wallet, don't you? You said you did. You weren't lying to me, were you?"

"Doppel, you know the code is not in his wallet. We don't have the code. Is there another way? What about taking out all the power spheres?"

"Sure, that would work, but ten hours later the atoms of the Fortress will be converted to pure energy, leaving a five hundred foot deep crater in the ground."

"Whoa, it will explode?"

"That's one word for it. You should expand your vocabulary. Ever heard of a thesaurus? It's a book that's filled with lots of other big words. You should check it out."

Odo gritted his teeth. "One moment, please. Sephie, may I speak with you privately?"

Sephie was doing a poor job of hiding her grin. "Of course, Odo Whitley."

The two friends stepped behind the control panel.

"Why is he being so rude? I'm not rude like that, am I? You can tell me if I am. It won't bother me."

"Of course you're not rude like that. I think his previous personality is mixed in with yours."

"Can you fix it? Make him not rude? He asked me if I knew what a thesaurus was, said I should expand my vocabulary. I know what a thesaurus is."

"It's too dangerous, it might make things worse. At least now he's not trying to kill us, and he did say he would help us shut down the fortress."

277

"I have an excellent vocabulary. Lots of people have said that. Lots of people. I know what a thesaurus is, Sephie. I have three of them in my library."

"Odo Whitley, you have to ignore what he says. I think you're brilliant, one of the smartest people I know."

"Really?"

"Yes, really. If Doppel called you a grapefruit, would that mean you were a grapefruit?"

"Of course not, that's silly, but I see where you're going with this. His words don't change what I am."

"His words don't change what you are, but if you're not careful they can change the way you think about yourself. When I was little I thought my orange hair was beautiful, but when Brandon Crouch started making fun of it, I changed. I was embarrassed by my hair until I realized his opinion meant nothing. He was just a mean, angry person trying to make me feel bad about myself. He was the one with the problem, not me."

"I like your hair, Sephie. I think it's really cute."

"Thanks, Odo."

Doppel poked his head over the control panel.

"Are we going to shut this place down, or are you going the spend the rest of the day jabbering about Sephie's super cute hair?"

Chapter 42

Not Yet

"Doppel said once we take out the power spheres we have ten hours until the Fortress of Rain explodes, or should I say, instantly dissociates into pure energy." Odo looked pointedly at Doppel, raising one eyebrow.

Doppel shook his head. "I said ten days, not ten hours."

"No, you distinctly said we had ten hours. You most certainly did not say ten days."

"I most certainly did say–"

Sephie held up her hand. "Stop. Doppel, are you certain we have ten days?"

"Absolutely. Ten days, not ten minutes, as Odo incorrectly suggested."

"I said ten hours, not ten minutes."

"All right, let's think about this, Odo Whitley. Once we shut it down, the rain will stop, but Emerus will still be flooded. And if you think about it, there's nothing to keep the Piscorians from coming back and building another rain machine."

"Don't forget about all the electrolysis cubes scattered across Emerus. They'll keep converting the floodwaters to hydrogen and oxygen. It will take time, but the waters will recede."

"Good point. That means we just need to think of a way to stop the Piscorians from returning."

"Doppel, can you send messages to the Piscorians?"

"Anything for you, Sephie. Your hair looks super cute today."

Odo's eyes narrowed.

"Is there any way to stop the Piscorians from coming back? Something you could tell them?"

"I could say there's been an infestation of Horobotites."

"What are those? Are they scary?"

"You don't want to know."

"But it will keep the Piscorians away?"

"They won't come within a hundred light years of Emerus. How are those Taste-E Kakes coming along?"

Odo glared at Doppel. "Just a quick question, my old friend Doppel. How are you going to eat Taste-E Kakes when you don't have a mouth?"

Doppel reached up and touched his face. "Whoa, you're right. How did I miss that? Okay, forget the cakes, let's shut this place down."

"You'll send a message about the Horobotite infestation?"

"Done and done. Let's rock and roll."

"Why are you saying that? I never say that."

"You want to say it, but you don't because you're afraid Sephie might laugh at you."

Sephie looked at Odo, her eyebrows raised.

Odo gave a dark look. "We don't have time for this. I'm going to let everyone in so they can help us take out the power spheres."

"Let's rock and roll, Odo Whitley."

Odo gave Sephie a sideways look, marching over to the door and swinging it open.

The others entered, stopping when they saw Doppel. "What is that?"

"It's nothing to be afraid of, just a Piscorian automaton. He's going to help us shut the plant down. Okay, Odo Whitley, what's the plan?"

"To deactivate the plant we have to take out the power spheres from the six towers. We dispose of them in the dome behind the fortress. Doppel can show us how to do that."

Odo headed to the first tower. "When you press this violet tab, a big tray will slide out with a blue sphere on it."

Doppel called out, "Hey, forgot to mention if all the power spheres aren't taken out at precisely the same moment, the fortress will be instantly converted to pure energy."

Odo gave a yelp. "What? How could you forget to tell us that? The plant will explode? That seems really important, not something you'd forget."

Doppel shrugged. "Hey, I forgot I didn't have a mouth. I'm human, I forget stuff. Try showing a little empathy for the less fortunate. Be more like Sephie, she's nice to everyone, even forgetful people."

Odo stared daggers at Doppel. Sephie intervened. "Okay, you heard Doppel. We need someone at each of the towers. Clara and Arthur, you can take out a sphere together."

"Okay."

"Everyone take your place at a tower. Tap the violet disk, and a tray will slide out with the power sphere on it. Don't touch it until I say to."

Six panels slid open and six trays whirred out.

"When I say three, everyone pull their sphere off the tray."

Doppel added, "Almost forgot, don't drop it. That would be bad. Five hundred foot crater."

"One, two, THREE!"

Odo glanced around the room. Everyone was holding a sphere. "We did it!"

Doppel gathered up the spheres, placing them in a large crate. "Sephie, I'll take these out to the dome for you and deactivate them."

"Thanks, Doppel."

Silas sank down on a crate. "We did it, we actually did it. We rescued Mirus, Clara, and Arthur, and we shut down the Fortress of Rain."

Mirus pulled out his brass goggles and the small blue sphere Kalumnia had given him. "You're certain you don't need these to get back home?"

Sephie shook her head. "Odo and I will use our homestones to bring everyone back. We'll arrive in

Wikerus Praevian's house."

Arthur turned to his dad. "Will we be living in the future?"

Mirus nodded. "It looks that way. Odo has been telling me some amazing stories about the new technology. You can watch color movies on little boxes in your house. It's incredible."

Arthur was clearly not thrilled with the idea. "What about my friends? What about Mama and Joseph?"

Mirus put his hand on Arthur's shoulder. "I'm sorry, we don't have a choice."

Odo's heart sank when he saw the look on Clara's face.

"Don't give up hope, maybe our friend Wikerus Praevian can help you. He has some amazing powers, he might be able to send you back to 1921. I'll talk to him as soon as we get back."

Clara touched Odo's arm. "Thank you, Odo. That's so nice of you. You're so sweet."

Sephie glared at Clara. "Everyone outside, now."

The adventurers stepped out into the bright sunshine, Odo pointing to the horizon. "The black clouds are gone, I can see the ocean. No more rain."

Sephie called out, "Okay, time to go home. Everyone stand in a circle and hold hands. Odo and I will use our homestones to shift us back to Earth. It's not scary at all, one second you're here, the next second you'll be standing in Wikerus Praevian' sitting room."

When the adventurers had formed a circle, Sephie took out her homestone, but stopped abruptly, tilting her head, listening. She turned to Odo. "We can't go home yet, Odo Whitley. We have to go back and talk to the Council of Three."

"Why would we do that? Those are the guys who tried to kill us. We stopped the rain, it's time to go home. We're done here."

"We're not done here. We have to talk to them, it's important. Silas, you need to come with us. Mirus, Clara, and Arthur, you stay here with Doppel. We'll be back in a few days. You'll be safe inside the Fortress."

Mirus nodded. "I understand. We'll be waiting for you."

Doppel waved to Sephie. "See you soon. Be careful, okay? I miss you already."

Odo's jaw tightened.

Chapter 43

Gotta Go

"You can see the whole mountain now that the black cloud is gone. This is amazing, but I still don't get why you want to go back and see the Council of Three."

"I'm not exactly sure, I just know we have to."

"On the bright side, there's no reason for them to kill us anymore, since we already stopped the rain. Emerus is going to change whether they like it or not."

Silas nodded. "You're right about that. The flood waters should recede pretty quickly. Those electrolysis plants are huge, and there are a lot of them. They were positioned in flooded areas, not in the original ocean, so they'll shut down once floodwaters are gone."

"It was weird to see Mirus in person. Your grandpa looks the same age as your dad."

"And I look the same age as Arthur and Clara. They'll probably be going to our school. I could be sitting next to my uncle in math class."

Odo laughed. "Your dad is going to be so surprised. It's going to be a big change, that's for sure."

The warm Emerusian sun was shining down on the three adventurers later that afternoon as they strolled through the forest.

"These trees are amazing. I like hiking through the forest now that the rain has stopped. I wonder if the Altusians will move out of their caves?"

"That would be bad news for the Council of Three. It would bring a quick end to their life of luxury."

"Shhh! Someone's coming, duck down."

The three friends hid behind one of the trees. Odo peered around the trunk. "It's okay, a bunch of Altusians pulling wagons. They're not warriors, no weapons."

They stepped out from behind the tree, waving to the group.

One of the Altusians let out a cry. "The Chosen Ones! They're alive! It's a miracle!" The villagers dropped everything and ran toward them, falling to their knees.

"The Council said you had failed, that you had been killed by wild animals, but you are alive, and the rain has stopped. It is a miracle never to be forgotten, a tale to be told by storytellers until the end of time."

"It wasn't exactly a miracle, the Council of Three was just a little confused about what happened. We did stop the rain though, and the flood water should recede within a year or two. Where are you going?"

"You are far too humble, great Chosen One. Your deeds here shall be remembered forever. We are leaving the caves, returning to the forests and farms and cities. The flood waters are already receding, the ground rich and fertile. We will become farmers, selling our crops at market, no longer living in caves like animals."

Sephie was clearly embarrassed by the kneeling Altusians. "Please stand up, there's no need to kneel, we were happy to help you. We're on our way to speak with the Council of Three before we return to our home."

One of the villagers spit on the ground. "A pox on the Council of Three. We have seen how they live, their decadent luxury, feasting on delicacies while the rest of us starved ."

"Is everyone leaving?"

"Everyone has left except the Council of Three, their guards, and Kalumnia the Seer."

"They are the ones we need to speak to."

"Bless you, Chosen Ones, you have saved our lives, saved our world."

"Thanks, but we're not really–"

"Odo, we should go."

He waved to the kneeling villagers. "Gotta go, good luck with the farming."

One the villagers repeated Odo's words with quiet reverence. "*Gotta go, good luck with the farming.* These words of the Chosen One named Odo shall live on forever."

With a hurried wave the three adventurers turned and set off for the gorge.

"Whoa, that was rough. I don't know what they

think we are, but we're nothing like that. We just came here to rescue Silas' family, we're not Chosen Ones."

"I guess they need to believe in things like that, Odo Whitley. It gives them comfort. It is kind of amazing that the Sinarians knew over a year ago that we would be coming here. They told Kalumnia exactly what was going to happen."

"Maybe they just traveled into the future and saw what was going to happen, like I traveled into the past and saw Arthur and Clara."

"Do you hear what you're saying, Odo Whitley? How many people on Earth would think traveling to the future was not miraculous?"

"You do make a good point. I must be getting used to being a superhero, all the weird stuff just seems normal now."

Silas nodded. "Me too. I couldn't believe it when we shifted to Emerus; it seemed like magic. But after I thought about it, I realized shifting is just a quick way to travel from one place to another. I've read about lost tribes in the jungle who think airplanes flying overhead are magical beings."

"It's all just science."

"Shhh, more villagers heading this way. I don't want to go through this again." They darted behind a tree, concealing themselves until the Altusians had passed.

Their journey ended the next afternoon when the three friends reached the gorge. Silas peered over the edge.

"Incredible, at least a mile deep."

Sephie attempted a smile. "How do we get down

there?"

"We slide down a rope. Easy enough."

"I guess I could do that. How far down do we go? I had my eyes closed before."

"Maybe a few hundred feet. Then we cross on the rope bridge."

"The rope bridge, I forgot about the rope bridge."

"Are you okay? You look a little pale."

"I'm fine, Odo Whitley. I have to do this."

Silas studied the network of caves on the opposite side of the gorge. "That big tunnel is the entrance to the Council of Three's cave. We take two ropes down, walk along that ledge for about a hundred feet, then cross on the rope bridge."

"Perfect, sounds great." Sephie's heart was thumping. "Silas, you lead the way and we'll follow." She drew a quick symbol and three pairs of heavy gloves blinked into existence. "These will protect our hands when we slide down."

"Sephie, you can stay up here if you want. We could give them your message."

"Thanks, but I don't know why I need to see them yet. I'll be fine."

Silas' eyes were suddenly focused on something behind Odo and Sephie. "I don't think we'll need to climb down those ropes."

Odo and Sephie whipped around to see Kalumnia, the Council of Three, and a dozen heavily armed warriors standing behind them.

Chapter 44

The Final Prophecy

Kalumnia stepped forward, gesturing grandly to Odo, Sephie, and Silas.

"Just as I said they would in my staggeringly accurate prophecy, the Chosen Ones have made their triumphant return after stopping the rain. Once again I have proven myself to be the greatest seer this world has ever known."

One of the green robed Council members sneered at Kalumnia. "You said no such thing, you pompous fraud. There was nothing in your prophecy about them succeeding. You said they would die at the hands of my guard. You were wrong. You have failed us."

Kalumnia smiled graciously. "Perhaps I mistakenly gave you an earlier, less complete version of the prophecy. The great and magnificent Kalumnia understands how fluid the events of this world can be, but he sees all. My final prophecy clearly states the Chosen Ones shall stop the rains, the world of Emerus entering a great renaissance, standing on the glorious shoulders of Those Who Came Before."

The Council member curled his lip. "I should have you thrown into the gorge for your treasonous lies." He turned to Odo, Sephie, and Silas, his face darkening. "I suppose you are here for a reward? Perhaps a lovely chest of gold and gems, or a grand parade, a thousand cheering Altusians tossing flower petals as you ride past? You most certainly shall have a reward, but unfortunately for you, it lies at the bottom of the gorge. Guards, take them!"

Odo let out a screech. "Run!"

"No, Odo Whitley. This is why we're here."

The guards formed a deadly circle of razor sharp spears and arrows around the three friends.

Odo whispered, "Sephie, use your powers! Get us out of this."

Sephie called out, "The Chosen Ones do not fear death."

Kalumnia's expression did not change.

The Council member gave an icy smile. "Such inspiring words of bravery, so deeply moving. I do hope you will keep those particular words in mind as you plummet to your death on the jagged rocks below. Guards, throw her into the gorge. We shall see just how brave our little orange haired Chosen One is."

Kalumnia stepped forward. "You will not harm her.

I will not allow it. Your rule as greedy and arrogant tyrants has come to an end. The Council of Three is no more, your subjects have abandoned you. You stand alone now, three trifling old doddering Altusians soon to be forgotten in the dustbin of time."

The Council member let out a bloodcurdling scream of rage. "Throw him in the gorge! Now! I command it!"

The guards grabbed Kalumnia, dragging him to the edge of the chasm. He cried out, "You will regret this!"

The Council member snorted. "Not as much as you will."

Odo grabbed Sephie's arm. "Sephie, stop them! You have to stop them!"

"No, this is what must happen."

The guards hurled Kalumnia over the edge.

"So much for the great and powerful seer known as Kalumnia. Curious that he didn't foresee his own death on the rocks below."

Odo noticed a pale blue light coming from Sephie's hand. She pointed to the gorge. "Perhaps that is why he did not foresee his death."

As one, the Council of Three turned, letting out a singular gasp, the guards staggering back in terror. Kalumnia was floating in the air above the gorge, his face a mask of dark and fearsome anger.

The guards dropped their weapons and ran.

"Get back here! Kill him! I command it!"

Kalumnia floated toward them, landing in front of the Council of Three, his anger gone, replaced by an unnerving calm.

"I will spare your lives, but know this. You are old fools, blind to the depth and complexity of the world you live in. Your gold and gems are illusions, vaporous shadows hiding the true treasures that lie beneath all things, treasures which cannot be touched or seen or stuffed into a chest and hidden in a cave."

Odo and Silas stood spellbound, unable to take their eyes off Kalumnia.

Sephie whispered to Odo, "Sorry, Kalumnia made me promise not to tell you the last part of the prophecy."

The Council of Three slowly backed away, then turned and ran, their green robes flapping in the breeze.

Odo ran over to Kalumnia. "Did you know Sephie was going to float you up from the gorge?"

He gave a sweeping wave with one arm. "The great and magnificent Kalumnia knows all. Fear not, little Chosen One, I shall not harm you with my astonishing mystical powers."

"What?"

"Of course I knew, the Sinarians told me a year ago. I gave only a small portion of their prophecy to the Council of Three."

"What are you going to do now?"

"Now that my career as a magnificent mystical seer has come to an abrupt end, I shall be seeking employment elsewhere. The Sinarians believe I would make an excellent ruler, noting my deep understanding of people and my innate ability to motivate them. I won't bore you with the rest of their prophecy, but in a few years the Emerus you see before you shall be miraculously transformed, with my old friend Augur playing an important part in restoring the technologies of Those Who Came Before."

"You'll make an amazing ruler. Maybe we'll come back in a few years to see the new Emerus."

"You shall be welcomed guests always. This world owes you a great debt, one which can never be repaid."

"Thanks, we were glad to help. We should probably get going. The others are waiting for us at the Fortress of Rain."

"Of course, your friends are waiting. Silas, do remember that no matter what happens in life, all things are exactly as they should be at every moment in time. There is a hidden order that lies beneath the apparent chaos of our world."

"Thanks, I'll remember that."

After their farewells to Kalumnia, the three companions set off on the long trek back to the Fortress of Rain.

"I hope they aren't worried, it took longer than I thought it would."

"They're probably having fun chatting with Doppel. He has a great personality, doesn't he? Very likable fellow."

"Not very good taste in movies though. Can you believe he said Forgotten Memories was predictable?"

TOM HOFFMAN

"Right, I was thinking maybe you should change his personality. It's a little spooky that he's so much like me."

"He's growing on me, Odo Whitley. He might not like the same movies I do, but he says the nicest things to me. I think he likes me. A lot."

Chapter 45

Vanished

They trekked through the vast forests and up the rocky slopes, making their way back to the Fortress of Rain.

"I can't wait to show Arthur and Clara all the cool technology we have on Earth. They've never flown in an airplane, never seen a television. Clara said they listen to shows on the radio. Can you imagine? They do have movies but they're black and white, not color."

"It's going to take time for them to adjust to all the changes."

"Probably not too long, they both seemed excited about it."

"Hey, there's Doppel sitting on that rock."

Doppel turned when he heard their voices. "Hi Sephie! How did everything go?"

"It went great, thanks. Where is everyone?"

"They went on a hike but they'll be back soon.

Arthur and Clara wanted to see the big slugs again before they left."

Odo grimaced. "Why?"

"That's what I said. Seriously, those things are so creepy."

"I feel like I'm talking to myself. This is weird."

"Completely weird. You should change your voice. It's driving me crazy."

"I can't change my voice, this is the one I was born with. You're the one who should change your voice. It's not even your real voice."

"Why should I change mine? You're the one who–"

Sephie groaned. "You need to stop, both of you."

Silas called out, "They're back!"

Odo turned to see Mirus, Arthur and Clara. "Did you find any big slugs?"

"We saw four of them! Arthur wanted to ride on one, but Papa wouldn't let him. We saw three of the big blue frogs, but Fluffy chased them away."

Arthur nodded. "I wish they'd been the fire breathing ones. That would have been fun. This is just like Professor Challenger in *The Lost World*."

"You like Sir Arthur Conan Doyle? He's my favorite author. I love Sherlock Holmes."

Sephie laughed, "You'll have plenty of time to talk when we get back. Is everyone ready to go?"

Mirus nodded. "You're certain you'll be able to take us with you when you shift?"

"Absolutely, Wikerus Praevian told me exactly what to do. We form a circle, hold hands, and I use my homestone to shift us back. We should all arrive at exactly the same moment, still holding hands."

Doppel approached Sephie. "How long will you be gone, Sephie?"

"We're going to be gone for a long time, Doppel. I told Kalumnia we'd probably come back to visit in a couple of years."

"I'll stand here and wait for you."

Sephie's face softened."Doppel, you should go find Kalumnia. He's looking for people to help him rebuild Emerus, and he'd be lucky to have someone as amazing as you. He said he's going to be staying at the gorge for a few more weeks. I promise we'll find you when we come back. I promise."

"I'll do it, I'll help him rebuild Emerus. Piscorian technology is far more advanced than anything the Emerusians ever had."

"That sounds wonderful. I know you two will become the best of friends. I can't wait to come back and see what you've done." Sephie gave Doppel a long hug.

The six adventurers formed a circle, Clara holding Fluffy.

"Here we go, everyone hold hands, don't let go."

At precisely the moment Sephie's homestone began to change color she felt a hand on her shoulder.

"Sephie, I forgot, do you know exactly when you're—"

With a brilliant flash of light they vanished.

When Odo appeared in Wikerus' sitting room, he became aware of two things; the absence of Mirus,

Clara, and Arthur, and the presence of Doppel, his hand still resting on Sephie's shoulder.

Doppel glanced around the sitting room. "What is this place? I like it. Lots of books, nice furniture. Looks comfy." He stepped over to a bookshelf, running a finger across the dusty bindings, pulling out a heavy leather bound volume.

"This one looks interesting." He slumped down in Wikerus Praevian's favorite stuffed chair, putting his feet up on a glass coffee table.

Silas was distraught. "Where are they? Where are Mirus and Arthur and Clara? What happened to them?"

"I don't know. They should be here, I did everything I was supposed to."

Odo turned to see Wikerus striding down the hall-way.

"You're back. You didn't find them?"

"We found them, but they vanished when we shifted back. We held hands in a circle, just like you said to do."

Wikerus stopped when he saw Doppel. "Why is there an automaton in my chair? Why is he reading one of my books?"

Doppel glanced up at Wikerus. "Whoa, you're old. Where'd you get all the cool books?"

"Why does he sound like Odo?"

"We'll explain everything later; we need to get home before our parents start to worry. The automaton's name is Doppel. Can he stay with you for a few days?"

"Just for a few days. I will contact the Sinarians and

ask them about Mirus, Arthur, and Clara. I'm certain they'll have an explanation. They'll be fine, nothing to worry about."

Sephie waved to Doppel. "See you later, Doppel."

He glanced up from his book, waving back. "See you soon. I like your hair, it's super cute."

"Um… thanks, Doppel. Bye!"

Odo, Sephie, and Silas dashed out the door and headed down Expergo Street.

"Why does he keep saying your hair is cute? It's kind of weird that a robot would say that."

"It's not weird at all, he has your personality. He says the same things you would say."

Odo was not certain he liked this. The last thing he wanted was for Doppel to be blabbing out something that would embarrass him, something he wasn't ready to tell Sephie.

Silas had not spoken since they left Wikerus' house. "Do you think they're still alive?"

"I honestly don't know. Wikerus thought they'd be fine, but I'm not sure how the passage of time would affect them. They were from the past, not from our present, and shifting always brings us back to about an hour after we left."

"I hope they're okay, not lost in some weird dimension."

"Wikerus said he would talk to the Sinarians. I promise we'll find out what happened to them and where they are."

Chapter 46

The Letter

The three friends headed home, Sephie's house the first stop.

"Bye Odo! Bye Silas! I'll see you at school tomorrow."

Odo's house came next. Silas stopped when he saw the Ghost Sailor on the front porch, motioning for him to come in.

"Hey, Odo, can I come in for a minute? I should probably call my dad and let him know I'm on my way home. You know how he worries."

"Sure, come on in."

The two friends stepped through the doorway.

"I'm home! Odo Whitley is in the house!"

"Odo, I told you there's no need to say that." Petunia stepped around the corner, stopping when she saw Silas.

"You must be Silas. Odo said he was going to the

movies with you and Sephie. How was the show?"

"Um... good... lots of adventure."

"You should join us for dinner. Would your parents mind?"

"That's nice of you to ask, but I should probably..." The Ghost Sailor appeared behind Petunia, nodding his head up and down. "...probably call my parents to make sure it's okay."

"Wonderful, dinner will be ready in about an hour."

Odo flopped down on the couch after Silas had called his mom. "I'm exhausted. I can't believe we really did it, we shut down the Fortress of Rain."

The Ghost Sailor was pointing to a large black book under the coffee table.

"I hope Mirus, Arthur, and Clara are okay. Maybe they went back to their own time or something."

"Maybe."

The Ghost Sailor was gesturing emphatically toward the black book under the table.

"Silas, are you okay?"

Silas leaned over and whispered, "Don't freak out, but the Ghost Sailor is here. He's in the room and he wants me to look at that black book under the table. He was on Emerus the whole time we were there. He saved our lives a couple of times and showed me which way we should go. He's the one who led me to the light-house and the gold power spheres."

"He was on Emerus? How is that possible? We need to find out who he is. That black book is an old photo album." Odo pulled it out from under the table and opened it.

"He wants you to turn the pages."

One by one Odo flipped through the book while Silas watched the ghost.

"Stop! That's him! The guy in the sailor uniform standing next to the old car."

"I don't know who that is. Let's go ask my mom."

Odo and Silas found Petunia at the kitchen table reading a magazine.

"Mom, we were just looking through this old photo album. Who's the guy in the sailor uniform?"

Petunia gave a wistful smile when she saw it, touching the photo. "That's Daddy when he was in the navy during the war. He wore his uniform every year in the Fourth of July parade."

Odo and Silas glanced at each other.

"I didn't know your dad was in the navy."

"He served in World War Two. He died two years before you were born. I still have his uniform and war medals tucked away in the attic. I know it's silly, but I do feel like he's watching over me. Sometimes if I close my eyes it feels like he's standing right next to me. Your dad says I'm crazy."

"You're not crazy. I believe it; I think he's here with us."

"Thanks, sweetie, that's nice of you to say. You two scoot along while I make dinner."

Petunia was still looking at the photo when they left, her dad standing next to her.

Silas headed home after dinner. The car was gone,

his parents out, so he used the key under the flower pot to unlock the door. He flopped down on the couch, flipping on the television.

"That was exhausting, I could fall asleep right here."

He leaned back against the soft cushions, his eyes drooping. He was drifting off to sleep when he heard footsteps coming down the stairs. He woke with a start, his eyes wide.

"It's the Lady in Black, but she's wearing a yellow dress." He watched her descend, step by step.

"She's not in mourning clothes. That means we must have changed the past when we rescued Mirus. But why is she still here?"

A chill shot through Silas when the ghost turned, looking directly at him.

"You didn't go to the movies with your mom and dad?"

Silas' voice was a hoarse whisper. "What?"

"You sound dreadful, are you sick? Wait, are you watching another scary movie? You look like you saw a ghost." She laughed, giving him a wink. "Grandpa told me you see them. I promised him I wouldn't tell your parents. It took me a long time to get used to Grandpa's ghost friends. They still make me a little nervous, even though he says they're nice. Oh, before I forget, you got a letter today from Grandpa, all the way from Africa. Can you imagine being that far away from home?"

Silas was having a difficult time processing what he was seeing and hearing. He stammered, "A letter from Grandpa Mirus?"

"It's on the entryway table. Are you sure you're all right?"

"Just kind of tired, that's all. I just woke up."

"Are you all set for tomorrow? Won't it be fun to see Uncle Arthur and Aunt Clara? Your father is so excited, it's been almost two years since they came to visit."

Silas' thoughts were a whirlwind. Mirus, Arthur, and Clara must have returned safely to their own time. That meant his grandma was never accused of murdering them. He jumped up from the couch, darting over to the entryway table, eyeing the wrinkled yellow envelope addressed to Mr. Silas Ward. He tore it open, pulling out the letter.

Grandma Sarah headed to the kitchen. "I'll make you a nice snack while you read Grandpa's letter."

"Thanks, Grandma." Silas realized he had never said those words before. He liked having a grandma. He liked it a lot. He plopped down on the couch and began to read.

Dear Silas,

If I have timed it correctly, you should be reading this letter on the day of your return from Emerus. As you may already know, Arthur, Clara, Fluffy, and I returned safely to our own time, an hour after we had left. Your grandma never knew we were gone. It would probably be best not to tell her. I know this is a big surprise for you, suddenly having so many new relatives. You have seven cousins now. You won't remember anything about this timeline from before your trip to Emerus. You won't remember growing up with grandparents, aunts, uncles, and cousins, but I didn't forget about you, I took lots of pictures. When I get back from Africa we can go through all the albums. It was such a joy watching you grow up.

Silas, I know you can see ghosts. I see them also, and I can communicate with them. In this timeline I taught you how to talk to them, but you won't remember any of that. It will take a bit of practice, but you were always a quick learner. Make sure you go down to the basement and see your workshop. I think you will be pleasantly surprised by what you find there!

During my captivity on Emerus I learned a great deal from Kalumnia about the ancient technologies, and your friend Doppel was most informative regarding the technical aspects of the Piscorian water production facility. That's why I'm in Africa. Ten years ago we installed two small rain machines in the Sahara Desert, transforming it into a rainforest.

Arthur and Clara will arrive tomorrow to help you transition into the new timeline. They'll tell you about your cousins so you'll know who's who. Clara, Arthur, and I are the only ones who know about Emerus, how you and Sephie and Odo rescued us. Welcome to your new life!

With lots of love,
Grandpa Mirus

"I have cousins?" He stopped, studying the ten

symbols at the bottom of the letter, a seemingly random series of stars, squares, triangles, and circles.

"I wonder what that is? Grandpa drew them, so it must mean something. It's probably a code, but I don't have a clue what it's for. I guess I have to wait till he gets back." He called out, "Grandma, I'm going to run down to my workshop for a minute."

"Don't be long, your sandwiches are almost ready."

"I won't."

Silas froze when he opened the basement door. "We have an elevator?" He stepped inside, studying a glowing keypad on the wall. "There's no way these are floor numbers."

He tapped one of the buttons. Nothing happened.

"Wait, the symbols in Grandpa's letter, he knew I wouldn't remember the key code."

Silas pulled out the letter, studying the row of symbols.

"The keypad has numbers, but these are symbols, geometric shapes. Each symbol must represent a number, but which ones? I need to find a pattern, something they all have in common."

Silas stared at the symbols for almost a minute.

"Got it! Very clever, Grandpa. All the shapes except the circle have corners. The circle is zero, no corners. The triangle has three corners, square has four, and the stars have five, six, and seven points."

Silas entered the ten digit code into the elevator. He jumped when he heard the voice.

"State your name."

"Who is this?"

"State your name."

"Silas Ward."

"Voice print verified. Welcome, Silas."

The door whirred shut, the elevator descending.

Silas stepped into a brightly illuminated workshop, long gleaming counters covered with dozens of complex pieces of machinery and scientific instruments.

"What is this place?"

The voice from the elevator answered.

"This is your workshop."

"Who are you?"

"I am a modified engineered intelligence network taken from a deactivated Atroxian automaton."

"Who brought you here? Who built this place?"

"You and your grandfather brought me back from Atroxia four years ago. Are you not feeling well, Silas?"

"I'm fine. I was just... kind of thinking out loud, that's all. Do you know what all these machines do?"

"Of course, I helped you build most of them. Are you not feeling well?"

Silas stepped over to one of the long workbenches, studying a glass case on the wall.

"Those are the goggles Grandpa invented, the ones he used to get to Emerus."

"Clumsy and primitive when compared to the current ones."

"The current ones?"

TOM HOFFMAN

"You remember, on the shelf below the display."

"They look like normal glasses."

"Quite so, an elegant design if I do say so, voice activated and currently able to view three hundred and eleven dimensions."

Silas slid a stool out and took a seat. "Grandpa was right, it's going to take time to process all this. What's this glass jar filled with folded papers?"

"Are you certain you are all right, Silas? The contents of that jar do not seem like something you would forget. Would you like me to scan your brain?"

"Okay, the thing is, when I came home from Emerus, I entered a different timeline. This is all new to me, none of it existed in my old timeline."

"Ah, I completely understand. The jar is filled with notes from your girlfriend Nia. You have been going out with her for six months."

Chapter 47

This Ends Now

Odo, Sephie, and Silas were huddled together around Odo's locker.

"You've been going out with Nia for six months?'

"We go to the movies with you guys every Saturday. I read the notes in the jar and pieced it all together, plus I had a long talk with the engineered intelligence in my workshop. Six months ago I asked Nia out and she said yes. She really likes math a lot."

Sephie beamed. "That's great, Silas. What kind of movies does she like?"

Odo groaned. "Don't start."

"One of the notes said how much she liked one called *Forgotten Memories*. She said it was really romantic."

Sephie gave Odo her best smirky smile.

"Fine, she likes the same movies you do. Oh, I stopped by to see how Wikerus and Doppel are doing.

They're getting along pretty well. Mrs. Preke said she's going to teach Doppel some manners. We'll see how that goes. I'm not sure anything is going to change Doppel."

"Did he mention anything about how cute my hair is? He really likes me a lot, you know."

The bell rang before Odo could give his hilarious reply, the three friends heading off to their classes.

Silas raced down the hall toward his math class, stopping when he saw Brandon Crouch heading toward him.

"Hey, warthog! Where you going??"

Silas realized at that moment just how much the trip to Emerus had changed him. He had traveled to another dimension, faced fire breathing frogs and giant slugs, sailed an alien ship across a vast and mysterious sea. Heavily armed Altusian warriors and flying Flatlanders had tried to kill them, not to mention their encounter with Doppel and his heavy particle fusion beam. He turned to face Brandon Crouch. This was going to end now.

Brandon ran up to him, holding up a paper for him to see.

"I got a B! The first one I've ever gotten in math. Thanks for helping me study."

Silas tried to process this most unexpected turn of events.

"That's great. Nice job." He saw the ghost lady standing behind Brandon, heard the words *thank you* in his thoughts. He knew she was Brandon's mom.

Brandon leaned over to Silas, whispering, "Thanks for telling me about my mom, all the things she says. I went sort of crazy after she died. I was so angry at the world, just like she said. It was awful, and my dad… well… you know what he's like. That made things a lot worse. He's been nicer since my grades started improving, but he still won't talk about my mom."

Silas nodded. "You should be really proud of yourself."

"You said you'd help me study for the final?"

"Just say when."

"Thanks, warthog. You're the best."

* * * *

When the bell sounded at the end of science class, Odo Whitley flipped open his backpack.

"Pretty empty in there without my old sidekick Watson. I bet he was the only time traveling cat in history. I miss that crazy cat. The good news is I can go back anytime I want and visit him using the old family photo." He put his book away, glancing over at Sephie, pausing when he saw the curious grin on her face.

"Why are you grinning like that?"

"Grinning like what? Was I grinning?"

"You're still grinning."

"Gotta go. Oh, we're going to Madam Beffy's Diner after school with Silas and Nia. You can get a giant cinnamon roll."

"You're still grinning."

"Really?" She tossed a folded piece of paper onto Odo's desk as she left.

Odo stared at the note, knowing it held the explanation for Sephie's goofy grin. A smile crept across his face when he read it.

I stopped by to check on Doppel yesterday.
Imagine how surprised I was when he
told me he was falling in love with me.
I told him I already had a boyfriend.

If you enjoyed reading

*The Translucent Boy and
the Cat Who Ran Out of Time*

please leave a short review or rating
on Amazon.com
Reviews are the lifeblood of indie publishers –
we can't survive without them!

If you have any comments or suggestions
or would like to be notified of upcoming book
releases and Free Kindle book day promotions,
please email me at
OrvilleMouse@gmail.com

Follow me at:
www.facebook.com/TomHoffmanAuthor/

Best wishes until we meet again,

Tom Hoffman

ABOUT THE AUTHOR

Tom Hoffman received a B.S. in psychology
from Georgetown University in 1972
and a B.A. in 1980 from the now-defunct
Oregon College of Art. He has lived in Alaska
with his wife since 1973. They have two
adult children and two adorable
grandchildren. Tom was a graphic designer
and artist for over 35 years.
Redirecting his imagination from art to
writing, he wrote his first novel,
The Eleventh Ring, at age 63.

Made in the USA
Las Vegas, NV
12 December 2021

PRAISE FOR
Love's New Beginnings

This is the perfect start to the series and a perfect book for
the Christmas season.

Jenny, Reader

Love's New Beginnings is a tender, gentle, faith-filled romance
that will sweep the reader into the world of two uncertain
characters and the captivating Wyoming Sunrise series.

Madisyn Carlin, Author

A lighthearted read set in the mountains of Wyoming Territory,
you'll be left smiling and sighing throughout its entirety. Perfect
for readers of Janette Oke.

Abbigail Raine B., Author

In today's world, the chance of finding good clean fiction that is
sweet and a joy to read is rare indeed...I highly recommend this
book and series.

Chat With Vera, Blogger

PRAISE FOR
Forgotten Memories

With themes of forgiveness, grace, and second chances, this story is sure to touch your heart.

Cover Lover Book Review, Blogger

This was the first time I have read a book by the author, Penny Zeller and I was captivated from page one.

Michelle, Reviewer

This book is a wonderful read! It's well written and holds your attention from the first page until the last.

Ann, Reviewer

Fantastic book! The story line is unique and the setting comes alive with Penny's descriptions. The characters are so realistic and relatable.

Jeanette, Reviewer

WYOMING SUNRISE
BOOK 2

Dreams of the Heart

PENNY ZELLER

Maplebrook

ALSO BY PENNY ZELLER

Maplebrook Publishing

Standalone Books
Love in Disguise
Love in the Headlines
Freedom's Flight

Wyoming Sunrise
Love's New Beginnings
Forgotten Memories
Dreams of the Heart
When Love Comes

Love Letters from Ellis Creek
Love from Afar
Love Unforeseen
Love Most Certain

Chokecherry Heights
Henry and Evaline (Prequel)
Love Under Construction

Horizon Series
Over the Horizon

Whitaker House Publishing

Montana Skies
McKenzie
Kaydie
Hailee

Barbour Publishing

Love from Afar
*(The Secret Admirer
Romance Collection)*

Freedom's Flight
*(The Underground Railroad
Brides Collection)*

Beacon Hill Press
(Nonfiction)

77 Ways Your Family Can
Make a Difference

Dedicated to all of who have been hurt by another and have found peace and healing in the arms of our Savior.

And what doth the LORD require of thee, but to do justly, and to love mercy, and to walk humbly with thy God?
Micah 6:8

CHAPTER ONE

POPLAR SPRINGS, WYOMING, 1894

WHY WAS HE ALWAYS watching her? Scrutinizing her? Did he think her a ne'er-do-well? That she was part of the messes her pa found himself in?

Deputy Eliason was a lawman, after all.

Hannah shifted her attention toward the street lined with multiple saloons, a brothel, mercantile, dress shop, the new restaurant, barbershop, and sheriff's office. So many people had come and gone in the years she'd lived here. Businesses closed and businesses opened, especially saloons, which dominated the town. As such, she knew so few of the townsfolk.

She ventured a gaze in the deputy's direction. His attention remained fixed on her.

Had his ma never taught him it wasn't proper manners to stare?

Several men stumbled in and out of the Sticker Weed Saloon. Her own pa either gambled or frittered away on whiskey all the money he earned from working for Mayor Roessler.

Deputy Eliason stood on the boardwalk outside of the sheriff's office. She knew what he must think of her. He was a man of the law and she was the daughter of

1

a no-good drunk. And not only that, but her appearance must look a fright. Instinctively, she reached up to smooth her hair, hair that she'd never had the chance to fix before Pa hastened her to town. Her dismal calico no longer held the pattern, but instead was threadbare with years of wear.

More than once, Hannah found some dingy scraps of material and sewed them on to the bottom of her dress, adding to its length. Thankfully, she never grew wider. There wasn't enough food for that. And being fairly flat on top made it easy to wear the same dress for several years.

Indeed, what must someone as upstanding and handsome as Deputy Eliason think of her?

Balancing on the edge of the wagon wheel, she climbed down and paused on the boardwalk, deciding where she should go. If she hurried, Hannah would have a few minutes to marvel at the clothing in the dress shop and maybe even explore the new items at the mercantile before each store closed. Starting toward her destination, she again met Deputy Eliason's stare. Did he have nothing better to do than to watch her?

He tipped his hat and nodded. Could that be a slight smile forming across his lips? Her cheeks flamed and Hannah pretended to be preoccupied with a pebble on the ground.

A few moments later, she pushed open the door of Nellie's Dress Shop and moseyed inside. Gorgeous gowns met her perusal, including a delicate cream-colored satin dress with numerous gathers and fancy ruffles. Lace adorned the two bottom layers. Hannah rubbed the smooth, delicate fabric between her index finger and thumb. Up close, she could see miniature designs—tiny flowers perhaps? She moved closer and inhaled. The dress even smelled new.

Unlike her own stained and tattered garment.

Hannah closed her eyes and tried to envision herself in such an elegant fashion. Maybe her hair would be curled or wound around her head in a thick plaited braid. Or maybe she'd don a fancy hat like she'd seen some of the wealthy ladies in town wear. She would purchase a pair of shoes to go with the dress and she'd walk around as if she was somebody.

Instead of a nobody.

Hannah continued to run her fingers along the material, delighting in its softness in contrast to the rough fabric of her own dress.

It was then that she noticed Claudelle Roessler and her mother standing nearby staring at her. Claudelle whispered something to her mother. Mrs. Roessler nodded and approached the owner, Nellie Quirke.

Hannah strained to hear their words, thoughts conflicting within her of both desiring to know what was being said, and yet dreading it at the same time.

"Is *she* going to purchase that dress?" Mrs. Roessler asked, tilting her head in Hannah's direction. Claudelle shuddered, likely for added effect.

Miss Quirke's eye met Hannah's. "I'm not sure."

"You know full well she's not," said Mrs. Roessler. "You should preclude her from handling the gowns and fabrics lest she soil them."

3

Hannah swallowed the lump that formed in her throat. Mrs. Roessler and Claudelle had never taken kindly to her.

"Miss Bane, if you don't mind..." Miss Quirke began.

"Yes, ma'am, I was just leaving."

Tears stung her eyes as Hannah rushed toward the door. She'd never treat people the way she'd been treated by the Roesslers. Never.

Hannah retreated down the boardwalk, the misting tears blinding her vision. So preoccupied with what had just happened, she wasn't paying attention and bumped into someone.

She tottered and wobbled until a hand on her elbow steadied her.

"Are you all right, miss?"

Hannah looked up at the man who was forever watching her. Only this time it wasn't from a distance. There was something in his hazel eyes that she couldn't ascertain. Compassion? Pity? Sympathy?

"I'm all right, thank you."

Deputy Eliason held his gentle grasp on her elbow for a second longer before releasing it.

What must he think of her?

He'd seen the tears in her eyes when they collided. A glance through the dress shop window and John Mark figured he knew the reason for Miss Bane's sadness. Claudelle Roessler caught his eye and fluttered her lashes at him. His sister, Charlotte, would say Miss Roessler had set her cap for him. He cringed at the thought.

Claudelle Roessler may be a comely woman, but John Mark would never be interested in a woman who mistreated others as she had Miss Bane.

John Mark heard a ruckus behind him. Frank and Hank Maloney bumbled toward him, words hurled back and forth between them. "Deputy Eliason," called Frank, his hoarse voice hinting at desperation.

"Hello, Frank and Hank. What can I do for you today?" John Mark took a deep breath and prepared for another benign quarrel between the elderly twin brothers. The two were a testament that not everything occurring in Poplar Springs was nefarious in nature. And while the men were exaggerated and, at times, absurd, it gave John Mark a reprieve from more serious matters.

"There's an argument and Hank started it."

"Did not."

"Did so."

"Gentlemen. How about we resolve this peacefully?"

The men proceeded to outstare each other.

Hank shook his bald head. "No can do, Deputy. This time Frank has really gone and done it."

"*I've* gone and done it?" Frank, twice the size and two inches shorter than his scrawny brother, stood next to Hank and jabbed a finger into his shoulder. "You're the one who decided to wear my boot."

"One at a time tell me the problem so I can help you resolve it."

Frank and Hank began to talk at once, Hank's higher-pitched voice rising above Frank's gravelly growl.

"Hank, you go first," John Mark requested.

Frank had something to say about that. "Why did you choose him first? Is it because he's older?"

It was going to be a long afternoon. John Mark nodded at passersby, suddenly wishing he could be rounding up horse thieves, catching outlaws, hauling drunks to the jail, or settling *real* disputes. "Hank, tell me what happened."

"See, I told you he was showing favortisms. Ain't fair." Frank crossed his thick arms across his chest and pouted.

Hank, on the other hand, stood taller, a smug look on his wrinkled face. "You see, Deputy, it's like this. When we woke up this morning and headed out to do the chores, I put on my boots like I always do."

"'Cept one of them boots ain't yours!"

"Is too."

"Is not."

"Gentlemen...let me see if I have this correct. Hank is wearing your boot, Frank?"

Hank's bulbous eyes bulged. "He just says I am."

"Because you are."

"Are you wearing Frank's boot, Hank?"

Hank peered down at his boots and John Mark immediately knew who would be winning this argument. While Hank's boots were both brown and somewhat worn, the boot on his right foot was larger. As such, the toe of the boot protruded farther than the toe of the boot on his left foot. "Hank..."

Guilt washed over Hank's face. "I was thinking one didn't fit near as well," he muttered. "My feet have always been somewhat cramped in my boots, but today, one didn't feel nearly as crowded."

Frank thrust his chest out and gloated. "See, told you so. And looky here, Deputy, my poor right foot is all bent and squeezed and my toes ain't comfortable one bit. Reckon my foot's asleep."

"Aww, you poor thing," chastised Hank. "My feet are both comfortable. Matter of fact, I might trade you both shoes."

Frank balled his fists at his sides. "Oh, no you won't. You ain't stealing my shoes like you stole my whirligig when we was young'uns."

John Mark was not going to go back into the past with these men and all of their perceived transgressions against each other. If he did, it would be his next birthday before this matter was settled. "All right, men, trade shoes so that both of you are wearing your own." John Mark leaned against the side of the barbershop and waited for the two not-so-identical twins to switch their boots. "There. All settled."

"Told you Deputy Eliason was a smart whippersnapper," said Hank. "He's always solving people's problems."

Frank nodded. "And I told you that you were wrong and I was right."

That started another disagreement.

"Have a good day, gentlemen." John Mark slipped away and headed toward the jail before the two could ask him to resolve another of their differences.

"The horses are hitched. It's time to go!"

Hannah finished hanging Pa's shirt on the clothesline the following afternoon. "Coming, Pa." She darted toward the wagon and attempted to climb in just as Pa beckoned the horses. Half in the wagon and half out, Hannah hung on, her thin arms struggling for a secure hold on the buckboard as her feet dragged. She closed her eyes for a minute, willing her legs not to get caught in the turning wheel. *Why couldn't Pa wait one second before commanding the horses? Does he wish to bring injury to me?*

Finally, Hannah was able to hoist herself into the wagon. Heart racing, she willed herself to calm. She gripped the side of the buckboard and stared straight ahead as Pa drove the wagon at a speed faster than was prudent.

Pa never spoke during those times into town, or much of any other time for that matter. Unless he was ordering Hannah about or verbally abusing her. Today was no different. He focused his attention on the road, his cigar dangling precariously from his mouth. Hannah tried not to inhale. The cigar's sickly odor had a way of causing nausea.

They passed the neighbor's house, then vacant, flat ranch land before entering Poplar Springs. The town bustled with activity, mostly from men rushing to the saloons for their nightly fix of liquor. Pa brought the wagon to an abrupt halt and sauntered into the Sticker Weed without so much as a word to Hannah.

Hannah didn't need instructions—she already knew what Pa expected of her. It was the same routine several nights each week. She was to wait the four or five hours in town, occupying herself in some boring way, until he was ready to be driven home. Most times, she had to solicit the assistance of other men from the saloon to heave her father into the back of the wagon so she could haul him home. His loss of consciousness made it difficult for Hannah to manage him on her own.

She'd once made the mistake of not waiting for him. Hannah instead drove home and busied herself with chores. When Pa awoke facedown the next morning in the middle of the street, he made it clear that would be the last time she'd make that mistake.

Hannah sat in the wagon for a moment just watching the activity on the street. She saw Claudelle Roessler and her mother emerge from the mercantile wearing dresses that were far too elaborate for the likes of a dirty Wyoming town. The oversized leg-o-mutton sleeves accentuated Claudelle's already slim waist. Fashionable hats topped their heads and both women carried several parcels. Hannah glanced down at her own rag of a dress. Someday she'd have a new one.

Someday.

If she ever got away from Pa.

Later, on the splintery bench outside of the Sticker Weed Saloon, she attempted to take her mind off of why she was there and instead focused on a plan to get away from Pa. The same questions filled her mind. Where would she go? Would anyone take her in? Would Pa find her and bring her back? How would she manage to escape?

She loved the Lord. Had dedicated her life to Him and worshipped Him from a young age. Hannah had adhered to the verse in First Thessalonians that said, *"pray without ceasing."* But the Lord hadn't heard her on this matter.

He hadn't rescued her from her pa, even after all of these years.

If only God would hear her prayers like He heard the prayers of others.

Hannah perused the surrounding area. Poplar Springs boasted a thriving community, but most of the commerce existed in a handful of places: the numerous saloons, the brothel across the street from the Sticker Weed, and the mercantile.

A bearded man stumbled out of the saloon and into the street, narrowly avoiding a collision with an oncoming wagon. A few seconds later, he staggered into the brothel.

Worry, so often a part of her daily life, threatened to overtake her thoughts. Would Hannah find herself in such desperate straits that brothel or saloon work was what she must succumb to?

Lord, please...please hear my prayers.

The orange and pink hues of the sunset warned nightfall would soon arrive. Boisterous music from the saloon filled the air and the smell of something cooking—venison stew perhaps—waffled from the new restaurant. Hannah's stomach growled. When was the last time she had eaten?

She couldn't remember.

As she approached the end of the street, someone tugged on her sleeve.

"Ma'am? Have you seen Deputy Eliason?"

A little brown-haired boy, no older than five or six years old, peered up at her, his tearful voice matching the expression on his face.

"I'm sorry, I haven't." Hannah scanned the street both ways. Odd that she hadn't seen the deputy this evening.

"Then can *you* help me?"

The desperation in his voice tugged at her heart. She kneeled beside him. "Yes, I can help you."

"I lost him."

"Him?"

"Yes. He was just here and now I lost him." The boy folded his arms across his skinny body and a whimper escaped his lips. No one else paid him any mind, the world around him oblivious to his pain.

Had he lost his pa? His brother? "What is your name?"

"Ambrose. Mr. Ambrose Miller."

"I'm Miss Hannah and I will help you find him. Can you tell me...when did you last see him and what is his name?" If it was his pa, was he in the saloon? Had his younger brother wandered off? Where was Ambrose's ma? A group of three men exited the saloon. A woman hurried past with her two children. A few men on horses rode down the street.

"His name is Grumbles."

"Grumbles? Is he your..."

"He's my pet pig."

Hannah's jaw dropped. "Your pet pig?"

"Yes, and he was just right here with me like he always is. Now I can't find him." Ambrose rubbed at his eye with a dirty hand.

"We'll find him. Let's see…where would a pig go?" But as soon as she uttered the promise, she regretted it. Nightfall would soon be upon them. How would they ever find a missing animal? The pig could be anywhere by now.

Ambrose reached for her hand. "Thank you, Miss Hannah. Let's start over yonder." He pointed toward the livery.

The ache in her heart expanded when Ambrose tugged her along toward the livery. Something about the gesture reminded her of her brothers.

And how she'd never see them again.

Ten minutes later, they'd entered and exited the livery with no sign of Grumbles. Ambrose provided a vivid description of his pet to every passerby as they went from one end of town to the other. They'd even gone as far as the Roessler's Dry Goods on the edge of town. "Ambrose, I think we should continue our search tomorrow." The sun set long ago and the only bright lights were from the saloons and brothel.

"But, Miss Hannah…" the boy's voice wavered. "I can't go home without Grumbles."

"Maybe he already returned home. Your ma and pa will be so worried. Come on, I'll walk you home." It wasn't safe for a young child to be out wandering the streets this late.

Ambrose shook his head. "Don't have me a ma and pa, and Grandpa was sleeping when I left. He's probably still sleeping. I need to find Grumbles."

A deep voice behind them caused Hannah to jump.

"Miss Bane? Ambrose?"

"Deputy! Deputy!" Ambrose ran toward the lawman. "I need your help in finding Grumbles. Me and Miss Hannah have been looking all over for him."

The deputy ruffled Ambrose's hair. "I'll help you, but you best get home. Your grandpa will be worried."

"Can't go home yet. Not until I find Grumbles." Although it was a dimly-lit night, Hannah could see the rigid determination on the young boy's face.

"Why don't I take you home and I'll use my Pinkerton detective skills to find Grumbles."

Ambrose pondered that for a moment. "Do you promise?"

"I promise to do my utmost best."

"But do you promise you'll find him? Grumbles is afraid of the dark."

"If he can be found, I'll find him."

Ambrose wrapped his arms around Deputy Eliason's waist. "I know you will, Deputy. My grandpa says you're the best lawman this side of the Miss-sippi."

Deputy Eliason chuckled and Hannah was in awe of the interaction between the two. Pa never treated her brothers in such a manner. Granted, they were Ramona's before she married Pa, but even so, there had never been any sort of kindness between her father and the boys.

"Miss Bane, it's not safe for you to be out alone at night either," he said, interrupting her thoughts about Pa and her brothers.

Being alone at night was something she did regularly while she waited for her father. Even before the deputy recently moved to Poplar Springs, wishing time away while sitting on the bench outside the Sticker Weed was a significant part of her daily life.

"There's no one in the sheriff's office right now. Why don't you wait there while I take Ambrose home?"

Before she could object, Ambrose interjected. "And after you take me home, you'll find Grumbles, right?"

"I'll do my best."

That seemed to satisfy the young boy and as the three of them walked toward the sheriff's office, Ambrose again reached for her hand.

The pain in her heart hit her with almost unbearable force. Would she ever know the joy of motherhood? The blessing of raising a child of her own?

And would she even know how to be a ma? After all, with the exception of Ramona's short-lived marriage to Pa, she'd never known a mother.

Chapter Two

John Mark strolled into the church and sat in one of the back pews as the reverend was announcing upcoming events. He peered around the humble sanctuary. Few people frequented the church services, which surprised him given the high rate of attendance at his former church in Willow Falls. In a town the size of Poplar Springs, which was just slightly more populated than Willow Falls, there should have been more participation.

But Poplar Springs was a wild town, much like many of the other towns in Wyoming. Willow Falls, Prune Creek, and perhaps Nelsonville were the exceptions.

While he'd lived in Poplar Springs less than two months, John Mark surmised that attending church was not a high priority for the residents. Unfortunately, to the town's detriment, Reverend Fleming alternated his preaching between Poplar Springs and Bowman, the nearest town with a population of only fifty people but no permanent church location. As such, the reverend hadn't cemented many relationships during his three-month tenure in Poplar Springs. The inconsistency of sermons, coupled with the apathetic attitude of the overwhelming majority of the townsfolk, failed to produce a thriving congregation.

The whitewashed pews had the appearance of being built in a haphazard manner. Their unpretentious design was rustic and worn, despite being constructed two years prior. John Mark shifted, causing the pew to creak and groan.

Reverend Fleming announced the first hymn, and the parishioners stood. John Mark struggled to his feet, every bone in his body weary from last night. He'd never run so much as of late and had never ridden so fast. Both due to chasing stagecoach robbers who decided to shoot first and then steal. In the end, three of the gang were caught and remanded to the Poplar Springs jail. One had been killed in a shootout with Sheriff Winslow, and the other escaped under Deputy Gaston's watch.

John Mark massaged the back of his neck, attempting to ease the tension that settled there. Two people from the stagecoach had lost their lives to the merciless and well-known gang. Two innocent people who never imagined last night was their last on earth.

He attempted to focus on the hymn while allowing his eyes to travel over the few congregants. A newcomer to the town, he made it his goal to meet the residents and hoped to, at some point, develop friendships. The Alvarados, an elderly couple who owned the mercantile, stood in the front on the left-hand side next to John Mark's new friend, Silas. Behind them stood the newcomers to the town and owners of a restaurant, Mr. and Mrs. Pearson and their brood, along with Mr. Pearson's mother, Grandmother Pearson.

In the first row on the right-hand side was Mrs. Fleming and her baby daughter. Next to them, young Ambrose, and his grandfather, Mr. Miller. Sheriff Winslow, his wife, and their twin sons stood behind them.

Also on the left, Wally Pritchard, a man about John Mark's age and an interesting character John Mark was still attempting to understand, stood, his attention fully directed toward the reverend. Mr. Pritchard's slim, wiry body gave the false notion of him being puny, when in fact he was more than capable of defending what he believed in, or so Winslow had said. "A force to be reckoned with", were Winslow's exact words. John Mark's only interaction with Wally Pritchard thus far was the two times he'd arrested him and thrown him in jail—once for stealing and once for trespassing—both crimes that occurred at Roessler's Dry Goods. John Mark's first impression was that Pritchard was dishonest and might have a habit of stretchin' the blanket a bit. Or maybe he was just evasive about where he'd come from and how he possessed an abundance of insight into criminal activity. Based on his consistent gaze in a certain direction, the man had an affection for the oldest Pearson daughter.

At least Pritchard was in church. That should help alleviate some of the concerns Mr. Pearson might have if he knew of Pritchard's fondness for his daughter.

In the pew with Pritchard were Hank and Frank, the twin brothers, dressed in their Sunday finery. On the opposite side stood a fashionable older woman, Widow Holmes. A man would have to be blind to fail to notice that Hank exhibited a penchant toward the woman.

The door creaked open. Hannah Bane entered and stood in front of the last pew on the left-hand side, directly across from John Mark. She wore a faded dress and tattered boots and clutched a worn Bible. Their eyes connected and she stared at him for a moment until she blinked, straightened her posture, and returned her attention to Reverend Fleming.

What was her story?

He knew her pa was the town drunkard and spent a considerable amount of time at the Sticker Weed Saloon. As John Mark watched Miss Bane, something in his heart jolted. She reminded him of the time he'd rescued a baby bird that had fallen from its nest. Frightened. Timid. In need of care.

John Mark couldn't hear her, but he could see that Miss Bane's lips moved to the words of the hymn. She closed her eyes and he thought he saw a tear glistening on her cheek. John Mark recalled how patient she'd been with Ambrose. He'd taken to her right away, and Ambrose was a particular sort.

After singing a few more hymns, the congregants took a seat and Reverend Fleming led the prayer, took the offertory, and preached his sermon. John Mark opened his Bible to the passage. Miss Bane did as well, her head bent forward in rapt attention to the pages of God's Word.

John Mark appreciated the reverend's sermons, although he carried a substantial bias toward his own pa's preaching.

"The Lord is clear that stealing is wrong," Reverend Fleming was saying. Wally Pritchard tugged at his collar and shifted in his seat. Good. Maybe the reverend's wise words would influence Pritchard the next time he decided to steal a crate full of canned food from Roessler's Dry Goods.

When he finished his sermon, the reverend led another prayer and John Mark lifted his own requests to the Lord. That God would use him to make a difference in Poplar Springs, that God would keep him and his family healthy and safe, and that God would help Miss Bane.

After the prayer, the parishioners filed out of the church, pausing to shake Reverend Fleming's hand. Mrs. Fleming, carrying her baby and a basket, spoke to Miss Bane. She lowered her voice, but John Mark heard every word.

"How are you today, Hannah?"

"I'm fine, thank you, Mrs. Fleming."

But John Mark could see something troubled Miss Bane. He figured Mrs. Fleming saw it too.

"Here's some food and a pair of socks."

"Thank you."

Mrs. Fleming handed her the basket and the baby babbled, causing a slight smile to light Miss Bane's face.

"Please," Mrs. Fleming continued. "Stash it somewhere for when...for when *you're* hungry."

Miss Bane blinked rapidly and nodded. "I will."

"For *you*," the reverend's wife reiterated.

John Mark made a note to speak with the reverend and his wife about how the church could come together and continue to help Miss Bane.

He realized he was staring and averted his attention to his hat in his hands. He best head home and get some

19

shut-eye before it was his turn again to keep an eye on the town. There was one sheriff and eight deputies for all of Poplar Springs County, but they needed at least one more full-time deputy in Poplar Springs. Winslow and Gaston oftentimes traveled to other parts of the expansive county. John Mark nodded at both women and strolled toward the door, stopping to shake Reverend Fleming's hand before entering the cloudy day.

"Say, Deputy Eliason, how did it go with that there stagecoach robbery?" Frank asked.

Hank's attention remained fixed on Widow Holmes, who walked toward her house not far from the church.

"We caught three of the gang members."

Frank's eyes enlarged. "You don't say? Now that's somethin' I oughta share with the townsfolk."

When John Mark raised an eyebrow, Frank continued, "Oh, not that I'm a leaky mouth or nothin, but that oughta make us all feel a bit safer."

"The truth is you are a leaky mouth," snorted Hank.

"You don't got no right to say nothin' 'bout what I is or what I ain't, seeing as how I'm talkin' to the deputy while you take a year-long gander at Widow Holmes."

Was that a blush John Mark saw on Hank's weathered face? "Speakin' of womenfolk, it's high time you got yourself a wife, Deputy. Not that you look like you're starvin' or nothin', but..."

John Mark involuntarily patted his stomach. Ma told him he'd lost weight the last time he'd returned home for a visit. She'd fretted and worried and then fretted some more before putting a year's worth of food in front of him for one meal. But then, with his height and broad shoulders, John Mark might appear a more robust person to someone like Hank with his scrawny build and lack of muscle.

"You do need a wife," agreed Frank. "What's takin' you so long to find one? You been here several weeks already."

John Mark hadn't seen a woman in town that he cared to court, let alone marry. Poplar Springs women, few as they were, didn't capture his attention. That, combined with his dangerous job as a deputy sheriff, made it unwise to marry when he could lose his life to an outlaw.

"You're gonna be old and decrepit with no wife." Hank shook his head as if John Mark's life as he knew it would soon come to a dismal end.

"Wait a minute, Hank and Frank, have you two ever been married?"

"Can't say as we have." Frank looped his fingers through his suspenders, accentuating his round, portly stomach. "Why do you ask?"

John Mark chuckled and looked over in time to see Miss Bane untether her horse, mount it, and ride away, clutching the basket from Mrs. Fleming. "I...well, because you two are harassing me about being married, but you two are old and..."

"Don't say it," said Hank. "Frank gets a burr in his saddle when folks tell him he's decrepit."

Frank placed his hands on his hips and scowled. "If I'm decrepit, then you are too."

"Reckon I'd like to stay and find out who's decrepit and who's not, but I best go," said John Mark. Without awaiting a response, he was about to untether his own horse when Ambrose ran toward him.

"Deputy! Deputy!" The little boy leaned over, hands on his legs, attempting to catch his breath.

"What is it, Ambrose?"

Ambrose took a deep breath before answering. "I just wanted to thank you again for finding Grumbles. I missed him so much and thought he was losted forever."

John Mark laughed at Ambrose's exuberance. "You're welcome. Glad he could be found."

Mr. Miller, Ambrose's grandfather, ambled their way. "Mighty grateful for what you done," he said.

"Happy to help, Mr. Miller." John Mark pondered suggesting a closer eye be kept on Ambrose, but the grandfather's appearance took him aback. The pallor of Mr. Miller's face, combined with his sunken cheekbones, the weakness in his voice, and the way he leaned heavily on his cane, concerned John Mark. "How have you been?" he asked.

"Fair to middling."

The fatigue etched in Mr. Miller's tired eyes prompted John Mark to figure a way he could aid the man with Ambrose's care. But how? He worked numerous hours a day and sometimes into the night when Winslow and Gaston were traversing the county. A shade of concern emerged on the boy's face. "Ambrose, would you mind giving your grandpa and me a minute?"

"Yes, sir." Ambrose skipped off toward the Flemings.

"Mr. Miller, are you feeling well enough to care for Ambrose?"

John Mark thought he saw a flash of irritation on the elderly man's face before he pasted on a smile. "Of course, I am. I'm his grandfather. It's my job to care for him. Now today, I'm not feeling the best. Think I had me a bad meal last night that didn't sit well in my gut. With a little rest this afternoon, I'll be right as rain." He paused. "Now, I best take the boy and get home. He'll be wanting the noonday meal soon."

John Mark bid Mr. Miller farewell and he lifted two people up in prayer.

Ambrose. And Miss Bane.

And for God's guidance on how he could help them both.

CHAPTER THREE

HANNAH SCOOPED RABBIT STEW into two bowls and set the pan of biscuits on the table. The reverend and his wife delivered food earlier that day, and Hannah always appreciated the alternating Sundays Reverend Fleming was in Poplar Springs to preach. Until recently, the town lacked a consistent pastor.

Unbeknownst to Pa, she'd been able to indulge in the loaf of bread, jelly, and canned peas Mrs. Fleming gave her two Sundays ago, albeit with guilt. Today, Pa had been standing nearby when the reverend handed her the food.

Of course, Pa hadn't so much as mentioned a "thank you." He'd barely acknowledged the Reverend and Mrs. Fleming, other than to mutter "Best you quit thinkin' we're in need of charity."

But Hannah had reveled in the couple's generosity. It would be a welcome change from watery beans and moldy potatoes. She poured the fresh milk from the borrowed pitcher into the glasses. Her mouth watered at just the thought of eating such a fine supper.

She closed her eyes, bowed her head, and gave thanks for the reverend and his wife's benevolence. While she loved the Lord with all her being, she wasn't sure He always heard her prayers. But she hoped her prayers of gratitude reached Him.

A scraping sound pulled her from her prayer and her eyes fluttered open to see Pa pouring some of her stew into his own bowl.

"If you ain't gonna eat it, I will," he said.

"I was blessing the meal first." She dared not say more if she wished to avoid her father's wrath.

Pa pushed her now half-full bowl toward her and began to slurp his own stew. He released an obnoxious belch and tilted the bowl toward his face, guzzling the remainder of his meal. If Hannah wasn't so famished, she would have lost her appetite.

But she may very well not have another chance to eat such a palatable meal in the near future, so she tamped down the nausea, filled her spoon with stew, and savored a bite. She closed her eyes and relished the flavor of carrots, rabbit, onions, and potatoes.

Pa interrupted her thoughts with another belch followed by harsh words. "If your ma was here, I'd be eatin' this kinda food all the time."

She'd heard a similar sentiment a million times, although most of the time he complained about the food she prepared and compared it to what he would be eating if Ma was alive.

Hannah acknowledged his comment, but said nothing. She sipped some of the frothy milk, the refreshing beverage providing much-needed moisture for her parched throat.

"Course, your ma would be here if it weren't for you."

No matter how many times Pa uttered the words, they still stung as if it were the first time she'd heard them.

"Get me some more milk," he ordered.

Hannah hastily guzzled the remainder of her own milk, detesting the unladylike sound of her swilling, but knowing the second she emerged from her chair to pour Pa some more milk, hers would disappear. Nearly choking and regretting she'd not be able to enjoy drinking the beverage, Hannah retrieved the pitcher.

Two glasses later, Pa finished the milk from the reverend and his wife.

"Please take me with you." Hannah clung to Ramona, her arms wrapped around her stepmother's waist.

"I can't."

"Please."

Irvin sniffled and wiped his nose with the back of his hand. "Why can't Hannah come?"

Hannah begged him to continue his pleading, but instead, he started to cry. Her other brother sat on the horse, his face expressionless as always. Ever since his accident, three years before Ramona married Pa, he'd "not been right in the head." Ramona was a doting ma to him and Irvin, but Pa hadn't taken kindly to a ten-year-old who couldn't partake in chores.

"We have to go before your pa gets home." Ramona attempted to remove Hannah's clasped hands from their clutch on her. But Hannah clung all the more, her tears dampening her stepmother's dress.

"Ramona, please can I come?"

"No, Hannah, you cannot. Now, please, let go."

But Hannah continued to cling to the only woman who'd been remotely like a mother to her. At twelve-years-old, Hannah understood why Ramona was leaving. Her father failed to be forthright with Ramona even in the beginning. Hannah witnessed Pa's temper and the subsequent abuse of his wife on more than one occasion. While they'd only been married a short time, Ramona had seen a side of Harold Bane no one ought to see.

She was wise in deciding to leave.

"I'll behave myself. I'll watch the boys and take care of them. I'll do all the cooking and washing. Just please don't leave me here."

Ramona fixed her attention on the road, her anxiety obvious. Hannah knew her stepmother must leave before Pa returned or she'd lose her chance.

"You're not my child, Hannah. You must stay here."

"But..."

In a rougher-than-necessary push, Ramona shoved Hannah from her and hurried toward her waiting horse. She placed Irvin on the horse with his brother, mounted her own, and led them down the road in the opposite direction of town. Ramona peered over her shoulder four times but never turned around.

Hannah jolted from the memory that haunted her, Pa's stained shirt suspended idly in her hand.

Seeing Ambrose thrice in recent days precipitated the uninvited and unwanted memory. He reminded her so much of her brothers, especially four-year-old Irvin. And while they did not resemble each other, Ambrose had the same inquisitive personality as Irvin.

Still shaken from her recollection, Hannah took a deep breath and willed herself to continue to scrub the stubborn stain that marred Pa's ragged shirt.

She'd never seen Ramona or her brothers again after that fateful day.

John Mark traipsed through town on his daily rounds. Poplar Springs, founded in 1879 and named after the flowing springs at the edge of town, had seen better days. Crime was rampant. Shootouts common. There were numerous saloons and a brothel, but only one church in the town of four hundred.

Unlike some Wyoming towns with railroad lines, Poplar Springs still used the stagecoach to deliver passengers to their destinations—a stagecoach route that was frequently robbed and deemed unsafe by many.

The scenery was breathtaking with high mountain peaks and clear sparkling rivers. The town had potential to be revitalized into what could be a law-abiding community of ranchers and other hardworking folks.

Just as he did in people, John Mark saw the potential in Poplar Springs. It wasn't too late. But not if Mayor Roessler continued to be in charge. Winslow insinuated the mayor was involved in shady interactions, but couldn't prove it. John Mark aimed to do what he could to reveal any unscrupulous dealings. He had a hunch several of the less-than-stellar individuals in Poplar Springs worked for Mayor Roessler, including

Harold Bane. What these men partook in while in the mayor's employ, John Mark had no idea. Yet.

John Mark greeted everyone he passed. If he was to earn the trust of the residents, he needed to be friendly and approachable. More than anything, he wanted to earn their respect and show them he was a dependable lawman.

He rounded the corner and saw Miss Bane and her pa driving through town. A few moments later, Harold Bane climbed from the wagon and stalked into the Sticker Weed Saloon.

John Mark walked to the side of the wagon. "Miss Bane, can I assist you from the wagon?"

He noted her hesitancy and was about to go on his way when she offered her hand. "I wanted to thank you for helping Ambrose Miller the other day when he lost Grumbles."

Miss Bane's eyebrows drew together. "Were you able to find him?"

"I was. Can't say that, as a deputy, I have too many requests to find pet pigs." He smiled, hoping to alleviate some of her obvious nervousness. She was taller than he expected and appeared to be close to his age. Her eyes darted toward the saloon and anger arose in John Mark at the way Miss Bane's father treated her.

"Look, Miss Bane..."

She returned her focus to him, sadness in her pale green eyes.

"I...uh...look, I know your pa spends a lot of time in the saloon. It's not safe for you to always be out here in the evenings. There are..." he paused, thinking of the types of folks he dealt with on a daily basis. "There are some despicable characters. Perhaps you'd like to sit in the sheriff's office for a time while I do my rounds."

It was obvious from her expression that his words took her aback. Had he made her feel uncomfortable? But he'd previously mentioned the same suggestion. "If you'd like, that is. I am gone much of the time and there's no one in the jail right now. If I do have to arrest someone, that would change, but at least it's safer than sitting on the bench outside the saloon."

"I appreciate your concern, deputy, but I'm fine." Miss Bane's voice wavered and she once again reminded him of that fragile little bird he'd rescued as a boy. But John Mark doubted Miss Bane was fragile. From what he'd seen, she'd have to be a strong woman to withstand the life into which she'd been born. For the hundredth time, he wondered why more folks in town didn't help her. Assist her. Interact with her. Sure, the reverend and his wife spoke to her and took her food, but what of the many others in the town?

"If you're sure."

"I'm sure. But I do appreciate your offer."

John Mark touched the brim of his hat. "Let me know if you need anything."

As long as he was able, John Mark vowed to continue protecting her from afar.

Chapter Four

JOHN MARK LOCKED THE cell behind Wally Pritchard.

Pritchard plopped on the cot and placed his hands behind his head as if taking a peaceful nap in a jail cell was an everyday occurrence.

"You've really got to get this thievery under control," John Mark told him.

Pritchard avoided his eye and stared at the ceiling. "Sure thing, Deputy."

"Even if we don't much care for an individual, it's not right to steal."

Pritchard exhaled a frustrated sigh. "Are you by any chance a preacher's son?"

"I am and I'm being serious. One of these days, a judge is going to send you to prison. And Winslow isn't going to keep giving you chance after chance to redeem yourself."

How many times had Pritchard landed himself in the jail cell? How many times had Winslow or Gaston arrested him before John Mark's arrival?

"You wouldn't understand," Pritchard muttered.

"Wouldn't understand what?"

"Nothing."

John Mark sauntered toward his desk and took a seat. A pile of wanted posters graced the top, along with a typewriter and magnifying glass. His tin cup with a meager amount of cold coffee remaining in the bottom of it reminded him of the busy day. He leaned back in his chair and propped his feet on the crowded desk. "Tell me what I wouldn't understand."

"A man's gotta do things every now and then. To set things to right."

"Like stealing?"

"Could be." Pritchard crossed his legs at the ankles and whistled a tune.

He liked Pritchard with his silly sense of humor. But why the stealing?

A few years older than John Mark's twenty-three, they may have been friends in school if Pritchard had attended in Willow Falls. He saw potential in Pritchard. But his constant thievery from Roessler's Dry Goods was unacceptable. And John Mark didn't need to be a preacher's kid to know it.

At five feet, five inches and one-hundred-thirty pounds, Pritchard's spindly and wiry stature was a little more than half of John Mark's sturdy, muscular build at six feet, three inches and two-hundred-forty pounds.

"Well?" John Mark asked. "Why the stealing?"

Pritchard cleared his throat and sat up on the cot. "It's like this, J.M." He paused. "If I tell you, you have to keep it between us."

Pritchard was the only one who had ever called John Mark "J.M.," and he did so with such a nonchalant and casual flair that to an observer, it would appear they'd been friends all their lives.

"If I'm called to testify if you ever go before the judge..."

"Right. Reckon I forgot about that. All right, so let's just say I'm trying to change my ways, but if it's a necessity, I won't be able to."

"Makes no sense, Pritchard."

His prisoner shrugged. "You going on your rounds tonight?"

"Yes, I always do. I'll be leaving here in about ten minutes or so, but I'll be back in time for supper."

"With food from the restaurant?" Pritchard's blond brows rose into his forehead.

"Perhaps." Pearson's Restaurant was paid by the town to provide suppers for the sheriff and his two Poplar Springs deputies as well as three meals a day for the prisoners. "Is the grub the reason you stay here so often?"

Pritchard chuckled, a boisterous laugh for such a slight man. "You know how I feel about the restaurant food, especially when Miss Pearson prepares it."

"Ah, yes, the woman who has captured your fancy." John Mark shook his head. "She'll never give you a second glance as long as you're a lawbreaker."

An expression of concern flashed over Pritchard's face, but he recovered quickly. "She's a mighty fine woman, and I aim to someday win her heart."

"With a stolen necklace?"

"Not a bad idea, J.M. Not a bad idea at all."

Pritchard must have noticed John Mark's scowl because he retracted his statement. "Just joshing you. I only steal food these days, and besides, I wouldn't be stealing a gift for Miss Pearson. I'd work for it and present it to her all gentlemanly-like."

John Mark removed his legs from atop his desk and stood. "I'm going to do my rounds. Behave yourself."

Not every prisoner could be trusted, but Pritchard was as harmless as they came. Sure, he could run fast and was an accurate shot, but he wouldn't attempt to escape. Not if Miss Pearson's cooking was in his future.

Hannah shook her leg to alleviate the pins-and-needles sensation from sitting on the bench. She limped down the boardwalk, knowing most establishments would be closed. This was her least favorite time of the evening. Nothing to do and nowhere to go. The winters would be worse when she'd be forced to huddle just inside the saloon doors. Perhaps she would take the deputy's suggestion and wait inside the sheriff's office. It was a better alternative to the saloon or waiting outside in the cold.

She'd attempted to escape from her pa once, and that had been the last time she'd risked such a feat. Without a horse, she hadn't gotten far. It was a late night, and after fearing for her life twice due to belligerent men from the saloon, Hannah took off at a fast pace down the boardwalk and in the opposite direction of home. It would take her days to walk to where she believed Nelsonville to be, but at least she'd be on her way. No matter that the crisp fall air during the day and cold temperatures at nights were a threat.

Her heart had raced that night as she ran down the road and darkness had closed in around her once she exited the town. In the direction she traveled, homes were few and far between. She stepped on something sharp and felt it through her dilapidated boot—a rock perhaps—and she had lifted her foot, hopping on one leg for several seconds as she willed the pain to subside.

Hannah remembered wondering if she was still on the road, or if she had detoured off into the weeds. She had started to run again, and recalled the piney scent of the trees filling the air.

Less than ten minutes after she'd left town, a wagon came upon her. Yin and Mander, both her pa's friends, hauled her into the wagon and drove her back to town. Back to Pa.

The beating that night left two scars on her upper back. They had healed with time, but her heart never had. Yet, Pa hadn't broken her spirit. She would never allow that to happen.

Three years later, Hannah didn't dare try to run again. Her pa would always find her, and he had enough of his henchmen to assist him in that endeavor.

That was before Deputy Eliason arrived in Poplar Springs. Funny how he entered her mind at times like these. Probably because she expected to see him at any moment making his rounds. Much better to see him than Deputy Gaston, a calloused and mean-spirited man. She should know. Deputy Gaston associated with the likes of Oslo Dunn and Red Beard, which she found peculiar for a lawman.

While she didn't trust Deputy Eliason, he didn't scare her like Pa, Yin, Mander, Oslo Dunn, Red Beard, Gaston, or even Mayor Roessler. Something about him was different.

Hannah passed by one of the alleyways and peered into the darkness before crossing to the other side of the street. A chill traveled up her spine. Nothing good came from being out this late at night, but what choice did she have? Meander around or remain on the bench outside the saloon and subject herself to crude comments from uncouth men.

She passed the jail, paused, then turned around. She could go there. Deputy Eliason made it clear she could stay inside whenever she needed to while he was doing his rounds. Hannah peered inside and that's when she saw someone on the cot in the cell. He was facedown so she couldn't determine who he was, but his snores, noisier than what she imagined a train whistle to be, thundered through the small building.

So as not to awaken the prisoner, Hannah tiptoed backward, shut the door, and went on her way.

Pearson's Restaurant came into view and encouragement swelled within her when she noticed the lights still on, even at this late hour. She'd never visited the restaurant before, but she'd heard the food was delectable. Perhaps they would allow her to work for room and board and she could finally find a way to support herself without Pa.

She peered into the front window. Inside, workers bustled about. She'd heard folks talking about the new family that had recently moved here from Indiana and opened the restaurant, and although she'd seen them at church, she'd never met them. Most times, she exited the church as quickly as possible to arrive home again before Pa noticed her absence. And never once had she ever partaken in any of the church potlucks or other activities.

Hannah tried the doorknob. It was unlocked.

She debated her options. Wander inside and ask if they had any jobs available or wait until next time when she could muster up more courage?

She chose the former.

Taking a deep breath, she opened the door. Lively camaraderie echoed throughout the room, along with the clanging of pots and pans. The aroma of cornbread mingled with another heavenly scent. Beef, perhaps? Her stomach growled in response and Hannah instinctively pressed a hand to her stomach.

An older woman bustled around the kitchen while two boys and three young women assisted her in a variety of duties.

One of the women, about her age, smiled as she entered. "May I help you?" she asked.

If only she had a few coins to purchase a meal! To sit at one of the tables and partake was almost too great an ambition. She swallowed the thought and answered the woman's question. "I was wondering if I might speak to the owner."

"That would be my parents," the cheerful woman with a red apron answered. "If you'll come this way, I'll lead you to them. I'm Ina Pearson."

"Hannah Bane." She waited warily for the dreaded words she'd heard countless times before: *"Surely not the daughter of that ne'er-do-well, Harold Bane."*

When no further response came, she followed Ina to the back of the restaurant. "Ma, we have a guest who'd like to speak with you."

A guest.

No one had ever referred to her in such a way before. The words buoyed her spirits and she straightened her shoulders. She could succeed at her endeavor. She could.

An older version of Ina greeted her. "I'm Mrs. Pearson. How may I help you?"

"I..." the words stuck in her throat and Hannah willed herself to speak them. "I was wondering if...if you might have a job opening available. I'm a real hard worker. You don't even have to pay me much or anything. Just room and board. That would be all."

Mrs. Pearson's forehead creased. Hannah pressed the wrinkles from her dress and attempted to stand taller. "I'll work hard, ma'am. I can cook and clean and I never complain."

"Oh, sweet child, I'm sure you are a hard worker. But the truth of the matter is, I don't have any job openings at the moment."

Hannah bit back the tears. She'd not cry. There were other places besides Pearson's Restaurant who might hire her.

But you've been to nearly all of them.

"Are you sure?" she asked.

Mrs. Pearson wiped her hands on her apron. "Can I get you something to eat?"

"I'm sorry, but no, thank you. I...do you think you'll be hiring soon?"

The older woman shook her head. "It's not that I don't think you'd be a suitable employee, but we have five children and my husband and I, plus my husband's mother, working and living here. We all share in the work as well as the upstairs living quarters, and it's extremely crowded. I'm so sorry." She rested a hand on Hannah's arm. "Might I get you a plate of food to eat? We have leftovers from tonight. It would be no charge."

No charge?

But could she accept charity?

On the one hand, Hannah disliked pity, but on the other, she *was* starving. "Yes, ma'am, if you don't mind."

"Not at all." Mrs. Pearson led her to one of the tables and within minutes, brought Hannah a plate of rump roast and a slice of cornbread.

The meal was even tastier than the rabbit stew from the reverend a few nights ago, and Hannah attempted to refrain from devouring it. When she finished, Hannah thanked Mrs. Pearson and Ina and slipped out once again into the night.

CHAPTER FIVE

JOHN MARK APPROACHED THE Sticker Weed Saloon. He expected to see Miss Bane sitting outside on the bench waiting for her pa; however, the bench was vacant. It was already edging on darkness and worry filled his thoughts. Poplar Springs wasn't safe at night for a young woman, not even on a less-rowdy Tuesday night.

He fixed his gaze to the left, then swiveled his head to the right, and again to the left. A drunkard limped along the boardwalk, tottering on unsteady legs and singing a garbled song that made no sense. In the other direction, a group of men in a circle slung whiskey down their throats. A horse with a lone rider trotted down the street and a stray dog sniffed his way toward his next meal.

But there was no sign of Miss Bane.

As he was about to embark on a search for her, he heard the familiar and obnoxious voice of Harold Bane coming from the saloon. John Mark veered toward the swinging doors, his back against the building to avoid being seen. Piano music played in the background, no match for Harold's booming voice. The strong odor of alcohol permeated through the air, mingling with the stench of pipe tobacco and body odor. John Mark's eyes watered and the temptation to leave was significant. However, something in Harold's tone lent to more than just his usual ramblings. That and the offensive responses from the men in his company.

"You owe me so much money, you ain't never gonna be able to pay it." John Mark recognized the deep, nauseating baritone voice of Oslo Dunn.

"Don't owe you as much as you say," retorted Harold.

John Mark had been called into the saloon on many occasions to attempt to keep the peace. Usually someone had already taken care of the matter using physical means by the time someone else fetched John Mark. Several times in his short tenure as deputy he hauled a man away for fighting or for assault. It was part of his job to observe the ongoings at the saloons, especially the Sticker Weed, which was by far the most notorious.

"You pay up tonight or something very bad will happen to you and that daughter of yours."

John Mark's attention perked and he was about to march into the saloon and have a discussion with Oslo Dunn about threatening to harm an innocent woman.

But his feet stalled at Harold's next words.

"Tell ya what. Do you think Hannah's a comely woman?"

"Mebe."

"How 'bout Friday night you and me have the card game of all card games. I win, I owe ya nothin' and my debt is forgiven. You win, and you have my blessin' to take Hannah as your wife."

The piano player ceased playing and a hush fell over the raucous saloon.

John Mark stilled. Harold was about to gamble his daughter away to the likes of Oslo? He balled his fists. There was no doubt in his mind that Harold would lose. Folks didn't often win against Oslo, who had made a reputation for himself of not only being a thief—and a sinister one at that—but also a cheat.

And what of Hannah? Shouldn't she be given a choice of whether she wished to marry someone as dishonorable as Oslo Dunn?

"You don't say..." boomed Oslo. "Whatcha gonna do when she's not here no more to take you home after you have too much whiskey?"

"Not gonna worry none because you ain't gonna win." Harold's slurred words were magnified against the otherwise hushed silence.

Oslo released a rumbling guffaw and a few others chimed in. "You think so, do ya? Well, guess you and me will be related soon 'nuff. But I ain't gonna just let that money you owe go away. If you lose, you still gotta pay some of it back. Least half."

"A quarter. You get Hannah and I pay you a quarter of what I owe."

Oslo scratched his head. "I dunno."

"You get my daughter for your wife. That there is better than all I owe. She can cook and clean and she don't eat much."

John Mark's heartbeat pounded in his ears and a mixture of fury, concern, and ambition overcame him.

A strangled prayer consisting of a hasty, "Lord, please help me with what I'm about to do," fell from his lips. Before any rational thoughts could infiltrate his mind,

John Mark stomped through the swinging doors and into the Sticker Weed. His boots clomped on the wood floor, the only sound echoing throughout the building.

He found Harold Bane and Oslo Dunn without much trouble. They lounged at a table with three other men. Harold was little more than a breath away from passing out, his head nodding and his hands shaking as he attempted to lift the glass of whiskey to his lips. "Whatcha want, Deputy?" He belched, the jolt spilling the whiskey across the front of his already-soiled shirt.

"I have a deal to make you, Harold."

"Man ain't in no position to make deals," said a scoundrel named Yin.

"Let him finish," barked the bartender, swiping a dirty rag across the counter.

A saloon girl winked at him. "Hello, handsome. Care for a drink?"

John Mark ignored the woman and instead focused on Harold. "I'll make you a deal, Harold. I'll take Oslo's place Friday night."

"Oslo's place where?" Harold asked.

Oslo narrowed his eyes at John Mark. "Why would you go and take my place? I'm the one who's owed money from this here drunk." The huge man with greasy white-blond hair had no place to talk about drunkenness. His flushed face and bloodshot eyes gave proof of his own inebriation.

An alarm rang in John Mark's mind, but he ignored it. Sweat trickled down his spine and his heart raced. The words tumbled from his mouth before he could stop them. "How much does Harold owe you?"

"Fifty dollars and some change."

John Mark inhaled sharply. His weekly wages were a third of that amount. He quickly contemplated what he could sell to earn that kind of money. Nothing came to mind.

"All right. If I win, Harold, you can give me your blessing to marry your daughter and I'll pay Oslo fifteen dollars to pay back in full what you owe him."

Oslo shook his head. "But he owes me fifty dollars. How am I winnin' in this? If I play Harold, I get both the wife and some money."

"You'll never see any of the money," said John Mark.

"But at least I get a wife."

Ideas to counteract Oslo's words failed to come. How could he convince the man to allow him to take his place and be the one to play the card game against Harold? "You don't get the wife, but you get the fifteen dollars. That's more than you have now and more than you'll ever see from Harold."

Oslo appeared to contemplate John Mark's offer. "Tell ya what. You throw in that hat and we have ourselves a deal."

"My hat?"

"Yep."

John Mark fingered the brim of his black hat. The hat Ma and Pa had purchased for him in celebration of his new job as deputy sheriff. The hat they'd paid a pretty penny for. Could he relinquish it?

Yes, to save a life he could. Without hesitation.

"All right. The hat is yours as well as the fifteen dollars to pay Harold's debt. Friday night, seven o'clock, me against Harold."

"And what do I get if I win?" Harold growled. "Seems only Oslo gets somethin'. What about me?"

Harold's whiny voice grated in John Mark's ears. What could he offer Harold to allow him to be the one to challenge him in order to save Miss Bane? "If you win, you are free from debt since I'll still pay Oslo the fifteen dollars, which will pay your debt in full."

"Reckon that suits me." Harold shook John Mark's hand.

"Friday night it is," agreed Oslo. He reached a beefy hand toward John Mark. "Everyone," he slurred. "In two days, Harold and the deputy go against each other in a card game. We all know the deputy ain't the gambling type. He's a lawman and a preacher's boy. So when Harold wins, I get fifteen dollars and a hat from the deputy here to pay off Harold's debt." Oslo puffed out his chest, causing his ample gut to protrude even more.

John Mark straightened. "And if I win against Harold, I win his blessing to make Miss Bane my wife. I'll also pay Oslo the fifteen dollars and give him my hat for allowing me to be the one to challenge Harold." Even when he uttered the words they sounded a bit discombobulated, but as long as he could free Miss Bane from her father, all would be well. The poor woman wouldn't be betrothed to Oslo Dunn, a depraved and evil man with a wicked temper and a nasty drinking habit.

Miss Bane would never choose to marry someone so wretched. And she had every right to choose whom she wanted to marry.

CHAPTER SIX

JOHN MARK NEARLY COLLIDED with one of the Pearson boys as the youngster bounded through the door of the sheriff's office. "Supper is on the desk, sir. Sorry it's late, but we were extra busy at the restaurant this evening."

"Is that for me?" Pritchard sat up in his cot and pointed at the plate.

"Could be."

"Reckon you've probably already eaten. What is it, prit near ten o'clock?"

John Mark glanced at the mantle clock collecting dust and set the plate on the desk. He had already eaten his sandwich several hours ago, but he wouldn't let Pritchard know that. First, he needed to have a discussion with the man who now stood facing him at the bars of the cell. If Pritchard was any skinnier, he'd slip through those bars and escape. "I have a favor to ask you," he said.

"Well, you and me are friends, so what can I help you with?"

John Mark wouldn't go so far as to say they were *friends*, although Pritchard was by far the most pleasant prisoner he'd had to supervise. He drew up a chair and planted himself backwards on it, facing Pritchard. "Reckon I need you to teach me how to gamble."

"Have you gone and lost your mind while doing your rounds?" Pritchard gaped and his eyes bulged on his narrow face.

"Not exactly. Well, maybe." To play a card game against Harold might not seem significant given the fact Harold would likely be drunk at the time, but it was a concern because John Mark had never played cards. Nor had he cared to. He was raised to believe any type of gambling was wrong. But sometimes desperation to help someone caused one to do absurd things.

Things such as participate in a card game in just three days.

Lord, reckon I'd best ask forgiveness ahead of time.

"Why would you want to gamble?" Pritchard splayed his hands palms up and his mouth hung open several seconds before he finally closed it and pursed his lips. "Might I give you some advice, Son?" he asked.

Son? Pritchard was no more than a couple of years older than John Mark. Hardly enough of an age difference to be his elder. More like his equal.

"Whether you want it or not, I'm giving you some advice." Pritchard raised a pointy finger and shook it at John Mark. "Don't even get started at gambling. It will become an addiction and ruin your life. Doesn't the Bible say something about it being a sin to have a love for money? Well, gambling will do that to you. And furthermore..." a vein popped out in his forehead. "I will not, in good conscience, teach you how to partake in it.

I've seen how this vice can ruin a man, and I'll not cause someone else to stumble. No can do. Won't do it." He folded his arms across his narrow chest.

John Mark began to chuckle at Pritchard's serious demeanor.

"It's not a laughing matter, J.M. Now, can I have some of that food from the restaurant? I've been sitting in this cell languishing for the better part of the evening."

John Mark rested his arms on the back of the chair and leaned forward. "I wouldn't ask you to teach me something I don't agree with if it wasn't absolutely necessary."

"Absolutely necessary?"

"Yes."

Pritchard appeared to ponder John Mark's statement. "Why do you need to know how to play cards?"

"If I tell you, it remains between us."

The man bobbed his head a little too quickly. "I promise."

It wasn't as if the entire saloon didn't already know what was to occur in three days. However, John Mark wouldn't want to do anything to embarrass Miss Bane. "I mean it, Pritchard. You have to keep it between us."

"Why all the concern, J.M.? Don't worry. I won't tell a soul. Provided you give me some food."

John Mark blew out the breath he'd been holding. "All right. You have to teach me because I am challenging Harold Bane at the saloon Friday evening."

Pritchard spoke no words, but instead stood facing John Mark with his mouth gaping open as if he'd been frozen in time. Finally he spoke. "Why would you want to challenge anyone, much less Harold Bane, to a game of cards? The man's a drunk and he's evil as they come in the way he treats his daughter."

For all of Pritchard's faults, he was a compassionate sort. "Exactly. He was going to challenge Oslo Dunn for Miss Bane's hand in marriage, but I couldn't allow that to happen. So I offered to take Oslo's place. If I win, I win Harold's blessing to marry Miss Bane."

Pritchard paced the jail cell several times, taking three steps forward, pivoting, then taking three more steps, all the while scratching his head. "You've got to save her, J.M."

"I aim to, but here's the problem. I've never played cards and have never cared to. Even though Harold will be drunk, he could still win. Then there's a chance Miss Bane would still have to marry Oslo. Will you help me?"

"You bet your five horses and six cows I will."

"Good. When can we start?"

Pritchard nodded toward the desk. "After I finish supper."

"Now, I don't want to learn how to cheat. I don't believe that's right."

"Nor do I."

Given Pritchard's history, John Mark wasn't so sure of that, but he didn't argue. Instead, he opened the cell door and handed his prisoner the plate of food. If it had been any other criminal, he would have had to be more cautious. But Pritchard wasn't like most criminals. Beneath his puny exterior was a heart for others.

Pritchard devoured the food as if he hadn't eaten in weeks. "One of these days, I'm going ask Miss Pearson's pa if I can court her."

"Doubt that would happen given your criminally-minded past."

"Criminally-minded past, pshaw. Anyway, this is after I'm reformed." Pritchard took another bite. "Say, if you win this card game and *you will*, that would mean you have to marry Miss Bane. Do you even know her?"

"No, but I'm not necessarily going to marry her." Pritchard attempted to interrupt, but John Mark help up his hand. "I'm going to ask her if that's what she wants. Harold gave his word that if I win, I get his blessing to marry his daughter. I will do that *if* that's what she wants. If not, I will support her in whatever decision she makes provided it keeps her away from her pa."

Pritchard downed the two pieces of cornbread without a breath in between. "If you marry Miss Bane, you're going to break several hearts. Seems the eligible women in Poplar Springs have set their cap for you. Claudelle Roessler, for one, and who's the one working for the seamstress over on Third Street?"

"I'm not concerned, Pritchard. I have no interest in those women." Wasn't it just last month when he'd returned to Willow Falls and Charlotte had given him a ribbing about falling in love and getting married before he was twenty-five? He had vehemently denied wanting to marry until he was at least thirty and had his own place. And maybe by then, he'd even be the sheriff. But no, he'd never set his mind on getting married at twenty-three, no matter what that featherbrained sister of his said. He would remain steadfast in his decision to remain a bachelor.

Unless it meant saving Hannah Bane's life.

"Do you even have a deck of cards?"

Pritchard's voice interrupted John Mark's musings. "No, don't believe I do."

The other man rolled his eyes. "I'm still living above the barbershop until I can fix up that dilapidated cabin on my ranch. Go to the room above the barbershop, and in the top drawer of the bureau is a deck. Bring it back and I'll teach you how to play."

John Mark didn't need extra prompting. Time was of utmost importance.

CHAPTER SEVEN

HANNAH RETURNED TO THE bench after her visit at Pearson's Restaurant. Someday she would ask if she could stay in the restaurant while Pa downed the whiskey and gambled his money away. She would persuade Mrs. Pearson to allow her to do so in exchange for assisting with the clean-up after supper was served.

She just had to work up the courage.

Pa bellowed belligerent words while staggering through the swinging doors of the saloon. Hannah dreaded the thought of going home.

Her father toppled over and collapsed to the ground, his usual drunken stupor giving way to unconsciousness.

Several men, nearly as drunk, chortled as they emerged from the saloon behind him. "Look at ol' Bane. Could never hold his liquor."

They stood around him and mocked him before Oslo Dunn grabbed Pa's arms and Red Beard his legs. Yin, likely for good measure, assisted as well. They tossed him into the back of the wagon. "Best get him home," slurred Mander, another of Pa's cohorts, and a skinny-legged, big-bellied man with dark eyes, thick bushy eyebrows, and a frightening demeanor.

Hannah rose and Red Beard sauntered toward her. "You might need my help to unload him, and you know I'd be happy to oblige." Even in the darkness with only the light of the saloon, Hannah could imagine his roving eye.

Gooseflesh pricked her arms and her heart raced. Something about the man left her unsettled.

"I'll be following them out to the Bane place to assist with unloading Mr. Bane," a voice from somewhere behind them said.

Hannah turned to see Deputy Eliason. "You men all go home and sleep it off. I'll take care of Bane."

"But I already offered," countered Red Beard.

"And I already told you I'll be assisting Miss Bane."

Deputy Eliason gave no opportunity for Red Beard to argue. "I'll get my horse and meet you on the road," he told Hannah.

Moments later, Hannah beckoned the horses toward home. She detested traveling at night in the darkness on the lonely road. Tonight was a cloudier and darker night than usual. Coyotes and wolves howled and Hannah thought she saw eyes peering at her through the trees. The night had cooled considerably and she shivered.

She turned and fixed her eyes briefly on the road behind her. In the moonlight, she could make out the shape of a man on a horse.

Thank You, Lord, that Deputy Eliason is following me rather than Red Beard.

After what seemed an insurmountable period of time, Hannah drove the horses to the front of the Bane house. She didn't need lights to envision the dark and dreary abode. She tugged on the reins and the horses stopped.

Deputy Eliason stood next to the wagon. He gently lifted her from it, and for the briefest of moments, she reveled in the safety of his closeness.

All too soon, he placed her on the ground. "I'll bring your pa in," he said.

"Thank you, Deputy. Thank you for not allowing Red Beard..." Her voice trailed and embarrassment flooded her. How often had she delivered Pa from the saloon to the house on her own? Without incident? Too often to count.

"You're welcome, Miss Bane."

For perhaps the first time, Hannah noticed Deputy Eliason had a nice voice, not a harsh, barking, and demeaning one like Pa's. From what she'd observed, he didn't utter crass words that no one, especially a woman, should be privy to. Rather, Deputy Eliason's voice was confident, robust, and respectful.

"I'll unhitch the horses," she offered.

"No need, ma'am. I'm happy to oblige. Let me haul your pa into the house and then I'll take care of the horses."

"If you're certain."

"Don't mind at all."

Hannah opened the door and lit a lamp. Deputy Eliason walked through the door, Pa draped over his shoulder as though a mere sack of potatoes.

In the flickering light, she was reminded once again the strength the deputy possessed, not only physically, but also in character.

But you can't be sure he's a man of integrity. She attempted to brush the niggling voice aside, but knew all too well the façade a man could exhibit. A façade that hid the truth beneath a seemingly upright demeanor.

"Where should I put him?"

Deputy Eliason's words interrupted her thoughts and she realized she'd been staring. She returned her attention to the deputy's question and pointed toward Pa's room. "You can place him in here."

The deputy flung Pa back over his shoulder in the opposite direction and onto the bed. A pungent odor permeated the air and Hannah nearly gagged at the common stench of whisky mixed with cigar smoke and body odor. A stench she'd never grow accustomed to.

"I'll take care of the horses. Bolt the door after I leave."

The fact that he cared about her safety stirred something within her and Hannah nodded, her voice temporarily nonexistent. She followed him to the door.

Deputy Eliason touched the brim of his hat. "Good night, Miss Bane."

As tired as she was, Hannah found sleep illusive. Pa's thunderous snoring was the only sound in the house. She turned to one side, then to the other, willing herself to get some much-needed shut-eye. Pa's volatile mood would no doubt make tomorrow another distressing day.

She fought the disconcerting thoughts that oftentimes made their presence known at this hour when she ought to be welcoming some much-needed shut-eye. What if Deputy Eliason hadn't been there to offer his assistance with Pa? What if Red Beard had been the one to follow her home? What if...

Hannah flipped over onto her back. For the first time in a long while, her stomach didn't growl as she beckoned sleep. On the contrary, the food at the restaurant, appetizing and delectable, had provided a satisfaction surpassing even Mrs. Fleming's rabbit stew.

She reached for Ma's Bible and pressed it to her chest, wishing she had light. But she couldn't very well use the lamp and read to calm her overactive mind. She'd done that once, believing Pa to be asleep. He'd somehow seen the crack of light beneath her door and gave her a tongue-lashing that included threats to discard Ma's Bible.

No, instead Hannah would do her best to recall the verses she'd memorized throughout her time in the Word. And she would pray.

More "what-ifs" found their way into her mind instead, initiating the battle of questions that so often plagued her.

Tears slid down her face, wetting her cheeks and landing on her blanket. What would it have been like if Ma had lived? If Hannah hadn't been the cause of Ma's death in childbirth? What would it have been like if Ramona had stayed? If she'd loved Hannah as some stepmothers loved their new children? What if Ramona had taken Hannah with her? What if there was some way to escape from Pa and start a new life? A life of freedom? What if someday she would be able to have a family of her own? Would she be a good ma? Would she even know how to be a ma? Could a man ever love her the way she'd witnessed Reverend Fleming cherish his wife?

Deputy Eliason came to mind. While there weren't many unmarried women in Poplar Springs, especially those who weren't elderly widows, nearly all were fond of the deputy and sought his attention. Especially Claudelle Roessler. Would someone such as the deputy ever find someone like Hannah worthy of his affection?

The tears continued to stream down her face and she did her best to remain quiet in her weeping, lest she awaken Pa.

Returning the Bible to the upturned log beside her bed, Hannah slipped from beneath her threadbare blanket and kneeled, the hard wood floor digging into her bony knees. "Lord," she whispered. "I'm not sure if You can hear me, but if by chance You can and you are listening..."

She knew from her time in the Bible and from the reverend's sermons that God *did* hear prayers. But her mind wrestled with that fact as He had never answered one of hers.

"Lord," she breathed, "If You do answer prayers, even mine, might You hear the words of my heart?" Her body shook and she put her face in her hands. "Please don't let Pa hear me," she said, her voice muffled through her hands.

Hannah sniffled and once again folded her hands. "Lord, if You do hear prayers, might I please pray for a miracle? Might you hear my desperate pleas?"

Of course there was no audible answer from the Lord. The only sound was Pa's snoring.

She hadn't awakened him.

Her knees ached from the hard floor, but Hannah once again lifted her requests to her Heavenly Father. "Might I pray that You would guide me and show me a way to leave Pa?" Would the Lord see fit to grant her request? "I lay my life in Your hands, Lord. I beg You to help me. I can work hard. Please let someone hire me and allow me to have room and board." Her words came as a string of blabbering. "I know You created the earth and all that is in it. You formed mountains and created people and gave us the beautiful rivers and trees. I know You can..." her voice broke. "I know You can help me, Lord. I just...I just need Your help. Show me what to do. Please give me peace." Hannah hunched over the bed, her body trembling and her shaking hands still folded.

After some time, she stilled, a flood of calm temporarily rushing over her. Hannah climbed back onto her bed and closed her eyes.

This time she fell fast asleep.

Friday would soon arrive, and after working through the night, John Mark was eager for some shut-eye. At least now he had three days off before he returned to work on Monday. That was his schedule this week. But he aimed to ask Sheriff Winslow for several days off because if all went according to plan, he would need to take Hannah to Willow Falls to meet his family if she chose to marry him.

If all went according to plan. Ma was fond of quoting Proverbs 16:9, *"A man's heart deviseth his way: but the LORD directeth his steps."*

His heart was devising his way all right. Marrying a woman he didn't even know after partaking in gambling. But even though the method was unorthodox and wouldn't be his preferred approach to the situation, John Mark knew God would direct his steps.

But while exhaustion tugged at every inch of him, John Mark could not sleep. He rolled over in bed, rehashing the rules of the card game and the surefire tips on how to win, courtesy of Wally Pritchard. He'd had to grasp the entire lesson, which took place in the wee hours of the night, because there would be no other time to learn.

And he needed his rest so he would be alert and successful. Miss Bane's future depended on him.

Thoughts crammed his mind. Would Harold remember John Mark was to challenge him, rather than Oslo Dunn? Would John Mark win? Would Miss Bane accept the freedom John Mark would secure for her? If so, would she choose to marry him or would she choose to reside elsewhere with her newfound liberty? If she chose him, would she be happy as his wife? Would he be happy as her husband? Did she share any of her father's undesirable traits? If he and Miss Bane weren't suited for each other, could he honor his wedding vows and live a life of misery? What would Ma and Pa say?

Light peeked in the house through the faded curtain, and outside the obnoxious rooster crowed for the fifth time in a row. He swung his long legs over the side of the bed. Perhaps sleep would come later.

He placed the kettle on the stove, brewed a cup of coffee, and sliced himself some bread off the loaf Widow Holmes had given him yesterday. When he was a youngster, he would joke with his older brother, Caleb, about eating only bread crusts and crackers. Now John Mark was living a similar existence. He missed Ma's cooking, and although Pearson's Restaurant was a reasonable alternative, it didn't compare.

After breakfast, he would venture into town and stop by the bank to withdraw some money from his meager savings. Someday he aimed to own his own home, maybe even purchase the one he lived in now from Mr. Valdez.

An hour later, breakfast eaten and chores completed, John Mark saddled his horse and rode the mile to town. At the outskirts, he stopped and gazed at the wooden sign teetering on the splintered post that announced one was entering the town of Poplar Springs. He dismounted, straightened the post, and packed more dirt and a few rocks around it to stabilize it.

Folks visited on the boardwalk and wagons clamored down the main street. Somewhere someone cooked breakfast, causing a savory aroma to fill the air. While tempted to stop at Pearson's Restaurant for something to eat, John Mark resisted. The card game alone would be an impediment. If he hoped to support a wife, he needed to save his pennies.

He tied his horse to the post outside Poplar Springs Bank and wandered inside to withdraw the fifteen dollars. When he returned to the boardwalk, he head a familiar voice call his name. Ambrose waved, his pet pig on a leash behind him.

"Ambrose, how are you today?"

"I'm just tracking me down some hornswogglers." He placed a thumb through the top of an oversized belt that had been wrapped around his waist thrice. Ambrose wore his grandpa's old and soiled cowboy hat and boots that were a few sizes too big. "You know what it's like, Deputy, to always have to keep the law in this here town of lawlessness."

John Mark chuckled. "Yes, I do know what that's like."

"Say, are you fixin' to go get something to eat?" A hopeful glint lit Ambrose's eyes.

"Did you eat before you left the house?"

Ambrose shook his head. "No, sir. Grandpa wasn't feeling well, so I let him sleep."

"Well, I reckon it's high time you and I got some breakfast then."

"Can Grumbles come too?" Ambrose puffed out his chest and stood a little taller. "I'm the sheriff and he's my deputy."

John Mark chuckled at Ambrose's declaration and eyed the plump pink-and-black pig with its curly tail and rope tether attached to a collar around its neck. "He can, but I think he will have to wait outside."

Ambrose ate enough for both he and John Mark. The scrawny youngster, who had been raised by his grandpa since the time he was two years old, had a voracious appetite with little to show for it. John Mark suspected Mr. Miller struggled to provide food for he and Ambrose, and with his health steadily declining, there would come a day when the young boy would again be orphaned. The thought worried him.

"How many people have you put in jail today?" Ambrose asked, leaning across the table at Pearson's Restaurant.

"I'm not at work today, but I did have a prisoner yesterday."

"And was he a rapscallion of the worstest sorts?"

John Mark would hardly consider Pritchard a rapscallion, but he did need to change his ways. "That's a mighty big word for such a young fellow."

"I learned it from Grandpa. That's what he calls the mayor," Ambrose whispered.

Hopefully, Mr. Miller kept his opinions of the mayor to himself. There was little doubt in John Mark's mind that the public official was behind some shady dealings.

Ambrose pressed his face against the nearby window of the restaurant. "Oh, look, it's Mr. Pritchard!"

"How do you know Mr. Pritchard?" *And why is he released from jail so soon?*

"He's been at our house...to visit." Ambrose squirmed in his chair and avoided John Mark's eye. John Mark didn't need to be a man of the law to recognize shifty behavior when he saw it.

Pritchard was a likeable fellow, so it didn't surprise John Mark that he would visit Mr. Miller and his grandson, but what was of some concern was Ambrose's apparent attempt to conceal that information.

After Ambrose finished two helpings, he bid John Mark goodbye with a plate of breakfast for his grandpa.

And John Mark returned to the bank to withdraw nearly all of the remainder of his savings.

Chapter Eight

John Mark had just exited the bank when he saw Reverend Fleming outside the mercantile holding a package of peppermint sticks. Thoughts of his own father entered his mind. If Pa were here, John Mark could ask him the million and five questions on his mind about his decision to assist Miss Bane.

Should he seek the reverend's advice?

"Hello, Deputy," Reverend Fleming said.

"Hello, Reverend. I see you have a fondness for peppermint sticks." John Mark didn't know the reverend well, but from what he did know, he found the preacher to be of reputable character.

Reverend Fleming chuckled. "No, these aren't for me. These are for my lovely bride." He paused and whispered, "She's with child, hasn't been feeling well, and has been asking for peppermint sticks nearly every day. She insists they quell the nausea. I'm grateful Mrs. Alvarado gives me a discount for being such a loyal customer."

John Mark could imagine the reverend didn't make much by way of earnings with the low number of congregants who attended on the Sundays he was in Poplar Springs. He also hadn't realized the reverend was about to be a pa again, but menfolk didn't commonly discuss such matters.

When he married someday, would he make quick jaunts to the mercantile to procure peppermint sticks for his wife? The thought of marriage and being a father embarrassed him and muddled his thoughts. He swallowed the sizeable lump in his throat as Hannah Bane's face flashed in his mind. Perhaps he should have thought things out a little better before deciding to gamble for her pa's blessing to marry her. Surely there might have been another way to help her.

John Mark needed to change the topic of discussion to another matter on his mind. "Say, Reverend, I've noticed there's a lot of need in Poplar Springs."

"That there is."

When Pa would hear of someone in need, his demeanor would indicate concern and he would do what he could to fulfill the need. He hoped Reverend Fleming would have the same reaction. "I've been especially concerned about Miss Bane and Ambrose Miller."

The pastor's eyebrows drew together and his demeanor reflected compassion. He peered down at the peppermint sticks in his hand. "As have I. The missus and I have devoted ourselves to praying for both of them, along with several others in the town. And while prayer is the most important, we've also attempted to find other ways to help both of them. We've taken food to them on numerous occasions as has ..." the reverend paused mid-sentence. "I never want to neglect the flock, especially those in need, yet I believe I may have done just that. I've agonized many times about how to minister to both towns effectively in light of all the demands and challenges, especially since I don't reside in Poplar Springs the entire week. Couple that with the baby, the missus not feeling well as of late, and the cramped parsonage..." He sighed. "Please forgive me, Deputy. I don't mean to complain. I'm just attempting to settle into this calling the Lord recently placed on my life. But you have my word that I intend to do what I can to see to the needs of the townsfolk."

John Mark recalled clearly the obligations his own pa shouldered—and continued to shoulder—as a pastor. Reverend Fleming was near John Mark's age and likely overwhelmed by his new responsibilities, in addition to having recently moved to Poplar Springs. "My pa is a preacher and I witnessed his frustrations and distress at the immense nature of his calling at times." He placed a firm hand on Reverend Fleming's shoulder. "We're fortunate to have you in Poplar Springs."

"I appreciate that, Deputy. Reckon I better get these to the missus before she wonders if I traveled to Montana to secure them."

Hannah clutched her basket and started toward the chicken coop in search of eggs. Unfortunately, the two hens left rarely laid well. Pa would be in soon and he would demand a breakfast. How she was supposed to achieve that with no food was beyond her. She prayed God would provide even one egg, and set out for the coop.

On her way, she stopped in the barn to see the horses. How many times had she contemplated climbing on one and riding plumb out of Poplar Springs and away from Pa? The temptation had been great. Were it not for the fact that being a horse thief would land her in jail, she might be on her way to freedom the next time Pa left to carry out the nefarious business of Mayor Roessler.

Just as Hannah stepped inside the barn, she heard the sound of horses' hooves. She peeked through the door to see two riders approaching, and immediately recognized them as Yin and Mander.

Hannah slimmed herself against the barn wall and listened to the loud voices of the ne'er- do-wells who frequently visited Pa. While Yin and Mander were cruel and reprehensible, they were no match for Oslo Dunn and Red Beard.

Yin spoke first. "The boss wants us to go out to the Daly place and get some more cash from him."

"We just went out there. Why go again?" Pa asked.

Mander chortled a loud and obnoxious laugh Hannah could recognize blindfolded. "You know the mayor. When he wants something he gets it. He *really* wants Daly's land. After all, it's on the river with a steady supply of water. Get Daly to pay more money if he wants us to leave him alone. You know how this works."

"Besides," said Yin. "Ain't our job to question what the boss wants."

"True, and I haven't never been paid as well as he pays us. 'Sides, it's always right fun to see others squirm," Pa said, his own voice harsh and disdainful. "How long you reckon it'll take?"

Yin blew out a deep breath. "Shouldn't take long."

"Good. I got me an important meeting at the saloon tomorrow night and I gotta practice for it tonight."

Mander chortled again. "That's right, Bane, you do. Prit near forgot about that." He lowered his voice, but Hannah could still hear him. "Does your daughter know about it?"

"No, she don't, and I aim to keep it that way. Won't she be surprised?"

"Surprised ain't the word I'd use for it," said Yin. "She's not gonna be happy."

"Don't care not even a little bit."

Pa's words jabbed at her heart. What was it he was planning? What was it that he didn't care about with regards to her feelings?

"I need to fetch my horse and I'll be ready."

"Hurry yourself up. That ain't the only place Roessler wants us to visit today."

Hannah panicked. If Pa found her in the barn when she ought to be making breakfast, or worse, if he found her eavesdropping...

There was no exiting the barn without passing Pa as he entered. She searched the vacant building for a place to hide.

Hannah scurried up the rickety ladder toward the loft, which was filled with old smelly hay, much of it covered in droppings from the birds who flew in through the hole in the ceiling. Her foot nearly slipped as she made her way from the distance between the last rung to the loft.

Pa's footsteps sounded. Would he see her? Would he enter the house and find her missing? Would he wonder where his breakfast was and why she hadn't yet prepared it?

Hannah flattened herself on her stomach, and she nearly gagged on the stale stench of the hay.

Pa shuffled through the barn and presumably toward his horse. Hannah's heartbeat sounded in her ears.

Could Pa hear it too?

Nausea roiled in her belly and she fought the urge to hyperventilate. *Lord, please don't let Pa see me. Please don't let him go back to the house and look for me.*

She couldn't see him, but she did hear his footsteps stop. Was he saddling his horse? Was he looking her way? Had he seen her hiding in the loft?

Her legs shook and her shoulders tensed. She held her breath despite the fact that it threatened to escape in quick short bursts.

Finally, after what seemed like hours, Hannah heard the clop-clop of a horse's hooves. Likely Pa leading the horse from the barn. She dared not move for several minutes. What if Pa came back?

When she surmised it safe to retreat from her hiding place, Hannah slowly rose and climbed down the ladder. It was only by God's grace that Pa hadn't returned, hadn't gone to the house in search for her, and hadn't discovered her in the barn. She whispered a prayer of gratitude and headed back to the house.

Pa's words lingered in her mind. What did he have planned for her?

John Mark had just returned home and was fixing to start chores when he saw a rider in the distance.

Of all the folks he thought it could be, the one person he wasn't expecting for a visit was his own father.

His pa waved and dismounted, and it was in times like these that John Mark realized how much he missed Pa.

"You remember Jack from school? I was passing through on my way to Bowman to marry him and his fiancée and thought I'd stop by."

"It's always good to see you, Pa." John Mark embraced his father.

"It's good to see you too." His father took a seat next to John Mark on the porch in one of the wooden chairs.

John Mark leaned back and crossed his feet at his ankles. "How is Ma?"

"She's fine. Been extra busy lately with the sewing she's been taking in."

"And Charlotte? Caleb and Annie?"

"They're all fine too." Pa shook his head. "Cyrus Keller asked Charlotte to court him."

"Cyrus Keller? Pa, I'm not sure I like that idea."

"I know how protective you are of Charlotte, Son."

John Mark gazed out across the field. Protective, yes. And now very concerned. "I went to school with Cyrus. He's not worthy of Charlotte."

Pa said nothing for a few moments. While there were times John Mark didn't agree with his father, he always respected the fact that Pa took time to think, and likely pray, before opening his mouth. Something John Mark hoped he'd become adept at someday.

Finally, Pa spoke. "It has taken your ma and me some time to grow accustomed to Cyrus."

"But you've given Charlotte your blessing?" There he went again, speaking before he could think about it. "Pa..."

"I know. We have concerns as well. Your ma and I have been in constant prayer. You'll understand as a parent someday that some decisions are difficult."

John Mark recalled Cyrus from his last years in school in Willow Falls. The man was an impolite and overbearing cad if there ever was one. Maybe when John Mark returned home for a visit, he could talk some sense into his sister.

"I know you're concerned for your sister, and that's one of the things your ma and I love about you—your protective nature. I assure you that Charlotte and Cyrus have agreed to an extended courtship. It is my prayer that the Lord will make it clear whether or not Charlotte should marry him in that time."

"Is he in charge of the Keller Ranch yet?"

"His parents recently gave him several hundred acres of his own."

John Mark had never liked Cyrus and even less now that the man was courting his sister.

"Caleb and Annie are expecting another little one, and your ma is overjoyed at the thought of being a grandma again. She sure spoils the other three." Pa's eyes crinkled at the corners. "Of course, it is pretty special being a grandpa too."

The thought of being an uncle again brought a smile to John Mark's face. "Glad to hear they're doing well. I hope to visit Willow Falls again soon."

"How are things here?"

John Mark again stared out into the field where the annoying rooster had taken up the habit of running back and forth. "Reckon they're fine."

"Sounds to me like you might have a few thoughts on your mind."

It was something that weighed heavily, and John Mark would covet Pa's advice. "It's this woman in town named Hannah Bane. Her pa is an ill-tempered sort, a wicked drunkard who mistreats her." He thought of Miss Bane—her tattered clothing, worn boots, and the haunted expression in her eyes.

"It grieves me to hear of people like that."

John Mark gazed into the eyes so much like his own. Pa had a tender heart toward the less fortunate, something he'd emulated throughout John Mark's life. "I don't know what to do, Pa. We've arrested Harold Bane a time or two, sometimes just to sleep off the whiskey, other times because of fights in the saloon, and I think he's a ne'er-do-well and is in cahoots with some of the other men in town and their nefarious schemes, but..." his voice trailed. Would Miss Bane accept his offer to marry her? Should he tell Pa of his plans?

"One of the other things I love about you, Son, is your heart of compassion. You've always been that way. You love justice and you love to do what's right."

"I want to help her."

Pa nodded and bowed his head, likely seeking God's direction before responding to John Mark's statement. "Have you discussed your concerns with the reverend?"

"I have. He and his wife take meals to her sometimes, and I've also attempted to see if there's somewhere she might stay. But, Pa, Poplar Springs isn't like Willow Falls. This town has far fewer kind citizens and far more lawlessness. I've suggested she come to the sheriff's office for safety if there are no prisoners while she waits for her pa to stumble out of the saloon most nights of the week in a drunken stupor. I can't keep her safe while she's wandering the streets, but I can when she's in the sheriff's office. But that's only when I'm on duty and doing my rounds. I make sure I'm never there alone with her and do all I can to protect her reputation. When I'm off-duty, I make a trip to town and watch from afar to ensure she's safe. Other than that..."

Pa rested a reassuring hand on John Mark's shoulder. "Sounds like you're doing all you can."

"Not all I can. I also..." but he stopped short of telling Pa about his plan to challenge Harold to a card game in order to win Miss Bane's freedom. As gracious a man as Pa was, there were some things he ought not yet know.

Because Pa might try to talk John Mark out of his rescue mission.

And John Mark couldn't have that. Not when he was so close to liberating Miss Bane from her father.

"Yes?" Pa asked, interrupting John Mark's thoughts.

"I just want to do all I can."

They sat in silence for a few minutes. "Do you remember," asked Pa, "when you were a youngster and you rescued that baby bird that fell from its nest?"

John Mark remembered as if it were yesterday. The defenseless little robin he'd lifted in his hand, barely reaching it in time before the mangy cat who lurked nearby. He'd fed the bird, cared for it, and prayed for it. Most birds didn't survive without their mothers, but that one had, and when the time came, it flew away into the wild where it belonged. "Yes, I do."

"You did a mighty fine job rescuing and tending to that bird. Your ma and I were so proud of you."

"And Charlotte wanted to keep it for a pet."

Pa chuckled. "Yes, well, Charlotte had other plans for it, but God's plans were best. He allowed it to survive and return to the life He'd chosen for it." Pa paused. "I guess what I'm trying to say is that God has a plan for Miss Bane. He has a plan for her life. She's not like the bird where you can easily rescue her from the nest. But you can provide a watchful eye and food when possible, encourage the reverend and others in town to become more involved in helping her, and most importantly, pray for her. Pray that God will provide a way of escape from her pa."

What would Pa say if he knew *John Mark* would be the one rescuing Miss Bane from the nest? Would he agree it was a wise choice? Or tell John Mark to make alternative plans?

"The verse in Proverbs comes to mind," Pa continued. "*Trust in the Lord with all thine heart; and lean not unto thine own understanding. In all thy ways acknowledge him, and he shall direct thy paths.'* Seek and submit to Him your plans in this situation and He will guide you."

If John Mark won the card game, would God guide him in marriage if that's what Miss Bane chose? Would He lead her toward accepting John Mark's proposal? Would He guide John Mark in finding somewhere else for her to live if she didn't choose to marry him? Would he be making the right decision if Miss Bane did choose marriage?

"I just want to do the right thing," John Mark said, more to himself than to Pa.

"Of course you do, Son, and the Lord knows that, and He knows how much you care for others. He's the one who created that benevolent heart within you."

"But sometimes I want to give Harold Bane a taste of what it's like to be his daughter. I'm sorry, Pa, but I do want to seek revenge on him for Miss Bane's sake sometimes."

Pa's voice held neither condemnation nor judgment when he spoke. "We've all struggled with the temptation to make things right and to take revenge into our own hands, but it's not the way of the Lord. Revenge is His."

"I know."

"Tell me, does Miss Bane know the Lord?"

John Mark recalled seeing her sitting by herself in the back pew at church, her head buried in her Bible. Her mouth moving to the words of the hymn, even though he couldn't hear her. Her tenderness toward Ambrose.

"I believe so." Did Miss Bane know the Lord loved her and cared for her? That He had a plan for *her* life?

"I best be on my way to make it to Bowman before nightfall, but I do want to pray for you and for Miss Bane. Lord, we lift up this matter to You. Please give John Mark wisdom. Direct his paths. Prompt him to lean on you in the matter of helping Miss Bane. And, Lord, we lift Miss Bane up to You and ask for Your protection against her father and for You to wrap Your peace and love around her. We know Your plans are not our plans and we pray for Your will to be done in this matter."

A tug at John Mark's heart reminded him of the very fact that, depending on the outcome of tomorrow night's card game, God might use him to rescue Hannah Bane and give her a chance at a new life.

No sooner had John Mark's pa left when Silas, Nowell, and Pritchard arrived at the house.

In the days since John Mark moved to Willow Falls, he'd been fortunate to find friends in Silas and Nowell whom Winslow indicated had upstanding character. John Mark was still contemplating Pritchard's integrity.

According to Winslow, Silas and Nowell had been friends for years and both hailed from Texas. Tall, wiry, and a sure shot, Nowell would make an exceptional deputy. Silas was muscular with broad shoulders and thick wrists. He'd done a stint on the wrong side of the law, became a Christian a few years ago, turned his life around, and never looked back. He, too, would make an excellent deputy.

But as of yet, Winslow hadn't been able to convince either of them that the life as a lawman was their calling. Both had ranches to operate, and that was their first priority.

And then there was Pritchard. A friendly fellow with what Winslow termed a "generous heart." John Mark still didn't know what to think of a man who spent a considerable amount of time in jail, but was always released. Always without a hearing before a judge.

"We heard you were planning a visit to the saloon tomorrow," Nowell said, walking toward John Mark. "I never thought I'd see the day."

News traveled fast in Poplar Springs. "Do I have you to thank for sharing that piece of information, Pritchard?"

Pritchard's eyes flickered with suspicion. "Can't say as I let on in an obvious way, but..."

Nowell chuckled. "There's nothing about you that ain't obvious."

"The reason we're here is because we aim, with your permission of course, to be there tomorrow in case anyone gives you any guff." Silas's powerful presence would intimidate anyone. He was a valuable one to have on your side.

"I think it's admirable of you, J.M., for helping that Hannah Bane woman like this," said Pritchard.

"Peculiar way to find a wife, but I tend to agree," said Silas. "Women aren't too plentiful in these parts. Anyhow, after Pritchard told us, we figured Harold might go back on his word. Four is better than one when it comes to dealing with Bane and his cronies."

John Mark grinned. What did he do to deserve such loyal friends? Ones he'd not known for long at that. "Say, Pritchard, when did you get released from jail?"

"Winslow liberated me from the confines of that dank cell this morning when he came on duty. Said I really shouldn't even be there after all. We had us a long talk, and sure enough, I was found innocent and released."

As if Winslow could make such a determination.

John Mark didn't mention the fact that Pritchard had been caught in the act of once again stealing food from Roessler's Dry Goods. "Well, I'm much obliged for your loyalty. All three of you."

Nowell slapped him on the back. "That's what friends are for. But have you given any thought as to what you're getting into? You don't even know Miss Bane. She's comely and all, but...Pritchard here says if you win the game, you'll have Harold's blessing to marry his daughter."

"Know her well enough to know she needs to escape from her pa. Besides, once I win her freedom, she can do as she pleases. There's nothing that says she has to marry me."

Concern rippled through John Mark. Would he win against Harold?

"Sounds fair enough to me and I'm sure she'll be much appreciative," Silas added.

Pritchard kicked at a pebble on the ground. "Say, J.M., I was meaning to ask you the other night if you could put in a good word for me to Miss Pearson. Reckon it would help my credibility to have the deputy sing my praises."

"Sing your praises?" Silas scowled. "You're a fine fellow and all, but you aren't worthy of a woman like Ina Pearson."

Pritchard slugged Silas in the arm, a hit that barely budged Silas's muscular physique. "I'm more than worthy. Just underappreciated is all."

The men howled with laughter at Pritchard's declaration.

"Don't know if I can put in much of a good word," said John Mark. "I don't often eat at the restaurant. The Pearson boys deliver my supper each evening I'm on duty."

"Next time you see her or Mr. Pearson, would you let them know what an upstanding young man I am?' Pritchard puffed out his puny chest.

Nowell shook his head. "Upstanding? You're just lucky Winslow lets you go every time you're caught. On a more serious note, things are getting worse with the thievery. I lost several head of cattle last week."

Nowell's comment troubled John Mark although he and Winslow had made progress on investigating the matter. "I've heard about the thievery and also some mumblings about people having to pay to maintain their safety."

"I've heard that too," said Silas. "My hunch is Roessler is behind it."

Pritchard shook his head. "Not a hunch. It's the truth. That man's as crooked as they come."

John Mark knew he and Winslow would have to prove Roessler was involved in the rampant crimes that occurred in Poplar Springs. But the mayor was a powerful man with many friends and even more loyal followers.

Chapter Nine

HANNAH TOOK A SEAT on the bench and thought of her prayer once again that God would somehow rescue her from having to reside with Pa. If she could find a job, she could save money and travel to somewhere else and start over.

Somewhere where no one knew her.

A fresh start was the dream of her heart and she desired it so badly at times she could focus on little else.

But who would hire her? She'd tried nearly every business in Poplar Springs with the exception of the brothel and the saloons, and she wasn't yet desperate enough to seek employment at those types of establishments.

Hannah knew God was real. Knew what Jesus had done for her. Knew He heard her prayers. She just wasn't sure why He deemed hers unanswerable.

Oslo Dunn strutted toward her and stopped when he reached the bench. He leered as usual, his dark, close-set eyes causing nausea to rise in her throat.

Hannah gulped several shallow breaths of air, her heart pounding.

He plopped his rotund self on the bench beside her, the stink of whiskey, body odor, and tobacco mingling and emanating from him. Hannah stiffened, scooted as far as she could to the edge of the bench, and angled herself back, attempting to put more space between them.

Oslo tugged at his bushy beard and chortled a wicked and throaty laugh that matched his evil persona. He opened his mouth to say something, then closed it, apparently changing his mind, and instead reached up and ran a rough thumb across her cheek. An evil smirk, highlighting several missing teeth, covered his bearded face.

Hannah held her breath and did her best to display the confidence she didn't possess. She looked him in the eye praying there would never be a time when he confronted her in a desolate location. For what would she do then?

Passersby gave no indication they saw or were troubled by the happenings.

"Mr. Dunn?" A familiar voice from behind Hannah addressed the man.

"Whatcha want, Deputy?"

"Time for you to move on and leave Miss Bane alone."

Hannah released the breath she'd been holding.

"Ain't doin' nothin' wrong, Deputy." Oslo's eyes narrowed.

Deputy Eliason walked around to where Oslo Dunn sat. "Miss Bane, is everything all right?"

She nodded mutely.

Oslo stood, nearly butting his chest against Deputy Eliason's. "You don't scare me none."

"Never was my intention to scare you. Just to keep the law."

They stood chest to chest, the tension mounting as the seconds ticked by. Deputy Eliason was at least a foot taller than Oslo and a foot narrower. She watched his hand rest on his revolver. She witnessed a shootout once on the main street in town. One man died that day. She offered a prayer for the Lord to keep the deputy safe.

"I'll be going now." Oslo took a step backwards while maintaining his gaze on the deputy. When he was out of sight, Deputy Eliason turned toward her.

"Miss Bane, staying out here when it's nearly dark isn't safe."

They'd had this conversation before, but she appreciated his concern. And more than that, she appreciated his willingness to come to her aid against Oslo Dunn. Eyes full of compassion connected with hers and there was a sudden, peculiar fluttering in her belly. She'd never known a man to be a honorable and a gentleman. But Deputy Eliason was both.

And handsome too.

But she pushed the thought aside. Someone as dapper as Deputy Eliason would never take an interest in the likes of her.

No, she'd never met anyone like the deputy who stood before her. A man inclined to defend her against the ilk of Poplar Springs. A man who had no idea he was her hero.

John Mark leafed through the wanted posters on his desk. A notorious gang wanted for train robberies in the southern part of the state. Three other men wanted, one for horse thieving, one for cattle rustling, and the other for fraud. Detailed descriptions ranged from false teeth and sallow coloring, to short necks and stooped shoulders. From dark complexions, to droopy mustaches and plentiful graying chin whiskers. There were rewards for most, some of which could make a man temporarily wealthy.

Frank and Hank Maloney shuffled in, an animated feud in progress. "Not the way I 'member it," snarled Frank. "We'll have the deputy here settle the matter once and for all."

John Mark could sense the beginnings of a headache. While the twins amused him, they could also be a persistent and bothersome duo.

"Deputy, we have something for you to unriddle." Hank slammed a tin cup on John Mark's desk.

Frank shook his head. "Ain't nothing to unriddle. More like deal harshly with a dishonest and double-crossing criminal."

"I ain't no criminal, Frank. Just 'cause you remember somethin' differently that I do don't make me no criminal."

John Mark stood and squared his shoulders. He ought to be grateful he only had to deal with resolving yet another dispute between the brothers rather than assist in apprehending a trio of bank robbers, as was the case yesterday after his meeting with Pritchard, Silas, and Nowell. "Gentlemen, what seems to be the problem?"

"See, I told you he'd understand." Hank tossed his brother a smug grin.

"Deputy, once upon a time back in Missoura, our parents left us some possessions after they up and died.

Hank here got Ma's prize frying pan. Still using it to this day. I got this here cup. It was Pa's."

"And you don't reap the rewards of the frying pan?" Hank shook a narrow fist at his brother. "Seems prit near every day you have some fried eggs. That was for the both of us. The tin cup was left to *just* me. And let me be the first to say you by far eat enough for the two of us."

John Mark took a deep breath as he listened to the brothers argue. Hank with his shiny bald head and Frank with his mop of short, wiry gray hair, were as different as brothers could be. He lifted the tin cup. Apparently it had sentimental value because the mercantile offered such cups for a reasonable price.

Another idea entered his mind. "Say, gentlemen, I have the perfect resolution."

"You don't say?" Hank leaned toward him. "See, Frank, it was a grand idea to come to the sheriff's office and have this resolved. Told you so."

"Not so fast. We need to hear what he has to say first. Besides, Pa left me that cup since I'm the eldest."

"There's always been debate on whose the eldest and you know that. Ma said I was born first and Pa said you were born first."

"Your parents taught you well the art of arguing," muttered John Mark.

"What was that?" Frank asked.

"Yeah, Frank don't hear as well as he use to."

That commenced into another argument about Frank needing a hearing trumpet. John Mark held up his hand. "Gentlemen, I can't resolve this matter if you continue with your quarreling."

The men hushed, but John Mark could see it took great effort to remain silent. "How old are you two?" he asked.

"I'm sixty four and he's almost sixty four," Hank chortled.

"You're a clodhopper, Hank. You know we're both the same age."

John Mark again held up his hand before that could cause another squabble. "Now, here's what we'll do. I want you both to go to the smithy and have him slice this tin cup in half. Give one half to Frank and the other to Hank. There. Problem solved."

This was the first time John Mark had seen them in any form of agreement, as their mouths both hung open in shock. They looked at each other, then at John Mark, then back to each other. "Reckon that's not such a grand idea," said Hank. "You go ahead and have the tin cup, Frank. I'll take the fryin' pan."

"But you'll share the fryin' pan, right?" Frank asked.

"If you'll share the tin cup."

The two men shook on the matter. "You're a wise one, Deputy. Guess that's what happens when you're a preacher's son. Matter of fact, that sounds like something in the Bible we once read. Anyhow, thank you for resolving this matter."

If only everything could be that easy to resolve.

What if John Mark hadn't been there yesterday when Oslo Dunn made improper advances toward Miss Bane? He might not be the next time. And one day, Oslo might not take "no" for an answer.

Frank and Hank were in agreeable conversation when they bid him farewell and left the sheriff's office.

Not a moment later, Ambrose and Grumbles traipsed in, followed by a harried Hannah Bane.

Concern enveloped him.

Ambrose was chatting about something, but John Mark's focus was on Miss Bane. She stood in front of his desk, arms wrapped around herself and looking over her shoulder out the window.

Something was amiss.

He rose and veered around his desk to stand in front of her.

"My deputy here and me was wondering how many people you've put in jail today. Have there been any gunfights? Did the good guys win?" Ambrose's cowboy hat was slung over one eye and he'd pinned a homemade paper star on his plaid shirt.

John Mark's uneasiness of seeing Miss Bane rush into the sheriff's office in a nervous state was briefly interrupted by Ambrose's barrage of questions. "No gunfights today," he said, resting a hand on the young boy's shoulder. "Would you and Grumbles mind giving me a minute? I need to speak with Miss Bane."

Ambrose whipped his head around to see Miss Bane, causing his oversized hat to fall down over the other eye as well. He shoved it up with his hand. "All right. I'll just wait over here by the jail." He tugged on Grumbles's leash and stood a few feet away.

"Can I help you, Miss Bane?"

She peered at him warily, her eyes wide. "I need to tell you something." Her voice was barely above a whisper.

"Did someone hurt you?"

Miss Bane shook her head. "No."

He let out a release of breath and offered a prayer of gratitude. "You're safe here to tell me whatever needs to be said."

Hannah Bane glanced over at Ambrose, whose attention was solely on Grumbles and his intermittent snorts as Ambrose relayed some silly story to the pig. She then refocused her gaze on John Mark. "It's something I overheard." Her eyes strayed to the window towards a passerby.

Why was she so afraid? "You overheard something?"

"Pa can't know I talked to you."

John Mark and Winslow had long suspected Harold Bane was involved in some immoral activities, along with several other men in Poplar Springs. But he didn't let on. "He won't."

Miss Bane blinked rapidly. Did she believe him?

"Did you overhear your pa talking?"

She nodded. "Yes. He, Mander, and Yin were planning to pay a visit to Mr. Daly and threaten him if he doesn't do their bidding." She peered back at Ambrose, who paid her no mind, but was busily pretending to "lock up" an outlaw in the cell. Miss Bane lowered her voice. "It would seem they are doing the mayor's bidding in blackmailing Mr. Daly into paying money to be left alone. They paid a visit to him."

John Mark regularly heard murmurings about Mayor Roessler, and Silas, Nowell, and Pritchard confirmed as much yesterday. Sheriff Winslow spoke a few times about his concerns about the mayor's "activities," although no one yet had been able to prove anything. And Winslow had told John Mark they weren't sharing their information with Deputy Gaston. Extortion, blackmailing, cattle rustling, assault, and even murder were suspected of the man who claimed to care about the town he presided over.

With regards to Deputy Gaston...was that the reason Winslow so often assigned the other deputy to work in one of the other towns in the county?

"I just thought you should know."

Her voice brought him back to the conversation. She stood within arm's length of him, still obviously afraid, likely of who might find out that she'd overheard. "Did anyone notice you?"

"No. But these men are ruthless." She avoided his eye. Was she ashamed that her own pa would be involved in such a scheme?

Blackmailing wasn't anywhere near as serious an offense as mistreating your daughter. The distress in her eyes and her pale face indicated she feared more than just her father. And rightfully so. Her courage caused him to respect her even more than he already did. "Miss Bane, thank you for coming in today. I assure you that this information will remain confidential. I will tell the sheriff about these men blackmailing Daly, but I won't say who told me."

For the first time since she entered the sheriff's office, Miss Bane's shoulders softened and her arms loosened and eventually fell to her sides. "Thank you, Deputy."

"You did a brave thing today by bringing this to my attention. Hopefully someday, Poplar Springs will be a safer place to live."

"It'll never be safe. It's full of lawlessness and corruption."

If only the words she spoke were false. If only John Mark could change things in Poplar Springs for people such as Miss Bane. To a place like Willow Falls. And while the town he loved wasn't perfect and still struggled with criminal activity from time to time, under Sheriff Townsend's watch, the town and the entire county was much safer than Poplar Springs.

"Reckon I aim to make it my goal that Poplar Springs is someday a friendly place where criminal misdeeds are the rarity."

Miss Bane offered a weak smile. "That's a fine way of looking at things, but for as long as I've lived here, Poplar Springs has been a rough place where most folks live out of necessity, rather than their choosing."

John Mark thought of his own journey to the town so opposite from Willow Falls. He never would have chosen to reside here were it not for the deputy position. Miss Bane obviously had no choice in where she resided. But if he won tonight, and he prayed he would, she *would* have an option on where to live.

Tonight. Only mere hours away.

And if he didn't win...

"Deputy Eliason? Grumbles and me was wonderin' if it's time for the noonday meal yet." Ambrose rubbed his stomach. "I'm what Grandpa calls 'a hungry young'un.'"

Miss Bane's smile widened. "He's such an adorable pig. What made you decide to name him Grumbles?"

"It's because when he oinks, it sounds like he's grumbling, or at least that's what Grandpa says." Ambrose bent down and patted the pig on the head. "His full name is Deputy Grumbles. Me and him solve all kinds of crimes in Poplar Springs. Say, Deputy Eliason, do you have any food? I sure am hungry."

John Mark could have figured the young boy would be hungry. "As a matter of fact, I do." He strolled over to his desk and removed a sandwich from the top drawer. Hopefully Ambrose was hungry enough that he wouldn't realize it wasn't the best tasting, given John Mark forgot to stop at the mercantile for a few necessities yesterday.

The boy unwrapped the sandwich, blessed the food, and scarfed three-fourths of it. "That sure was tasty, Deputy Eliason. Do you have another one?" He paused and veered his attention to Miss Bane. "Oops, where are my manners? Would you like some, ma'am?" He held out the last bit of his meal.

Miss Bane's face brightened. "Thank you, but..."

Ambrose would have none of her excuses. He transferred the meager portion of sandwich from his grubby hands into hers.

The tenderness in the woman's face impressed upon John Mark as he watched the interaction between the two. "Thank you kindly. I don't mind if I do."

Ambrose's delighted expression, combined with a clapping of his hands and a little boy giggle, caused Miss Bane to laugh as well. She placed the two bites into her mouth, likely herself attempting not to scarf down the scant portion.

And John Mark wished he'd brought four sandwiches instead of the one.

"Quite scrumptious, thank you, Ambrose. You are a kind and thoughtful young man."

Ambrose giggled again, jelly smeared on one cheek. "You're welcome, Miss Hannah. Say, Deputy Eliason, are you sure you don't have more food?"

"I'm sorry, Ambrose, that's the only sandwich I have. But I think I might manage to find a penny in my pocket for a peppermint stick at the mercantile."

Ambrose's face lit up. "Really? Did you hear that, Grumbles?"

John Mark handed him the penny and Ambrose bounded out the door.

A wistful expression crossed Miss Bane's face, and a thought entered John Mark's mind. What if she could work for Ambrose's ailing grandpa and take care of the both of them?

But as soon as it entered his mind, John Mark brushed it aside. While Miss Bane could work for room and board, there would be no way for Mr. Miller to feed another mouth. He and Ambrose were just scraping by.

If John Mark did win Miss Bane's freedom from her pa, would she remain in Poplar Springs?

Chapter Ten

THAT EVENING ON THE bench outside the saloon, Hannah prayed no less than thirty times that Oslo Dunn would leave her be.

She thought of the day's events. While he hadn't said as much, Hannah figured Deputy Eliason already knew about Pa's nefarious activities and that he worked for Mayor Roessler. And while Hannah had suspected for some time that Pa's "work" for the mayor was of an unscrupulous nature, she'd never felt compelled to confide in anyone until now.

For some reason, she trusted the deputy.

Trepidation overwhelmed her at telling him about what she'd overheard, but knew he'd be the best of the three lawmen due to his apparent upstanding character. Sheriff Winslow was polite, although rather brusque. Something about Deputy Gaston caused suspicion.

Hannah's concerns had been many. Would Deputy Eliason believe her? Would someone walk by and hear as she told him? Would there be retaliation from Pa, the mayor, or the other men if they discovered what she'd done?

She often wondered how Pa had enough money to drink whiskey and gamble several nights a week. He didn't win often, so receiving an income from playing cards was not a likely scenario. Instead, he lost regularly and their meager belongings had begun to disappear, probably to pay debts. First the two extra horses, including the one Hannah rode a time or two when she was younger. Then the plow. Then Ma's brooch. That had been the most painful. She'd hoped to always have that as a reminder, along with Ma's Bible. Several chickens and the milk cow were soon gone from their farm.

Hannah suspected Pa would wager her if he could.

When she'd walked home earlier that day, Pa, thankfully, was nowhere to be found. If he had been, she was armed with several excuses since Pa rarely allowed her to go to town. When she drove him home after a night at the saloon was the only time she used the wagon. To attend church while Pa was still sleeping off his alcohol was the only time she rode one of the horses.

Her stomach growled. The piece of sandwich from Ambrose earlier today was hardly enough to sustain her. The little boy had won her heart in a short amount of time with his charismatic personality and generous nature. He obviously admired Deputy Eliason.

Hannah's thoughts settled on the lawman. He was considerate of and patient with Ambrose and would make a devoted father someday.

Unlike her own pa.

Someone pounded on the keys of the saloon's piano to the tune of *Oh! Susanna*, a tune Hannah knew by heart. Men hustled past her, most ignoring her. A woman from the brothel with her immodest, cleavage-bearing dress, painted face, and a bottle of whiskey in one hand, propositioned a heavyset bald man.

Hannah shivered. *Lord, please don't let that be what I must become. Please let there be an alternative to living with Pa...please rescue me.* It was the same prayer she prayed every night she sat outside the saloon. Surely the One who created the world from nothing and who took the sins upon Himself could perform a miracle and deliver her from her circumstances.

Surely she'd not have to succumb to the same dreadful existence as some of the other women in town.

In less than four months, winter would be upon them and Pa would frequent the saloon less often. He detested cold weather. But that hadn't stopped him from coming into town about once a week to imbibe.

She wasn't sure which was worse. Coming to town nearly every night during the week for Pa's habit or having no escape when confined with him at home for hours on end.

Deputy Eliason, Mr. Pritchard, and two other men strolled past. Mr. Pritchard nodded. Deputy Eliason's eyes briefly met hers, and he touched the brim of his hat. He didn't appear to be on duty tonight, especially since she'd seen the crass Deputy Gaston near the dry goods store earlier.

She watched the direction in which they ambled. Deputy Eliason cast her another glance. Was he concerned she was on the bench by her lonesome once again? She knew he worried about her and she appreciated his concern.

When all four of them enter the saloon, her heart fell. She didn't know the two strangers, and while Mr. Pritchard had been so generous in bringing her and Pa food many times over the past several months, she wasn't too surprised he would enter a saloon. Perhaps because most men in town did. However, why would Deputy Eliason patronize such a place?

Hannah thought he was of moral character. Religious even, since she'd seen him in church. That he was different. Somehow set apart from the rest of the men in Poplar Springs.

But he was no different at all.

The profound disappointment caught her unaware. Would Deputy Eliason imbibe like her father always did? Emerge drunk and mean? Hit those he supposedly loved as Pa quite often did?

While she knew so little about the deputy, she had both assumed and hoped he was a man of honor and nothing like her pa.

Hannah's crestfallen expression was nearly his undoing. Why couldn't she have been visiting the mercantile or Pearson's Restaurant when he entered the saloon? What must she think? Did she assume him a drunkard like her pa?

"Ready for this?" Pritchard asked, jolting John Mark from his thoughts.

"I think so."

"Just remember what I taught you."

John Mark hoped he could recall Pritchard's lesson, especially as the tension mounted. So much depended on him and the first and only card game he would ever play.

Hannah's future depended on his ability to win.

Silas scanned the saloon, a revolver on his hip, and Nowell flanked John Mark on the other side, at the ready should the need arise. If John Mark could rely on the loyalty of anyone, he could depend on Silas and Nowell.

"Well, well. You done showed up." Oslo's toothless sneer and confident swagger reminded John Mark of Oslo's behavior the other night with Miss Bane and anger flooded his veins. He clenched his fists at his sides, fighting his irritation. He needed to temper himself and remain calm and composed.

This might be the only way to win Hannah Bane's freedom.

Oslo shoved him on the shoulder, a move likely intended to intimidate him, but it had no such effect. For one, John Mark was stronger. For two, sober.

Harold Bane slouched at one of the tables, a scowl on his narrow, weathered face. Miss Bane must have gotten her looks from her ma, because besides the tall frame and pale green eyes, she looked nothing like her pa. His eyes were harsh and close-set unlike Miss Bane's, which were warm and evenly-spaced.

John Mark dismissed the disturbing thought that he'd noticed her eyes and focused on the situation in which he'd found himself. A vile and putrid odor consisting of whiskey, unwashed bodies, and a hint of manure overwhelmed the dim room. Somewhere nearby a woman had taken to crooning an off-key song. An unknown older man in a dingy gray shirt puffed on a cigar, making a swirly circle float on the already-hazy air.

"'Bout time you showed up. Thought you was gonna be a yellow-livered coward." Harold squinted and rubbed his scruffy, graying beard and what appeared to be a food particle flicked onto the table. Red Beard, who lounged next to him, sniggered.

John Mark had never been called a coward and he didn't ever intend to be known as one. He took a seat across from Harold. "Just to reiterate..." he began. "If I win, I have your blessing to marry Miss Bane and I'll also pay Oslo fifteen dollars to cover your gambling debt."

Oslo took a step forward and broadened his stance. "And your hat."

"Yes, and my hat." *Sorry, Ma and Pa.*

"Ain't no one dumber than you. If you win, you still agree to pay my debt and give up your hat? What a ninny," chortled Harold, a whiff of his foul breath reaching John Mark from across the table.

John Mark didn't bother to argue. If it took him paying Harold's debt and relinquishing one of his most prized possessions, so be it.

"What're you two doin' here, Silas and Nowell? Ain't no one invited the neither of you." Harold spat the words, a wad of phlegm landing on Red Beard's hairy arm.

Silas pulled out the chair directly beside John Mark and took a seat while Pritchard and Nowell remained standing.

Several other men crowded around and Oslo took the seat on the other side of Harold, filling the last remaining seat at the table.

"Bring me another drink," Harold bellowed and thumped the table with a puny fist.

A saloon girl slinked up next to him and handed him a bottle of whiskey. "And how much do you win when you defeat the deputy?" She fluttered her eyelashes at him, no doubt possessing an ulterior motive.

A low rumbling tone rose in Harold's throat. "Yeah, what do I win?"

"You get to keep Hannah," offered Oslo.

Her name, mentioned as an afterthought and as though she was a possession, caused a fresh swell of anger to rise within John Mark. How could anyone view her as a possession or an afterthought? Or view any woman in that manner? He'd prayed often throughout the night last night that God would hold his tongue, even in the midst of defending those who could not defend themselves.

Like Hannah Bane.

"Can I get *you* something to drink, sweetie?" a saloon girl asked.

"No, thank you."

"What? No whiskey for the preacher's boy?" Red Beard taunted, his uneven eyes casting a mocking glare.

John Mark had never touched the stuff and never would. From his peripheral, he noticed his three friends passing on accepting whiskey as well. They would all need their wits about them if things should turn unruly.

Harold guzzled his drink and asked for another before announcing he was ready for the game to begin. John Mark thanked God for his own clarity of mind.

"Hey, who's gonna deal?" Harold asked, his speech already slurred.

"How 'bout Pritchard?" Oslo asked. "You ain't no friend of the law so you're impartial."

Red Beard guffawed and held a dirty hand to his ample stomach. "Yeah, he ain't no friend of the law. Done spent more time in a jail cell in one week than I have in a year."

John Mark attempted to conceal his relief at their choice of a dealer.

"Sure," said Pritchard, stepping forward and tucking his thumbs beneath his suspender straps. "I'll do it."

"Figured you would. Didn't you used to do it all the time?"

Pritchard ignored Red Beard's remark and whistled as he shuffled the cards. Typical Pritchard. If he was nervous, he never showed it.

"Where ya been lately anyhow?" Oslo eyed Pritchard, who shuffled a deck of cards with skill.

Pritchard's face beamed. "In jail. Good to be out today to watch this game. Heard stakes were high."

"You done heard right," garbled Harold.

"I gots me a question," Red Beard said. "What if the preacher's boy here don't marry Hannah? Can I have her as my own wife?"

John Mark narrowed his eyes at the man who'd done more time in the Poplar Springs jail than anyone in town as far as John Mark knew. Even Pritchard, despite Red

Beard's argument to the contrary. Most oftentimes it was due to assault or saloon brawls.

"I'll be marrying her," John Mark said, his voice sounding more confident than he felt.

"Let's say if he don't marry her tomorrow, he don't marry her at all. Then you can have my blessing to marry her." Harold nodded toward Red Beard.

"Wait..." began John Mark, then thought better of it.

Pritchard shuffled the deck of cards one more time. "Are we ready, gentlemen?" Without waiting for a reply, he dealt the cards. "There'll be no cheating under my watch," he said, to which Oslo snickered.

"Your watch? You know you got a reputation in these parts for being less than honest. But I also know you ain't no half-wit." A few of the men murmured their thoughts of agreement to Red Beard's words.

"No, I'm not a half-wit," agreed Pritchard.

"But he's a cheater? And he's dealin'?" Harold sat up straighter in his chair only to slump again.

John Mark held his breath. If Pritchard dealt the cards, he had a chance of winning because he knew Pritchard *would be* honest in this situation. Whatever Pritchard's past consisted of, he was attempting to change. If someone else shuffled and dealt, John Mark's chances of victory declined significantly.

As they began to play, John Mark searched his memory for Pritchard's tips. The game continued and a considerable crowd had gathered around the table. Many were placing bets of their own that Harold would win.

Sweat trickled down John Mark's back. Never had he imagined he'd spend time in a saloon. Never had he desired to. The only time he darkened the door of such a place was to settle a dispute or arrest someone, although most arrests occurred in front of the saloon on the boardwalk or in the middle of the street.

Never had he imagined he'd play cards. It went against everything he believed in. *Lord, please forgive me.*

Yet here he sat, playing a game he'd just learned and attempting to win the blessing to marry a woman he barely knew.

Charlotte would call him an addlebrained ninnyhammer. He could even hear her say it.

His heart thumped in his chest a lot faster than it ought, and John Mark did his best to focus on the game. If Harold won, someone else—someone like Oslo Dunn or Red Beard—could potentially try their hand at winning against Harold. An easy feat for the experienced gambler, especially one who aspired to cheating.

Lord, reckon this is the oddest request I've ever made, but can you please let me win?

Pa always said you could bring any concern to the Lord, big or small. But could you bring a concern such as this to Him?

Finally, after what seemed a lifetime in the shadowy confines of filth known as the saloon, John Mark slammed down the winning hand.

The game was over.

He let out a deep breath and thanked God for His providence, while Harold released a stream of oaths that burned John Mark's ears.

Silas grabbed John Mark's arm and raised it above his head. "Men, we have ourselves a winner!"

Oslo Dunn plucked John Mark's hat from his head and placed it on his own. Harold argued about who the fifteen dollars went to, and John Mark just wanted to get out of the saloon without any trouble and take Miss Bane somewhere safe.

"Remember," said Red Beard. "You gotta marry her tomorrow or I get Harold's blessing to make her my own wife."

The cavalier theft of Miss Bane's choices sickened John Mark. Bile rose in his throat at the thought that such a tender and innocent woman might be forced to marry someone as calloused as Red Beard.

The first thing he would ask her when he retrieved her from the bench in front of the saloon was whether or not she wished to marry him. The choice was hers and hers alone. He would make sure she had other options if she declined his offer to wed her.

But John Mark would do everything in his power to make sure she didn't ever have to marry the likes of Red Beard, Oslo Dunn, or any other of the ilk so prevalent in the town he called home.

Hannah heard loud cheers in the saloon and she folded her arms across her chest. The night dragged on. Pearson's Restaurant had already closed, as had the mercantile. Alone on the bench, she hoped Pa would finish his gambling soon so she could take him home.

Deputy Eliason, Mr. Pritchard, and the two other men emerged from the saloon sometime later. The deputy was no longer wearing his hat and a strained expression covered his face. Had he lost a lot of money due to gambling and drinking? If so, it would be a well-deserved comeuppance. Pa was constantly losing the meager amount of money and possessions they had because of his penchant for sinful behavior at the saloon.

She was surprised he hadn't lost their farm yet. What would he gamble away next? Her?

The thought caused her to tremble.

Pa would never do that. Would he?

Deputy Eliason and his friends neared her. "Miss Bane?" he asked.

"Yes?" Had Pa finally succumbed to his alcohol? Had there been a brawl with her father being the loser?

"I...uh..." The deputy shifted his feet. She'd never seen him nervous before. Always self-assured, confident, and perhaps even arrogant, but not nervous.

"Is it my pa?"

Mr. Pritchard raised a brow. "Want me to tell her, J.M.?"

J.M.?

The deputy shook his head, his lips pressed slightly together and a troubled expression in his eyes. Had something happened to Pa? The thought caused a mixture of emotions. She picked at a thread on her dress.

"Miss Bane," Deputy Eliason's voice interrupted her concerns.

Her gaze settled on him. He was a handsome man and seemingly kind, although the fact he was in the saloon disturbed her greatly. His integrity had slipped a notch in her eyes.

Hannah's thoughts returned to her pa. "Yes?"

"Miss Bane, I challenged your pa in a card game and...reckon I won."

So he did gamble. Hannah's shoulders slumped and she broke eye contact as disappointment nagged at her. She swallowed hard. Why had she thought him to be an upstanding and God-fearing man? But then he *had* entered the saloon. She should have been prepared for his answer. "All right," Hannah said, her voice sounding monotone to her ears. Why was he telling her this?

Two of the men excused themselves, leaving only Deputy Eliason and Mr. Pritchard.

"Reckon what I'm about to say might not be easy to hear."

Hannah watched Mr. Pritchard nudge him. "You can do it, J.M."

Deputy Eliason took a deep breath and straightened his posture. "Hannah Bane, will you marry me?"

CHAPTER ELEVEN

HAD HANNAH HEARD HIM correctly? Likely her brain was discombobulated from waiting on the bench for such a lengthy time. Weariness engulfed her.

Why would someone like Deputy Eliason ask her to marry him? Either she needed a hearing trumpet to better comprehend his words or she desperately needed some shut-eye.

Maybe both.

"Begging your pardon?" she asked. Marry a man she thought to be upstanding, but now realized he was little better than her pa and engaged in gambling and alcohol?

No, thank you.

Mr. Pritchard smirked. "Perhaps we should start at the beginning. J.M. here won your freedom."

"Won my freedom?"

Even in the shadowy night, Hannah could see Mr. Pritchard's full grin, which covered the entirety of his oval face. "As sure as the sun comes up each morning."

Several men emerged from the saloon, staggering in their drunkenness, their loud voices competing against the rambunctious noises of the saloon. One man fell on the ground and his friends moved him toward the building and propped him against it.

"Perhaps we could discuss this matter as we walk to Pearson's Restaurant," suggested Deputy Eliason.

"They're closed." It was nearing ten o'clock, two hours after the last meal was served. "Besides, I need to wait for my pa." Even as she mentioned it, she dreaded the dismal tradition of carting her father home each evening in his drunken stupor.

Mr. Pritchard shrugged. "If you marry J.M. tomorrow, you'll never have to go home to your pa's house again."

Why would she marry Deputy Eliason? And why would he ask her to do so? What did it mean he won her freedom? She squinted. "Begging your pardon, Mr. Pritchard?"

"You two know each other?" A confused expression crossed Deputy Eliason's face.

Mr. Pritchard chuckled. "Been out to visit Miss Bane and her pa a time or two."

"You never made mention of that." Deputy Eliason shrugged. "The choice is entirely up to you, Miss Bane. I won your freedom from living with your pa tonight when I won the card game. But you're free to do as you wish. Either way, you no longer have to return home."

Hannah sucked in a breath. While the news of never having to return home was an answer to prayer, it also caused her considerable consternation. For where would she go? Unless she married a man she barely knew.

Mr. Pritchard whispered something inaudible to Deputy Eliason and he nodded.

Pa stumbled from the saloon, assisted by Oslo Dunn on one side and Red Beard on the other. Pa's arms were stretched between the two of them, his feet intermittently dragging on the ground. "Get in the wagon, Hannah Bane," Pa bellowed, his speech slurred and his head lolling.

"Mr. Bane, I believe I won your blessing to marry Miss Bane fair and square," said Deputy Eliason.

Pa's eyes hardened. "Not if she don't wanna marry your sorry self."

"I'll marry him," Hannah squeaked, uttering the words before her mind had a chance to fully ponder them.

"By tomorrow," Red Beard shot John Mark a nasty glare. "Or..."

Hannah stood, her heart pounding in her ears.

"Don't be thinkin' you'll get any of your belongings. You leave with him, you leave forever and don't you never come back. Ain't nothing at the house is yours no more." Pa hawked and spat hitting Red Beard's boot.

Hannah had two possessions in the house. Her Bible and a quilt given her by the reverend's wife. The only thing she truly cared about was her Bible because it had once been Ma's.

"Ready?" Deputy Eliason asked.

"What're you doin' here, Pritchard? Preacher's son gonna arrest you again?" Pa's head flopped to one side.

Mr. Pritchard guffawed. "Something like that," he said.

Hannah planted herself between Mr. Pritchard and Deputy Eliason. "I'll thank you kindly, Pa, to have Red Beard and Mr. Dunn take you home."

Never had she been so courageous when speaking to Pa. A beating would have been forthcoming if she had.

Deputy Eliason nodded at her to proceed walking and she did. She cast a wary glance behind her.

"By tomorrow," reiterated Red Beard.

The night and the circumstances added to the chill in the air and Hannah shivered. Had she made the right decision? The jumble of emotions exhausted her. Relief because she no longer had to return home and face Pa. Fear because of the unknown realization she would be marrying a stranger.

Concern due to the fact that Deputy Eliason apparently gambled as well. Had he imbibed? Would he become like Pa? Trepidation because the deputy could marry anyone, but now he must marry her.

Hannah had no idea how to be a wife.

She lifted her eyes to the star-filled sky and prayed the Lord would go before her.

John Mark had been relieved when Hannah Bane accepted his marriage proposal. If for nothing else than to free her from the prison she resided in at the hands of her father.

Pritchard jabbered on faster than a man running from a mountain lion about this and that while Miss Bane remained silent.

Periodically, John Mark peered behind him to see if anyone followed. Had Harold succumbed to a state of unconscious drunkenness? Would Oslo and Red Beard leave things well enough alone?

The dark night invited criminal activity and John Mark kept his wits about him. He cupped Miss Bane's elbow and led her down the boardwalk to the center of town and to Pearson's Restaurant.

No lights shone in the restaurant or the cramped upstairs area where the new residents of Poplar Springs—eight Pearson family members—resided in two rooms, each the size of John Mark's porch. Mr. and Mrs. Pearson, their three daughters, two young sons, and Mr. Pearson's elderly mother all called the humble building home. It didn't take much knowledge to figure out that the Pearson house was filled to capacity. But it was the first place that came to mind.

The family was likely already asleep and John Mark regretted interrupting their much-needed rest. But he needed somewhere safe for Hannah to stay until tomorrow when...

He gulped. Tomorrow she would reside with him at his place.

John Mark tapped on the restaurant door. A lantern light flickered. He turned and observed Pritchard standing on tiptoe and attempting to see around he and Miss Bane. John Mark faced the door again, but heard an intermittent thudding sound against the boardwalk. He swiveled to see Pritchard jumping up and down.

How did the man have so much energy at this time of night?

"Just trying to see around you, J.M. Sure do hope I can say a word or two to Miss Pearson."

"At ten o'clock at night? If she's wise, she'll be getting some shut-eye."

Pritchard was not dissuaded. "I really would like to court her."

"Given your fondness for the town jail, it's one thing to fancy her, and quite another to want to court her."

Pritchard shrugged, likely a smirk on his face. Did he take anything seriously?

The man took his part-time residence behind bars so cavalierly.

"I've got my own ranch, small, but it's growing, so I could support her. I have ambition and hope to be the mayor of this here illustrious town someday. In addition, I'm charming and dapper."

A soft giggle from Miss Bane diverted John Mark's attention from Pritchard's hopes of courting Miss Pearson, and while it was dark and difficult to see her clearly, he couldn't help but stare. He wondered how often she had ever experienced happiness. When her eyes met his, he veered his attention back to the door and again knocked.

"All in all, I'm a respectable and principled gentleman, and I know the Bible front to back," Pritchard quipped.

"You know the Bible beginning to end except for that very critical portion in Exodus about not stealing," said John Mark.

A brighter light shone and Mr. Pearson opened the door. John Mark caught a glimpse of fear in Miss Bane's face. Would she change her mind?

He should have contacted the Pearson family beforehand and asked if Miss Bane could possibly stay with them. John Mark wouldn't have had to give details, but it would have been prudent to arrange this before this late hour. But the thought hadn't even entered his mind.

"Deputy Eliason, what brings you here at this time of night?" Mr. Pearson rubbed his eyes.

"Sir, I apologize, for bothering you at this late hour, but may we come in?" He glanced behind him in the darkness. Best that Oslo Dunn and Red Beard didn't know where Miss Bane would be staying tonight.

Mr. Pearson, always gracious, stepped aside and motioned for them to enter. John Mark dwarfed the short round man.

Miss Bane lingered toward the door and a thought clicked in John Mark's mind. He'd forgotten to ask her if staying with the Pearson family would be amenable to her. "Excuse me just a moment, Mr. Pearson."

He leaned and whispered to Miss Bane, "Is it agreeable to you to stay with the Pearsons until tomorrow, should they have the room?"

She nodded, but a look of distress crossed her face. Was he making the right decision?

John Mark then explained the situation to Mr. Pearson, leaving out most details, but including the critical part of he and Miss Bane getting married tomorrow and could she stay here until then.

Mr. Pearson grimaced. "We've got no space..." he paused. "But yes, if you don't mind cramped quarters and sleeping on a blanket on the floor, Miss Bane, then you may stay until tomorrow."

"Thank you, sir," she said, weariness in her voice.

"I'd love to have been able to offer you somewhere to stay on a more permanent basis, but with Grandmother Pearson here now, we've even less room."

"I understand, Mr. Pearson. I'm grateful for a place to stay for tonight." Miss Bane's gaze met John Mark's and a rosy blush had crept into her cheeks.

He couldn't imagine how awkward this must be for her. Pawned on others with nowhere to go. At the mercy of the new restaurant owners. Until tomorrow when his home would be her home.

It was agreed that the Pearson family would deliver Hannah to the church tomorrow at noon for her wedding to Deputy Eliason.

There was still time to recant her decision. Still time to return to Pa. Still time to borrow a pair of shoes—perhaps from Ina—that weren't holey and worn out and run as far and as fast as she could out of town or even borrow a horse and flee.

But no. This was an answer to prayer—to be free from the bondage of Pa's abuse. To start anew. Even though the answer had come in the form of a deputy sheriff securing her freedom through winning at a game of cards. Yes, that dream of her heart was now a reality.

God had heard her pleas.

Ina's whisper greeted her. "You can sleep between Mary and me." She pointed to a spot on the floor and scooted over her own bedroll. A curtain separated Ina, her two sisters, and her grandma—the only one with a bed—from two other makeshift sections, presumably her brothers and the other, her parents.

Hannah unfolded the blanket Mrs. Pearson had given her and settled in for the night. Ina turned toward her and propped herself up on one elbow. "Is it true you're marrying Deputy Eliason tomorrow?"

She'd only just met Ina a few days ago, and had spoken to her maybe twice. But she could hear the woman's excited smile in her voice.

"Yes."

"I thought that's what I overheard. Not that I was eavesdropping, mind you. All right, maybe I was." Ina plopped on her pillow then quickly propped herself up again. "What a thrilling episode in your life! Deputy Eliason is so dapper and kind too. I keep praying the Lord has someone in mind for me. I'm already nearly twenty-three and considered a spinster." Ina's voice changed from vivacious to troubled. "How I hope He has someone planned for me."

"What about Mr. Pritchard?" Hadn't the young man expressed interest in Ina?

There was silence, except for an unintelligible mumble from her grandmother in between gargled snores. "I've not given Mr. Pritchard much thought. But I do believe he's been in jail before."

Hannah surmised the reason Mr. Pritchard had landed himself in jail, but she would never divulge the information she'd been privy to.

Grandmother Pearson mumbled what sounded like a scolding because someone forgot to remove the clothes from the clothesline and they fell on the ground in the dirt. Her rebuke was mixed with random snorts and intermittent snoring. "You pick those up now!"

Ina stifled a giggle. "Grandmother Pearson is always mumbling something in her sleep. Usually it's because someone snatched food off the plate before supper, someone picked one of her flowers, or something fell from the clothesline. She's the sweetest woman, but she does have her list of frustrations."

Hannah settled into the narrow space sandwiched between Ina and her sister with barely enough room to turn from one side to the other. Her thoughts returned to Ina's grandmother who sounded like a witty sort. Never would Hannah's paternal grandma, whom she'd only met once, be considered "the sweetest woman," and her "list of frustrations" measured from Wyoming to the eastern seaboard. Envy tugged at Hannah and she shoved it aside. If she was ever blessed enough to become a grandma someday, she'd be nothing like her own.

A grandmother? It could be possible far into the future if she truly did marry Deputy Eliason and all that transpired tonight wasn't just some fanciful dream.

"Good night, Hannah," Ina said, and within minutes, her soft breathing meshed with Grandmother Pearson's mutters and the subtle snores of Ina's two sisters.

Hannah stared into the darkness, willing sleep to come. But the questions rammed through her mind. Would Pa or one of his cronies decide before the vows were made to retrieve her and return her to the Bane home? Had she made the right decision? Would the deputy like her as his wife? Would she like him as her husband? When morning came, would Deputy Eliason realize his error and rescind his offer for matrimony? Did he frequent the saloon often? Would he be anything like Pa? The never-ending barrage of questions tortured her restless mind.

If God, in His mercy, had seen fit to rescue her from Pa, then He would lead and guide her through a marriage to Deputy Eliason.

Wouldn't He?

Chapter Twelve

THE PEARSON FAMILY AWOKE early the next morning and it wasn't long before the aroma of baking bread waffled through the air.

Hannah inhaled as her stomach simultaneously growled. She rested for the merest of seconds before two thoughts flooded her mind: she ought to be helping the Pearsons since they so graciously allowed her to stay here last night.

And second...

Today she would become Deputy Eliason's wife.

Her heart lurched as the realization set in.

Would he follow through with his promise? Would he be a kind and thoughtful husband? Memories of Pa courting Ramona collided with her thoughts of Deputy Eliason and fear rippled through her.

Maybe she should be the one to recant on her promise to marry him. So very much was at stake. But the alternative was worse.

Hannah folded her blanket and stacked it near Grandmother Pearson's freshly-made bed. She best hurry downstairs to assist in preparing food for what she presumed would be a lively breakfast crowd.

Ina met her on the stairs. "I was just coming to help you," Hannah said.

"Oh, no, you don't." Ina placed her hands on Hannah's shoulders and started to turn her around. "This is your wedding day, and Ma and I already determined you'll do nothing but prepare for this momentous occasion."

"But you have been so kind to me. Forgiving me for waking you in the middle of the night and permitting me to stay here with no advance notice. Please allow me to earn my keep."

Grandmother Pearson slowly and meticulously traversed the stairs, taking one at a time, pausing with both feet on each step before repeating it all again. "You just go right back upstairs," she said and pointed with her free hand toward the doorway.

Hannah reversed direction, the thoughts of her upcoming wedding fresh on her mind. Most women had months to prepare.

She had a few hours.

"I have just the idea for a dress," Ina beamed. She clasped her hands together, her blue eyes sparkling.

A dress. Hannah hadn't even given that important item any thought.

Grandmother Pearson shuffled toward her, a blue handkerchief in her hand. "Something borrowed, something blue. This will be the 'something blue.'" She handed the handkerchief to Hannah.

"And something borrowed will be my dress," said Ina.

Hannah didn't want to appear ungrateful, nor did she wish to deflate Ina's enthusiasm, but she wasn't sure how well one of her new friend's dresses would fit. Ina was short, maybe five feet, one inch, and amply plump. Her dress would likely come to Hannah's kneecaps and would be ill-fitting and loose. But Hannah was ever so appreciative for a friend, especially a friend who would be so willing to share on such short notice, so she smiled and said, "Thank you, Ina."

"Why don't you fetch that dress, dearie, and let's see what alterations need to be made," said Grandmother Pearson. She bunched her mouth into a lopsided pucker and furrowed her brow. "We will also need your brothers to haul up some water for a bath. We haven't much time so we best scurry along."

A flurry of activity ensued with the tub placed in Mr. and Mrs. Pearson's "room" for privacy. Soon Hannah sank below the water, guilt mixing with euphoria. She couldn't recall the last time she'd had a real bath. Closing her eyes, she allowed herself to revel in its warmth. The Pearson family had been so charitable toward her. She hoped she could someday return the favor.

After washing her hair, Hannah emerged from the tub and pondered her reflection in the mirror above a worn two-drawer bureau.

Lord, please guide me. If this isn't Your will for me, please make it clear.

Marriage had not ever really been something Hannah ever desired. She recalled in her later years of school, her female classmates yearning to be married. They planned their weddings and set their caps for the most handsome boys in school, which were few since the entire school boasted fourteen pupils.

Even though Hannah celebrated her twenty-second birthday a few months ago, she wasn't so nearly concerned about being a spinster as Ina was. To her, marriage was not something to be coveted, but rather something to be abhorred. Hannah had watched the treatment Ramona received at her pa's hands. Observed the abuse, both emotional and physical, that her stepmother endured simply for making a vow.

Pa was a hateful, vindictive, and abusive man. Many times Hannah sought to escape from him, and now finally God had answered her prayer. Yet, guilt clung at the edges of her heart at leaving her father to fend for himself both in day-to-day duties and after a drunken binge.

Hannah brushed her thick brown hair. She wished she were comely like Ina with her wispy wheat-colored hair and pretty round face. Or dainty with delicate features like Claudelle Roessler.

Eligible women were scarce in Poplar Springs, yet no man had ever desired her hand in marriage. She just wasn't pretty enough. Hannah leaned closer to the ornate oval mirror. Her eyes were a pale green like grass just beginning to come to life after a dormant winter. Freckles dotted her nose. She was much too tall and willowy, not curvaceous like Ina or slender and feminine like Claudelle. Would Deputy Eliason ever think her a somewhat handsome woman?

He was a dapper man, to be certain. There were times when she attempted not to stare. But dapper appearances did not equate to godly character.

Worry again wormed its way into her heart. Would he regret his decision to ask her for her hand in marriage? Would he find her unlovable? Would she be tending to his unconscious self on the way home from bouts of drinking as she had with Pa?

"Hannah?" Ina's voice interrupted her apprehension.

"Yes?"

Ina peered around the curtain, flour dotting her cheeks. "Grandmother Pearson would like you to try on the dress so she can make alterations."

"I can't thank you enough for allowing me to stay the night and for loaning me your dress and the bath..." Hannah's voice faltered.

"There now," said Ina. She folded Hannah into a hug.

Hannah clung to her newfound friend as tears trailed down her cheeks. God had answered one of the dreams of her heart when she crossed paths with Ina Pearson. The dream of having a friend.

John Mark finished his chores then swept the floor and tidied up the cabin. Someday he would muster the courage to ask Valdez if he could buy it. Things would change once he brought home a wife.

Would Hannah want to live here? Would she be content as a deputy's wife? Could he properly support her? John Mark gazed at the clock. Pa should be traveling back anytime. He'd prayed a dozen times that he'd be able to fully explain to Pa the seriousness of the situation. Would Pa be agreeable? Would he dissuade John

Mark? Would he have an alternative idea? Somewhere in the tangled mass of nerves residing in John Mark's mind, the verse in James sprang to mind about seeking wisdom. *"If any of you lack wisdom, let him ask of God, that giveth to all men liberally, and upbraideth not; and it shall be given him."*

Oh, John Mark needed wisdom, all right.

He'd always had a strong marriage to emulate—that of his parents. Would his marriage to Hannah Bane, a woman he didn't even really know—even remotely resemble that? Would she grow to love him in time and would he grow to love her? Was it God's will that he marry Miss Bane or had John Mark sidestepped God's plan and meandered along his own path?

John Mark stepped onto the porch and straightened the two chairs. Would he and Miss Bane sit in them after a demanding day and reminisce about their future as he'd seen Ma and Pa do at home? Would they ice skate in the winter? Someday have children?

He hoped to imitate Pa. Loving, chivalrous, and thoughtful. He'd rarely seen his parents argue. He knew they themselves were not perfect, but to have a marriage like theirs was his wish. He'd seen many times the love expressed between them. The sacrifices on both sides. Ma's patience at being married to a man of the cloth whose life was often dictated by the unending needs of his congregation.

And so it would be for John Mark and his job as a deputy sheriff. A dangerous job that, at times, took him out of town to the rest of the expansive county, and one demanding a fair amount of time. Ma was Pa's partner in ministry. Would Miss Bane share the same devoted and unselfish partnership with John Mark?

The crazy rooster crowed, stalked toward the porch, and crowed again. He regarded John Mark and reached a spurred claw up one stair then another. John Mark reached for the broom just in case the capricious rooster had any ideas. "Go your way, rooster," he bellowed. Why was it always a showdown with this addlepated fowl? John Mark had dealt with horse thieves, cattle rustlers, outlaws, gunslingers, and the like, yet none perturbed him like the annoying rooster making its way up the porch toward him. Was there not a day that went by when the bird didn't attempt to chase him?

"I'm getting a dog," he muttered. A dog that would keep the rooster compliant. "Reckon I see you being part of supper in the future."

The rooster paid him no mind and hastily dashed toward him. John Mark swatted at him with the broom. The animal stopped, stared at him, and raised a leg, his claw dangling in midair as if the rooster contemplated his next move.

"Behave or you're going to become fixings for a stew," John Mark warned.

The rooster ignored him and continued to stare, beady eyes unblinking.

It wasn't that the rooster was mean or a menace. Just cantankerous. And he was an excellent protector of the hens. But he and John Mark shared some sort of unspoken disdain for each other.

Pa rounded the corner then and rode toward the house.

And John Mark's stomach pitted into tight coils. Would Pa understand his predicament?

CHAPTER THIRTEEN

THE ROOSTER, AS IF he hadn't just been the crabby sort toward John Mark, stepped off the porch as if to greet Pa.

And John Mark prayed once again for guidance.

"How was the wedding?" John Mark asked as Pa dismounted.

Pa chuckled. "A rather sizeable one. I think Jack and his new wife invited nearly everyone in Wyoming. Thought maybe if you weren't on duty today, we could get some fishing in and then, if you don't mind, I could bed down here for the night before heading to Willow Falls first thing tomorrow morning."

John Mark rubbed his sweaty palms together. Telling Pa about the latest turn of events gnawed at his insides something awful. He tempered his rapid breathing. *Lord, reckon this might be a good time to seek Your help.*

Pa's brow knitted. "Is everything all right, Son?"

If only Pa wasn't so perceptive. "Yes." But John Mark's utterance sounded more like the times when Pa would chastise him for causing a disturbance at school and then ask if John Mark learned his lesson.

If only that's all this was. Another occurrence in the life of an ornery young'un instead of a man about to relay to his father the most addlebrained idea ever undertaken in Eliason history. He took a deep breath, willed his heart rate to stop pounding out of his chest, and shoved his hands into his trouser pockets. Trepidation filled him from head to toe.

And then came the internal dialogue. Always an advantages-versus-disadvantages situation with the arguments for and against equally weighed in the mind of a bewildered and befuddled young man.

You've really gone and gotten yourself into a quagmire this time, John Mark.

Yeah, but Pa's always been a good listener.

True, but he's not going to like what he hears this time.

Hasn't been the worst he's ever heard. Remember all those pranks you played on Charlotte?

This is worse.

All right. What about the time you told your entire family you wanted to be a sheriff? Remember Pa's jaw dropping and resting on the table?

"John Mark?"

He silenced his internal argument. "So, how was the trip?"

A change of subject to delay the unavoidable. Always worked.

Temporarily.

Pa slung his pack on the porch and took a seat in one of the chairs. "Long. Dusty. I can't wait to return to Willow Falls. Not that I'm complaining, but for some reason, the journey seemed lengthier than usual."

127

"I'll get you a cup of milk."

Plod along doing other important things. The perfect postponement.

Briefly.

He stepped inside the cabin and poured Pa a tall glass of milk from the pitcher, grabbed him a piece of bread from the loaf someone had dropped off at the sheriff's office for the "poor young man with no wife," and returned to the porch.

"Thank you." Pa bowed his head and blessed the meager meal.

"So, Pa, how was the weather during your trip?"

Talk about the weather always diverted the topic.

Momentarily.

But Pa was neither dissuaded nor deterred. "Something tells me there's a mighty heavy load on your mind."

Heavy didn't begin to describe the circumstance. John Mark attempted to shove aside the apprehension. This was Pa. The most godly man he'd ever known. The one who loved him unconditionally. "Yes. Yes, there is."

"Would you care to take a load off?"

"Reckon I would."

Pa faced him. "I've been told a time or two that I'm a good listener."

John Mark blew out the deep breath formerly trapped in his lungs. "I...well...I...uh..." He jiggled his leg, causing the chair to shake. "Let me put it like this. I...you see...uh..."

"This isn't like you at all, Son. Are you in some kind of trouble? If so, I'll do what I can to assist you."

He was in some kind of trouble, all right. Made a promise and now wavered between carrying it through or changing his mind.

Only, he wouldn't change his mind because Miss Bane needed him.

"Pa, can you marry Miss Bane and me before you go back to Willow Falls tomorrow?"

Pa's bearded jaw dropped. "I beg your pardon?"

"I've always wanted you to be the one to perform the wedding ceremony for me one day."

The crust of bread was suspended in air in Pa's right hand and his eyebrows disappeared into his hairline. "Miss Bane? The one with the mean father? When did you start courting? Why didn't you tell me this last time? And can this wait until another day? You know your ma would like to be present."

The third part of the question was the easiest one to answer. "No, it has to be today." He pulled out his timepiece. "In two hours to be exact."

John Mark had never seen Pa's eyes bulge in such a way. Once deep-set hazel eyes now protruded and rounded. "Two hours?"

"Yes, sir."

"John Mark Solomon Eliason, I'd be much appreciative if you would explain yourself."

The use of his full name brought back a flood of memories. None of them fond. He rolled his shoulders in an effort to release the tension and faced Pa. "It's like this, Pa. Yes, Miss Bane is the woman whose father mistreats her. I asked for her hand in marriage."

Pa's mouth opened, but no words emerged as several seconds ticked by. He bowed his head, likely praying, maybe for wisdom for himself in handling the situation. Or maybe praying for his daft son.

"I should start at the beginning."

"That would be a right fine idea."

So John Mark told Pa once again about Hannah Bane and her father. All seemed well, and Pa appeared to understand.

Then, as rapidly as his mouth would move so maybe Pa would miss part of the explanation, he recounted the last few days. Even in his own ears, John Mark's words sounded jumbled, disorganized, and discombobulated. "And, of course, Miss Bane said 'yes', and seeing as how I have to marry her today per the terms of the agreement, I'm left with no choice but to become her husband." John Mark held his breath, awaiting Pa's response.

"I see."

"It's really not so bad, Pa. She's nice and all and it'll work out."

Pa steepled his fingers beneath his chin. "And is Miss Bane a Christian?"

"Yes, and before you ask, I have prayed about this." *Probably not as much as I should have, but...*

Pa nodded. "Prayer is always the best practice. But have you truly sought God's will on this matter? Did you pray first and then act, or did you act first and then pray?"

His conscience pricked him and John Mark cleared his throat. "More so the latter."

"Marriage can be difficult. Are you ready to commit to this and take a vow before God to remain faithful and loving all the days of your life?"

"I am."

"Ephesians 5:25 can be a challenge under the best of circumstances, let alone when you enter the marriage as near strangers. *'Husbands, love your wives, even as Christ also loved the church, and gave himself for it.'* That's how we are to love our wives. Are you prepared to, with the Lord's help, love Miss Bane in this way?"

The sweat beaded on his brow. Could he be in obedience and love her that way?

"When we marry, we are called to love and cherish our wives all the days of our lives. Now, we won't do it perfectly." Pa paused and stared out into the open field. "Thank the Good Lord for His grace as I've not always loved your Ma the way she ought to be loved. We've had our disagreements and I've given into my own selfishness more times than I care to admit." Pa returned his gaze to John Mark. "Marriage is a wonderful gift from God. It takes two people with different personalities, different dreams, and different ideas and meshes them into a partnership like none other. It takes work, forgiveness, grace, and plenty of time on our knees in prayer. Are you ready to make that commitment to Miss Bane?"

For all John Mark's worry, had he failed to grasp the true gravity of the situation? Could he love Miss Bane the way God intended? Could he love her even if she never loved him? Could he take the one life he had been given and make that life a partnership with a woman he barely knew?

"That's one of the primary purposes of courtship," said Pa. "Marriage isn't something to be done in haste."

"Yes, sir, I agree."

"Could you perhaps reconsider and court her for a time before entering into marriage?"

He thought of Red Beard. Would the man hold him to his word? Likely so. And there had been many witnesses to the agreement. Where would Hannah live while they courted? He mentally listed off the folks in his mind who could help, even entertaining the thought of Hannah residing with Ma and Pa for a time.

But no. The fact remained. He'd made a promise, and as a man of his word, he best keep it. No matter what the stakes. "Pa, we need to marry today."

Pa tugged at his beard and lifted his eyes heavenward. One thing about Pa was that he was constantly seeking God's wisdom, likely doing that again now. "All right, but your ma will have my hide and then some if I marry you without her present. Sure you can't wait until you pay a visit to Willow Falls? She'll want to arrange it at the church and invite friends..."

"Ma will understand." But John Mark wasn't so sure. Ma was a merciful woman, but for her second son to marry without her in attendance? When she didn't even know there was a young lady in the picture? A thought then pricked the edges of his mind. "Perhaps Ma could have a get-together with townsfolk when we reach Willow Falls. I could ask Miss Bane if she'd be willing to travel there tomorrow. Winslow gave me a few days off for my wedding."

"That might work."

"Besides, Miss Bane would want to be married here with her friends present." But did she really have any friends? John Mark never witnessed anyone coming to her aid with the exception of Reverend Fleming and his wife and maybe Pritchard. John Mark had heard plenty of rude comments about her, but few stepped forward to assist her in leaving the life she'd been born into.

"All right," said Pa. "Never heard of a matrimony gambling situation, but God can use all things for good."

John Mark knew the verse from Romans well, especially since it was a verse Pa quoted often in his sermons when discussing going through life's trials. *A matrimony gambling situation?* Surely, Pa didn't think... "Don't worry, Pa. I will never again darken the doors of the saloon unless it's to settle an argument or haul someone to jail. And I've repented of it."

"I may not agree with the way you proceeded with this, but I trust your decision. You're a prudent man and I know you wouldn't make a risky decision without prayer and mulling it over. And I do believe it's a wise idea for the two of you to come to Willow Falls when you're able. Whether that's tomorrow or sometime in the near future. Your ma would like to meet the woman her son has chosen for his bride."

John Mark crossed his feet at the ankles and leaned back, feeling some relief after discussing the issue with Pa. "I'll ask Miss Bane if she'd be amenable to leaving tomorrow morning. We could travel with you."

"Looks like you're about to have company," said Pa, nodding toward a rider on a horse in the distance.

John Mark's relief was short-lived as concerned thoughts crammed his mind once again. Had Miss Bane changed her mind? Had something happened in town and Winslow needed his assistance? Had the cattle rustlers struck again?

Pritchard stopped his horse in front of the house and dismounted. "Hey there, J.M., got good news for you."

John Mark released a sigh of relief. "What is it?"

"I took it upon myself to speak with the reverend and the church is yours at noon for the wedding. He'll marry you if you need him to." A broad smile lit Pritchard's face. "And when I went to the restaurant to eat breakfast, I asked Miss Pearson if she'd be in attendance. She said yes."

John Mark hadn't even thought about asking to borrow the church. "Sensible thinking, Pritchard. Thanks."

"Not a problem." Pritchard stuck his thumbs through his belt loops and his eyes strayed toward Pa.

"This here is my father, Reverend Solomon Eliason. Pa, this is Wally Pritchard, an acquaintance of mine."

"Acquaintance? More like friends." Pritchard shrugged. "But nice to meet you anyhow, Rev."

Pa stood and reached a hand toward Pritchard. "Nice to meet you as well."

Pritchard removed his timepiece from his pocket. "Reckon it's just over an hour before you make the biggest decision of your life. Anything else I can do to help?"

Just over an hour? Why was it suddenly more challenging to breathe? Had the air gotten thinner?

"J.M.? You still with me?"

"Yes, uh, no, there's nothing more to do. However, my pa here is going to marry Miss Bane and me."

"Do you have a best man? If you need one to stand up in your favor, I'd oblige."

The one John Mark truly wanted to be his best man was his brother. If only he hadn't shook on the promise to marry Hannah today.

But what was done was done. Hopefully Caleb would understand.

"Sure, Pritchard."

Pritchard grinned. "Never been a best man before, but I reckon I can do it. Well, I better go. Pleasure to meet you, Rev." Pritchard headed toward his horse, then turned around. "Say, maybe you could pay me a visit after the wedding. I'm in need of some wise counsel."

The man could use all the wise counsel available, but John Mark didn't say as much.

Hannah slipped into the green calico dress. The material felt so new and crisp although Ina apologized for having worn it several times for church.

Hannah cared not that Ina had worn the dress before. For her, to be able to wear something other than her faded and threadbare dress was more than she could ever hope for.

The dress hung off her, several inches too wide. The length did, indeed, hit her at the knee, her five-feet-eight height quite a stretch from Ina's short stature.

"But goodness," gasped Grandmother Pearson. "I may need more than a few hours to fix this dilemma. Who knew there would be such a difference in figures?" She held a gnarled finger to her mouth and her eyes darted about.

"Oh, dear," Ina whispered. "Is there something that can be done, Grandmother?"

Her grandma lowered her spectacles on the bridge of her nose and squinted. "Yes. Yes, I believe so. I can take in the sides of the dress with a tuck here and there. The stitches can easily be removed after the wedding so Ina can wear it again." She nodded her head. "Yes, that's what I'll do."

"And for the length?" asked Ina.

"The length?" Grandmother Pearson's brow furrowed. "Oh, yes, the length. You are a tall and lithe woman. But not to worry. I will sew a swath of fabric onto the bottom of the dress and extend the length. I can again remove the stitches once the wedding is over."

Hannah pondered her statement. "It seems like such an inconvenience. I can wear my brown dress if need be."

"Goodness, child! Wherever did you get such a dismal idea? You deserve a special dress. My only regret is that I do not have time to sew you your own." Grandmother Pearson lifted her chin. "I was once a renowned seamstress in Kansas, you know."

"Thank you, ma'am. I am most grateful."

"I know, dearie, and this will be most memorable." She glanced around the room. "I need to pilfer through the leftover fabric in the chest downstairs for some scraps. Or..." Her focus landed on the patchwork quilt on Mr. and

Mrs. Pearson's bed. "Do you like the colors of that quilt? I believe I may still have some fabric left."

Hannah did not want to appear ungrateful, for it was a blessing to have someone else's grandmother care enough to ensure her wedding dress was special, but would a portion of it resemble a patchwork quilt? Inwardly she cringed.

"Why don't you allow Ina and me to take measurements? Then you can slip out of that dress and permit me to use my famous stitching skills." Grandmother Pearson shuffled forward and slipped an arm around Hannah's waist.

Hannah reveled in the older woman's affection and leaned into the hug. What would it have been like to have a grandma who loved her?

"I will do whatever I can to make this dress exactly what you've always dreamed your wedding dress would be. Not traditional like the ones at the millinery, because I haven't any satin. Nor will it be white with lace. However, it will be charming in its own right, a dress that a beautiful girl such as yourself will be proud to wear." Grandmother Pearson squeezed Hannah's waist in a hug so tender and so meaningful Hannah knew that whatever the end result of the dress, this brief time with Grandmother Pearson would make it worth it.

In just over an hour, Hannah would be a married woman. A married woman wed to Deputy John Mark Eliason. To say she was fraught with nerves would severely understate the worries and apprehension she was experiencing.

She sat in front of Mrs. Pearson's worn bureau with the tiny mirror while Ina brushed her hair and chatted nonstop, a permanent giggle mug planted on her round face. What would she do were it not for the friendship she'd found in the woman who graciously assisted her in preparation for her wedding?

"You could do far worse, Hannah," Ina was saying as she twisted a section of Hannah's hair, wound it around Hannah's head, then changed her mind and brushed it out again.

Hannah thought of Deputy Eliason and his easygoing smile and protective manner over her. An image of him entered her mind. He was rugged with his broad shoulders and long legs. He likely could marry any woman, but now he would be marrying her.

Guilt assailed her.

"Perhaps he ought to think of marrying someone else," she muttered, not intending for Ina to hear her.

Ina stopped brushing her hair and peered around to be in Hannah's line of vision. "Hannah Bane, soon to be Hannah Eliason, don't you dare say such a thing. He has chosen you and for good reason."

"To free me from Pa and perhaps having to marry someone of the likes of Red Beard or Oslo Dunn?" she shivered.

"Those are as worthwhile reasons as any, although not quite conventional." Ina attempted a different hairstyle, then placed the brush on the bureau. "And while that may be the case, I believe you and John Mark Eliason could very well fall in love someday." She held her hand to her heart and swooned. "Isn't it so romantic to marry a deputy?"

It might be romantic, but what if she didn't like him after becoming his wife? What if *he* didn't like *her*? Wedding vows were designed to be permanent.

Unless you are Ramona, a little voice hissed in her head. While it was painful that Ramona left Pa and took Hannah's brothers, but not her, and divorce was scandalous, Ramona had made the right decision. Hannah fully believed that in the case of the abuse Ramona suffered at Pa's hand, she was justified in leaving. What if Deputy Eliason turned abusive? What if he pretended to be an upstanding man, as her pa had to Ramona, only to have a sullen and wicked personality? What then?

She shoved aside the dismal thoughts. God had provided a rescue from Pa. He would help her. Wouldn't He?

Ina resumed brushing her hair again. "You have such lovely hair. I'm trying to decide between two different styles I recently saw in an advertisement in the catalog at the mercantile. Oh, my, you should see some of the styles now becoming fashionable." She paused. "I do believe I shall send one of my brothers on a hunt for wildflowers. Wouldn't those be lovely intertwined in your hair?"

A knock at the door sounded, followed by Grandmother Pearson poking her head around the corner. "Ina? Mr. Pritchard is here and would like a word with you and Hannah."

"Oh, but goodness!" Ina fumbled and accidentally yanked on Hannah's hair. "Thank you, Grandmother Pearson. Will you tell him I—we'll—be right down?"

"Yes, I shall. He's a cordial young man. Perhaps you ought to take a notice of him, Ina." The elderly woman hobbled toward the stairs.

A bright grin lit Ina's face. "Perhaps I shall." She put a finger to her chin. "But he has spent time in jail..."

"I believe that was all a misunderstanding," said Hannah.

"You do? Well, that is such a relief. I aim to marry a godly man who is an upstanding and a respectable member of society."

Hannah wriggled into her dress and followed Ina down the stairs and into the restaurant. The aroma of eggs lingered in the air from the breakfast meal. Mr. Pritchard stood near one of the tables. Was it Hannah's imagination or did he stand a bit taller and puff himself up when Ina drew near?

The man had always been kind in Hannah's estimation. He'd delivered food to her and Pa numerous times and Hannah suspected he assisted other downtrodden folks in town as well. Someone said he owned a small ranch with a few head of cattle, but other tongues wagged about how Mr. Pritchard spent more time in jail for theft than at his humble cabin or his temporary home above the barbershop.

"Miss Pearson, Miss Bane." Mr. Pritchard strutted forward, removed his hat, and did a slight bow, as though he might have hailed from the city rather than the Wild West.

"Mr. Pritchard, what brings you to the restaurant?" Ina's smile covered her entire face, causing her squinty eyes to nearly disappear. A red blush covered her cheeks.

Mr. Pritchard took a few steps toward them. "I am on duty as a messenger for Deputy Eliason." His formality caused both Hannah and Ina to laugh.

"A messenger? For the deputy?" Ina asked.

"Yes. He would like me to ask Miss Bane if she is content with his pa, the esteemed Reverend Solomon Eliason, presiding over their wedding in..." Mr. Pritchard removed his timepiece from his trouser pocket. "In less than an hour."

Ina held a hand to her bosom. "I do declare, Mr. Pritchard, but you speak as though you are a man of great wealth from New York or Chicago."

"And you, my fair lady, have you ever met such a gent?"

Ina tittered, her plump cheeks reddening all the more. "Why, I most certainly have met a few of them here in the restaurant from time to time as they travel through to another destination. But you, Mr. Pritchard, do you hail from a city?"

Mr. Pritchard chuckled and looped his thumbs through suspenders that gave the appearance of fighting to hold up his trousers on his thin frame. "Actually, Miss Pearson, I do. I once resided in the city of Boston."

"Pray tell, for how long?"

"Two weeks."

There was an obvious interest between Ina and Mr. Pritchard, and Hannah felt like she was intruding on a special moment. Seconds ticked by with the only sound being the clanging of pots and pans in the kitchen and a horse neighing on the street outside.

Finally, Mr. Pritchard spoke again. "Miss Bane, is it acceptable to you to have the esteemed Reverend Solomon

Eliason performing your wedding vows at the church? If not, tell me posthaste so I can make alternative arrangements."

Hannah had heard Deputy Eliason was the son of a preacher. "His pa is in Poplar Springs?"

"Yes, ma'am, he is. And what will your answer be?" But Mr. Pritchard didn't cast even the slightest glance in Hannah's direction. Rather, his attention remained fixed on Ina.

"That is acceptable to me, yes."

A whole additional flood of concerns filled her mind. Would Deputy Eliason's pa find her to be a suitable wife for his son?

"Very well." Mr. Pritchard slapped his hat on his head. "I will see both of you soon." With one final nod in Ina's direction, he left the restaurant.

Ina meandered toward the front window and watched him go, her swooning quite obvious to the onlooker.

If only things had been different for Hannah. If they had been, she might have known the joy and thrill of falling in love with a potential suitor.

She fought the envy that rose within her and chose instead to focus on the blessing of God's deliverance from her father by way of a sheriff's deputy named John Mark Eliason.

Chapter Fourteen

Hannah faced Deputy Eliason at the front of the lone Poplar Springs church. To her surprise and appreciation, she recognized several familiar faces. Reverend Solomon, the entire Pearson family, Mr. Pritchard, Reverend Fleming and his wife and baby, and the two friends of Deputy Eliason who joined him at the saloon all attended.

A tumbleweed of emotions occupied her thoughts. Had her life been different, would she, as a young girl, have imagined the details of her wedding? The hopes? The dreams? The anticipation? Would she have dreamed of a pa in the pew smiling, tears in his eyes? A pa who was proud of his daughter and wished her the best on her happy day? A ma who prayed for her before the momentous occasion? An elegant wedding gown like the one she saw in the window of Nellie's Dress Shop? A handsome beau who would take her in his arms and declare his love for her?

While her newfound friends sat in the pews, there was no pa to be proud of her, no ma to pray with her, and there was no elegant gown. Deputy Eliason was a handsome beau, if she could call him her beau, but it was doubtful he would take her in his arms and declare his love for her, for he barely knew her.

And while she couldn't fathom what he might gain from the proposition of marrying the town drunk's daughter, she knew for her it was only a marriage of convenience.

The convenience of freedom.

She turned briefly to see Ina, Grandmother Pearson, and Mr. Pritchard engaged in lively conversation. Ina's cheeks reddened and her giggle emanated throughout the church. Mr. Pritchard gazed upon her as if she were the most beautiful woman he'd ever seen. He was smitten for certain, and Hannah hoped—and would remember to pray—that he was worthy of her new friend.

"Miss Bane?"

She returned her gaze to the front of the church and to Reverend Eliason who'd just spoken her name in a hushed tone.

"Yes, Reverend Eliason?"

His kind eyes, so like his son's, crinkled at the corners. "Please, call me Reverend Solomon." He paused. "I do need to ask both you and John Mark a question before we begin."

She held her breath. What would the reverend ask?

"Hannah, may I call you Hannah?"

Hannah nodded.

"Do you wish to proceed with the wedding today? Neither John Mark nor I wish for you to feel as though you are being coerced into something you don't wish to do. If you would prefer, you can forego the wedding and we can find you somewhere else to live. Maybe in Willow Falls."

"No, sir. I am fine with marrying Deputy Eliason." But as soon as she said it, a worrisome thought nearly choked her for the hundredth time. Was the deputy having second thoughts about marrying her? Should she ask the reverend to ask Deputy Eliason first? Perhaps he'd changed his mind.

She stole a glance his direction. His mouth curved into a smile. "Please, call me John Mark."

"I—yes, John Mark." How foolish of her to continue to refer to her soon-to-be-husband as Deputy Eliason. He must think her daft.

"Very well, Hannah. And, John Mark, are you having any reservations about taking Hannah as your wife today? Perhaps you two could enter into a courtship and marry at a later date."

John Mark fidgeted.

And Hannah fretted.

Was John Mark about to change his mind about marrying her today? Would he agree to court her and marry her later? She had nowhere else to go to get away from her father. The thought of returning to her father or Pa promising her hand in marriage to one of the scoundrels he imbibed with horrified her. The images of Oslo Dunn, Red Beard, Mander, and Yin flashed across her mind.

"I would like to marry Hannah today if she'll have me."

A whoosh of breath escaped her lips. *If she would have him?* Of course she would choose him as a husband, provided he didn't become like Pa. Ramona's image entered her mind and how Pa had lied to her about who he really was. "Yes," she squeaked.

"Very well." Reverend Solomon closed his eyes briefly. Was he praying? Was he concerned about his son's choice?

He opened his eyes a moment later and announced that the ceremony would begin. Silence ensued except for the reverend's voice, and Hannah feared everyone could hear her loudly-thumping heart.

The next few minutes were a blur. She recalled Reverend Solomon reading a few passages from the Bible, then her answering, "I do" when he asked if she'd take John Mark to be her husband. She vaguely heard him direct his question to John Mark, and John Mark answering and placing a thin gold band on her finger.

Had he noticed how her hand shook?

"I now pronounce you man and wife." Reverend Solomon paused for a moment before adding, "You may kiss your bride."

John Mark took a step toward her. She closed her eyes. Might they delay this part until they knew each other as more than just mere acquaintances? More than just him as her protector?

His lips brushed hers and her knees wobbled. While she did imagine her wedding day to be memorable, losing consciousness would not be the kind of memory she wished to create.

"Hannah?" John Mark whispered.

Her eyes fluttered opened. He was again standing where he'd stood when the ceremony started and Ina and Grandmother Pearson stood on the other side of her,

Ina's arms outstretched. "Congratulations!" She pulled Hannah into a hug. "Borrow the dress for as long as you need," she whispered.

Grandmother Pearson gave her a hug next. "You're a beautiful bride, Hannah," she said.

Mr. Pritchard shook John Mark's hand, and the remainder of the guests offered their congratulations.

And as she and John Mark left the church, Hannah sent the prayer on her heart toward Heaven. *Lord, please let this have been the right decision and please let me be a good wife to John Mark.*

John Mark had heard the tales of how fast wedding ceremonies were performed, despite a woman's hankering to spend countless hours on preparations and plan it months in advance.

The tales were true. In less than an hour from the time he entered the church to the time he left with Hannah, he'd become a married man.

Lord, please let me have made the right decision. Let me be worthy of Hannah.

As he was about to assist Hannah into the wagon, a familiar voice called out to him. "I done changed my mind, Deputy."

Harold stood against his wagon, a flask in his hand.

"It's too late, Mr. Bane. I've already married your daughter."

"Ain't too late. She belongs at home. Who's gonna cook me supper?"

Hannah edged closer to John Mark and he took her hand in his. "Reckon that's something you'll need to figure out."

"You cheated at the game," griped Harold.

"No, sir, I didn't." John Mark was still amazed he'd won, and while he aimed never to partake in another card game, he knew for certain he hadn't cheated. He assisted Hannah into the wagon and flicked the reins.

Harold teetered aside, bellowed something unintelligible, and stumbled toward the boardwalk.

"Thank you," whispered Hannah.

"You have nothing to fear from that man any longer." John Mark would need to pray he'd be able to keep himself tempered if Harold decided to arrive at his home for a visit. He wouldn't be there when on duty. Would Hannah be safe? He would need to make certain she was competent with the Winchester rifle in case Harold sent any of his cronies for a visit.

Pa once told him that a man must always fight for his wife's honor. Protect it. Protect *her*. Love her the way Christ loved the church.

A tall order, but he would try.

He cast a glance her way. Her attention was to her right, toward the passing scenery. Pa told him on the way to the church that it wouldn't be easy to begin a marriage this way. But one thing John Mark had never lacked was determination. "I was thinking about us traveling to Willow Falls tomorrow with Pa. I'd like you to meet my family."

She whipped her head toward him so quickly he feared she might bounce from the wagon. "I—"

"I'd like them to meet you. You'll get along right fine with them. Ma, well after she has my hide and then some for marrying without her present," he chuckled, his voice sounding nervous in his own ears. "She's a considerate and kind woman and very gracious." At least, he hoped she was gracious after she discovered John Mark's decision. "And then there's my sister, Charlotte. She can be featherbrained at times, but I wouldn't trade her for anything. Caleb, my brother, and his wife, Annie, live just up the road from my parents' house. They have three daughters and another one soon to be born. I'm sure you'll like them all."

He awaited her answer, but a few more seconds would tick by before he received it. Finally she spoke, her voice hushed. "All right."

"Or we can wait until another time, I just think it best while I have a few days off from upholding the law."

"No, it's fine. I would like to meet your family." But her voice faltered.

John Mark returned his attention to the road. From the corner of his eye, he saw her stare straight ahead, an expression of trepidation lining her pretty features.

And she was pretty.

"Pa said he would meet us tomorrow morning at sunrise. He's staying at Pritchard's tonight. Apparently Pritchard has a million and five questions for Pa and needed some advice. Poor Pa won't likely get any sleep tonight with Pritchard prattling on like some hen."

A hint of a smile formed on her lips. "Mr. Pritchard does seem to like to talk."

"Yes, he does. He's a church bell for sure." Normally that term only referred to a woman and her incessant rambling, but at times, when Pritchard had a story to tell, it could apply to him as well.

They arrived at the cabin, the rooster perched on the porch awaiting them. "Watch out for the rooster. He's harmless, but he is a nuisance."

John Mark climbed from the wagon, rounded it, and reached up to assist Hannah. She took his hand, hers small and delicate in his own.

Would he grow to like her?

Or even someday grow to love her?

CHAPTER FIFTEEN

THERE WAS ONLY ONE other time Hannah remembered sleeping so soundly and that was the previous night at the Pearson home. When she awoke in the morning, Hannah stared at the ceiling of the unfamiliar home, wondering for the briefest of moments where she was.

She braced herself on one elbow. The room housed the bed, a wooden crate with a Bible and a few other possessions, and a stack of clothes folded neatly in the corner. The sunrise, barely obscured by a faded yellow curtain, streamed into the room.

Other than a rooster crowing outside, all was calm.

Hannah stretched her arms above her head then rested them on her stomach.

That's when her eye caught the thin gold band on her left hand.

Finally, recognition commenced.

It hadn't been a dream that she married Deputy Eliason, or rather, John Mark, but a real occurrence.

And if she wanted to surprise him before he awoke for their journey to Willow Falls, she best endeavor to proceed with her plan.

Hannah swung her legs over the side of the bed and stood. She tiptoed to the closed door, opened it, and peeked into the main area of the home. John Mark slept on the floor near the unlit fireplace, his soft snores filling the air.

She closed the door and efficiently slipped Ina's dress over her head, ran a comb through her tangled hair, pulled it into a braid, and tiptoed toward the kitchen. A swift perusal of the table revealed one egg in the bowl.

One egg would hardly do.

Hannah slipped on her worn boots and headed toward the chicken coop. The promise of a new day beckoned her.

What had Ina said? That she needed to have a wedding gift for her husband? If she'd had more time, she could have sewn him a new shirt or a pair of socks. She had no money, but if she'd known in advance she would be getting married, perhaps one of the shop owners in town would have paid her to sweep the boardwalk. It would have made just enough money to purchase her husband a trinket at the mercantile.

No, there had been no time to even contemplate gifts. Ina's declaration had come as a surprise, and Hannah found herself with a case of the nerves trying to figure a gift she could make at a moment's notice.

The idea had come to her right after she'd said her prayers and right before she'd nodded off last night.

She would prepare a meal of scrambled eggs for John Mark. It was likely he hadn't had a homecooked meal for some time, unless he ate breakfast at Pearson's Restaurant.

But what if he abhors your cooking like Pa does?

The nagging voice echoed through her mind, and Hannah nearly stopped on her way to the coop. What if John Mark complained and growled at her efforts to cook him a meal? What if she burned the eggs? What if there were no eggs in the coop?

No. There had to be eggs and she would do her best to prepare the scrambled eggs in a perfect manner. She took a deep breath and with forced resolve, continued toward the chicken coop.

A rustling noise sounded behind her and she jumped. Cautiously, she turned, dreading whom she might see.

But when she saw a rooster standing there watching her, she let out a sigh of relief. "Oh, but goodness! You gave me a fright."

The rooster tilted his head from side to side and peered at her. Hannah continued toward the henhouse with the rooster following. She turned again and he stopped and eyed her once more. They'd once owned a mean rooster who spurred Pa near the corral. The impetuous animal's life was cut short.

But the red-and-brown rooster with his floppy red comb and claw-like beak didn't appear to be the foolhardy sort. To the contrary. He almost looked to be smiling.

"You need a name," she said.

He bobbed his head as if to agree.

"Yes, I shall call you Clarence. It suits you."

She laughed at the thought of naming John Mark's animals. Hannah would keep that little morsel of information to herself until she could discern how he would respond.

Clarence continued following her as she entered the henhouse.

The hens clucked loudly at her intrusion. Grabbing several eggs, she placed them in the bowl, then started back on her way toward the house, the rooster again following.

Hannah quietly strolled up the porch steps and into the house. John Mark remained on the floor sleeping. As noiselessly as possible, she removed one of the two pans from the shelf and set about preparing breakfast, hoping she'd have it completed before John Mark awoke and Reverend Solomon arrived to accompany them to Willow Falls.

Soon the aroma of eggs filled the house and she watched as John Mark stirred. "What is that delicious smell?" he muttered.

He peered at her, confusion alighting his eyes. Had he momentarily forgotten he married her yesterday? Would he be disappointed when his recollection returned?

"Good morning," Hannah said.

"Good morning." His disheveled hair stood up at odd angles and his sleepy countenance endeared him to her. John Mark was a dapper fellow even upon first waking.

Hannah realized she was staring and immediately averted her gaze to the stove. "Supper will be ready soon!" she said, the words tumbling from her mouth before she gave them a second thought.

"Supper? Did I sleep so long that I missed breakfast and the noonday meal?" From the corner of her eye, she could see his confusion.

"Supper? Oh, dear. I mean, no, not supper, and not the noonday meal, but breakfast, yes, breakfast is nearly ready." Her words came out a jumbled mess. Would he think his new bride a mumbling dolt?

She dared not look his way for fear something else utterly asinine would escape her mouth. Instead, Hannah busied herself with finishing a sizable heap of scrambled eggs.

She hoped John Mark was hungry.

"I'll just wash up and be right back," he said, his voice still lined with early-morning croakiness.

Hannah nodded, gave the eggs one more stir, and set the pan off to the side to allow them to set. How she wished she had time to make a batch of homemade bread! At least she'd found a pitcher of milk in the icebox, for she'd not had time to milk the cow.

She watched outside the window as John Mark filled a pitcher with water from the pump and returned to the house to splash water on his face. His back to her, she noticed the wide expanse of his shoulders.

Would John Mark prove to be a man of godly character? She reminded herself that many men were handsome in appearance and lacking in Biblical temperament.

Hannah heaped a generous mound of eggs on a metal plate and set it at one of the place settings on the table. She poured a full cup of milk and positioned it in front of the plate, along with a fork. Then she scooped a meager portion of the remaining eggs from the pan onto a plate for herself and poured a quarter cup of milk. She would leave the rest of the eggs in the pan in case John Mark desired seconds.

"Is there anything I can do to help?" John Mark's voice brought her back to the present.

"I—no—I'm fine, thank you." She waited for him to sit at the table in case he wanted her to retrieve something else for her as Pa always did.

"Will you be joining me?" he asked.

Hannah nodded and took a seat across from him.

John Mark blessed the meal. His humble words of gratitude for the simple meal mesmerized her and warmed her heart. She'd never heard a man pray over a meal before.

Hannah held her breath as John Mark ate his first bite. She prepared herself for the barrage of derogatory comments about the meal. When none came, she released the tension in her shoulders.

"These eggs are delicious. Thank you, Hannah."

She watched, not sure if she should start eating or save her portion in case what he had and what was left in the pan weren't enough. Her stomach growled, and Hannah hoped he hadn't heard the disconcerting grumble.

John Mark stopped eating. "Aren't you going to eat?" He stared at her plate. "Are you not hungry?" he asked, his voice gentle and calm.

"I..." what could she say? What *should* she say? Pa rarely allowed her to have an opinion.

His dark brows knitted together. He stood and wandered over to the pan on the stove. Lifting it, he returned to the table. "Would you like more? There's plenty."

"I wanted you to get your fill." Her voice caught in her throat.

"I have a lot on my plate. As a matter of fact, it's likely..." but he stopped short and eyed her as if not sure what to say. Finally, John Mark continued. "Please. Have more. It's a long trip to Willow Falls with not many stops in between. Nelsonville is the first town on the way, but it'll be hours before we reach it for the noonday meal."

"Are you sure?"

John Mark nodded and scooped a lofty amount of eggs from the pan onto her plate.

Hannah took a deep breath, lifted her fork, and took a bite. The eggs melted on her tongue and she relished the taste. Glancing down at her plate, gratitude filled her heart that there was a sufficient amount to fill her stomach. She took a bite, then another, doing her best to remain ladylike, but struggling to maintain an eating speed that complied with proper etiquette.

When she looked up, she noticed him watching her, and she slowed her eating.

"Thank you for making breakfast this morning."

She felt the red creep up her face and she shifted in the chair. "It's your wedding present." The words tumbled from her mouth before she could rein them in. Would he be happy with his gift? Would he rather have received a new shirt or knife from the mercantile?

"A right fine wedding present at that." He smiled, his eyes crinkling at the corners as he did so.

And Hannah's heart felt lighter than it had in forever.

John Mark hitched the horses to the wagon. Pa would arrive any minute, and while Pa was a patient man in most senses of the word, he did appreciate punctuality.

Several minutes later, Pa dismounted and walked toward John Mark. "Good morning, Son."

"Good morning. Did Pritchard bombard you with a million questions?"

Pa chuckled. "That he did. Reckon he had a question or two about growing in his faith."

"Ah, well, you're the one to talk with about such matters."

"That I am. Are you and Hannah about ready to leave for Willow Falls?"

John Mark nodded just as Hannah emerged from the house. The rooster followed her calmly, as if a pet rather than the nuisance he was.

Once they both climbed in the wagon, they began their trip. It didn't matter how many times John Mark made the journey between Poplar Springs and Willow Falls, he never tired of the breathtaking scenery designed by an imaginative Creator. In the distance, timbered hills gave way to snow-capped mountains. Alpine valleys—littered with the remaining pink, purple, yellow, and white summer wildflowers—drew his gaze from the road ahead. Cattle covered the hills and valleys, and the grass, while now yellowing, was blessedly sufficient this year due to the overabundance of rain from a wet spring.

If one didn't know of Poplar Springs' lawlessness, they might think they had arrived in one of the most beautiful places on earth. A vast corridor expanded from Poplar Springs and Bowman on the far end; to Nelsonville and Willow Falls on the opposite end; and Prune Creek just over the mountain. This part of Wyoming beckoned the traveler, as well as the long-time homesteader, to stay awhile and feast their eyes upon the magnificent offerings.

When the opportunity opened for a deputy sheriff in Poplar Springs, John Mark nearly leapt before he prayed. After all, wasn't that God's answer to the passion within his heart? The dream to uphold justice and make a difference? And yet, when John Mark arrived in Poplar Springs, it was immediately evident that it was not a calm and mostly-peaceful town like Willow Falls.

But there was hope.

There was always hope.

And John Mark aimed to do what he could to harness the minute amount of lawfulness the town offered. Sheriff Winslow agreed and had been a mentor to John Mark, as had Sheriff Townsend in Willow Falls.

God had a plan for Poplar Springs and for the lives of those who resided there. John Mark prayed the Lord would use him in fulfillment of that plan.

He stole a glance at Hannah's profile. She was pretty with her delicate features and large, wistful eyes that guarded her soul. The gift of the breakfast she'd made tugged at him. He hadn't yet purchased a gift for her for their wedding and hoped to do so once they reached Willow Falls. Perhaps Pa would be amenable to riding ahead without them and warning Ma of what was to come.

"Thank you again for the meal this morning, Hannah. It was a right fine one."

She turned to face him, her normally pale skin flushed. "You're welcome."

"Don't fret about meeting my family," he said, hoping to ease any apprehension she may have. If it were him meeting her family for the first time, he would experience a degree of nervousness.

"I hope they like me."

He almost didn't hear her muted response over the creaking of the wagon wheels, the roaring of the nearby river, and the sound of birds chirping in the trees. "They will. Reckon I've already mentioned a bit about my family. Ma is a selfless woman—always doing something kind for someone. I don't think she's ever met a soul she didn't cotton to. And as I mentioned before, you'll like Charlotte. She's boisterous and opinionated and smart. But she's also charitable and tenderhearted. Don't tell her I told you anything but the boisterous and opinionated part, though." He chuckled. "We do like to annoy each other from time to time."

A soft smile lit her face and John Mark wondered how he'd never seen her as the beauty she was. Of course, Pa would lecture him about outer appearances and reiterate that all beauty fades with time. That it's the character and integrity of a woman that mattered. But Ma was both pretty and full of integrity, so John Mark knew there were such women who possessed both characteristics.

"And then there's my brother, Caleb, and his wife, Annie. I've never met a man who can fix or build anything like Caleb. Annie was mine and Charlotte's teacher before she married Caleb. She was the best teacher we had and made sure we knew about every vocabulary word and each of their four hundred definitions. They have three daughters. Esther is the only one old enough to eat peppermint sticks, but I imagine when the other two are old enough, I'll be somewhat penniless bringing surprises for them when we visit."

It occurred to him that he'd naturally included Hannah in his future. The thought both surprised him and gave him hope for the vows they'd made in their unconventional situation. Theirs was not even rivaled by marriages such as that of the Corbetts. Mr. Corbett found his wife through a mail-order bride advertisement. The serious young woman had arrived from Maine and perfectly balanced Mr. Corbett's more laidback personality.

His mind returned to bringing Esther, Lena, and Lola treats during their visits. The three had just gained an aunt in Hannah. And Hannah had gained a family of eight.

They continued toward Willow Falls, Pa a few horse lengths between them. John Mark wanted to converse with Hannah. Wanted to get to know this woman God had blessed him with. Wanted her to know he was interested in things that mattered to her.

But how?

First, he needed to precipitate the conversation. While he didn't know much about Hannah, he surmised she was shy.

Another way they likely differed.

He searched his mind until a topic surged to the forefront. "Reckon the sun is shining brightly today."

As soon as he uttered the words, John Mark inwardly cringed. Anyone could see it was pleasant weather, and wasn't that something folks spoke of when they were attempting to remedy an awkward silence?

"Yes, it is."

John Mark steered the horses around a sizeable hole in the road. "So, when is your birthday?"

His topics were improving. Even Charlotte would be proud.

"It's March fifteenth. And yours?"

"November eighth."

Good. Now he knew when her birthday was. He tucked that nugget of information into his memory. Pa always told him to remember two important dates. Your wife's birthday and your anniversary. "Just keeps a marriage happier," he'd said at the time.

John Mark wouldn't soon forget their wedding anniversary and he hoped he wouldn't forget her birthday.

Hannah was a woman of few words, and he surmised that she would never be considered a chattering church bell like so many women. "Do you have a favorite animal?"

"I've never owned a pet, but I am quite fond of dogs. I also like chickens and Clarence seems friendly."

"Clarence?"

Hannah covered her mouth with a hand. "Rather, the rooster."

"You named him Clarence?"

Wariness flickered in Hannah's eyes. Was she concerned he would be vexed by her decision to name the ornery bird? "Interesting," he said.

Her shoulders immediately relaxed. "Are you all right with me naming him?"

John Mark shrugged. "He's a bothersome creature, but...Clarence?" Hannah's creativity amused him and he chuckled.

"He just reminded me of a Clarence. He's a rather likable fellow, and he followed me to the barn and back." A slight smile shone on her face.

"Are we talking about the same rooster? Red-and-brown with a red comb? Nosy and annoying? Thinks he owns the place?"

A faint giggle erupted, and John Mark wondered if he may have imagined it.

And then the oddest yearning occurred within him.

The yearning to be the one to make Hannah smile and laugh on more than just a rare occasion.

Chapter Sixteen

THE RIDE IN THE wagon with John Mark was a pleasurable one. She'd always been bashful, and Hannah appreciated him initiating the conversation, although a huge part of her feared she'd say something featherbrained and make him regret marrying her.

They stopped in a town called Nelsonville for the noonday meal before continuing toward Willow Falls. The journey was slow and arduous, and at first, Hannah pondered why they didn't saddle the horses and take them instead of the wagon.

Reverend Solomon answered that question when he and John Mark spoke of a bureau John Mark's parents were giving him because they no longer needed it.

She'd been relieved he found the breakfast tasty and that he'd even thanked her for it. Hannah would hold that memory in her heart. She was also thankful he wasn't angry, nor did he mock her for naming the rooster. As a child, Hannah had named many of the chickens. But she never told Pa.

A sign indicating their arrival into Willow Falls announced a population slightly less than Poplar Springs. The town, tucked at the base of the mountains, was bustling with folks strolling up and down the boardwalk. Nerves assailed her and she prayed for God's peace. A verse she'd memorized from Ma's Bible flooded her mind and she allowed the words to soothe her anxious heart and to combat the fear enveloping her. *"Peace I leave with you, my peace I give unto you: not as the world giveth, give I unto you. Let not your heart be troubled, neither let it be afraid."*

John Mark parked the wagon at the mercantile. "Pa will ride ahead and let Ma know we're coming for a visit. I do need to go into the mercantile for a moment. I'll be right back." He climbed from the wagon and strode into the building.

Willow Falls was a busy place, much like Poplar Springs, but Willow Falls seemed more orderly. She only counted two saloons. There was a church, a school, livery stable, sheriff's office, a barbershop, and a bank. Someone built a few benches and planted a patch of flowers near the church. A stream flowed adjacent to it and several children played nearby.

A woman and a man about her age strolled down the boardwalk and stopped outside the mercantile. The woman giggled and placed a hand on the man's arm, smiling coyly at him. Hannah observed such behavior many a time from her place on the bench.

The man returned the red-haired woman's flirtatious overtures, even leaning forward and whispering something in her ear, which caused her to flutter her eyelashes at him. He lifted her hand to his lips and she tittered again.

John Mark emerged from the mercantile a few minutes later. "John Mark," the woman trilled. "How have you been?"

The man touched the brim of his hat and bid the woman goodbye. "Eliason," he grunted, before striding down the boardwalk toward the livery.

"I've missed seeing you in Willow Falls," the woman said. She placed a hand on his arm and fluttered her lashes at him, much as she had done with the man. "Have you thought of me often?"

"Truth of the matter is, Violet..."

"You think of me all the time?" Her eyes enlarged and she placed a hand to her bosom. "I hear you're a sheriff's deputy over in Poplar Springs. Do tell. What's that like?"

"Busy. Poplar Springs is a mite bit different than here."

Violet closed the space between them. "I have really missed you, John Mark. You know I've set my cap for you."

"And not Cyrus?"

"Pish posh," said Violet. She twirled a tendril of hair between her finger and thumb. "He would be my second choice."

Hannah attempted to divert her attention to something else other than the coquettish woman and her antics.

"Truth is, Violet, I'm married and I'd like to introduce you to my wife."

Hannah felt the heat climb up her neck and onto her cheeks. She glanced down at her wedding dress, or rather, Ina's dress. It was, by all standards, a fine dress. But nothing like the latest fashion Violet wore.

The woman joined John Mark and they walked to Hannah's side of the wagon. "This is my wife, Hannah. Hannah, this is Violet. She and I went to school together."

Violet's eyes narrowed and her lips pursed. "Well, you never did tell me you got married, John Mark. I didn't even know you were courting." Violet's gaze traveled from the top of Hannah's mussed hair to her worn and holey shoes and embarrassment again flooded her.

"We best be going. If you'll excuse us." John Mark touched the brim of his hat, and in one brisk movement climbed into the wagon and tucked a burlap sack onto the seat between them.

As they drove away, Hannah dared to peer over her shoulder at Violet. The woman glowered, looking down her nose at Hannah.

"Don't worry about her," John Mark said. "But I'll be having a word or two with Cyrus when I see him next."

An immense flood of relief overcame her. Violet's affection for John Mark was one-sided.

John Mark pursed his lips. "He's supposed to be courting my sister, not allowing Violet to hang off his arm. I saw them outside the window while I was in the mercantile." A muscle in his jaw pulsed.

And Hannah realized something else about John Mark.

He was protective of those he cared about.

John Mark steered the wagon around the curve leading toward his parents' home. "Sorry it took me so long in the mercantile. Frederick likes to babble."

It then occurred to him that Hannah wouldn't know who Frederick was or any of these people he had known for most of his life. "When Mr. and Mrs. Morton moved out of Willow Falls a few years back, their son, Frederick, became the owner of the mercantile. He was actually one of my ma's pupils, and according to her, he's always been talkative and adept at spinning yarns." John Mark chuckled as he recalled some of the stories Ma had shared with him, Caleb, and Charlotte about Frederick and his creative yarns. "Humorous thing is that his wife, Millicent, is long-winded as well. I've always wondered how either of them gets a word in during their conversations."

Speaking of conversations, John Mark needed to discuss the gathering Ma would likely want to arrange to celebrate their marriage. Would Hannah be agreeable? Her countenance was one of reticence and he wanted to be respectful of that. "Uh...so my pa wanted us to discuss the get-together my ma might suggest. Would you be amenable to one?"

Seconds ticked by with only the sound of the wagon wheels creaking against the hardened earth and the sound of birds twittering in the trees. Finally, she responded in a hushed voice. "Yes, if that's what your ma would like."

"Ma would want what we want. And she might not be...she might not be thrilled that..." he struggled for the words. "Well, that I married so hastily and without her there."

John Mark heard Hannah's sharp intake of breath and instantly regretted his choice of words. "What I mean to say is that she'll like you and all, but she would have rather attended the wedding."

Hannah's eyes had widened and she clutched the side of the buckboard. He focused on her for a brief moment before returning his attention toward the road. "That is, while Ma is a shyer woman, she is also hospitable and would want everyone to celebrate our marriage with us."

"Oh."

He wasn't making this conversation any better. How would they ever discuss important matters in their marriage if John Mark couldn't even discuss a gathering? "It will be like a potluck, and everyone will be congratulating us. And if you don't—if we don't—want to have a gathering, Ma will be fine with that."

Would everyone in attendance wonder why no one knew he'd been courting a woman in Poplar Springs?

"I...I guess that would be all right."

John Mark slowed the wagon to a stop and turned toward her. Hannah had removed her tight grasp from the side of the wagon and smoothed her skirt. "Hannah, I realize you won't know anyone except Pa and me..." The awkwardness of the situation hung in the air. "If you'd rather we not have the get-together, I understand, and so will Ma. She will be proud of you and want everyone to meet you, but..."

Her gaze met his and he saw the trepidation in the depths of her eyes. "I just...I've never met any of them and I'm not sure they'll like me."

"They'll like you." And he knew they would.

"All right."

John Mark wasn't convinced. Perhaps he could discuss it with Ma and ask that they wait until a later date after Hannah had at least met his family and some of his close friends. He recalled how she waited so quietly outside the saloon, barely speaking to anyone.

He beckoned the horses and they continued toward the Eliason home. John Mark's thoughts turned toward Charlotte and what he'd seen outside the window when he was in the mercantile. He prayed for the Lord's wisdom in speaking with his sister. It could have been an innocent dalliance, but John Mark wasn't willing to take the chance. Violet's flirtatious overtures were common, always had been. But if Cyrus was Charlotte's beau, he should have refused those overtures.

Charlotte deserved better.

Even if telling her about Cyrus and Violet broke her heart.

John Mark had never liked Cyrus. That was no secret. But in John Mark's mind, it would be better to find out the kind of rapscallion the man was *before* the wedding vows.

The burlap sack shifted and he redirected his thoughts to Hannah. Would she like the gift he'd purchased for her? Thankfully, Pritchard, the unlikely knower of all things, had mentioned the necessity of buying a wedding gift. The thought hadn't even crossed John Mark's mind.

But then, marriage hadn't been at the forefront of his thoughts until a few days ago.

When John Mark entered the mercantile, he'd been hoping to find a music box for Hannah. However, there were none to be had that he could afford. He'd stood pondering the ornate one made of wood and bronze with the bird figurine atop it, but knew the chances of paying for it in a reasonable amount of time, even on account, would be slim.

Wisdom dictated he search and find something less expensive and plan to purchase a music box for Hannah in the future.

The future.

He knew God was sovereign and foreknew every event in every human life from beginning to end and all parts in between, and while there was solace in that, John Mark worried about his future with Hannah.

Pulling on the reins, John Mark again stopped the wagon by the side of the road. It would be best to present her with the gift now before they reached his parents' home. He lifted the burlap sack that cleverly hid Hannah's gift.

"Here is a wedding present. For you." He clumsily handed her the sack.

Her eyes doubled in size and she hesitantly took the sack from him. Hannah opened it and retrieved the first of two gifts, a wooden sewing box. She set the sack on the seat between them and opened the box.

"There are scissors, a thimble, a needle case, and thread..."

"John Mark, thank you." Hannah's voice quivered and she blinked several times.

"Do you like it?"

She nodded and fingered each of the items within the box. "Thank you."

"I wasn't sure what to buy you, so..."

"It's perfect."

John Mark fiddled with the reins. "There's another gift in the sack."

"Really?" Her face brightened, mixing with a stray tear. Hannah reached inside the bag and removed the pink ribbon.

"It's a hair ribbon. For your hair." John Mark inwardly groaned at his obvious statement. Why had he all of a sudden become so nervous around her?

Hannah ran her long fingers along the edge of the ribbon, smoothing a crease. "Thank you." She tugged her braid to the side where it rested on her shoulder and tied the ribbon at the bottom.

"The color suits you," John Mark blurted. Of course, he figured anyone as pretty as Hannah could have any color suit her. But the pink ribbon did perfectly contrast her silky brown hair.

Hannah's smile grew with his words and she sat a little taller and a little straighter.

CHAPTER SEVENTEEN

HANNAH HELD THE SEWING box carefully. She rubbed her finger over the wood and opened it no less than five times to peer at its contents. She had never before owned a sewing box. And she had never before received a gift such as this.

Her breakfast gift to John Mark suddenly seemed so insignificant compared to the gift he had given her.

A memory entered her mind unannounced. Pa had sent for Ramona and her sons after corresponding with her for several months. When she arrived that day on the stage, he presented her with a bottle of perfume from Roessler's Dry Goods. To Ramona and the unknowing observer, such an expensive gift indicated Pa's undying devotion to the woman he'd met through an advertisement where he sought a mail-order bride. Ramona's expression of surprise and delight would be forever embedded in Hannah's mind. As would the day Pa removed the perfume bottle from the bureau in their room and threw it at the wall in a drunken rage. The rose-scented aroma filled the entire house for several days after that.

And Hannah still couldn't bear the smell of roses even after all this time.

Her chest constricted. Would John Mark be the same as Pa? Was she a fool for agreeing to marry him? Pa and Ramona had only known each other for a few months by correspondence and exactly two days in person before the preacher married them.

And now Hannah was a married woman to a man she barely knew, just as Ramona had scarcely known Pa. Would she discover he wasn't who he proclaimed to be? Would his family like her? Would they accept her? John Mark had said his ma would be displeased at not attending the wedding. Would she place the blame on Hannah?

Hannah wiped her palms on the front of her dress, well, rather, Ina's dress. She'd need to return it when they arrived back in Poplar Springs. She shifted on the buckboard and bit her lip. Had agreeing to marry John Mark been a good idea?

"We're almost there," he said. "See that house? It's my brother, Caleb's."

She followed the direction he pointed. Numerous cattle dotted the landscape, and in the near distance stood a house with two towering trees, a barn, and a nearby chicken coop. Two thick logs on either side supported a crafted wood sign and the words *Eliason Ranch*.

Would Caleb's brother and his wife like her? Would they welcome her into the family?

A few moments later, another house came into view surrounded by several trees and a garden. Hannah's nervousness increased. A woman stood on the porch and waved.

"I'll introduce you to Ma before I unhitch the horses," John Mark said.

She appreciated his thoughtfulness and attempted to ignore the headache forming from the tension in her shoulders.

John Mark assisted her from the wagon and led her to the porch. "This is my ma, Lydie Eliason. Ma, this is my wife, Hannah."

It would be some time before she became accustomed to being a "wife" and John Mark's words caused her breath to hitch. Would she awaken at any moment and still be at Pa's house?

"It's a pleasure to meet you." Mrs. Eliason, a petite and slender woman in her forties with dark hair and the same infectious smile as John Mark, invited Hannah inside. "Please do come in. Charlotte is calling on a friend and should be home soon."

Hannah perused the house's interior. It wasn't that it was fancy, for it wasn't. Nor was it ostentatious in any way. Rather, it was modest, but tasteful. Homey and warm. An aroma of baking bread lingered in the air, and a few pieces of China rested on a shelf near a table with six chairs. Colorful curtains hung on the windows and a quilt rested on the chair by the fireplace. She closed her eyes and imagined what it must be like to live in such finery.

When she again opened her eyes, Mrs. Eliason stood before her, a smile alighting her face. "Would you care for a cup of coffee?"

"Yes, please." She would try her best to hide her overwhelming nerves and make a favorable impression on John Mark's ma.

Mrs. Eliason filled two cups with coffee and invited Hannah to take a seat at the table. The scent itself was enough to satiate her. She sipped the beverage, allowing the warmth to slide peacefully down her throat.

Only one other time had she ever tasted coffee.

The recollection clouded her memory. Ramona had purchased an expensive packet of coffee from the mercantile with her own funds as a surprise for Pa's birthday.

Ramona had anticipated the special occasion and bustled about the kitchen, singing in her melodic voice a happy tune as she prepared the two cups of coffee. One for Pa and one for herself.

Hannah had begged Ramona for the teeniest sip from the cup awaiting Pa. Ramona acquiesced and Hannah knew she'd never tasted anything finer, second only to a cup of fresh milk.

Ramona had pressed the wrinkles from her dress and patted her hair, but her primping would be for naught.

Pa had stomped into the house and complained that there should never be a snowstorm in the middle of June, even though such things weren't uncommon. Hannah and her brothers peered from the other room and Hannah had prayed Pa would at least offer a word of thanks to Ramona.

Pa slammed the door, causing the entire house to shake. He then left a watery mess on the floor as he thundered toward the table.

"What's this?" he had bellowed.

As if the memory occurred yesterday, Hannah recalled Irvin trembling and covering his eyes with his hands. "It's all right, little brother," she had whispered, pulling him close.

Ramona had flinched and her posture sagged. "Happy birthday, Harold," she had murmured, her hushed and trembling voice contrasting Pa's harsh tone.

Pa had slammed a fist on the table, causing the coffee to slosh over the sides of the cup. His uttered oaths combined with chastisement belittling Ramona for wasting money burned Hannah's ears. While Hannah may have become accustomed to Pa's fearsome outbursts over the years, they never ceased to terrify her. And while Ramona's considerate gesture went unappreciated by Pa, Hannah had never forgotten the aroma or the taste of the coffee.

Hannah took a deep breath and reminded herself she no longer had to return to Pa's house and experience his volatile temper. Her hands trembled and she placed the cup of coffee on the table.

Mrs. Eliason's voice returned Hannah fully to the present. "It's wonderful to meet you," she said.

"It's wonderful to meet you as well." Hannah's voice shook and she gathered her emotions. *Lord, please help me not to allow such remembrances of the past to ruin the present.* "Mrs. Eliason?"

"Yes?"

"I—" Hannah paused, not sure how to ask the question that plagued her. "I—I hope you're not vexed because

John Mark and I were married without you in attendance."

"I'll be honest, I was disappointed when Solomon first told me. A wedding is an important event, and I did want to be there when my son took that step in life. But then I remembered that John Mark is a grown man and must make his own decisions." A smile that lit up her entire countenance spread across her face. "Having said that, if you and John Mark are in agreeance, I would love to organize an informal potluck tomorrow with family and close friends to celebrate this momentous occasion."

Did Mrs. Eliason know the story behind her marriage to John Mark? Did she know her son had gambled and won Pa's blessing to marry her? That she and John Mark barely knew each other?

"Now," Mrs. Eliason continued, "the choice of whether or not to have a gathering is entirely up to you and John Mark. If you'd rather not, I completely understand. Although I selfishly would like our friends to meet you, it is your decision, and I am agreeable with whatever you decide."

"Thank you, Mrs. Eliason."

"Please, call me Lydie."

Hannah savored another sip. Concerns swirled through her mind. Should she utter such apprehensions aloud? "Lydie?" Pa's episode with the coffee re-entered her mind.

"Yes?"

"Is John Mark prone to temper?"

Lydie's brows furrowed. Was she taken aback by Hannah's boldness?

"John Mark does have a temper, mainly when he sees someone mistreated." She stared at the ceiling for a moment. "Once he started a brawl with another boy and Solomon had to bring him home early from school. Although John Mark did have the propensity to play many pranks during his boyhood years, naughty behavior was not customary for him. When he arrived home, John Mark told us the boy he'd scuffled with was a bully and had been mocking a fellow student because he had a limp. But other than that, no, I wouldn't say he's prone to temper. He's a big man, built just like Solomon, only taller, but he's a gentle soul."

"And does he imbibe?" Her voice squeaked in her own ears, Hannah's words falling freely from her mouth, something so otherwise uncharacteristic of her. But John Mark had entered the saloon that day he challenged Pa. Had he imbibed with the rest of the men? She held her breath as she awaited Lydie's answer.

Lydie shook her head. "No."

Hannah exhaled the breath she was holding, her fears somewhat alleviated. If Lydie was correct—and she certainly should know her son better than anyone—John Mark was not like Pa in the sense of his violent temper or his drinking. But was how he presented himself different than the person he was? Like what Ramona had believed about Pa? Anxiety pummeled through her again.

"John Mark is a fine young man. His pa and I couldn't be prouder of him. But John Mark isn't perfect, just as no one is." Lydie took a sip of her coffee. "I recall when I first began to court Solomon." A smile crossed her face. "He was so smart, so handsome, and so thoughtful. I'd never known a man quite like him before. I didn't remember much of my own father since my parents died when I was little and I was raised by my aunts, Fern and Myrtle. I thought for certain God had blessed me with the perfect husband."

Hannah directed her attention to Lydie, eagerly awaiting the rest of the woman's story.

"Of course, no one is perfect. As a matter of fact, I didn't much care for Solomon when I first met him due to a misunderstanding. But in a short amount of time, I came to love him. As much as I would have liked to think he was flawless, I couldn't be more incorrect. Just as I am not flawless. We both found that out about each other during our first fight. It was two days after we married and it was over potatoes."

"Potatoes?"

"Yes. An absurd argument, but it made me realize that as wonderful as Solomon is, he, like me, has his idiosyncrasies." She laughed. "After the potato incident, I wrote my two aunts a letter. Aunt Myrtle, the more outspoken of the two, responded, telling me that, while she and Aunt Fern appreciated me taking the time to write to them, it was never a virtuous idea to complain about your husband to others. She suggested in no uncertain terms that I resolve our differences regarding the potatoes posthaste, just Solomon and me. Of course by the time I received the letter, the potato debacle was already settled."

Hannah allowed herself to cautiously laugh. She imagined in her mind a much younger Lydie and Reverend

Solomon arguing over potatoes and a spunky aunt giving her opinion.

"I do hope you have the benefit of meeting the aunts someday. They are truly a plucky and spirited duo." She paused. "Are both of your parents living?"

Hannah thought of the mother she never knew and the stepmother who'd deserted her. Even now, the heartache of being left behind was an ache that would never subside. But at least Ramona and her sons hadn't had to continue to endure her father. "My ma died giving birth to me, and my pa married Ramona when I was twelve. When she found out who Pa really was—" Hannah's voice trailed and she looked away. She attempted to reconcile her fears about John Mark with Lydie's reassurances.

"I'm so sorry." Lydie reached over and placed a hand on Hannah's arm. "I know you and John Mark weren't able to court before your marriage. You weren't able to get to know each other and spend time together the way betrothed couples do. But I can assure you that John Mark would never lay a hand on you, nor will he imbibe. Although he *can* be fiercely stubborn and ornery at times."

Hannah wiped a tear that slid down her cheek. Trust was difficult. Both trusting John Mark and trusting the gracious woman sitting before her.

CHAPTER EIGHTEEN

JOHN MARK UNHITCHED THE horses, his mind on the day's events. While Hannah seemed thrilled after he presented her with the gift, she'd said few words the rest of the way home. Had he erred in his decision to purchase a sewing kit for her? Would she have preferred a music box?

Who could understand women?

John Mark entered the barn, a feeling of nostalgia overtaking him. Chores or fetching the horses were his main reasons for visiting the barn. Other times it was for a talking-to from Pa over a mischievous event John Mark had partaken in. And still other times—many times—it was to seek Pa's wisdom, of which he always had an abundance.

Today it was for the latter.

Pa was mucking out the stalls when John Mark entered. "Hey, Pa."

"How did it go in town?"

John Mark thought of Violet and Cyrus and irritation rippled through him. He'd need to discuss that with Pa as well. "I stopped in at the mercantile. I'd forgotten how much Frederick likes to talk."

Pa chuckled. "That, he does. His pa was always a talk-ative sort. Seems the apple doesn't fall far from the tree, as the saying goes."

"That's true. I recall Mr. Morton clucking on like a hen." How had time gone by so fast? Wasn't it just yes-terday that John Mark was accompanying Pa to fetch supplies? Now he was a married man.

Unbelievable.

"Say, Pa, how did Ma take it when you told her about the wedding?" He knew how important milestones were to his mother and she thrived on being a part of the things that mattered to her children.

"She was disappointed at first but understands and knows the situation."

Relief flooded John Mark. "What did she think about me gambling for Hannah's freedom?"

"While it wasn't the most conventional way to find a wife, you know your ma and her tender heart for others. While she'd never condone gambling, she understands why you did what you did, just as I do."

"Thank you, Pa."

Silence lingered in the barn for the next few minutes. When John Mark was younger, he figured it out that Pa was quiet on purpose because he was waiting for John Mark to share what was on his mind.

His thoughts then took a different direction. "Pa?"

"Yes, Son?"

John Mark stared at the hay on the barn floor and pondered his next words. "What if—what if I never do love Hannah the way God calls us to love our wives?

What if she and I don't get along? Or she doesn't like me? Or what if she's a contemptible woman?"

Pa stopped what he was doing and leaned an elbow on his pitchfork. "That's a lot of what-ifs, Son."

"I just—how do I know I did the right thing in rescuing her?" Pa's opinion mattered.

"You knew the life she lived and knew something ought to be done. And you prayed about it."

John Mark wiped his sweaty palms on the front of his trousers. Had there been any other option? "Yes, sir, on all those things. But forever is a long time to be married to someone. What if I chose the wrong someone?"

"Marriage is not an easy thing, even under the best of circumstances. It's sharing your life with someone—a completely different person with a different personality. It's putting someone else above yourself and wanting what's best for them. It's loving someone even when they're unlovable."

John Mark's heart constricted for a moment at Pa's words. How could he ever succeed at all of this? Why hadn't he thought about this more thoroughly? "I know she needed her freedom, but I guess a part of me was thinking—maybe even hoping—she'd choose not to marry me, but instead choose to start a new life in a different way. Not that I don't like her, I do. I just..." He recalled Hannah's joy when he gave her the wedding gift. How could he *not* want that?

Pa said nothing for a time, but bowed his head, likely to pray. That was the thing about Pa. He rarely spoke more than a word or two without seeking the Lord's guidance first. "I've told you before how your ma didn't much care for me when we first met, right?"

"You did."

"And I wanted more than anything to apologize to her for our misunderstanding. And then I fell in love with her. We were young. Younger than you and Hannah. But I knew—I can't really explain it—but I knew she was the one for me. We courted and married. We've had some difficult times in our married years and one of those things I had to remember was that life is never perfect. Oh, my life with your ma is the best thing I'll ever experience this side of Heaven, and I love her more than I love anyone. But she's not perfect and I'm certainly not perfect. Marriage is something two people work at daily to achieve a union pleasing to God. You and Hannah have started things differently than most. But that doesn't mean it won't work. It doesn't mean she won't someday love you and you won't someday love her."

"But right now we don't even know each other well enough to like each other."

Pa stroked his beard. "That's true, and you're not the first to enter into a marriage of convenience. But when God is the center of any relationship, whether it be a marriage or a friendship, it has the best chance of success. You both have to aim to make Him the center of all you do. Of how you treat each other. And of how you live your lives together and apart." Pa paused. "Hannah has been through a lot in her life. Things have not been easy. She's been mistreated, abused, and I would venture to say she's never been loved. She will struggle with things. You grew up with a family who loved you, while she didn't have that."

"I know. I've witnessed the way her pa treats her."

"Exactly. So you know that while she's struggling with things—struggling even more so with a new marriage and a new life than you are—you must be patient with her. Remind her you are there for her. Right now more than anything, she needs a friend. And as I always say, it helps a whole lot if you like the one you're married to in addition to loving them."

John Mark considered Pa's words. Could he be patient with Hannah? Be there for her in times of need? Attempt to understand what she'd been through and her past, so opposite from his own? The pressure weighed heavily on him. "What if I fail?"

"You will. I've failed your ma more times than I can count. And, as you know, we often fail our Lord. But that's when you seek her forgiveness, ask for the Lord's guidance and wisdom, and continue on. A good marriage is worth fighting for."

Pa reached over and gripped John Mark's shoulder. "Your ma and I will be praying for you both and we are here for you whenever you need us. One other thing I might suggest is to help Hannah secure female friendships. I'm sure she, your ma, Charlotte, and Annie will become fast friends. She also needs friends in Poplar Springs. Womenfolk she can talk to and rely upon, especially in those long hours when you're upholding the law."

"Ina Pearson seems to be a dependable friend, although she and her family just moved to Poplar Springs.

She is the one Hannah stayed with the night before our wedding. Miss Pearson lives with her family in a tiny space above their restaurant, but she and Hannah are about the same age. Perhaps I can encourage that friendship and maybe one with Reverend Fleming's and Winslow's wives as well."

"Worthwhile plans for sure."

Pa waited a few more minutes, likely to see if John Mark had anything else on his mind. He did need to talk to his father about Cyrus, but that would have to wait. For now, John Mark's thoughts were full of all Pa had said and with the hopes he'd remember the vast wisdom in those words.

Lydie snapped her fingers. "I just thought of something! Wait here a moment." She sprang from her chair and hurried to another room in the house, leaving Hannah alone with her thoughts. She prayed God would guide her in this new freedom He'd given her. Thoughts collided in her mind and insecurities surfaced, although speaking with John Mark's ma had done much to alleviate the fear of an uncertain future.

"I don't want to speak out of turn." Lydie reappeared, something behind her back. "But do you have something to wear for the festivities tomorrow?"

"I was just going to wear this." Hannah had grown accustomed to Ina's dress. It would need a washing after today's travel on the dusty road, but it was still a better option than her brown threadbare dress.

Lydie's face glowed with a bright smile. "If you would like—and the decision is entirely up to you—I have a dress you could wear." Lydie brought her hands from behind her back and displayed a dress. Hannah gasped. It was the most beautiful one she had ever seen—even more so than the ones at the dress shop in Poplar Springs. Pale pink, it boasted a delicate pleated collar. Pearl-colored buttons lined the bodice and the lower sleeves.

Hannah drew a deep breath. "It's so elegant."

"Yes, I agree. Would you like to wear it tomorrow? If you don't, it doesn't hurt my feelings..."

"I'd love to! If...if it's all right."

Lydie held the dress against Hannah, reaching her arms toward Hannah's shoulders. "I think with a few minor adjustments, this would fit perfectly."

Hannah swallowed hard. "This is a magnificent dress, but I couldn't ask you to alter it for me."

"I sewed this for a young lady in town. At the last minute, she changed her mind. You will look so lovely in it that I think it was meant for you."

"Thank you, Lydie, thank you so much." Her vision blurred with tears and she struggled to rein in the strong emotions that enveloped her.

"You are more than welcome. Let's take a few measurements and we'll work on it before supper."

That evening, John Mark's sister arrived home from a friend's house. Would the spirited Charlotte Eliason accept her?

After introductions, Charlotte asked, "Would you care to go for a stroll? I've been sitting most of the day partaking in needlework with a friend and a walk sounds most invigorating."

Hannah joined Charlotte and together they meandered down the tree-lined road.

"I must say I never imagined anyone would marry John Mark unless it was against her will." Charlotte giggled. "However did the two of you meet and why was I not apprised that he was courting someone?"

Obviously, no one had yet shared with Charlotte the details of Hannah and John Mark's marriage. Should she be the one to do so? Or should it be John Mark since it was his sister and the two were obviously close? "We met when I ran into him outside of the dress shop."

"Oh, how romantic!" Charlotte clasped her hands together. "Did you just know he was the one for you?"

If only they had met in such a circumstance. They could have courted and someday fallen in love, with marriage the natural progression. But would John Mark have desired to court her on his own had he not decided to free her from Pa? If their marriage hadn't been one of necessity for Hannah?

"I must say I am somewhat of a romantic. My brother, Caleb, and his wife, Annie, met when she became the new teacher—mine and John Mark's teacher—all those years ago and he pretended to be an old student in her class. My parents have a delightful story to tell of how they met. And now you and John Mark. I can see it now...you're walking out of the dress shop after finding just the right dress and you run plumb into this handsome stranger. Well, John Mark isn't handsome, but for this story, let's pretend he is. And you both just knew it was meant to be, hence the expedient courtship." Charlotte held her hand to her heart and swooned.

Hannah had never been in the presence of someone so spirited and enthusiastic, not even Ina. Charlotte's cheerful and buoyant personality was so opposite of her own timid and reserved nature. Yet, it was contagious and Hannah couldn't help feeling instantly comfortable around Charlotte despite the misunderstanding about her and John Mark's relationship. "I did run plumb into him and..." she recalled how he gently steadied her. How could Hannah have known at that moment that she would someday marry him?

Charlotte stopped and whirled toward her, her eyes bright with anticipation. "And..."

Should Hannah tell her how the story *really* happened? Would John Mark want to tell her? Would Charlotte be disappointed when she heard the truth? "Charlotte..."

"Yes? And before you tell me, was your pa agreeable with you marrying a deputy? It's such a hazardous job and all. And do you have brothers? Mine are both so protective of me and tend to interrogate any potential beaus. As a matter of fact, I'm dreading John Mark finding out about Cyrus. But that's a story for another time. Do tell...how did your family respond? Was your ma teary-eyed that her daughter was about to be married?"

Hannah knew her countenance fell at the mention of a mother. Would her ma have been teary-eyed? Would she have encouraged Hannah in this pursuit, or would she have insisted Hannah and John Mark court before marrying? Would her ma have even stayed with Pa after all these years?

"I..." How could she tell Charlotte that everything in her imaginative and creative story was false? That the story she'd concocted possessed not one ounce of truth?

Charlotte's smile evoked encouragement and Hannah took a deep breath before telling the *real* story. "My ma died when I was born."

"Oh, Hannah, I'm so sorry." Charlotte rested a hand on her arm.

"I never knew her. But I do miss her and wonder what she might have been like." One time she'd heard from her grandmother that she favored Ma in appearance. It hadn't been a cordial statement, but more of a derisive one. Pa's mother had stayed only a short time before leaving on the next stagecoach. Just long enough to remind Hannah that love was sparse in her family.

"Please accept my apology."

"You didn't know. But, Charlotte, I do need to tell you that the real story of how John Mark and I met is nothing like the one you imagined. Quite the opposite."

Hannah heard the wavering in her voice and realized how the thoughts of Ma had evoked a host of emotions, from heartbreak to a yearning for a mother who had lived; from fear of Charlotte's opinion of her; to worry that when she'd accepted John Mark's proposal it had altered his life and not for the better. Should she have instead asked that he take her to another town so she could start over and allow him to marry the woman of his choosing?

The compassion in Charlotte's expression, so characteristic of everyone Hannah had met so far in the Eliason family, provoked the threat of tears. Hannah bit her lip, prayed for courage, then shared a condensed version of her story. "John Mark offered me marriage as a way for me to escape my pa, an abhorrent and contemptible man." John Mark could make the choice to tell Charlotte about the card game. Hannah would not do anything to cause Charlotte's opinion of her brother to be tainted.

Charlotte's jaw dropped. "I had no idea. However, that sounds like something John Mark would do."

"Yes, and I appreciate that he did this for me. But I hope it wasn't the wrong decision for him." The words fell from her mouth before Hannah could stop them.

"I'm so sorry about your pa. I've heard of men like him and you have my deepest sympathies. As for John Mark, there are some things you should know about him."

Hannah emotionally prepared herself for the words Charlotte was about to speak. Oh, how she prayed John Mark would not be like Pa in any way.

"John Mark is a protector. He cares for those who have been mistreated, whether it's people or animals. That's one of the reasons he wanted to become a deputy. That and he is a firm believer in justice. It's admirable he wanted to protect you and keep you safe from your pa."

"But I don't want him to regret that he didn't have the chance to marry who he wanted."

"What if he wanted to marry you?"

Charlotte's words gave Hannah hope. "But we barely know each other."

"The other thing I can tell you about John Mark is that he never does anything he doesn't want to do. I've never met anyone so stubborn. We've always been close, although we don't always get along, but I do know he would protect me or Caleb, or Ma and Pa, or anyone he cared about no matter what."

"I do know all of the young unmarried women in Poplar Springs—not that there are many—but of those there are—they had their cap set for John Mark. But he married me." Why had she spoken about things so close to her heart with a stranger? What must Charlotte think of her?

"That does not surprise me because John Mark is a godly man who cares about others. However, he didn't choose to marry those women. He chose you."

She choked back the burning in her throat at Charlotte's words. "But what if by wanting to rescue me, he lost the chance to marry a woman he loves?"

"What if someday *you* will be the woman he loves? Is there anything that says you two can't grow to love each other?"

Could she grow to love John Mark? Probably so. He was, as Charlotte said, a godly man who cared for others. And he was dapper and strong and a hard worker. She doubted he'd ever allow her to starve the way Pa had. He could be easy to grow to love. But would John Mark ever come to love *her*? Plain, awkward, and timid *her*? And how would she ever be good enough for him? She hadn't been good enough for Pa, Ramona, Grandmother Bane, or even the townsfolk in Poplar Springs.

Charlotte wrapped an arm around her shoulder. "I think John Mark made a wise choice. You see, when I was a little girl, I asked every year for several years in a row that my parents would give me a sister for Christmas. While I love them dearly, two brothers can be a handful at times. All of that begging for a sister, yet one never arrived. Until Caleb married Annie. She's been the older sister I never had. And now with John Mark marrying you, I have two sisters. Who knew I could be so blessed?"

Hannah wanted to remind Charlotte that they'd just met, but something told her that it didn't matter to Charlotte. For, just as Lydie and Reverend Solomon had, the Eliason family had given Hannah something she'd never before had.

Acceptance.

CHAPTER NINETEEN

JOHN MARK ENTERED THE house, a bowl of eggs from the chicken coop in his hands. He placed it on the table.

And that's when he saw her.

She emerged from one of the bedrooms, and he stilled, the sight of her causing his breath to hitch.

Hannah was not just pretty, she was beautiful.

Sure, she was pretty at their wedding, but today...she wore a light pink dress and had tucked a cluster of flowers in her hair. Her face shone, especially her eyes.

John Mark's jaw dropped. A vocabulary word they'd had to spell years ago in school entered his mind.

Captivating.

Only in this instance, it wasn't used to describe the mountains surrounding Willow Falls when brushed with snow.

It was used to describe his wife.

Her eyes met his and it was then that he realized something Charlotte would term as "profound."

"I'm staring," he muttered, his voice sounding hoarse like it had the time Ma fed him garlic syrup to heal a nasty sore throat and cough.

A pleasant blush crept up Hannah's face and she busied herself with one of the many buttons on her dress. He'd embarrassed her. John Mark cleared his throat and focused his attention outside the window. "The people are coming."

His voice again sounded eerily reminiscent of a frog croaking. *The people are coming?* He wasn't a shy man or a man of few words. Matter of fact, John Mark was just the opposite. *"Personable,"* as Ma described him on more than one occasion.

"The people?" she asked.

"Uh, yes, the people. You know, the—" his muddle-headed brain struggled to retrieve a word far in the recesses of his mind. "The guests."

Lest Hannah think she married an oaf, John Mark instead peered at the plate of sugar cookies on the table—his favorite type of cookie. Next to the plate was a cake with white frosting all fancy-like. Ma had been busy that morning.

He reached toward the plate of cookies, in need of something to distract him from blundering more words in a situation that had rapidly become awkward. John Mark grasped the soft cookie in his hand. Ma would never notice one missing.

It was only after taking a bite of the cookie and hearing a soft giggle from Hannah that John Mark realized his error. When he'd reached for the cookie, the sleeve of his shirt brushed against the frosting on the cake and now a decent lot of it clung to his once freshly-laundered shirt. He winced. What had once been a perfect cake was now marred with a trench plowed through it.

Ma would have his hide and then some. No matter that it was a special occasion.

It was John Mark's turn to be embarrassed and his face burned. He popped the cookie in his mouth and grabbed a knife. If he could somehow smooth out the frosting, no one would be the wiser to his blunder. Gently smearing the frosting, he swirled it in a circular motion, attempting to cover the trench.

Hannah stood beside him now. "May I?" she asked, her voice so quiet he wasn't sure he'd heard her correctly.

He turned his gaze to her, noticing the unique and pleasing color of her eyes. A soft scent of lavender floated toward him, affecting his senses. "I—yes." John Mark handed her the knife.

With ease, Hannah swooped the frosting seamlessly into the trench, evening out the rough spots caused by his shirt. He watched her profile, bent with concentration and caution so as not to get her own sleeve in the cake. "That should do," she whispered.

Unless someone knew the former fate of the cake, they *wouldn't* know. "Thank you," he said, impressed by her ability to transform his error.

A smile formed on her lips as she looked up at him. "We shan't tell a soul."

Seconds ticked by before John Mark realized his vocal cords still functioned. "Yes, I mean, no. We won't." For the first time since the incident, he had noticed the frosting on his sleeve. "Reckon I should go change before the celebration."

Hannah realized she'd been holding her breath for a lengthy portion of the time she and John Mark stood near the cake and she attempted to rectify the frosting incident. He stood so close to her she feared she'd smear the frosting either on herself or into a worse mess. The man was even more handsome this close. Seeing him with his hair combed and wearing his light blue shirt and black button-up vest had almost been her undoing. She nearly fumbled her grasp on the knife. Bemoaning her butterfingers, Hannah attempted to collect herself.

And lest John Mark think he married a flibbertigibbet, Hannah stuck a steel rod in her spine and endeavored to stand as poised as she'd seen the higher-society ladies in town do.

He grinned at her, the dimple in his chin proving more prominent as he did so. "Reckon I should go change before the celebration," he repeated.

"Yes," she squeaked.

But neither moved.

"I'll just go now." John Mark hiked a thumb toward the door.

She watched as he left to tend to his shirt, her thoughts about the embarrassing situation interrupted when Reverend Solomon entered the home.

"Hello, Hannah. Are you about ready for the potluck?"

"Yes, I believe so."

As if to read her mind that she was in need of such, the reverend offered words of encouragement. "Now, I will tell you that my sweet Lydie has invited a lot of people. For someone who was shy when I first met her, she has become somewhat chatty with all of her numerous friends in town. Word has spread rapidly about John Mark marrying a woman from Poplar Springs, and everyone will be eager to meet you."

A shock of panic zipped through Hannah. What would they think of her? The Eliasons were well-known and well-thought-of in Willow Falls. The entire ordeal brought about a case of the nerves. Had she made a mistake by agreeing to it?

"It can be overwhelming when you've never met anyone before. I recall being nervous myself when I first moved here. But I think you'll find the folks of this town gracious and accommodating."

"Solomon?" Lydie bustled through the door. "Oh, there you are. I believe we are just about ready. Hannah, if you need anything, we're here for you." She took a step forward and drew Hannah into a hug. "Welcome to the family." Lydie's demeanor spoke of understanding and benevolence.

A niggling bit of apprehension filled her mind. Trust was difficult. Could she trust the Eliasons to be a part of her life?

CHAPTER TWENTY

GUESTS MILLED ABOUT AWAITING Pa's announcement about John Mark and Hannah's wedding. John Mark spied Cyrus tethering his horse and his muscles tensed. Cyrus strutted past the barn and toward him. "Have you seen Charlotte?" he asked.

"Not recently."

Cyrus quirked an eyebrow as if he didn't believe him.

"Speaking of Charlotte..." began John Mark before he could rein in his tongue.

"Yes?"

"I noticed you talking to Violet outside of the mercantile last night."

Cyrus's tart tone matched his defensive actions. "When is against the law to talk to Violet? Or is that a crime in Poplar Springs?"

"It's not."

"Then what seems to be the problem?" Cyrus folded his arms across his chest and took a step toward John Mark. If he intended to intimidate, he failed miserably. While Cyrus was strong and well-built, John Mark was the same, only a half-inch taller. As a matter of fact, he was certain he could also run faster and farther than Cyrus too, if need be.

John Mark took a step closer as well. "The problem as I see it is that you are courting my sister. Being overly friendly with another woman isn't acceptable, and you were being overly friendly with her." The image of Violet hanging off Cyrus's arm and the two exchanging flirtatious overtures flitted through his mind.

"And you do realize Charlotte is a grown woman who can look out for herself."

"I do. And you do realize it doesn't matter how old Charlotte is, whether she's twenty-one or ninety-two, she'll always have two older brothers to protect her."

Cyrus threw back his head and chortled, then sobered. "Yet, I don't see Caleb anywhere around attempting to cause a scene." He thumped John Mark in the shoulder. "You need to stay out of Charlotte's business. Besides, there's nothing wrong with me talking to Violet." He paused and narrowed his eyes. "Or do you fancy her?"

"Not in the least. You know I've never fancied Violet."

"Then do you still hold a grudge against me from that time in school?"

John Mark revisited the time when they were both ten and Cyrus blamed something he did on John Mark and the teacher believed him. The repercussions of Cyrus's lies and John Mark being wrongly accused were extensive, but John Mark had forgiven him. "No, I don't still hold a grudge. It's just that—"

"Just that what? For a preacher's son, aren't you supposed to be forgiving and all that?" Cyrus sneered, his already-dark eyes turning darker.

"I am forgiving. But if you hurt Charlotte in any way, I might not be."

Cyrus bridged the remaining gap between them and stuck out his chest. "Is that a threat?"

"Could be."

"A threat from the powerful deputy sheriff of *Poplar Springs*?" He spat the words. "What would the people think?"

Cyrus brought out the worst in John Mark. Always had. And not just because of the incident when they were ten. He and Cyrus had never gotten along, and it was made worse by Cyrus's supposed affections for Charlotte. He noticed his sister in the distance speaking with Mrs. Townsend and Mrs. Garrett, Doc's wife. John Mark would do whatever it took to protect her, and if Cyrus broke her heart, so help him...

Cyrus averted his gaze toward Charlotte. "It's beneficial for the heir of the wealthiest rancher in the area to have a pretty woman by his side. Charlotte is one comely woman." Cyrus's expression, akin to one John Mark had seen in the eyes of Oslo Dunn when he leered at Hannah, made his insides twist.

His heart rate increased. "Surely *even you* know that a woman is more than her appearance."

"She can cook and have children, so that's of considerable benefit as well."

John Mark met Cyrus's eye. "Charlotte, as all women do, deserves respect."

"Oh, she'll be respected. She'll have everything she wants. Sure, Charlotte may have to turn a blind eye to some of my, shall we say, indiscretions, but she'll learn. Just like my ma has had to learn with my pa."

John Mark's heart pounded heavy in his chest and he figured his face was redder than the strawberry preserves Ma canned in the fall. "What does Charlotte see in you? And how did you gain our pa's blessing to marry her?"

"Not too hard. You do recall my family is rather prominent in these parts, right? A few niceties here and there. Go to church and put on a respectable presentation. It's not too difficult." Cyrus muttered an oath under his breath. "Look, Eliason, I aim to marry Charlotte, and it would behoove you to mind your own business." He poked a finger into John Mark's collarbone in time with his words. "Mine and Charlotte's business is mine and Charlotte's business. Not everyone's business is your business, despite what you might think."

John Mark's muscles tensed. The temptation to ensure that Cyrus knew John Mark was serious about the matter was immense. He knew for certain if there was a brawl, he would win.

"What's the matter, John Mark? Am I upsetting you?" Cyrus's lip curled. "Can Deputy Eliason, the son of the perfect Reverend Solomon and the lawman of the disreputable town of Poplar Springs where outlaws outnumber the law-abiding citizens a hundred to one—a town where no one with all their faculties intact would want to reside—keep his head in the face of anger?" The goading continued with a few choice words reflecting Cyrus's obvious opinion of him.

John Mark wasn't sure he could keep his head in the face of anger, not without the Lord's help, anyway. So far

Cyrus had insulted both his sister and his father. John Mark held his chin high, thankful no one roaming about noticed their discussion as he'd do nothing to embarrass his family and Hannah. He prayed for self-control even as Cyrus continued to mock him while interjecting an uttered profanity every few words.

"Keep your nose out of it, John Mark."

"I'll not have you hurt Charlotte."

"And what will *you* do about it?"

Pa's voiced echoed through his mind. *"A man does his utmost best to exhibit integrity at all times, even under tense situations."* Pa might be able to adhere to that rule, but if Cyrus continued to press him, John Mark feared he might not be able to do so. A verse from Proverbs entered his thoughts: *"He that hath no rule over his own spirit is like a city that is broken down, and without walls."*

Lord, please help me to exhibit integrity.

"What's the matter, is there a bee in your bonnet?" Cyrus chided, his voice dropping to a hiss.

Just as John Mark was about to retort something a man with integrity should not retort, Charlotte strolled toward them.

"Is everything all right? John Mark?"

The worry in her face unsettled him. He hated causing anyone pain, much less his sister. "Yes, everything is fine."

Cyrus pasted a smile on his face and wrapped an arm around Charlotte, his actions reflective of a chameleon. "There you are, my beloved. I was just listening to John Mark lecture me about how I don't meet his qualifications of a beau for you."

"John Mark, is that true?" Charlotte's brow creased.

"Charlotte..."

"You know John Mark. He thinks everyone's business is his business."

Charlotte bobbed her head. "I do know that about you."

"Charlotte, if I could explain..."

"Nothing to explain," interjected Cyrus, his voice dripping with falseness. "John Mark doesn't want us to marry. And frankly, Charlotte, such a thought..." Cyrus put a fist to his heart with his free hand. "It hurts me right there, for I cannot even imagine my life without you in it."

Charlotte blinked rapidly and John Mark wanted to tell her not to believe a word Cyrus said. But the adoring look she gave him assured him his words would be futile. "Oh, Cyrus."

Cyrus planted a kiss on her cheek. "Do not worry your pretty head, my beloved. I won't allow John Mark or anyone else to put a stop to something that is meant to be."

While the Lord had given John Mark a way out of the predicament with Charlotte's arrival, John Mark's anger burned inside of him. How had his family not seen the truth behind Cyrus's façade? Before he could give it any more thought, Charlotte faced him, her eyes flashing.

"And as for you...that's the problem with you, John Mark. You don't know when to leave well enough alone."

John Mark opened his mouth to utter a response when he saw Hannah look his way. This was a special day for her—or at least he hoped it was—and he'd do nothing to ruin it. "We'll discuss this another time," he muttered and found his way toward Hannah just as Pa announced he had some important news he wished to share.

Doing his best to shake his mind from the confrontation with Cyrus, John Mark stood next to Hannah and peered at all of the guests. He knew such a crowd made Hannah uncomfortable. He knew them all, but she knew none of them, save for some of his family.

Pa motioned for everyone to gather around the table where the cake, sugar cookies, and punch bowl awaited guests. "I would like to thank you all for coming." He paused and put an arm around Ma. "Lydie and I are grateful for the opportunity to share this momentous occasion with you." Ma nodded and smiled up at him. Pa squeezed her a little closer. "We hope you will make Hannah feel welcome."

The townsfolk nodded their agreement. Hannah *would* be welcome in Willow Falls. She fiddled with a button on her dress and her eyes darted from one person to another in the modest crowd that gathered. The baby bird comparison again registered in his mind. She needed someone to care for her, and he hoped she'd allow him to be that person.

John Mark swallowed the lump in his throat. He would fight for her honor. Protect her. Give her the life she never had.

And someday, he hoped to love her the way Pa loved Ma.

She shrunk even more after Pa finished his speech and people lined up to greet her. Without a second thought to how she might react or if it was even the right thing to do, John Mark reached for her hand. He wanted to reassure her he was right here beside her when three dozen people she'd never met converged on her. While he might never understand one's propensity toward shyness, John Mark did hope to alleviate her discomfort somewhat.

Hannah gazed up at him, something indiscernible in her expression. He grinned and leaned toward her. "You're about to meet some of the finest folks in Willow Falls."

A slight smile lit her face and he recalled her soft laughter after he'd created a trail through the top of the cake with his sleeve.

"Uncle John Mark!" two little girls in matching pink calico dresses and bonnets ran toward him and wrapped their arms around his waist. He released his hand from Hannah's and bent over to lift a girl in each arm. Lena, the older of the two, pasted a slobbery kiss on his cheek while Lola patted his hair and giggled, her tiny eyes disappearing as she did so.

"Where have you been?" Lena asked. "We've miss-ed you."

Lola, at only two and not yet one for many words, nodded. "Yes," she said.

"Well, I've missed you two as well." He snuggled them close and Lena ran her hand along his chin. "You need to shave, Uncle John Mark. You're feeling like a pokeypine."

John Mark chuckled at her little girl accent. "Have you ever pet a porcupine?" He asked.

Lena put a finger to her chin and shook her head. "I don't think so."

"Well, there then, how do you know my chin feels like a porcupine?"

Lola giggled again. "Pokeypine," she said, as if the word tickled her tongue to say it. With the exception of her squinty eyes, she was an exact copy of Annie, while Lena favored Caleb.

Esther bounded toward them. "Hi, Uncle John Mark!"

"Esther, you're missing some teeth. What happened?"

"Uncle John Mark, you're silly. I lost-ed them."

John Mark feigned concern. "I sure hope you find them."

"I don't need those old ones anyway because Ma says I'll be getting new ones. Can you see them yet?" She tilted her head back and pointed to the spaces.

"Not yet, but I'll bet soon. By the way, girls, I have someone I want you both to meet."

"Who?" Lena asked, her eyes large.

"It's your Aunt Hannah."

Lena held her hands out, palms up. "Who's that?"

"Who dat?" Lola copied.

John Mark shifted to face Hannah. "This is your Aunt Hannah."

"Like Aunt Charlotte?" Esther asked.

"Yes, like Aunt Charlotte. Now you have two aunts."

Lola clapped her hands. "Two aunts," she proclaimed. She reached her chubby arms toward Hannah.

A moment of hesitation evaporated when Hannah opened her arms and Lola fell into them. The girl giggled, then placed both hands on Hannah's cheeks, cupping her face. "You pretty," she said.

Hannah's eyes shimmered. "Thank you. And what is your name?"

Lola tilted her head to one side and pointed at herself. "Me is Lola and I this many." She held up two fingers.

John Mark watched the interaction between Hannah and Lola. It was clear children liked her and she liked them and he recalled her rapport with Ambrose.

A fleeting thought entered his mind unannounced. Would they someday have children of their own?

Hannah liked Annie immediately. John Mark's sister-in-law embraced her much the same as Lydie and Charlotte had. Hannah shoved aside the fact that she'd never had friends until the recent friendship with Ina and now John Mark's family. Charlotte joined Hannah and Annie, and John Mark strolled over to where a group of menfolk stood talking about cattle.

Annie stuck a hand on her back, her round belly indicating her baby would soon be born. "We are so happy to have you in the family."

"And our prayers do go out to you for having to deal with John Mark every single day." Charlotte pursed her lips in her brother's direction. "Which reminds me, he and I need to have a talk."

"Oh, dear," laughed Annie. "Whatever has John Mark done *now*?"

Charlotte brushed aside Annie's comment. "Never mind that now. Let's celebrate our new sister."

Did they really mean for her to be their sister? Would they still feel that way when they came to know the *real* her? That she was a timid and awkward woman with a drunkard father and three possessions to her name, one of which included the dress she now wore? Perhaps she ought not to be so trusting of them. After all, Ramona had accepted her at first.

"Oh, goodness, the baby is kicking!" Annie reached for Charlotte's hand and placed it on her stomach.

She and Charlotte squealed in unison; their closeness apparent. "Would you like to feel?"

Hannah gingerly positioned her hand on Annie's belly. Sure enough, she felt the imprint of the baby's foot with the kick. "Oh, my," she whispered. Never had she felt anything like it. When Ramona married Pa, her boys were youngsters.

"Doc says she'll be born any day now."

"And you're so sure the baby is a girl?" Charlotte teased.

Annie nodded. "I could be wrong, but I think so."

Hannah marveled at the miracle of life. Would she someday know what it was like to be a mother?

John Mark devoured another cookie—he'd lost count of just how many of Ma's scrumptious treats he'd eaten—and ladled some punch into two cups, one for Hannah and one for himself.

After most of the guests left, Annie, Caleb, and Charlotte joined he and Hannah. "Have you heard from Russell?" he asked Caleb.

"I heard he's been looking to buy a ranch."

John Mark hadn't seen his best friend in some time. "In Willow Falls?"

Caleb shrugged. "Wherever he can find one for sale, provided it's in the northern part of the state near family."

"I heard that too," said Annie. "I chatted with his ma at the mercantile a few weeks ago and it seems he's also engaged."

"Russell? Engaged?" John Mark wished he'd kept in better touch.

"That's what his ma said." Annie turned to Hannah. "John Mark and Russell have been best friends forever and were quite the handful in my class."

Charlotte giggled. "That might be an understatement, Annie, and they were even worse before you came to teach. John Mark, do you remember when you and Russell glued the teacher's chair to the floor?"

Oh, he remembered, all right. And he recalled the punishment from Pa that went along with his transgression. "If I recall correctly, Tobias was an accomplice as well."

Charlotte shivered. "Goodness, but may we please not talk about Tobias Hallman? He was such a vexing fellow. Likely still is."

"Tobias was Charlotte's number one foe," said Caleb. "I recall her sharing about his antics many a time during supper."

"He was the most exasperating and irksome boy I've ever dealt with. John Mark and Russell were bad enough, but Tobias Hallman..."

"And..." chuckled John Mark, "Charlotte never refers to him as just 'Tobias.' It's always 'Tobias Hallman' as if there were five or six others with the same first name in Willow Falls."

Charlotte elbowed John Mark in the stomach. "Can we please change the topic of discussion?"

"Do you see why being a big brother to these two is an exhausting job at times? They bicker like no one else I've ever known." Caleb jokingly threw up his hands in exasperation.

A round of laughs echoed in the pleasant afternoon air. "Oh, you love us, Caleb."

"You're right, Charlotte, I do. On most days."

Another round of laughter followed. John Mark hoped Hannah felt welcome in his family and realized they all wanted her to be a part of the close-knit camaraderie they shared.

CHAPTER TWENTY-ONE

THE DAY AFTER JOHN Mark and Hannah returned from Willow Falls, John Mark worked outside mending a fence. The chore gave him time to think. He'd spoken with Pa again about Charlotte and Cyrus. While Pa indicated some concern, it hadn't been enough to forbid Charlotte to continue courting Cyrus.

Not that Charlotte would take well to being forbidden to see the man she claimed was the one she wanted to marry.

Pa figured Charlotte would see Cyrus for who he really was in time, or at least that was what Pa and Ma prayed for—that if it wasn't God's will for Charlotte to marry Cyrus, it would be made clear. Pa also prayed for Charlotte to have wisdom in the matter.

John Mark wasn't so sure Charlotte would be able to see Cyrus for who he really was. At least, not in her enamored state.

A noise in the distance caught his attention. He squinted. Hopefully Harold Bane wasn't coming to pay them a "visit." He set down his tools and walked toward the house. If it was Harold, John Mark would need to be prepared to protect Hannah.

Upon closer inspection, John Mark realized it was a buggy, rather than a wagon; Mayor Roessler and his daughter, Claudelle, rather than Harold.

"What brings you out this way?" he asked as the mayor climbed from the buggy and assisted Claudelle.

Claudelle batted her eyelashes at him and her interest baffled him. John Mark could no more offer her the luxuries of the life to which she was accustomed than turn Poplar Springs into a respectable town.

"I thought I would stop by for a visit, and Claudelle here wanted to join me. You remember Claudelle?"

John Mark touched the brim of the old hat he'd found in a trunk of belongings he discovered in the barn.

He extended a hand and the mayor shook it. "What can I do for you, Mayor?"

Mayor Roessler was a deceptive man with false charm and a healthy bank account. Some said he was a shrewd businessman and that was how he came into his fortune. John Mark held other suspicions. "It seems there's been some concern about the crime in Poplar Springs as of late."

"Yes, but from what I understand, it's been this way for a time. At least since the cattle wars were at their pinnacle."

"True, true. So have you heard anything about the increase in crime?" Mayor Roessler's eyes held a sinister light and he gave a facsimile of a smile.

"Just that there has been more cattle rustling and a lot of stagecoach robberies, and of course saloon brawls, assaults, and shootouts."

"Ah, that there has." The mayor's black handlebar mustache twitched.

Hannah emerged from what would soon be a garden area around the side of the house. When she saw them, she paused for a moment before starting toward the porch.

"What is the Bane woman doing here?" Mayor Roessler asked.

"Yes, indeed," added Claudelle, wrinkling her nose. "What are you doing here, Hannah Bane?"

Hannah, an expression of uncertainty on her face, peered from John Mark to Claudelle, then back to him. "Mayor and Claudelle, I'd like to introduce you to my wife."

"Your wife?" Claudelle's jaw dropped. "I was hoping that was just a rumor."

John Mark walked toward Hannah, offered his elbow, and led her the few steps to where the mayor and Claudelle stood.

A scowl breached Mayor Roessler's mouth. "You do know that as a deputy of Poplar Springs that you have a reputation to uphold."

Hannah flinched and John Mark covered her hand with his in an attempt to comfort her. "Yes, and I am a reputable man."

"Marrying Harold Bane's daughter will do you no favors in your standing in our town."

Claudelle's countenance turned sour and she glowered at Hannah.

"I'll not have you speak about my wife in any way that denotes disrespect. Now then, will that be all today, Mayor?"

"You need to watch yourself, Deputy Eliason. Would be a shame to have to replace you. Come along, Claudelle."

Moments later, the dust from the mayor's buggy indicated their progression toward town.

"I'm sorry for what Mayor Roessler said. He had no right."

The emotion Hannah sought to hide came to the forefront when he saw a single tear slide down her face. "Thank you. For defending me."

"I will always defend you, Hannah."

And he meant every word.

John Mark's statement the previous day about defending her penetrated deep into her heart. Trust didn't come easily for Hannah, but he was weakening her resolve with his actions and words. During their journey from Willow Falls, he had continued to ask her questions about herself, and she was beginning to overcome her hesitation in allowing anyone into her life for fear they would someday reject her. The Eliason family welcomed her and several times, Hannah imagined what it would be liked to be truly loved and accepted by them.

Mayor Roessler's disparaging words scarcely surprised her. The Roesslers, especially Claudelle, had never accepted Hannah. She surmised that Pa, while the mayor's employee, was no more favored by the prominent family than she was.

Her thoughts shifted toward her father. Would he someday relinquish his desire for whiskey and time spent at the saloon? Did Pa miss her? Did he regret his actions?

Would she someday be able to forgive him?

Hannah finished sweeping the house, folding the laundry, and returning the clean dishes to the shelf. The mantle clock indicated it was four o'clock. The time she had been anticipating all day.

The time when Pa would be at the saloon and her plan to retrieve Ma's Bible would be successful.

Finally, she would be able to read the precious words upon the pages of the book Ma once held. Yes, John Mark told her she may use his Bible any time, but she yearned for her own. Especially one with such sentimental value.

She wrote, "Went to get my Bible from Pa's house" on the slate John Mark had on the table for important reminders. If he came home before she returned, she didn't want him to worry.

The sooner she accomplished this matter, the better. Clarence joined her in her walk to the barn, the rooster always seemingly happy to see her. "Watch over the place while I'm gone, Clarence," she said.

The day was perfect for a ride and she closed her eyes for a brief moment and allowed the sun to warm her face. She reveled in the freedom to come and go as she pleased. The liberty to live somewhere without fear of physical and emotional abuse. The independence to live whatever calling God had placed on her life.

She reminded herself she must be efficient. Not only to return in time to prepare supper, but also because Pa could be unpredictable.

Pa's home came into view. She slowed the horse and gaped. Had Pa's house always been so dilapidated? It was as though she saw it for the first time with fresh eyes.

Sticks and brush greeted her along the path to the cabin. The chimney leaned to one side and part of the roof sank. The exterior needed a thorough whitewashing, and weeds, overgrowth, and debris near the front porch alerted her to use caution as Wyoming was home to many a rattler.

She swiveled her gaze about the homestead, looking for any signs of Pa. The barn door swung open, its hinges sounding in the gentle breeze. Two chickens clucked about the yellowed vegetation.

Hannah dismounted and tethered her horse. A glimpse into the barn indicated Pa's horse was gone. She scrambled up the stairs of the porch and peered into the window, just to be sure her father wasn't somewhere inside unconscious from a drinking binge.

Reassured he was gone, Hannah turned the rusted doorknob and stepped inside. The fetid odor assaulted her nostrils, a mixture of urine, body odor, and stale food. Her eyes watered and she scrunched up her nose. Dirty dishes lined the table and flies swarmed about. A mouse skittered across the floor.

A range of emotions pummeled her at once. From gratitude that she no longer lived there, to horror at the condition of the house. From pity for her father, to disgust that he would allow his daughter and himself to live in such conditions.

Refusing to allow the emotions to reign over her, Hannah rushed to her former bedroom. Her moth-eaten raggedy blanket was tucked tightly around the edges of her bed as she'd left it, and the quilt from Mrs. Fleming was folded neatly on top. Her Bible was on the upturned log, opened to the Psalms, the book she'd been reading on her last day here.

A noise captured her attention just as she was about to reach for her Bible. Through the dirty window, she saw Pa stomping toward the house.

And she froze.

There was no escape. She couldn't run through the front door, not with him already on the porch. There was nowhere to hide. Nothing to conceal her. The only bulky item in the house was the stove, and that was pressed against the wall.

Panic washed over her. Her heart raced and sweat beaded on her forehead. She prayed, even as her hope faltered.

Memories surfaced of her life before John Mark's rescue and her breathing came in rapid spurts.

"Who's here?" Pa thundered as he flung open the door and tramped inside.

Hannah stood in the doorway of her former room, ready to bolt past him when the opportunity arose.

If she could persuade her knees to stop shaking.

"Hannah Bane, is that you?"

Without awaiting her response, he stalked toward her, closing the distance between them.

Lord, please help me.

Pa's lip curled. "I see you've come back," he sneered, his weathered face becoming more distorted as he narrowed his eyes. The cords of his neck began to protrude and he muttered an oath.

Hannah swallowed hard. *Lord, help me be brave.* "I've come for my Bible." She detested that her voice shook as she uttered the words. This was not the time to allow Pa to believe he frightened her. She must conceal her fear.

"Ain't your Bible. It was your Ma's."

"Yes, and she gave it to me."

"No she didn't. She ain't never once said, 'Give it to that there child who was born.'" Pa clenched his jaw and bared what teeth he had left. "Now tell me, are you here again 'cause you don't want to be married to that worthless deputy no more?" He paused and an evil chortle escaped his lips. "I knew you'd come back."

Hannah shook her head, even as dizziness threatened. "I'm not back, Pa. Not now, not ever. I need only to retrieve my Bible and I'll be on my way."

"No, I don't think you will be on your way." He took another step toward her and his voice became a shout. "You never should have left!"

Pa raised a hand.

Hannah ducked, the memories of being hit flooding her mind. "No, Pa. I am not back and I never will be. Let me retrieve the Bible and go." Where the sudden surge of courage emerged, she wasn't sure, only that God was answering her prayers for bravery.

Pa shoved her hard against the wall and uttered a stream of curses that made her ears burn. She slid down the wall, unable to maintain footing, the Bible slipping from her grasp.

Hannah closed her eyes and braced herself for what was to come. She'd endured it before, and she'd endure it again.

But no such moment came. Instead, she heard a commotion, and when she opened her eyes, she noticed John Mark standing between her and Pa.

"John Mark?" she whispered.

Instead of answering her, John Mark directed his words toward Pa, his voice low and calm. The exact tone she'd witnessed him using when he arrested men during brawls outside the saloon. The same remarkable self-control she admired and had rarely observed in a man. "Listen to me carefully, Harold Bane. If you ever lay a hand on my wife again, I'll petition the judge to keep you locked away until your bones rot. Am I clear?"

His wife. Those words alone emboldened her. Pa couldn't hurt her anymore.

"She shouldn't be in my house," muttered Pa, his face slackening in defeat.

John Mark offered his hand. She took it and he assisted her to her feet. She tottered and he steadied her as she regained her balance.

She wanted to collapse into his arms—her newfound refuge. "Let's go home, Hannah," he said.

Before she could mention the Bible, John Mark again addressed Pa. "Leave her alone, Harold."

Moments later, Hannah and John Mark embarked for home. She could see from his profile—his firm jaw and his unwavering stare straight ahead—that he was displeased with her. So instead of attempting to initiate a conversation, Hannah remained quiet, her focus on the road ahead.

And what her new husband must think of her.

Did he think her a fool? A dolt? Unwise?

The concern about John Mark's thoughts of her nagged at her and contributed to her already-nervous countenance. The situation with Pa was volatile and it could have ended badly had John Mark not arrived when he did. Hannah would not have emerged unscathed.

When they reached the house, John Mark finally spoke. "I'll take care of the horses."

Hannah took that as her cue to retreat to the house and prepare supper. She warmed the leftover stew and ladled it into bowls. She then buttered two pieces of bread, and poured the milk.

John Mark entered the house, washed up, and blessed the meal, his strained voice indicating his displeasure.

Finally after what seemed an eternity, he spoke. "What were you thinking going to your pa's place, Hannah?"

His voice wasn't necessarily condemning, but neither was it his usual soothing tone.

"I knew Pa would be gone and I wanted to retrieve my ma's Bible." She thought of the irony that even though she'd carefully planned the situation and John Mark had arrived just in time, Hannah had still returned home without the precious possession.

John Mark's hazel eyes met hers. "But your pa wasn't gone, was he?"

"He was, but then he unexpectedly returned." Her voice shook and she wrung her hands in her lap.

"Why didn't you wait until I was home and I would have taken you?"

How could she explain that she needed that burst of freedom to prove she could do something on her own? That, truth be told, she hadn't even considered waiting for John Mark to arrive home first so he would take her?

Tears burned her eyes and she stirred the remainder of her stew. Would John Mark decide it wasn't worth being married to someone with imbecilic tendencies? Would he return her to Pa? Would their marriage be over before she had a chance to grow to love him?

John Mark scooted his chair from the table. "I'll be in the barn. Thank you for supper." Without a nod in her direction, he left the house.

Hannah sat for several minutes, tears falling into her stew. She never should have gone to Pa's house. Never should have believed she could outsmart him.

And never should have believed she would be a suitable wife for John Mark.

John Mark stalked out to the barn. He perched on the stool used for milking and put his face in his hands. What *had* Hannah been thinking? Had her time in Harold's home not been enough of a reminder to deter her from ever returning? Why hadn't she asked him to accompany her? Why...

When he'd arrived home from work and saw her note, he couldn't ride over to the Bane place fast enough. The thought of what Harold would do to her, especially in retaliation for marrying John Mark, weighed heavily on his mind. The man was evil and deserved far worse than a prison sentence for the way he'd treated his daughter.

And what if Hannah hadn't left the note and John Mark would have had no idea where to search for her? Harold's place would not have been first on his list.

He'd thought her possessing more wisdom than that.

Perhaps he ought to sleep in the barn tonight. Frustration, disappointment, irritation...they all made him poor company.

Lord, help me. I'm so unsure of this whole marriage thing. Why would she go there? She says for a Bible, but she could use mine. I would buy her another one if she wanted me to. Why would she risk harm to herself? She knows what kind of man her father is.

John Mark searched his mind for verses about marriage. There was a verse in Ephesians Pa spoke of often and that John Mark had memorized. *"Husbands, love your wives, even as Christ also loved the church, and gave himself for it."*

What he felt for Hannah was not yet love, but he did care for her. A lot.

Lord, I want to honor her. To someday love her. To defend her and fight for her. To be her protector.

The yearnings of his heart came forth in prayer. Would the Lord see fit to enable him to be the husband he was to be? Tonight when he'd found the note, a sense of urgency to rescue her coursed through him.

If her pa had hurt her...

The thought of losing her was almost too much to bear.

John Mark knew he had a strong sense of right and wrong. Words Pa once told him during one of their talks on the way to town just before he left for Poplar Springs entered his mind. And he knew a decision needed to be made, even if he preferred to wait until tomorrow.

"John Mark, God has given you discernment to differentiate between that which is wrong and that which is right. This is a good gift. He has given you a desire to fight for justice and to protect the downtrodden. I'm reminded of the verse in Micah which states, 'What doth the LORD require of thee, but to do justly, and to love mercy, and to walk humbly with thy God?' I am proud of you for doing justly, loving mercy, and walking humbly with our Lord. Always love justice. Seek it and strive for it. Love mercy and offer it willingly to others. Walk humbly with God and experience His unconditional love, mercy, and grace. But remember that the Lord also desires us to relinquish everything to Him. Do not try to do things in your own strength."

He closed his eyes and folded his hands and prayed once again. *Lord, make me the husband You desire me to be. Give me patience and mercy toward Hannah, even when she does things I think are foolish. Thank You for giving me self-control with Harold Bane tonight as I know that restraint came only from You. Please help me to see things the way Hannah sees them. Help me to understand her.*

As quickly as he prayed the last sentence, John Mark thought better of it and chuckled to himself. He recalled a time when Ma and Pa were in a disagreement. He overheard Pa's words "I will never understand some of your ways, Lydie."

Ma had responded with, "Nor will I understand yours, Solomon. This quarrel is utterly ridiculous."

Their disagreement had continued, respectfully of course, but John Mark sensed the irritation in both of their voices. But they had reconciled soon after.

Even if Pa likely still didn't understand some of Ma's ways and she didn't understand his.

So as it was with his parents, it would most assuredly be with him and Hannah. They might never understand each other, but they needed to reconcile.

He plopped down on the hay and clasped his hands behind his head. Nightfall would soon arrive. Perhaps he ought to stay in the barn tonight and mull some things over.

Pa had once preached a sermon about not letting the sun go down on your anger. John Mark had experienced anger tonight more than once. Yet, the words from Ephesians and the commentary Pa offered in his sermon flooded his mind.

After several more minutes, he stood and started toward the house, noting the breathtaking sunset over the mountains. If he was to not let the sun go down upon his wrath, he best reconcile with Hannah posthaste.

Hannah finished washing the dishes and attempted to fix a button that had fallen off the Sunday dress Lydie had made for her. The button had likely detached itself due to Hannah's preoccupation with tugging on it in times of nervousness.

She bowed her head and folded her hands. *Lord, I have no idea how to be a wife. I've never been one and have never witnessed a godly wife's example. Ramona tried, but no one can be the kind of wife she must be when married to Pa. Please help me to be the wife you want for me to be. Help me to be wise and not foolish. Please let John Mark wish to remain married to me and please let him forgive me.*

What if he didn't forgive her?

No, she mustn't think like that. Hadn't the reverend preached a sermon once about not bothering to pray if you didn't think God would answer?

While He might not answer in the way Hannah desired, He *would* answer.

And she would wait until He did. After all, she'd waited for the Lord's answer all those years she asked Him to rescue her from her father.

The door opened and John Mark entered. She averted her eyes to her stitching.

"Hannah?"

She looked up. "Yes?"

"Can we talk?"

She stood and set her dress on the chair. "I'm sorry for going to Pa's house." Her voice quivered and she willed herself not to cry again. For so many years, she'd been brave and hadn't shed a tear, not even when Pa had hurt her, withheld food, or belittled her.

Why then did Hannah find it so difficult to maintain her composure now?

John Mark took a step toward her. "I would have taken you."

"I..." Should she tell him she hadn't wanted him to take her? Would he think her a simpleton?

He waited patiently for her answer, and she saw the turmoil in his eyes. John Mark Eliason was a good man. She just needed to be worthy of him.

"I'm sorry. I just..." the words then tumbled from her mouth. "I only wanted to retrieve Ma's Bible. It's the only thing I have of hers and, while I know you offered me yours to use, it's not the same. I wanted to once again be able to hold the same Bible she once did. To study the same scriptures. To wonder what she was like and if she would have been proud of me..." A deluge of tears followed and her entire body shook. No matter how hard she fought the grief, the pain had a mind of its own. She stared at the floor through hazy vision, not wanting to capture the disappointment in his gaze.

"Hannah."

A tear hit the wooden floor. She couldn't meet his eye. "Yes?"

Before any further words could be uttered, he folded her into his arms. His firm-but- gentle embrace gave her the safety, security, and hope that she needed, if only for a brief time. The sobs wracked her and the harder she fought them, the more freely they came.

John Mark allowed her to cry, his strong arms remaining around her. Finally, after some time, he took a step back and she immediately missed his warmth. John Mark cupped her face with his hands. "When I saw your note, I was so worried that something would happen to you."

"I'm sorry I made you angry."

"I was angry at you, yes. Angry you would go without me. Angry that your pa could be there and hurt you and I couldn't save you. Angry that you would be hurt again." His voice hitched and she saw the tenderness settle in his eyes.

"I never meant to make you angry. Can I still be your wife?"

Pain captured his expression. Had she annoyed him again with her words?

"Hannah." He tenderly brushed the hairs that had escaped from her bun off her face. "Do you not know I made a vow when I married you?"

She nodded, hesitant about his next words.

"I made a vow to love, honor, and cherish you until death do us part. That means that while you might do foolish things and I might do foolish things, one thing remains. I made a promise to God. A promise to be your husband through everything we might go through."

"But..." she let the words soak in. He would stay married to her?

"Now that we've settled that matter, let's talk about the visit to your pa. Will you please promise me you won't go there again? I know the kind of man he is. I've arrested him more times than I can count for brawls, assaults, and such. He should have been arrested every time he hurt you. I know he's mean and vindictive and dangerous. I can surmise some of how he treated you during your growing-up years." He paused. "I'll help you get your Bible, but please promise me you won't return to your pa's house."

"I promise."

"Thank you."

"John Mark?"

"Yes?"

"Thank you for marrying me."

He folded her into an embrace again. "Thank you for agreeing to it."

Hannah sniffled again, recalling how she might not have made the decision she had. "I don't know how to be a wife. My stepmother, Ramona, she tried to be a wife to my pa, but he wasn't a respectable husband."

"And I don't know how to be a husband. Sure, I've witnessed my parents' loving marriage and their godly example, but..."

She pulled away and their eyes met. "I guess that makes two of us."

"Yes, and we'll learn together." John Mark peered about the house as if seeing it for the first time. "I like what you've done with the place."

"I want more than anything to make it a house like your parents' home. Warm, inviting, and comfortable."

John Mark smiled and something inside her jolted. "Yes, I like those things in a home, but I don't want a Lydie and Solomon home. I'd like to have a Hannah and John Mark home."

"I think I can do that. I think I can make such a home."

"Yes, I believe you can."

His confidence in her was all she needed.

Chapter Twenty-Two

HANNAH SADDLED THE HORSE and rode into town to return Ina's dress. Thoughts of John Mark and their conversation last night flooded her mind—his embrace, his tender words, and his forgiveness. Despite her tomfoolery, John Mark still wanted to be married to her—Hannah Bane—or rather, Hannah Eliason. And more than ever, she desired to be married to him.

That morning before he left for work, he'd reached for her hand. "I'll see you when I get home," he'd said. And she'd stood there, marveling at God's mercy to bless her with a husband who'd saved her from her pa more than once. A man who had begun to fill her thoughts and capture her heart in a short amount of time.

A flutter of excitement stirred in her belly. There was no way she could deny it. Hannah was falling in love with John Mark.

Before she visited Ina, she stopped by the post office to see if perhaps the expected letter from Lydie had arrived. "Yes, Mrs. Eliason, I do have a letter for you."

Hannah stalled for a moment, her new name still catching her by surprise. Finally, finding her voice again, she thanked the postal clerk when he handed her the envelope.

Sure enough, Lydie's recipe was tucked inside. Wouldn't John Mark be surprised when she baked him his favorite cookies?

Moments later, the aroma of meatloaf greeted her when she stepped through the restaurant's door.

Ina rushed toward her and embraced her in a hug. Such affection from others was so foreign to her, and Hannah attempted to ease the tension in her shoulders. "Do come and sit down." Ina led her to a table in the corner. "I'll be right back with some coffee and you can tell me all about your trip to Willow Falls."

Ina bustled about, chatting with a few of the customers before returning with two steaming cups of coffee. "Now, do tell me all about the recent happenings since you married Deputy Eliason." Her bright eyes shone of excitement.

"First, I want to return your dress to you. Freshly laundered and, if you'd like, I can remove the seams."

"Not a concern at all. Grandmother Pearson takes great pride in mending and alterations." Ina took the dress from Hannah and placed it on her lap.

"I'm so grateful you loaned it to me."

Ina giggled. "It was an adventure to have Grandmother Pearson alter it so it would fit someone who *isn't* short and plump."

Hannah allowed herself to giggle as well. Perhaps with more time spent with Ina, Charlotte, Lydie, and Annie, laughter would soon come easy to her, too.

A frown creased Ina's round face. "Are you sure you don't need to borrow it for a lengthier amount of time?"

How had Hannah stumbled upon such a generous friend? "Thank you, but I believe I will be fine. Charlotte, John Mark's sister, received several dresses from her aunts in Prune Creek. Apparently they found a trunk of dresses in the attic of their home. Charlotte gave me two of them, one of which I'm wearing."

"But goodness. She sounds like a delightful new friend, and the dress you're wearing is lovely."

"Charlotte *is* a delightful new friend. She's convivial and gregarious like you are, Ina. And John Mark's mother is so thoughtful as well." Hannah's words burst from her mouth so uncharacteristically and it amazed her how easily they came with her newfound friend. "Her name is Lydie. She sewed a dress for one of the townsfolk in Willow Falls, but the young woman decided she no longer wanted it. So, Lydie gave it to me. Oh, Ina, you should see it. It's the most elegant dress I've ever seen and far surpasses those at Nellie's Dress Shop. It's a pale pink with pearl-colored buttons and a pleated collar. I wore it when we had a potluck to celebrate our marriage, and I'll wear it Sunday to church."

Ina reached across the table and clasped Hannah's hands. "I'm so happy for you. God has blessed you richly with a new family."

Hannah thought about Ina's words. Yes, He had blessed her richly. She dismissed from her mind the troubling thoughts of the encounter with Pa and how she had made such a grave error. She would need to pray for God's protection over her mind where worrisome thoughts sometimes re-emerged unannounced. "Do tell me all that has happened for you in these past few days."

"Well..." Ina sat up a little straighter and a blush covered her cheeks. "Pritchard arrived at the restaurant the other day. Not that this is an unusual circumstance, mind you, for he comes here often." Her face deepened in color. "He requested to speak with Pa and asked if he could join our family for supper."

"What did your pa say?"

"Now, Pa is very protective. But he said that of course Pritchard could join us." Ina peered around and lowered her voice to a whisper. "I was able to overhear the conversation, not that I was eavesdropping, mind you, but..." Ina giggled. "All right, I was eavesdropping and am grateful my ears work so well because there was a bit of commotion in the kitchen. Anyhow, Pa told him that of course he could join us, but I can only imagine Pa's distressed countenance because the last man who asked if he could join us for supper asked for my hand in courtship."

"He did?"

"Yes, and he was a crazy old coot, well, not old, as he was only a few years older than me, but he was not the type of man Pa would want his daughter to court, nor the type his daughter would wish to court. But Pritchard... Pritchard is different." A dreamy expression crossed Ina's face. "Pa asked Pritchard what his intentions were and he told Pa that he would like to someday court me. Well, there was silence for a good long time between the two of them, but as for me, my heart was pounding something fierce. I couldn't believe Pritchard had a mind to court me." Ina swooned. "I was praying Pa would not turn him away."

Obviously for Ina, the excitement was nearly too much to bear, and Hannah appreciated Ina's boisterous theatrics, so different from her own subdued timidity. "What did your pa finally say?"

"He said he and Ma would have to become more acquainted with Pritchard before they'd ever allow me to court him, and Pritchard said, 'Yes, sir, I understand and that is why I aim to spend time with your family at the supper table.'" Ina's voice deepened a bit and her words rushed from her mouth so rapidly that Hannah had to pay close attention to catch them all. "And then Pa said he figured that would be fine for Pritchard to join us for supper, and he did, and I could barely eat my meal. I was spilling things all over myself, and you know I'm not the messy type."

Ina discussed Pritchard a few minutes more before Mrs. Pearson arrived at their table. "Hello, Hannah, what a pleasant surprise to see you here. We have leftover meatloaf. Would you care for some?"

Hannah's stomach growled at the mention, but she'd not impose on her new friends. "I've already eaten, but thank you."

"It's leftover and there's no charge," added Mrs. Pearson.

Hannah mulled over the offer as the noonday meal hadn't been enough to satiate her. "Are you sure?" she asked.

"I'll bring you a plate."

Before Hannah could say anything more, Mrs. Pearson disappeared into the kitchen and brought back a plate with several slices of meatloaf, far too much for one person. Hannah thought of John Mark. Wouldn't he be surprised to see her in the middle of the day? She divided the meatloaf and would deliver his portion after her visit with Ina.

"There's been something I've been needing to tell you." A pained expression shone on Ina's face. "I wish I had known the situation with your pa. Had I known—had my family known—we would have done all we could to help you. I remember when you stopped by and asked for a job. We have inquiries like that often. I just never knew...can you please forgive me?"

"Of course I forgive you. How could you have known?"

"I could have asked. My family and I could have noticed that you were destitute when you arrived that day in a threadbare dress seeking a job. We could have taken seriously the rumor about a young woman sitting outside the saloon day after day."

Hannah shook her head. "I tried hard not to let anyone know and besides, what could you have done? There's barely enough room here for your family."

"We could have made a way. We would have had we realized."

"Please, don't give it another thought. You helped me when I needed a place to stay before my wedding. You gave me your dress to borrow, even though it meant you would be without it. You fed me breakfast, fixed my hair, provided encouragement to me, and you didn't even know me."

236

Ina's distressed expression eased somewhat. "I just want you to know that from this moment on, if you should ever need anything, anything at all, I am here for you."

Her words meant more to Hannah than she could ever express. The Lord had answered the dream of her heart of having a friend several-fold.

When Hannah entered the sheriff's office, John Mark was flipping through some papers at his desk. Her heart lurched at the sight of him. He stood tall and confident with his holster belt wrapped around his slim waist and his muscular shoulders accentuated by his plaid shirt. Warmth seared her cheeks.

"Hannah, what brings you to town?"

She was becoming accustomed to his crooked smile and the way it caused the slight dimple in his chin to be more pronounced. After stuttering over herself for the first several seconds, Hannah finally managed to explain her visit to Ina and the subsequent gift of meatloaf from Mrs. Pearson. She held out the plate to him.

Genuine appreciation touched his features. "Thank you."

He prayed over the meal and a short, but comfortable silence followed as he ate the meatloaf, then took a step toward her and handed her the plate.

And she wondered what it would be like to be kissed by John Mark. Heat infused her face again. She wasn't even sure if he felt for her the way she was beginning—after such a short time—to feel for him.

"I should be home in time for supper. It's been a slower day."

But just as he finished speaking, Pritchard flung open the door of the sheriff's office. "J.M.? There's some disorderly conduct happening down at the Sticker Weed."

CHAPTER TWENTY-THREE

THAT SUNDAY MORNING, JOHN Mark brought in a bowl of eggs for breakfast. When Hannah took the eggs from him, something captured her attention.

She commenced to taking a second glimpse at his gray vest.

Sure enough, two buttons were askew. The top button, which was sewn in the wrong place, caused the fabric to pucker when buttoned. The next button was equally as mis-sewn. It was too far to the left and the buttonhole was stretched unmercifully to accommodate the distance between the button and the buttonhole. The two buttons were also different from the rest. Mismatched. While the others were black, one of the buttons was red and the other blue.

They would need to leave for church soon and she hadn't the privilege of wasting any time staring at lopsided buttons.

Yet her eyes continued to find their way to the vest while John Mark stood there telling her about how well the chickens were laying. And the entire crooked button scenario caused something to bubble up inside her.

Did John Mark know his Sunday best was poorly mended?

Ought he be told?

She attempted to hold back the snicker that rose from deep within. Laughing recently became a more common occurrence for her, what with Charlotte's stories about John Mark's antics as a young'un, Ina's lively recount of Pritchard's meeting with her pa, and now two buttons haphazardly attached to a garment.

Whimpers of mirth soon became full-out amusement. Did John Mark intend to wear the dreadfully-sewn vest to church? Who had stitched the buttons? Did he even realize the imperfect craftsmanship?

An unrefined snort escaped her lips. She covered her mouth as heat rushed up her neck and face. Had John Mark heard the impertinent snuffle?

How could he not when he stood in front of her?

Hannah turned aside, but made the mistake of viewing the haphazard buttons again.

"Hannah?"

The confused expression lighting his face was enough to cause more gales of laughter. Poor, poor man. The vest was already slightly too short and too tight, as though he wedged himself into it. Add to that the buttons...

"Hannah?"

"I'm sorry—sorry—John Mark, it's just that—it's just that—" but the words would not come. Instead, they remained lodged somewhere in her throat, trapped by what could only be termed as unladylike cackles. She placed the bowl of eggs on the table so as to avoid a casualty.

"Did I say something funny?" John Mark blinked his eyes rapidly, a slack expression lining his handsome features. He rubbed his jaw. "Do I have something on my face? Drool from last night?"

Hannah shook her head as the tears proceeded to stream from her eyes and down her cheeks. What must he think of such a ninny laughing at something so preposterous? "No, it's not—it's not drool."

Several seconds passed and finally Hannah regained her composure. "I'm sorry, John Mark. It's your buttons."

"My buttons?"

"Yes, on your vest."

John Mark put his chin to chest and peered down at the buttons. "Oh, those."

"Yes, do you know how that happened?" Hannah attempted to resist the temptation to burst into laughter again.

John Mark fingered the first button. "Yes, I do. I sewed them on."

"You?"

"I left the Sunday shirt I'm accustomed to wearing in Willow Falls during our visit. This was the only Sunday finery I own besides that one. Reckon I received it for Christmas about eight years ago and have only worn it one other time while in Poplar Springs. That's when I lost the two buttons."

Had she heard him correctly? "When did you sew on the buttons?"

"Been some time ago right when I first moved to Poplar Springs. But I figured today was as good a day as any to wear it. Just can't eat a whole lot for breakfast or I won't be breathing properly."

The fabric was indeed stretched. "I can help you with the buttons. It'll only take a moment. Perhaps that will allow the vest to fit better, at least for today."

"I'd be much obliged for that." He unbuttoned the vest and handed it to her. She averted her eyes while he did so, but it was difficult not to notice how the shirt he wore beneath the vest accentuated the broad expanse of his shoulders and muscular chest. "I'd just wear this white shirt, but there's a stain on it. Guess I should either buy a new Sunday shirt or retrieve my other one from Willow Falls."

Thankfully, she was an efficient seamstress. She couldn't do anything about the vest's size, but figured a slight stretching of the fabric couldn't hurt. Hannah pulled it slightly, hoping to stretch it just enough so John Mark could eat as much as he wanted to for breakfast.

When the unthinkable happened.

A seam on the side split. She gasped.

"That will make it fit easier," John Mark quipped, a twinkle in his eye.

"Oh, my, but I will fix that too. At least it was in the seam and won't take much effort to repair."

Hannah stitched together the ripped seam, finished the buttons, and handed it to John Mark so they could leave and still arrive to church on time. His fingers brushed hers in the exchange and she nearly dropped the vest.

He slipped it on and buttoned it, then stood tall, puffed out his chest, and exaggerated his posture. He held his chin high and tugged on his vest. "Tell me, Mrs. Eliason, how do I look?"

Hannah attempted to utter a response, but no words came. A fluttering sensation tumbled in her belly. "I—you—look tidy."

"Tidy?"

"Not...not tidy. What I meant to say is..."

John Mark smirked. "Untidy then? Disheveled?"

"No. Oh, but goodness. You—you look just fine." Her heart skittered. He looked just fine indeed.

When Hannah's rosy face glowed with delight, something overcame him.

She was beautiful.

He already knew that. Had figured that out when she wore the dress she now wore for the first time. That day at Ma and Pa's house during their wedding celebration.

But today with the joyful tears rolling down her cheeks, the uncharacteristic noises when she laughed the hardest, and the way her eyes crinkled at the corners and her mouth upturned into a wide grin, lighting her entire face...

Beautiful was not a strong enough word to describe her.

Her obvious happiness, even at the expense of him and his poorly-mended vest, brought him joy as well.

John Mark wanted her to be happy.

Wanted her to find joy in her life with him.

And then her flustered demeanor when he teased her about his appearance and the subsequent playful bantering...

He was drawn to her. No two ways about it.

Hannah took a step toward him and smoothed his lapel. Then her eyes met his.

He wanted to kiss her—

A pretty flush colored her cheeks and her eyes were bright and full of life.

"Hannah..." John Mark cupped her face gently in his hands and his eyes traveled to her mouth. "May I kiss you?"

"Yes," she whispered.

He leaned toward her.

But just as he was about to kiss her, a merciless crow filled the air. It drew both of their attentions from each other and toward the direction of the sound.

A perusal out the window identified the source.

Clarence the rooster.

The bird teetered, perched on the porch railing. Clarence peered at them, his head tilting from side to side.

Disappointed he missed the moment with Hannah and frustrated by the animal he'd never been fond of, he muttered, "What is it with that rooster?"

They left for church a few minutes later. The already-warm morning promised another sweltering late-summer day. John Mark glanced at Hannah's pro-

244

file. Her facial structure was daintily carved, but beneath her fragile beauty lurked an unexpected strength he had come to admire.

In recent days, John Mark had grown fond of her and had enjoyed their camaraderie this morning. A thought occurred to him then that he knew very little about her. Had they courted, he would have learned about her likes and dislikes, her family—besides her pa—and her hopes and dreams. But their marriage had been an unorthodox one with no courtship, and John Mark found himself wanting to know more about the woman he'd married.

"Do you have any family besides your pa?" he asked.

Hannah shifted on the buckboard and picked at one of the buttons on her dress. This trait, one that he'd come to realize indicated her unease, caused him to wish he hadn't asked her. But the yearning inside of John Mark for Hannah to trust him was immense.

After a few seconds ticked by, Hannah answered. "Yes, I have a grandmother. She came to live with us for a short while when I was a young girl. She wasn't a nice woman—not like Grandmother Pearson. Rather, she was harsh and impatient. I rarely did anything right in her eyes, and she left almost as soon as she arrived and returned home to Kansas. Pa blamed it on me that she left." She appeared to want to say more, but stayed silent.

"I'm sorry, Hannah." How painful for her to be blamed for something beyond her control. A story Pa mentioned years ago came to mind. "According to my pa, your grandmother sounds a lot like my great-grandfather. I'm glad I never had to meet him myself."

Should he continue to ask questions? He did want to know more about her. John Mark argued with himself before his curiosity won the inner debate. "No brothers or sisters?"

Hannah faced him, a flicker of pain in her eyes. Did she want to answer his questions? Was this inquiry a distressing one?

Just as he was about to rescind the question, she spoke. "When my pa married a woman named Ramona, she had two young boys that I consider my brothers." Hannah took a deep breath. "Pa met her through an advertisement that I wrote for him since he cannot read or write. I then penned the subsequent letters as well." She focused on something in the distance. "I should never have written the advertisement or the letters as they were all a bunch of lies. Pa wasn't a wealthy rancher with a pleasing disposition. Nor was he tall and handsome; and he most certainly did not have all his teeth. But I wrote what Pa insisted I write. Ramona believed it and arrived one day from Wisconsin with the boys. She swiftly realized Pa's dishonesty."

Hannah slouched her shoulders and crossed her arms over her stomach. "It didn't occur to me at the time, but over the years, I came to the realization that I could have written whatever I liked and Pa wouldn't have known the difference seeing as how he was illiterate."

John Mark could easily believe Harold Bane would use deceitful correspondence to seek a wife. And to have Hannah be a part of his scheme? A fresh round of sympathy for the woman he married filled his thoughts. He was about to change the topic of discussion when she continued.

"Ramona was cordial, but she wasn't like your ma. However, for the first time, I had food to eat, a clean dress, and braided hair. For the first time, I had someone to help me with my homework and quiz me on my vocabulary words."

"But she's not in your life now?"

"She left as soon as she could, and took the boys with her, of course."

John Mark slowed the wagon as he neared a particularly deep rut in the road. Should he press her to proceed? Obviously the memory was a disconcerting one. "You don't have to continue if you'd rather not."

"No, John Mark, you should know." Her voice wavered. "Ramona left that day with the boys and I begged her to take me with her. I promised I would behave, that I would help her care for my brothers, and that I would be no trouble at all. But she..."

Another tear dampened her face and John Mark's chest squeezed and a flutter of guilt rippled through him. What did a godly husband do in this type of circumstance? Especially when it was his fault for asking her to recall a grievous memory? What would Pa suggest he do? He offered a prayer for wisdom and that he'd not say or do anything to make Hannah more disheartened.

His mind reverted to the time when Aunt Fern was ill. The doctor in Prune Creek didn't expect her to live. Ma was beside herself with sorrow since Aunt Fern was one of two aunts who raised her and she couldn't be there to say goodbye. It was one of the few times John Mark witnessed Ma's seemingly unending tears. Pa had prayed with her, comforted her, and held her.

God healed Aunt Fern, but John Mark never forgot how he'd witnessed Pa's tender and loving compassion toward his bride, only one time of many.

John Mark would do the same. He slowed the wagon to a stop, clutched the reins in one hand, and faced her. "Hannah."

She peered up at him through dampened eyelashes. "It happened a long time ago," she whispered.

Should he tell her he understood? But he didn't understand. Not really. He sympathized and cared deeply for the pain she'd endured, but he'd grown up in a loving family so opposite of hers.

John Mark inclined toward her, indecision about his next step persisting in his mind. He wrapped the reins around the brake and pulled her to him. She rested her head on his chest. "I'm sorry you had to endure that."

"I must have done something wrong for her to not take me." Hannah's voice shook.

He held her to him and prayed for the right words to say. "No, she probably felt she couldn't because..." *you weren't her daughter.* But he'd not say as much, for Hannah surely thought she was, or at the very least, important enough for her stepmother not to leave her behind.

Minutes ticked by and John Mark searched for words that would comfort her. "Sometimes we don't understand the actions of others." He planted a kiss on the top of her head. "Ramona cared about you, but your pa wouldn't let her take you with her."

"He needn't have known." She spoke so softly John Mark thought he might not have even heard her correctly.

He knew as well as Hannah did that Harold would not allow someone to take her, even though he didn't deserve to be her father, but John Mark didn't say as much. He lifted her chin tenderly with his finger. Red, teary eyes met his gaze. "Hannah, just because Ramona refused to take you with her doesn't mean you did something wrong. She was scared of your pa and he wasn't who he insinuated he was in his letters to her. Ramona knew she had to protect her sons and she surely would have taken you with her if she could have."

"How do you know?" Her voice faltered.

John Mark wiped away a tear that slid down her face. "Because no one in their right mind would leave you behind."

John Mark's words warmed her and she savored them the remainder of their ride to church. Was he right? That someone could care for her enough not to leave her behind? Hannah knew God loved her and cared for her, and that His unconditional love had carried her through all those years of pain, anguish, heartbreak, loneliness, and rejection. Hannah knew the Lord would never leave her behind; that she was His and that nothing and no one could snatch the love of her Savior from her.

But Hannah had never heard such fierce words of devotion from another person.

Would she someday be able to trust those words fully?

When they reached the church a few minutes later, Reverend Fleming had already begun the services. John Mark assisted Hannah from the wagon.

"Thank you for listening," she said.

"That's what husbands do, or at least that's what I think husbands do. Although I haven't much experience as one." His humor in addition to his compassion lifted her heart. John Mark pressed the front of his vest. "How do the buttons look?"

"Much better than earlier this morning."

"That's because I had a professional seamstress sew them on instead of a deputy who should limit his time with a needle and thread." He offered his elbow. "Shall we go in?"

Hannah settled her hand on the crook of his elbow as if it were the most natural thing in the world. She marveled that in a short amount of time, she was beginning to feel more comfortable around her new husband.

She could have found freedom only to have married someone just like Pa, or even worse.

Instead, God had blessed her with a man named John Mark Eliason.

CHAPTER TWENTY-FOUR

AFTER CHURCH, AMBROSE RAN toward Hannah and John Mark. "Miss Hannah! Miss Hannah! I gots something for you."

Ambrose stopped for a minute to catch his breath before digging into the pocket of his trousers. "I found this here rock for you yesterday." He handed her a smooth, round, flat rock.

"Thank you, Ambrose. How sweet of you to think of me."

"I like rocks. I think they are fas-natin'." Ambrose dug into his pockets and produced several more rocks. "See, I found these on the way home. Me and Grumbles were out solving a crime."

"What kind of crime?"

"Oh, you know, the kind of crimes here in Poplar Springs. Someone stoled somethin' and Grumbles and me had to arrest him."

Hannah tousled his hair. "I'm thankful we have you and Grumbles to keep the folks of Poplar Springs safe."

"Aww, I know." Ambrose puffed out his thin chest. "Someday when I grow up, I'm gonna be just like Deputy Eliason. Maybe he and me can catch all them robbers and outlaws and put 'em in jail where they belong." He peered up at her. "Are you and the deputy gonna have you a noonday meal? 'Cause if you are, can I have something to eat with you?"

Hannah herself had been hungry so often in her life that she recognized the desperation in another and her heart broke for the little fellow. "Where's your grandpa?"

Ambrose pointed to Mr. Miller, who leaned against the church speaking with Reverend Fleming. "He's over yonder."

Did the Millers not have enough food? Perhaps Hannah should speak with John Mark about delivering some to them. "Won't your grandpa be hungry too?"

"Prob-ly. But I asked him if I could eat at your house and he said I could—if it's okay with you and Deputy Eliason."

Ambrose's hopeful expression melted her heart. When had the boy last eaten? Should she and John Mark invite Mr. Miller to their home for the noonday meal as well? Was Reverend Fleming aware of their need for food?

"Well, can I?"

After securing permission from Mr. Miller, who decided to return home for a short nap, Ambrose climbed into the wagon and sandwiched himself between Hannah and John Mark. He chatted the entire way home, and as they sat together on the buckboard, something stirred inside Hannah. Could this be in her future? Would the Lord someday see fit to bless her with a family of her own?

John Mark's profile spoke of confidence and inherent strength. Even from this angle, she could see the hint of a smile on his lips. The muscles in his arms strained against the fabric of his shirt as he held the reins.

There was so much more to John Mark than his handsome appearance, however. When he'd held her earlier during her distress over Ramona, he'd not judged her once. Instead, he comforted her, reassured her, and reminded her that he was a pillar of kindness in an otherwise harsh world. He worked hard and cared about truth and justice. And she appreciated John Mark's protective nature, sense of humor, and loyalty to his family.

She and John Mark would have shared a kiss this morning if it hadn't been for Clarence's untimely interruption.

A kiss from John Mark...heat whooshed up her face all over again.

"Can we have cake for the noonday meal, Miss Hannah?" Ambrose was asking.

"Yes."

"We can? We can have cake for the noonday meal?"

John Mark's hearty chuckle brought Hannah to the realization that in the midst of her discomfiture, she'd not properly heard Ambrose's inquiry.

"Pound cake is my favorite and can we have peppermint sticks too?"

The sparkle in Ambrose's eyes indicated both his enthusiasm and his surprise at her answer—an answer she needed to rectify. "While we can't have pound cake and peppermint sticks for the noonday meal, perhaps we can have another dessert after we eat the pot roast."

"Pot roast?" Ambrose folded his skinny arms across his body. "All right, Miss Hannah. That'll do." Not deterred by the change in meal plans, the youngster continued his chatter even as John Mark stopped the wagon.

John Mark assisted Hannah from the wagon, his hands lingering gently on her waist. Her heart thrummed in her chest as they stood for the briefest of moments in close proximity, their eyes locked. He released her waist and framed her face with his hands. All other noise ceased to exist when John Mark bent his head toward hers and tenderly brushed her lips with his.

The unexpected moment caught her unawares and was all too brief. Perhaps such an occurrence was only a figment of her imagination and had not actually happened. But why then did her heart race and tingles swirl in her stomach?

Ambrose tapped on her arm. "Miss Hannah?"

"Do you want to help me unhitch the wagon?" John Mark asked.

Ambrose shook his head. "No, thank you, sir. Can I help Miss Hannah with the noonday meal? My belly is rumblin' somethin' fierce."

John Mark reflected on the feelings he was beginning to have for Hannah. She wasn't just a beautiful woman, she was sweet, thoughtful, and generous. And this morning he'd seen a side of her he hadn't yet seen—he'd seen joy and happiness—and that attracted him to her all the more. The entire button incident and the entertaining interaction between them gave him hope that they could build on the unconventional beginnings of their marriage. Her tears at Ramona's leaving her behind and how she'd felt in his arms lingered in his mind. He wished he could erase the painful memories of her past.

After unhitching the horses, John Mark strode toward the house. From the porch, he saw Hannah and Ambrose at the table. Ambrose, perched in a chair on his knees was, as usual, jabbering as he stirred something in a bowl. Hannah nodded and smiled.

Their conversation lured him, and John Mark edged closer to the open door.

"How did you get so smart, Ambrose?"

"It's 'cause Grandpa read books to me when I was a young'un. 'Course, now he don't see so well. But he still tells me big words."

John Mark thought of Mr. Miller and his declining health and he worried for Ambrose.

The boy continued, "And do you know I'm gonna be six, Miss Hannah?"

"Goodness, but we'll have to have a birthday party for you."

"I would like that. And can we have pound cake?"

John Mark could imagine the sparkle in Hannah's eyes when she laughed at Ambrose's comment. She clearly adored the young boy.

"Yes, I think that would be a grand idea."

Ambrose stopped stirring whatever was in the bowl for a moment and rested his hand on Hannah's arm. "You know what, Miss Hannah?"

"Yes?"

"I think my ma was like you. Don't 'member her 'cause I was just a baby when she died, but I think she was just like you."

Hannah's sharp inhale revealed the effect Ambrose's comment had on her. "Oh, Ambrose." A sob escaped her throat.

"Miss Hannah, why do you have tears and why did your voice sound funny?"

"Because I—you—"

"Did I make you sad?"

John Mark could imagine Ambrose's furrowed brow.

"Oh, no, Ambrose. You didn't make me sad. Not at all. These are happy tears. We better finish these for John Mark before he returns from the barn."

"Who's John Mark?"

"John Mark is Deputy Eliason."

"He has so many names. That's pec-u-ler. I only gots me two names."

Hannah proceeded to explain to the boy how John Mark could have "so many names." And John Mark retreated toward the barn, his thoughts full of what he'd just witnessed.

Hannah removed the roast from the oven and prepared to bake the sugar cookies she and Ambrose prepared. Wouldn't John Mark be surprised when he entered the house to find his favorite dessert?

But apprehension filled her. Would he find the cookies tasty? Pa's continual criticism of her cooking infiltrated her thoughts at the most inopportune times. Would she ever be able to leave behind the pain caused by his words?

Ambrose fidgeted. "Sure am hankering for some cookies. Want me to go fetch Deputy Eliason?"

"Yes, please."

Several minutes later, the three of them sat around the table, John Mark on an overturned barrel. If they were to have Ambrose visit regularly, they'd surely need another chair.

"Ambrose, would you say the blessing?" John Mark asked.

At the important request, Ambrose sat upright in the chair. "Yes, sir. Dear Lord, please bless this meal to our bodies. And while it's not pound cake, I know what me and Miss Hannah made is gonna be tasty. Amen."

"After we eat, do you want to go fishing with me, Ambrose?"

Ambrose nearly fell out of his chair in his exuberance. "Yes, Deputy, I do! Do you think I could catch a shark? I learned all about sharks and the ocean from a story Grandpa told me once."

"We don't have sharks in Wyoming, but I bet we could catch us a trout for supper." To Hannah, he added, "Thank you for the pot roast. I believe I might need seconds."

Hannah appreciated John Mark's compliments about her cooking. She hoped he would find the cookies delicious as well.

"Guess what, Deputy Eliason? Me and Miss Hannah made you a s'prise, but I can't tell you what it is." Upon

Hannah's nod, Ambrose jumped from his chair and lifted the plate of cookies off the shelf. He carried them to the table. "You can go first, Deputy." Ambrose rubbed his palms together in anticipation as John Mark reached for a cookie.

Hannah held her breath as John Mark bit into it.

"Well?" Ambrose asked. "Is it the bestest you've ever tasted?"

"Yes, it is. You better have one, Ambrose, before I eat them all." The glint in John Mark's eye and his reach for a second cookie eased Hannah's concerns.

"May I, Miss Hannah?"

Before Hannah could nod his way, Ambrose devoured half of his cookie. "These are tasty, if I say so myself. Grandpa always says that when we eat the supper Mrs. Fleming brings us or the canned food from Mr. Pritchard."

"I think I better have another one," John Mark said. "Thank you for making these. Reckon it's one of the best surprises."

His words blessed her more than he could know. Their eyes locked, and the memory of the kiss they shared caused a warm heat to flush her cheeks. Would he kiss her again? She hoped so.

"Say," chirped Ambrose, "are you two having a staring game? 'Cause me and Grandpa once had a staring game and I won 'cause he blinked first."

Hannah looked away first and fixed her attention on a cookie crumb on the table. John Mark cleared his throat.

And barely waiting to catch his breath, Ambrose continued. "Say, Miss Hannah, are you gonna go fishing with us?"

Grateful for a change in topic, Hannah answered, "I think I'll stay here and read the book Ina lent me."

Several minutes later after they cleared the table and John Mark assisted her with the cleanup, he and Ambrose bounded out the door. She couldn't tell who was more ecstatic about going fishing: John Mark or Ambrose.

Hannah stood on the porch and waved them off. Clarence strutted next to Ambrose. "Say, Deputy, can that rooster come with us? I kinda like him."

John Mark shook his head. "I think we'll leave Clarence, the rooster, here."

"Clarence? I like that name. He's following us and I think he likes me."

The rooster had sidled up next to Ambrose just as he did with Hannah whenever she set about doing outdoor chores.

John Mark's response made Hannah laugh. "That bird seems to like just about everyone but me."

"Aww, he likes you, Deputy Eliason, don't cha, Clarence?" He reached down and attempted to pat Clarence on the head.

Then in an action that melted Hannah's heart, the boy put his hand in John Mark's and the two trotted toward the pond.

As Hannah settled into the chair on the porch with Ina's book in hand, a host of emotions from the day tugged at her—contentment, joy, grief over the memory of Ramona, gratitude for John Mark's care of her during that memory and that he appreciated the cookie surprise, and delight that they could come alongside a little boy who needed love and attention.

John Mark's image came to mind again—the kiss, the realization of his nearness, and their shared attention to each other.

On that day, Hannah lost her heart to John Mark Eliason.

Chapter Twenty-Five

JOHN MARK COMPLETED TWO of his more mundane and less desirable job duties—keeping the streets free of dead animals and manure. He moseyed back into the sheriff's office, his mind on anything but the numerous tasks that beckoned him. As a matter of fact, John Mark hadn't been able to focus on much of anything today except Hannah. Their day yesterday cemented in his mind the hope he had for their marriage. He prayed daily for it. That Hannah would come to trust him and that they would someday love each other.

The answers to both prayers seemed stronger possibilities than ever.

No one resided in the cell today and, for the most part, commotion in Poplar Springs proved less than usual. Days like this with little to no activity, while rare, did cause suspicion. Gaston was in Bowman today, and Winslow was hiring another deputy in a town on the northeastern edge of the county.

John Mark was about to undertake his rounds when a familiar—but unexpected person—sauntered through the door.

"Russell?"

"Hey, John Mark." Russell Jenkins shook his hand before taking a seat on the only cleared corner of the desk. "I saw Caleb at the mercantile in Willow Falls and he said I'd find you here working as a deputy sheriff. And here I thought you wanted to be a doctor."

John Mark chuckled. "You know me well enough to know I couldn't endure all the book learning that comes with that profession." He'd missed his friend and partner in mischievous behavior during their growing-up years. "I heard you were returning to this area, and I expected to see you in Willow Falls when I was there recently. What brings you to Poplar Springs of all places?" John Mark hadn't seen his childhood best friend since Russell left the state for a job opportunity.

Russell scratched his chin before he spoke, a habit he'd had for as long as John Mark had known him. "Remember how I was hoping to buy a ranch after I returned to Wyoming?"

"Yes?"

"I just purchased the Daly Ranch."

John Mark's jaw went slack. "As in the Daly Ranch here in Poplar Springs?"

"One and the same. There weren't any ranches for sale in Willow Falls or Nelsonville. Hadn't really given much thought to Poplar Springs until Caleb said you moved here. I nosed around a bit, found out about the Daly Ranch when I arrived in town this morning. Things moved faster than I anticipated. Planned on stopping by earlier to see you, but with visiting the ranch, talking to the owner, an appointment at the bank, and all the paperwork and such a man has to undertake just to own a piece of land these days, time got away from me. So here I am."

"Congratulations!"

Russell took a deep breath. "Wasn't an easy feat. Apparently, a man named Roessler wanted it, but fortunately for me, I knew Daly and was able to get my loan before Roessler could even make his offer."

A thorny knot of concern wound its way through John Mark's belly. "Roessler? As in Mayor Roessler?"

Russell shrugged. "Not sure. But I do know one thing. Now I can ask Amaya to marry me since I have my own place. And I can see it now..." Russell motioned his right hand in an arc movement. "*The Jenkins Ranch,* engraved on a wood sign for all to see."

"I'm happy for you, Russell, I am, but I doubt Roessler will take this well."

"He should have purchased it sooner. Would you like to come have a look at it? Lots of outbuildings, a decent house, chicken coop, and plenty of prime ranch land. The best thing about it is that I got it at a sensible price, one I could get a banknote for. Seems Daly was in a hurry to move to Bowman."

"Welcome to Poplar Springs, and yes, I would like to see your new ranch." John Mark again shook Russell's hand. He smiled for his friend's sake, but something about the sale of the Daly Ranch at a ridiculously low price, Daly's hasty departure, and the fact that Roessler wanted the ranch, left an uneasy feeling in the pit of his stomach.

Russell peered around the sheriff's office. "Caleb mentioned there's a lot of lawlessness here, but I don't aim to be in town much, what with running the ranch. And then if Amaya and I marry…" his lovesick expression told John Mark all he needed to know about his best friend's feelings for his fiancée.

"Congratulations on your upcoming wedding. I think you'll find you like marriage."

"Says the one who says he's not getting married until he's elderly."

"Not elderly. Just older." John Mark slugged his friend in the arm. "But I am married now. Caleb didn't tell you?"

"You're married?" Russell's eyebrows shot up into his forehead. "No, Caleb didn't tell me. He likely didn't get the chance because Frederick decided to join in on the conversation and changed the topic to something completely unrelated."

"Sounds like Frederick. Yes, I married a woman named Hannah. I'd like you to meet her."

Russell whistled. "Well, what do you know about that? I leave for a year to make some extra money, only to come back and find out my best friend is a married man. I'd certainly like to meet her. Would tomorrow evening work?"

"Sure would. We're living at the Valdez place about a mile from town. I like the proximity in case there's a situation, which in Poplar Springs, there are a lot of. At some point, I'd like to purchase it."

"Tell me about your Hannah."

John Mark stood and meandered toward the window. Passersby visited on the boardwalk and a drunk tottered in the middle of the street. "Hannah is a Christian, sweet, beautiful, and thoughtful." Her image entered his mind. He couldn't wait to see her this evening when he returned home. How had her day been? Was she settling into life with him?

"Sounds like you did well for yourself then. Is she from Poplar Springs?"

"She is."

"Your ma will have all three of her young'uns married from the sounds of it. I heard from Caleb that Charlotte and Cyrus are courting."

Irritation riveted through John Mark. "I'm against her marrying Cyrus. Ma and Pa don't see the problem, but you know as well as I do that Cyrus is a ne'er-do-well who won't treat Charlotte the way she deserves."

"Don't I know it. Charlotte deserves much better. 'Course, he does put on an impressive guise when he wants to fool someone. Your sister is smart. She'll see who he really is in time. And that's likely what your parents are hoping for."

"I'm sure it is. And we both know Charlotte. She's not only stubborn, but also has a habit of seeing the best in people."

"Two traits all Eliasons share." Russell scratched his chin again. "I'm amazed Cyrus and Violet aren't married. That would be the perfect match."

John Mark dismissed the thought that they both sounded like hens clucking on about the residents of Willow Falls. He was about to mention that he agreed with Russell's assessment when something across the street caught his eye. Mr. Nagel, the banker, followed by Mayor Roessler, emerged from the bank. Roessler pointed toward the far end of the street. Nagel said something, to which Roessler motioned to Red Beard who stood nearby. Nagel apparently changed his mind and abruptly retreated, his stubby legs carrying him faster than John Mark had ever witnessed.

What just happened?

Nagel kept his focus directly in front of him. Mr. Alvarado from the mercantile attempted to hail the banker with no success as Nagel continued down the boardwalk.

Had he been relieved of his job at the bank? If so, why?

The following day after a brief interaction with Nagel, John Mark learned he'd been fired due to selling the Daly Ranch to Russell rather than Mayor Roessler. He was still pondering the news and about to discuss it further with Sheriff Winslow when Old Man Skaggs burst through the door, his limp more pronounced with his hasty speed.

"Sheriff!"

Old Man Skaggs bent forward and placed his hands on his knees to catch his breath. "Sheriff, you gotta come real quick like."

Winslow placed a hand on his Colt Peacemaker. "What is it?"

"There's somethin' goin' on at the Daly place." Old Man Skaggs inhaled too much air and coughed several times before continuing. "I think it's a shootout. I was riding by there on my way to town and heard gunfire. Earlier this morn, a man named Russell something-or-other said he was gonna be my neighbor and that he was planning to be at the ranch today. And Daly, why, he already left this morn for Bowman."

John Mark's chest constricted and bile pooled in the back of his throat. Had Russell been caught in Roessler's crosshairs? For a moment, his lead-filled feet refused to move.

Winslow bellowed the words on John Mark's mind as they both stormed past Old Man Skaggs and toward their horses. "We need a posse. I'll round up Silas and Nowell. You find Pritchard."

Old Man Skaggs followed them out the door. "There was a bunch of 'em shootin' at the cabin. I think that Russell guy was holdin' 'em off all by his lonesome, but I didn't wait around to find out."

Thoughts—none of them good—pounded through John Mark's mind. They rounded up a posse, and headed east toward the Daly Ranch.

John Mark pulled ahead of the others, urging his horse as fast as safely possible. As he rounded the last curve to the ranch, he saw billows of smoke. "The house is on fire!" he shouted behind him. Not waiting to see if any of the others in the posse had kept up with him, John Mark pressed forward, praying that the Lord would keep Russell safe.

Flames shot from the roof and black smoke plumed toward the sky. The fire ignited sideways, threatening to spread to the barn.

The muscles in his shoulders tensed. Was anyone still in the house? Where was Russell? Where were those involved in the shootout? How had the fire started? The crackling of burning wood drew John Mark's attention toward the west side of the house where several dry pines were within feet of the burning building.

Anxiety coursed through him. He leapt from his horse and veered toward the pump. Aware that those bent on shooting at the house could be anywhere, but also wanting to extinguish the fire, John Mark did an efficient survey of the area as he ran.

There were no signs of the men and no sounds of gunfire.

He drew closer and the heat of the fire reminded him of its deadly force. "Ride to town and get help!" he yelled to no one in particular. "Russell!"

John Mark pumped the water into a bucket and rushed toward the house, joined by Winslow, Pritchard, Silas, and Nowell.

He stumbled on a rock in his path and water sloshed over the side of the bucket. A falling beam crashed to the ground, sending sparks raining. The overwhelming smoke choked him and he briefly held his shirt over his nose and mouth after emptying the first bucket.

John Mark rounded the side of the house, his thoughts intent on the fire and Russell's whereabouts. Old Man Skaggs mentioned he'd seen Russell earlier holding off some men in an apparent shootout. Where was he now? Had he left the ranch? Where were the other men?

Another scan of the area produced nothing but smoky air, trees, and outbuildings. Until...

He squinted, willing his vision to see clearly. And that's when he spied two familiar figures—Harold and Mander. A third person, Yin, ran around the side of the house while two others emerged from the opposite direction.

John Mark took shelter behind one of the outbuildings, hoping none of the men had seen him. He discreetly waved toward Winslow and Silas, who were behind him, to take cover.

Gunfire rose above the crackling of the fire. It was a matter of defense—shoot or be shot. The ruthless men had one goal in mind and it mattered not that two of the men in the line of fire were lawmen.

John Mark slimmed himself against the barn as a shootout commenced. Mander prepared to take a shot at Nowell, but not before John Mark took aim. Pritchard whipped around and sought refuge behind a trough. A sure shot, he covered Winslow as the sheriff flattened himself along the ground toward Harold, who staggered and fired his gun haphazardly at anything—or anyone—who moved.

"These guys aren't going to surrender," muttered Silas as he reloaded.

Five against five.

But while the outlaws may have had the advantage of surprise, they were no match for the posse.

A half hour later after an intense shootout that left three men, including Mander, dead, Sheriff Winslow arrested Harold and Yin. Thankfully everyone in the posse escaped injury.

The fire eased up some and Pritchard offered to ride to town to get help.

John Mark's muscles ached and exhaustion overtook him, but his determination forced him to forge ahead with the mission of extinguishing the fire before it spread. A handful of townsfolk arrived to assist.

He trampled through the overgrowth hauling bucket after bucket of water. He threw the water on the fire and took a wide berth around a row of pines to avoid colliding with three other men on their way to douse the cabin.

So consumed with his mission, John Mark nearly missed him.

He skidded to a stop and fell to his knees. "Russell!" His best friend's lifeless body was sprawled in the dirt atop a pile of brush, multiple bullet wounds evident.

They'd been too late.

"No!"

His reaction turned the heads of those hauling buckets. Winslow rushed toward him. "Eliason?" he asked.

John Mark pressed a palm to the tightening sensation in his chest. He forced his starved lungs to draw breath and his mind to rationalize what he'd seen.

No, not Russell. Not this way.

Winslow was discussing something about Silas and Pritchard guarding Harold and Yin and something else John Mark's muddled brain failed to comprehend. John Mark removed his vest and draped it over Russell to give him some semblance of respect, although the vest failed to cover much of him. The image of his friend implanted itself in his memory.

A choking sensation bubbled in his throat and if-onlies swarmed his mind. What if he'd arrived sooner? Been here when Yin and the others arrived? Thought to do more when he heard of Nagel's dismissal from the bank?

He stood and faced Winslow. "Why did they do this to him?"

"According to Yin, who decided to become a chattering hen all of a sudden, this gentleman was holed up in the house fending them off. Did a remarkable job considering there were five men to his one. Appeared to be a standoff until they started the place on fire. When he escaped through the back door, they put bullets in him."

John Mark scarcely heard Winslow's words. Instead, anger rose within him and the intense need for revenge took root in his heart.

Chapter Twenty-Six

HANNAH CARRIED A LANTERN to the porch and peered into the darkness. They were to have hosted a guest tonight—John Mark's best friend—but John Mark still hadn't arrived home. And although a sheriff's deputy's job demanded he be on duty at all times, he'd never been this late. An unshakable sense that something wasn't right heightened her concern, and she had prayed no less than fifteen times in the past hour.

She recalled verses she'd memorized from Ma's Bible about fear and worry. She recited both the verse found in First Peter and the one from Isaiah, beseeching the Lord's protection over her husband. *"Casting all your care upon him; for he careth for you...Fear thou not; for I am with thee: be not dismayed; for I am thy God: I will strengthen thee; yea, I will help thee; yea, I will uphold thee with the right hand of my righteousness."*

She wrapped her shawl tighter around her shoulders as the air turned chilly. Finally, she returned to the house, opened John Mark's worn Bible, and read the inscription:

To our beloved son, John Mark,

May you continually keep your eyes on Jesus in all things.
With Much Love,
Ma and Pa
November 8, 1883

The Bible's condition spoke of John Mark's frequent perusal. He'd underlined several verses and used a tattered scrap of paper as a bookmark in the book of Philippians. She turned there first, immersing herself in the familiar words.

Silence, except for the ticking of the clock and the rustling of trees outside, lent to her trepidation. Every few minutes between verses, she sought the time.

As she spent time in God's Word, a comforting peace enveloped her, a peace she could only attribute to the Lord. Hannah closed her eyes and rested against the back of the chair.

Some time later, she heard the thumping sounds of footsteps on the porch.

"John Mark!" Not caring about his soiled and smudged clothing, she wrapped her arms around his neck. Tears smarted in her eyes. "I was so worried about you."

The pungent odor of smoke struck her first. Then she noticed a cut grazing his cheek, surrounded by soot. His shirt was torn and his trousers filthy. Hannah would need to tend to the cut, but first she wanted to relish the fact that God had protected her husband.

John Mark wrapped his arms around her, and she could feel the weariness in his embrace.

"Russell is dead," he said, his tone flat.

"Russell?" She thought of the man John Mark spoke about frequently—his best friend from Willow Falls and the man who was to have eaten supper with them tonight.

"Shot by a bunch of pigeon-livered outlaws when he escaped the fire they set. Roessler wanted the land. Russell got in the way. They killed him."

His body tensed. Hannah had never understood any type of killing, especially the senseless variety. She took a slow step back from him. "Oh, John Mark, I am so sorry."

John Mark's jaw muscles firmed into a rigid line. "If I'd only been there sooner. I could have saved him."

"You don't know..."

"I do know." Anger laced his words. "Your pa was there. He helped kill my best friend."

The words took her aback. "I—I'm so sorry." Anything she could say would be inadequate. Her knees trembled and she pondered whether her legs would support her. Pa as an accomplice didn't astonish her, but it did send a terrifying jolt through her body. Hannah stepped backwards and steadied herself against the table. Her own father, responsible for taking a life. And not just any life, but the life of someone important to the person whom she cared about most.

John Mark said nothing, only fixed his attention on something beyond her.

The seconds ticked by. "I saved supper for you."

"I'm not hungry. I'll wash up outside and go to bed." His monotone voice, void of emotion and deeper than usual, bore witness to his pain.

"But what of the cut on your face?"

John Mark didn't respond. Instead he shuffled toward the door.

Hannah wanted to run to him, to wrap her arms around him again and to comfort him over his profound loss. To care for him and to let him know she was here if he needed to talk. To let him know she was praying for his loss.

After finishing her chores, she retreated to her bed and perched on the edge. The prayers came quickly, laced with desperation for the Lord to ease John Mark's grief.

Another thought entered Hannah's mind as she rested her head on her pillow. Did John Mark blame her for Russell's death?

After all, it was her father who killed him.

When morning came, Hannah found John Mark standing near the corral, absently fixating on something in the distance. For several minutes, he neither acknowledged her presence nor spoke. Finally, he turned toward her. Dark circles edged beneath his eyes and the corners of his mouth were drawn downward. His shoulders slumped, giving the appearance of defeat.

While Hannah knew little of his friendship with Russell, she did know they were close. The senseless killing—all in the name of securing Russell's land—was too much to bear, even for a strong man with a strong faith.

"John Mark?"

"Yes?"

"Breakfast is ready."

John Mark exhaled a deep breath. "I'm not hungry, Hannah, but thanks all the same."

She wanted to argue that he hadn't eaten since earlier in the day yesterday, but thought better of it.

"John Mark..."

But he'd shuffled toward the barn, his shoulders laden with the burdens weighing upon them. She started after him wanting to ease his pain, to pray with him, and to remind him she was there.

Clarence paraded toward her, but even his silly ways could not quell the torment that burrowed into her own heart at the sight of John Mark's anguish.

Hannah returned to the house, kneeled beside her bed, and folded her hands. She cried out to the One who could heal John Mark's sorrow. She prayed for his broken heart, for him to have peace in the midst of all that had occurred, and prayed she might be a help, not a hindrance. And that she would have wisdom in walking through this dark time with him.

Several moments later, she knew what she must do. "I have an errand in town. I'll be back soon," she told John Mark. His vacant stare made her wonder if he'd heard her.

Hannah welcomed the summer breeze as she rode toward town. The freedom to come and go as she wished invigorated her, and if it weren't for the concerns weighing heavily on her mind, she would have embraced the ride all the more. Yet, no matter how much she prayed otherwise, worry was her constant companion.

Poplar Springs was bustling, as usual. Hannah stepped inside the post office and noticed someone familiar at the counter. Her shrill voice was even more familiar.

"But I insist you send a telegram for me right away." The woman removed a handkerchief from her reticule and dabbed at her eyes.

"I'm sorry, Miss Roessler," said the postal clerk, "but unless you have another nickel, I won't be able to send the telegram."

"But I don't have another nickel. Can't you send it anyway?"

"I cannot."

Claudelle's high-pitched voice took on a sense of urgency. "If my father was still the mayor, he could have you fired for your refusal."

"But your father isn't still the mayor now, is he?" The postal clerk tilted his head to one side. "Now, Miss Roessler, if you don't have the funds to pay for the telegram, I must ask you to step aside and allow me to serve the next customer."

Without turning around to see who the next customer was, Claudelle removed a bracelet from her wrist. "Take this. It's worth far more than a nickel."

"With all due respect, I cannot take your bracelet in lieu of funds. Here are some options: why don't you send a letter? Or why don't you go to the mercantile or the dress shop and perhaps they will give you money in exchange for your bracelet? Then return here posthaste and I will be able to send the telegram." The postal clerk's exasperated tone indicated he'd been arguing with Claudelle prior to Hannah's arrival.

"You clearly don't understand. No one in town will purchase anything from a Roessler. Believe me when I tell you we have tried." Her voice shook. "You simply don't know what it's like to suddenly have a father and a brother with contemptible reputations. Please understand that I must reach my Uncle Arthur in Chicago immediately and ask him to send for Mother and me. And a letter simply will not do. Time is of the essence. Mother and I must leave this forsaken town."

Hannah counted the coins in her hand. If she gave a nickel to Claudelle, she would still have enough—just barely—to send her own telegram. She sidled alongside Claudelle and placed the nickel on the counter. "Will this allow her to send the telegram?" she asked.

"Indeed it will," said the postal clerk.

Claudelle's eyes widened. She gaped for several seconds before she spoke to the postal clerk. "Please send a telegram stating the following..." She gripped the counter for support. "Uncle Arthur. Stop. Emergency. Stop. Send for Mother and me immediately. Stop."

The postal clerk scribbled the words, accepted the money, then sent the telegram. Hannah took a step back to give Claudelle room and prepared herself for the barrage of mean-spiritedness that Claudelle was known for.

She stopped in front of Hannah.

Hannah pretended to be preoccupied, and when the other woman spoke, she flinched.

"Thank you," Claudelle said.

"You're welcome." Hannah despised the way her voice shuddered.

For several uncomfortable seconds, they stood facing each other. Finally, Claudelle removed the bracelet from her wrist. "Take this."

"Oh, I couldn't."

"You must. Do with it what you will. Sell it, give it to another, or keep it for yourself. Just, please, take it." She dropped the bracelet into Hannah's hand.

Without another word, Claudelle brushed past her and left the post office.

It took a few minutes for Hannah to collect herself as she fingered the bracelet in her hand. Never would she have imagined this outcome.

"Hello, Mrs. Eliason, what brings you here?" The postal clerk interrupted her thoughts.

"I'd like to send a telegram to Reverend Solomon Eliason in Willow Falls, please."

Hannah's hands shook as she retrieved the remainder of the funds she'd earned from supplying eggs to the mercantile over the past weeks. Such money was difficult to acquire and she pondered whether it was wasteful to spend it on a luxury such as a telegram.

But this was a necessity.

"What would you like for it to say?" the postal clerk asked, his pencil at the ready.

"Reverend Solomon. Stop. Please come to P.S. Stop. John Mark needs you. Stop." Perhaps talking with his pa—a man John Mark so obviously respected—would comfort him.

The postal clerk quirked an eyebrow. "Is everything all right with the deputy?"

Wishing to avoid providing fodder for the Poplar Springs robust rumor mill, Hannah simply answered, "He's working on a project."

"Ah, I see." To his credit, the postal clerk did not ask for details.

And Hannah sought the Lord's forgiveness that her answer was not entirely truthful.

She commenced her ride back home when the same worry from last night again niggled its way into her mind. Did John Mark blame her because Pa was involved in Russell's death? Did he regret marrying the daughter of a man who had his hand in taking another life?

When John Mark was of mind to hear her words, she would apologize for her pa's role in Russell's death and seek his forgiveness.

CHAPTER TWENTY-SEVEN

PA ARRIVED UNANNOUNCED THE next day and while John Mark was glad to see him, the last thing he desired was a sermon.

How many times had he replayed the entire scenario in his mind? Nothing was going to bring Russell back. Harold, Yin, Mander, or one of the other two men may have shot the guns and lit the fire, but John Mark was complicit as well for his lack of taking action when he could have.

The guilt smothered him.

"John Mark?"

"Look, Pa, I know you mean well..." John Mark's words trailed. He loved Pa, respected him, and valued his commitment to the Lord and to his family, but John Mark wasn't eager for a guest, even if it was his father. "Did Hannah ask you to come?"

"She did. Your wife is worried about you."

Hannah's concern was apparent, and John Mark regretted that he caused her any distress. He also bemoaned the fact that at that moment, Russell's death trounced all else, even his faith and Hannah.

But he was powerless to dwell on anything else.

Clarence crowed from somewhere nearby and a horse neighed. Both filled the intolerable silence—a silence that rarely occurred between him and Pa.

A firm hand on John Mark's shoulder, likely meant to alleviate his pain, instead caused him to stiffen.

"Look, Pa, I appreciate you riding all this way, but it was a waste of your time." John Mark's own words sounded foreign in his ears, but they needed to be said. Until he rectified the thoughts that tormented him since the moment he'd found Russell's lifeless body, he could focus on little else.

Pa removed his hand and John Mark figured he would take his leave.

That wasn't the case. "All right, John Mark Solomon Eliason, we need to talk."

Pa's stern expression and tone, combined with the use of John Mark's full name, brought John Mark to attention. "Pa..."

"We can talk here, on the porch, in the pasture somewhere, in the barn, or in the chicken coop. It doesn't matter to me the location, but we do need to talk."

Because it was Pa, John Mark would acquiesce. "All right. We can talk on the porch."

Hannah emerged from the house, two cups of coffee in her hands. Her swollen eyes told him she'd been crying. Knowing he'd likely been the cause crushed him and his chest constricted. He wanted to go to her, hold her, apologize for ignoring her and thinking only of himself and his concerns. But he couldn't. His feet remained solidly planted on the step of the porch, and when her solemn gaze lingered, John Mark was the first to look away.

"Thank you for the coffee, Hannah," Pa told her.

"Yes, thank you," John Mark muttered. He took a seat in the chair next to Pa's.

Pa said nothing for some time. A side-eye glimpse indicated Pa was likely praying. John Mark could use those prayers, yet he'd been unable to pray much himself in the hours after the shootout.

"Tell me about yesterday," Pa finally said.

"I—it was awful, Pa. I rode out there, knowing there was a shootout. When I saw all the flames, I never imagined..." John Mark paused, hating the emotion welling up in his throat. The image of Russell re-entered his mind. "I want revenge, Pa."

Would Pa quote verses from the Bible about revenge? Offer a lecture?

"You and Russell were close ever since you were youngsters. He was an honorable man and well-liked."

"Yes, and he was fixing to marry Amaya. They were going to live here in Poplar Springs on the Daly Ranch. Now that will never happen." Indignation rose within him. "I know who did this, and two of them—Yin and Harold are still alive. Locking them up, or even hanging them doesn't seem to be justice enough. Especially for Harold and the way he treated Hannah all those years." John Mark struggled through a drink of his coffee. "Look, Pa, I'm not very good company right now."

Pa stood and relocated his chair so he faced John Mark. "Son, there is nothing we can do to bring Russell back. Nothing. Taking revenge on Yin and Harold will not bring him back. Allowing the hate to remain inside of you will not bring them back."

"I know all this, Pa."

"You have always been one who seeks to set things to right. A man of justice and a man of truth. These are admirable qualities. I'd venture to say that you're one of the best deputies Wyoming has ever had because you care—truly care—about the people you serve."

John Mark knew where Pa's words would lead. He would encourage John Mark to not blemish the reputation he'd earned. "I..." He wanted to argue, to tell Pa that while he still knew right from wrong, some things—like Russell's death—needed to be atoned for. But the words wouldn't come.

"Russell's death was senseless. The men who did it should be punished to the fullest extent of the law, whatever that may be." Pa fixed his attention toward the sky for a moment before continuing. "You have every right to grieve Russell's horrific death. But you do not have a right to revenge. The Lord says revenge is His. Not ours, no matter how much we might like to think it is. No matter how we might think we could exact that revenge better than God can."

"But the anger...the injustice..."

"Yes, and anger is an emotion. It's when we allow that anger to cloud our judgment, to come between relationships, to affect our lives, or to escalate into sinful actions that it becomes problematic. No one is telling you not to be angry over Russell's death. No one is telling you to pretend it didn't happen. You *should* be upset that the life of an innocent man was stolen."

Pa placed his hands on John Mark's shoulders. "Son, you have always been an easygoing man. Stern when the need arose, but always amicable."

"I know this isn't like me. I know that."

"No, it's not, but sometimes life's events cause things to rise within us we didn't know were there. You will always grieve the loss of your best friend. You will always remember him. Someday when you go to Heaven, you'll see him again. But to seek to destroy the men who destroyed him doesn't honor Russell and it doesn't honor God."

A lump formed deep in John Mark's throat. "I know you're right."

Pa stood and John Mark rose to his feet. Pa hugged him. "I'm always here for you. It will take time to heal from this, but with God's help, you will heal."

Pa left early the next morning for Willow Falls to preside over a wedding. John Mark awoke after minimal shut-eye, his eyes gritty from lack of sleep. He rolled to one side and propped himself up on his elbow. Clarence crowed outside, his trademark cry reminding John Mark that, while Russell was gone, time moved on.

The aroma of bacon and eggs caused a rumble in his stomach. When was the last time he'd eaten? Hannah was at the stove, her back to him. He needed to apologize.

Lord, please give me the words to say to her. He rolled up his bedroll and strode toward her. "Hannah?"

Her reddened eyes, downturned facial features, and wilted shoulders gnawed at him. He hadn't been able to speak to her about Russell's death. Hadn't spoken much to her at all. And in his silence, John Mark knew he had hurt her.

"Good morning." Her voice wavered and she remained standing near the stove.

"Can we talk after breakfast?"

Hannah carried the plates to the table, then took a step toward him. He tenderly pulled her into a tentative embrace. His distance in the past day wasn't her fault. His growing feelings toward her hadn't stalled. She needed to know this. "Hannah," he whispered.

She nuzzled closer to him, likely in need of the comfort he provided. Comfort that told her all was well despite his standoffish behavior and clipped words, when he spoke at all. John Mark yearned to articulate to her his struggle with finding Russell at his new ranch and not being able to save him.

But he couldn't. Couldn't verbalize the pain and agony continually riveting through him.

Hannah was warm in his arms and he folded her into a tighter embrace. He closed his eyes and rested his chin on her head, praying for reconciliation, for her forgiveness, and for their future.

After some time, she pulled away from him, her eyes searching his. "I'm so sorry."

Her words caught him unawares. "Sorry?"

"That it was my pa who killed Russell." Her voice faltered. "How can you be married to a woman whose father killed your best friend?"

Hannah's words devastated him for he knew she blamed herself.

He attempted to pull her to him again, but she shook her head. "John Mark, I am sorry for what my pa did."

The agony in the depths of her eyes nearly undid him. John Mark reached for her hand. "Hannah, I don't blame you."

"But my pa was there."

"Yes, and I don't know who shot Russell as there were five men there."

"We all know Pa is an evil man. He would do what's necessary to carry out Roessler's wishes."

John Mark knew of Harold's propensity toward wickedness just from the way he mistreated his daughter. "If he shot Russell, that's not your fault. You aren't your pa."

Her lip trembled and her voice wobbled. "No, but I am his daughter."

"Hannah." He drew her to him again and this time she didn't resist. Her body shook and he placed his hand gently on the back of her head. "I don't blame you at all. I would never blame you. You didn't hold the gun, you didn't have the evil intent in your heart, and you didn't fire the weapon. You are not at fault for Russell's death. Hannah Eliason, you are not responsible for Russell's death," he repeated. "You are one of the kindest, most compassionate people I know. You are not to blame."

She stilled and John Mark prayed for continued wisdom. To know that she carried this burden with her the past couple of days shattered him. This woman who had lived a life of abuse, heartache, and rejection feared she disappointed him. And not only disappointed him, but that she was just like her father.

Hannah Eliason had nothing in common with Harold Bane.

"Hannah, I need to apologize to you for being despondent and distancing myself from you. I'm sorry I didn't eat the fine meals you made, and I'm sorry I wasn't here for you in your grief. Will you forgive me?"

She stared up at him, tears still glistening in her eyes. "I know you were grieving over Russell's death. I can't imagine the horror of finding him the way you did. I forgive you."

John Mark kissed the top of her forehead. "Thank you."

Standing there embracing her, he longed to kiss her. To rectify all that had happened between them. To demonstrate how much he cared for her. But John Mark didn't want to take advantage of the situation. Still, the way she felt in his arms, almost like it had always been meant to be, stirred something in him he couldn't articulate.

They'd known each other for such a brief time. Yet, in that time, they'd grown closer. Grown together.

He anticipated seeing her each morning and again each evening when he returned home. Treasured their conversations, their time attending church together, and the silly moments such as the button incident. She was beautiful in both appearance and heart, a woman of godly character.

He'd grown to love her.

Did Hannah feel the same?

He leaned toward her. Hannah tilted her head to one side and parted her lips. John Mark gently cupped her face, his thumb stroking her cheek as he bridged the distance between them. "Hannah," he breathed before his lips found hers.

Chapter Twenty-Eight

JOHN MARK WAS ABOUT to kiss Hannah a second time when a knock at the door sounded. "Eliason!"

He opened the door to find Gaston pacing on the porch, his dark eyes flashing. "Been a stagecoach robbery. The outlaws have a hideout somewhere between here and Bowman. Winslow wants us to find them."

It wasn't the ideal way to be notified of a stagecoach robbery, especially since he'd wanted to spend more time with Hannah.

"John Mark, please be careful."

He planted a kiss on her forehead. "I will."

"No time for that, Eliason. Winslow said these guys won't stay in the area forever."

Reminded they were not alone, John Mark reluctantly released Hannah. "I'll be back for supper," he said.

"Will you need anything to take with you?"

"*A woman needs to know you need her and that she's important to you.*" Pa's words echoed through his mind. Hannah needed to be needed, especially in this time of uncertainty.

"Could you pack a couple of sandwiches?"

Hannah nodded and hustled toward the kitchen. "It'll be but a minute."

Gaston butted his way through the door. "Look, Eliason, I said there's no time for this type of nonsense. We best get on the road and find this gang. Innocent blood has been shed from the robbery. I'm not thinking Winslow would take too kindly to you prolonging the situation."

John Mark knew the critical nature of finding the outlaws who committed the crimes and justice flowed heavily through his veins, but something about Gaston's tone annoyed him. "I'll meet you outside."

His coworker's intense glare lasted for several seconds before Gaston pivoted and left the house.

Hannah handed him the sandwiches. "Please be careful, John Mark. Please come back to me."

His heart clenched at the unsteadiness in her voice, and he grappled for more words to reassure her—to remind her of his devotion.

"I will always come back to you, Hannah."

Hannah stood on the deck, Clarence beside her, and watched as John Mark and Deputy Gaston rode away. She prayed for God's protection and safety.

John Mark's kisses just minutes earlier had taken her aback. His words comforted her that she was not to blame for Pa's role in killing Russell.

As they'd stood, their eyes locked, Hannah still cherishing the words he'd expressed, she had longed for John

Mark to kiss her. For them to fully mend any lingering rift between them. For him to reassure her he still desired her to be his wife.

Hannah closed her eyes and remembered the way she'd welcomed his kiss, how twirls of excitement rippled through her, and how her knees weakened, nearly failing to hold her upright. Her heart skittered when his lips found hers.

She relived the moment again, anticipating the next time.

Dirty dishes from breakfast beckoned her. Again inside, she peered around the home that had become hers to share with the husband God had blessed her with. Hannah had made new curtains, kept up with the sweeping, and scrubbed the floors once a week. She had never felt so eager to take care of Pa's house like she did her new home.

John Mark found a basket in the barn from the previous renters for her sewing. There she kept the kit he'd purchased for her. The bureau from Lydie and Reverend Solomon stood beside the bed, and she'd carefully stacked John Mark's shirts and trousers in the top drawer and her dresses in the bottom drawer. His Bible rested on the top of the bureau, making Hannah wish for Ma's Bible all the more. Although perhaps now that Pa would be taken to prison, the possibility of securing the precious possession was attainable.

Her attention veered toward the rifle above the mantle that John Mark taught her how to shoot. "Just in case you should need it," he'd told her. Hannah translated that to mean if Pa came for a visit.

She set her mind to the task of washing dishes when less than ten minutes later, she heard a sound outside. Clarence, who thought he was a watchdog, had taken to crowing.

And what Hannah saw outside the front window chilled her like nothing else.

Red Beard, Oslo Dunn, and one other man she only recognized from the saloon, were making their way toward the cabin.

CHAPTER TWENTY-NINE

KNOTS COILED IN JOHN Mark's stomach. Something wasn't right. He peered behind himself no less than six times as an eerie feeling of dread consumed him.

John Mark hastened his horse to keep up with Gaston's quickened pace. "The stagecoach robbery was today?"

"That's what I said."

Something hung just on the edges of his recollection. They rode another quarter mile when it came to him. A stagecoach arriving in Poplar Springs today was not on the schedule.

Red Beard and Oslo Dunn riding through the trees in the opposite direction toward his cabin confirmed his suspicions.

He'd been duped.

In a swift motion, he reversed course and headed toward his house.

"Wait! Where are you going?"

John Mark ignored the deafening echo of Gaston's voice.

Lord, please watch over Hannah.

He had no idea what scheme his fellow deputy was behind, but if it involved a ruse to remove him from his home, it worked.

But not for long.

John Mark pressed forward, pushing his horse as fast as was prudent. His heart raced in his ears in time with the hoofbeats on the hardened dry ground. If they injured Hannah...

The thundering hooves of a horse behind him reminded him Gaston was on the opposite side of the law. Agitation filled every part of him. The only thing worse than an outlaw was a traitor who pretended to be a law-abiding citizen.

His home came into sight and he saw three men taunting Hannah.

Even from this distance, he could hear Red Beard's spiteful laugh.

Fury engulfed him and acid rose in his throat. He'd barely stopped his horse when he dismounted and stalked toward Red Beard, Oslo Dunn, and a rail-thin man with ebony skin, who was known as Scowl.

"Leave her alone!" John Mark shouted. He placed a hand on his Colt Peacemaker, having it at the ready.

His Winchester, tossed on the ground not far from the house, caught his eye. They apparently managed to wrestle it from Hannah's grasp. He cringed at the thought of Hannah now defenseless and at the mercy of black-hearted cowards.

"Well, looky here. Deputy Eliason has shown up to save his wife, only it's not gonna happen." Red Beard shoved John Mark hard, causing John Mark to nearly lose his balance. He regained his footing and prepared to do what was necessary for Hannah to emerge from this unscathed.

The terror in her eyes broke him. She'd suffered mercilessly at the hands of her father for over twenty years. John Mark would do whatever it took to prevent her from ever having to suffer at the hands of a hateful man again.

Oslo Dunn caressed her cheek with his finger and got close into her face. "Always thought you were a pretty one."

"Leave her be!"

"You gotta a lot of guts waltzing on in here tellin' us how things oughta be." Oslo strode toward him and stuck his face in John Mark's. An acrid odor of onions mixed with boiled cabbage permeated the air. "You won't tell us what we will and won't do. But we do have a deal for you." The sneer caused Oslo's already-sizeable nostrils to expand all the more.

Gaston dismounted, and for the first time, John Mark recognized the wickedness in his barbed laugh. "Yep, we do have a deal for you, Eliason. Are you ready to hear it?" He strode toward Hannah and clutched her arm in a tight grip. "Guess you really don't have a choice if you want to your woman to live."

"How could you get embroiled in this, Gaston?" John Mark met the gaze of the man he'd ridden with on numerous occasions during stagecoach robberies. The man who worked alongside him to settle disputes in the saloon. The man who promised to uphold the law.

"You're a dimwit, Eliason." Gaston's words caused a round of chortles from the other three men. He removed his revolver from its holster and pointed it at Hannah. "Remove your gun and toss it on the ground toward Red Beard."

John Mark hesitated for the briefest of seconds.

"Do it, or I shoot her—and you know I will."

Gaston shoved the barrel edge into Hannah's side. The traitor had nothing to lose at this juncture. He likely was already involved in Russell's death and a host of other crimes at Mayor Roessler's request. John Mark removed his Colt and slid it on the ground. Red Beard retrieved it and stroked the end of the barrel. "Think I'll keep this for myself." He slid it into his waistband.

"Not fair," whined Oslo.

"Shut up the both of you," Gaston snarled. He tucked his own gun back into its holster. "Tell him how it's gonna be, Oslo."

Oslo strutted forward as if given an important task. "Here's what's gonna happen. You're gonna go into town and either free Yin, or if Winslow is there, convince him it wasn't Yin you saw out at the Daly Ranch. You're gonna tell him you was mistaken, that it wasn't Yin at all, but some other man. Then you see to it that Yin is released from jail. Or you could just open up the cell and set him free thataways too. Get Yin released and we'll release Hannah."

"Winslow was there. He saw that it was Yin. And Winslow isn't going to free him. Yin's wanted for murder." *And deserves to hang.*

Oslo exploded, his pursed lips, reddening face, and cold eyes giving testament to his fury. He balled his fists at his sides. "Yin don't deserve to be behind bars. You get him out or..." he jerked his thumb toward Hannah. "Or she gets the fate *you* deserve."

Every muscle in John Mark from his head to his toe tensed. He needed to exercise caution when it came to Oslo with his easily-provoked temper. But the words tumbled from his mouth unabated. "And Harold? You want him set free too?"

"Don't care none about Harold," sneered Oslo. "He's just a drunkard pawn. But Yin, he's one of us and is innocent. Was just followin' orders was all he was doin'"

Mayor Roessler's orders, no doubt. "Why don't you go into town and make the demand of Winslow yourselves?"

Gaston released Hannah and stormed toward John Mark. He jabbed him hard in the chest. "Listen here, Eliason. We say what's going to happen here, not you. If Winslow is going to listen to anyone, it'll be you. And if he won't listen to you, then you take your key, insert it into the lock, and *you* set Yin free."

His fellow deputy had to know that Winslow wouldn't just release Yin. But from his agitated state, Gaston likely wasn't thinking rationally. And why didn't Gaston use his own key to release Yin? Unless Winslow hadn't given him one, which was a possibility. John Mark nodded toward Hannah. "Let her go and I'll do whatever you want."

"No, you'll do what we want and then we'll let her go," sneered Red Beard. "And then, after Winslow releases Yin, we're gonna all ride out of here and you're not gonna follow us. Got that?"

"I'm not doing anything until you release Hannah." John Mark did his best to ignore the shaking in his legs and the tingling in his fingers. While setting Yin free was the last thing he wanted to do, he'd do whatever it took to ensure Hannah's safety.

Gaston's steely eyes met his. "Because you need a hearing trumpet to hear anything, let me tell you again." He raised his voice to a shout and annunciated his words slowly. "We'll. Let. Her. Go. Once. Yin. Has. Been. Released." He stomped toward Hannah and shoved her. She stumbled and nearly lost her balance.

The provocation was all John Mark needed and he rushed toward her, fury swelling within him.

"Whoa there, Eliason," hissed Red Beard. He planted himself between John Mark and Hannah. "Don't do nothin' you might regret. Remember, if we kill you, something *unfortunate* could happen to your woman."

Red Beard was rarely right about much, but he was correct in that John Mark needed to temper himself and keep himself alive. He begged the Lord for wisdom.

A staring match commenced between him and Red Beard. Seconds ticked by. "I'll tell you what. I'll go into town and attempt to convince Winslow to set Yin free. If he won't set him free, I'll open the cell myself."

"Now you're talking like a rational man," said Gaston. "We'll give you a half hour."

John Mark held up a finger. "Wait a minute. I wasn't finished. I'll do all that, but how about I give Oslo my horse in exchange for Hannah's freedom? I'll still ride into town on another horse I have in the barn, and see to it that Yin is released." He paused and beckoned the men to inspect his horse. "You'd have to go far to find a finer mount."

As if being identified as the one to receive John Mark's horse was a compliment, Oslo Dunn stood tall and thrust out his fleshy chest. "Might as well take me a look at this horse, even if we still ain't gonna set Hannah free until Yin gets here." He strode toward John Mark's horse and lifted a hoof. Gaston, Red Beard, and Scowl followed him. Oslo lifted one leg and inspected the hoof. "Don't see no cracks or nothin'."

John Mark's gaze connected with Hannah's. Would she take this as the chance to escape?

As if reading his mind, she inched toward Red Beard's sorrel quarter horse.

"Let me have a look-see at his mouth. Coat is shiny and his eyes are bright enough and ain't dull, I guess. Is he skittish at all?"

"No, he's as calm as they come." John Mark discreetly watched as Hannah efficiently, yet quietly, mounted the horse.

"Where'd you get him?" Scowl asked.

John Mark was about to answer when the neighing of a horse, followed by the pounding of hooves, directed the men's attention from him to Hannah.

"Hey!" Red Beard yelled. "That's my horse and what she done is horse thievery. She'll be hanged for that."

"Truth is, you stole it from that guy at the Daly Ranch," said Oslo.

Red Beard elbowed him hard in the ribs. "This is all your fault."

"I'll go after her," suggested Scowl.

Gaston aimed his gun toward Hannah and fired a shot. John Mark leapt into action and tackled him.

Over the next several minutes, a fight ensued. Gaston's revolver slid to the side, just out of John Mark's reach. He traded punches with the other deputy, who proved to be stronger and more robust than John Mark anticipated. He fended off Oslo at the same time, causing the rotund and sluggish man to lose consciousness from a hard hit. Scowl, thin and weaker, proved an easy defeat as well.

Gaston and Red Beard took advantage of the ratio with a combination of Gaston's swift thinking and prowess and Red Beard's size and strength. John Mark and Gaston wrestled on the ground, but whenever John Mark gained the upper hand, Red Beard would either kick or hit him. John Mark tasted blood more than once and figured it was from the hit he took to the nose. Scowl and Oslo joined in the fight again after several minutes, and Oslo yanked back John Mark's head and Scowl's fist aimed, but missed John Mark's face.

His ribs ached and his head pounded. Would Hannah think to seek reinforcements? Gaston flipped him over, the other deputy's endurance a shock. Round and round they went while John Mark attempted to fight off all four criminals. Time traveled slowly, as if the clock would stop and forget to start again. John Mark executed punch after punch and received quadruple the amount in return.

His surroundings spun as he managed to stagger to his feet. Gaston's face blurred as he and John Mark rounded each other. No amount of blinking staved off the ringing in his ears and the shadows edging his peripheral, but the longer he kept the men occupied, the better chance Hannah had at reaching Poplar Springs.

Red Beard and Scowl gripped his arms as he struggled to see straight, and Oslo aimed his gun at John Mark. "Want me to shoot him?"

"Not yet," said Gaston. "We still need him. But soon."

Oslo kept the gun trained on John Mark. "Can I have the honors when the time comes? Never did like him."

"Put your gun away," Gaston snapped.

John Mark almost managed to smile at the sound of Gaston's heavy breathing. He may be outnumbered, but at least he wasn't making it easy for them.

Oslo did as he was told and instead delivered another fisted blow. John Mark doubled over at the impact, his already-struggling lungs begging for air. "That's because I can't shoot ya yet."

Before John Mark could react, Gaston pummeled him again in the ribs. John Mark twisted and writhed, his own kick connecting with Gaston's kneecap. Despite the determination coursing through him, his weary state simply couldn't continue fending off the blows.

Red Beard's lip curled. "Always think you're so tough, dont'cha, Eliason?"

"I never did like you. You always thought you were better because you were the son of a preacher. Here's for always getting to stay in Poplar Springs while I had to travel elsewhere in the county to keep the law." Gaston struck him hard in the jaw.

Lord, please help me.

John Mark reassured Hannah he'd always come back to her, and he rather not break that promise.

Taking deep breaths despite the agony in his ribs, he set his jaw and wrenched one arm free, sending his elbow into Scowl's nose. Before the man's body hit the ground, John Mark nailed the underside of Oslo's jaw.

Before Gaston could react, John Mark yanked the other man's revolver from his holster. "You know I'm an accurate shot." He steadied the gun in his hands, willing his battered body to cooperate and not reveal the fact that right then, he would be unable to even hold a blade of grass steady.

Red Beard reached for his gun and fired a shot toward John Mark, grazing his left arm. Before Red Beard could shoot again, John Mark returned fire. His aim proved accurate and Red Beard dropped.

Movement flashed in the corner of his vision.

Gaston lunged toward him.

A gunshot took the other deputy down, but it wasn't John Mark's bullet.

Dust plumed around the hooves of a familiar horse as Pritchard rode up, posture easy and expression nonchalant. "How's your day going, J.M.?"

CHAPTER THIRTY

DOC THORSEN EMERGED FROM the bedroom, bag in hand. "I reckon he'll make a full recovery. Your most difficult task, Mrs. Eliason, will be ensuring he allows himself time to heal." He smirked. "Don't know your husband real well, but I imagine he's not the type to appreciate being confined for any length of time. I'll be back in a few hours to check on him."

Hannah struggled to formulate a verbal response to Doc's reassurances other than a "thank you." Dashing into the bedroom, she dropped to her knees by the side of the bed. "John Mark," she breathed, taking in his startling appearance.

Two black eyes, a cut lip, swollen face, and a bandaged arm and forehead attested to some of his various external injuries. Hannah covered her mouth with her palm. It was only by God's grace her husband survived the beating he suffered at the hands of Roessler's comrades.

She bent forward and nestled her cheek against his. "I rode as fast as I could."

John Mark lightly squeezed her hand. "You are the bravest woman I know. Thank you for what you did today," he rasped.

"I just...I just wasn't sure if when I returned..." Hannah's breath hitched. What if she had lost him today? What if the Lord had taken him home just as she was growing to love him? "I was so worried about you. I was so fearful they would kill you."

John Mark caressed her check with his uninjured hand. He spoke, his voice hoarse and strained. "Nah, my family would say I'm too stubborn for that." He paused and drew a ragged breath. "As long as I have anything to say about it, I'll never leave you, Hannah. I made that promise and I intend to keep it."

Hannah rested against him as the minutes ticked by before he spoke again. "Hannah?"

"Yes?"

"I love you."

Her heart leapt against her chest. "I love you too, John Mark."

"Milady," said a suspiciously recognizable voice. A giggle erupted before Pritchard and Ina waltzed through the door and toward John Mark. Ina's hand was tucked into Pritchard's elbow and the man's face glowed.

"I see you're resting as the doctor ordered," quipped Pritchard.

"Not much else I can do."

"Has Winslow stopped by yet?"

John Mark's day started with scrambled eggs and his favorite cookies for breakfast, courtesy of Hannah. The visitors hadn't stopped trickling in and it was only ten o'clock. "Let's see, Winslow, Silas, Nowell, Doc Thorsen, Hank, and Frank and their nonstop bickering…seems everyone in Poplar Springs has paid me a visit today."

"That's because we were concerned about losing the best deputy our town has."

"The only deputy."

Pritchard's trademark laugh reverberated through the room. "Yes, but not sure if anyone else has mentioned it yet, but Silas and Nowell are being deputized until Winslow can find some permanent deputies to replace Gaston and you while you heal."

"I'll be back to work in no time."

"Sure. Don't let a bullet wound, a few broken ribs, a swollen face, and two black eyes stop you from keeping the law in Poplar Springs."

"I won't. I aim to be up and back to making sure Poplar Springs is a safe place by next week."

Pritchard harumphed. "That's not what Doc said, although I'm sure Hannah would appreciate having you up and about sooner. You underfoot could get tedious."

"Glad to see your sense of humor remains intact after your heroic feat." John Mark paused. "Much obliged for what you did yesterday."

"Happy to help."

Ina gazed up at Pritchard, her devoted admiration as obvious as a beak on a chicken. "He is a hero, isn't he?"

"Because of my heroic deeds, Ina's pa allowed her to accompany me here. As of today, we're courting, and I plan to ask for her hand in marriage in the near future if she'll have me."

"Will you be asking Winslow to deputize you as well?"

"Nah. I work better undercover and from the surprised expression on your face, it appears I was effective. Besides, I have my aspirations on the political side of things. If Roessler is found guilty, and I have a hunch he will be, given all the rumors circulating through town, Poplar Springs is going to need a new mayor."

"Undercover? You the new mayor?"

Ina chose that moment to interject. "If you two will excuse me, I'm going to visit with Hannah. You should have seen her yesterday. You married a courageous woman."

"That I did." John Mark wouldn't forget how Hannah's bravery may have saved his life.

"John Mark, my parents and Grandmother Pearson send their regards." With that, Ina left the room in search of Hannah.

"Does Ina know what you're about to share?" John Mark asked.

"Yes, we discussed it on the way here. You don't need to worry about Ina. Her pa gave me permission to court her. And don't fret, J.M. I will be the fine upstanding young man you know me to be. I'll treat her with respect and in a way that pleases God."

"It's her pa you have to convince, not me."

Pritchard spun the chair around backwards and took a seat. "Yes, and I aim to. And about my being undercover—I'm a detective of sorts."

He had John Mark's attention now. "A detective of sorts? I thought you were a rancher."

"That too. Still working on growing my herd." Pritchard folded his arms across the back of the chair.

"But what about your stealing? How can you be working for the law and be a thief?"

"I'm not actually *working* for the law. You see, when I came to town I happened to overhear some information about Mayor Roessler. I told Winslow about it, and he asked if I'd be willing to share anything else I heard. I nominated myself an honorary detective, but I'm confident the sheriff agrees with that title. Only he and I knew about my eavesdropping, hanging out in the saloon and hearing about the ongoings, and what Roessler's son terms 'trespassing' because I'm at the dry goods store for hours on end listening to the interesting conversations there. Did you know that's where most of the ones involved meet? It's not the saloon, it's the dry goods store. And yes, before you ask, the culprits were Roessler and his son, Red Beard, Oslo Dunn, Harold, Yin, Mander, Scowl, and six other unscrupulous fellows."

John Mark always knew something was amiss with Pritchard, but he also suspected the man was on the right side of the law, just a bit misguided. "That still doesn't answer the question about you stealing. All the canned food, pickles, crackers, and the like. How can a man who's working for the law be on both sides of it?"

"Back up the wagon, J.M. You make me sound like an outlaw. The stealing was only a couple of times and that was more for revenge purposes since the mayor steals from our residents. You know, take back what was stolen and give it to people who need it? I've helped some exceptional folks in this town—including one you happen to love. Anyhow, I've ceased that—shall we call it, *profession*—and repented, thanks to your pa's wise counsel. He really gave me a lot to chew on during our visit after your wedding." Pritchard cleared his throat. "Seems he believes I should spend some time reading Exodus too and he made me memorize a verse in the Book of Mark as well—'*Thou knowest the commandments, Do not commit adultery, Do not kill, Do not steal, Do not bear false witness, Defraud not, Honour thy father and mother*'." Pritchard paused. "I was doing well with that entire verse with the exception of the stealing part. And no, before you say it, I wasn't hornswoggling anyone." He sighed. "Reckon I should tell you the whole story."

"This could take a while."

Pritchard wasn't dissuaded. "Seems to me like you have some time. You see, my pa was a Pinkerton detective for a time when I was a young'un. Dragged me around on some of his assignments. I learned from the best on how to keep an ear to the ground and an eye on the happenings. How do you think I learned how to play cards? It was a challenge for my pa to have a kid slowing him down, but I learned a lot. When I moved to Poplar Springs, I talked with Winslow about the situation with the stealing of cattle, the rustling, and the blackmailing. My guess from the beginning was that the mayor was involved. With him and the rest of the 'upstanding' characters to be brought before a jury in the coming months, I figure Poplar Springs will be a better place after they get their dues."

Justice for Russell wouldn't bring him back, but it *would* ease some of the pain.

Charlotte settled into the chair beside his bed. From the second she'd entered the room, John Mark could see the distress in her countenance. "Charlotte?"

"John Mark, thank the Lord you're all right." She reached a hand toward him. "When Sheriff Winslow sent a telegram to Pa, we weren't sure how bad it was. Ma would be here too but she and Mrs. Ledbetter are with Annie since the baby still isn't here yet and it could be any time now."

"Sheriff Winslow sent Pa a telegram?"

"He did. Ma was beside herself. Everyone knows being a deputy—especially in Poplar Springs—is a perilous job, but you could have been killed."

How many times had John Mark thanked the Lord for His protection, not only over himself, but especially over Hannah?

"There's something else I need to tell you." Charlotte bit her lip. "I'm sorry for our quarrel in Willow Falls. You were right about Cyrus."

John Mark hadn't wanted to be right if it meant pain for his sister. "I'm sorry too and especially sorry about Cyrus."

Her voice hitched. "I suppose it's better to find out now than after we're married."

"True." He waited for her to continue.

"I discovered that he and Violet are...he's not been faithful to me." Charlotte's chin trembled and she dabbed at her nose with her handkerchief. "I know you and Cyrus never saw eye-to-eye and that he wasn't a principled and respectable young man during our school days, but he seemed so charming and affable. I thought he loved me."

"Charlotte..."

Her shoulders slumped. "I really thought he loved me. Ma and Pa conferred with me on several occasions that I needed to pray for God's wisdom and guidance, especially for such an important issue as marriage, which I did. But I guess..." A tear slid down her face and John Mark patted her hand. "I guess I thought Cyrus had matured to a sensible and godly man. But it was all a façade."

"I'm sorry, Charlotte. I never wanted you to get hurt. I really hoped I was wrong."

Charlotte sighed, her shoulders shaking with her attempt to withhold her sobs. "He pretended to love the Lord, pretended to love me, and pretended I was the one he wanted to marry. All along, he was seeing Violet as well. Violet of all people!"

John Mark knew Charlotte and Violet had never been friends, and Charlotte was friends with nearly everyone. "Cyrus didn't deserve you."

"I apologize, John Mark. I came here to ensure you were all right after all you'd been through, not to converse about me."

"Isn't that what big brothers are for? To listen to and care for their little sisters?"

Charlotte half-laughed, half-sobbed. "Yes, and you and Caleb are the best big brothers a girl could ask for." She folded her hands in her lap. "Perhaps I was enthralled with the idea of being married and I really thought Cyrus was the one for me."

"I'll be honest and tell you I prayed, as I know Ma and Pa did as well, that God would guide you and make it clear if Cyrus wasn't the one you should marry."

"I appreciate your prayers, John Mark, and truth be told, I didn't want to hear anything from naysayers, but now, I'm much older and wiser." A glint sparkled in her eyes and he knew his sister would someday recover from her broken heart.

"Do you want me to let Cyrus know my feelings about him breaking my sister's heart?"

"Caleb said something similar. As much as it sounds tempting, no. Someday I'll forget about him and the several months of wasted time I spent courting him. I've been so foolish."

John Mark shifted, attempting to ignore the pain from his injuries. "Yes, you will forget about him someday. And, Charlotte?"

"Yes?"

"There's a man out there somewhere who will appreciate you, be faithful to you, and love you the way God intends. The funny, charismatic, kind, beautiful, and somewhat-dramatic woman you are."

"Somewhat-dramatic?"

John Mark attempted to chuckle, but the pain in his ribs caused it to resemble more of a grunt. "Yes, the somewhat-dramatic Charlotte Eliason. Notice I said 'somewhat.' Several years ago, I might not have even included that word."

Charlotte jabbed him on his uninjured shoulder. "And you're still somewhat vexing, John Mark Solomon Eliason." She took a deep breath and continued. "Ma suggested I go stay with Aunt Fern and Aunt Myrtle next spring. They require assistance, and Ma said visiting them will do my heart some good. They can definitely use some help with the upkeep of the Peabody home since they recently inherited it."

"Now that would be a sight to see—Aunt Fern, Aunt Myrtle, and Charlotte, all together in one town. Someone ought to warn the fine folks of Prune Creek."

Caleb arrived next. While the continual visits drained John Mark, he'd not have it any other way. He invited his brother—the one he'd always hoped to emulate—to sit in the chair Charlotte vacated. "I hear you're about to be a pa again in the next couple of days."

"Doc Garrett says our baby will be born anytime now."

"From what Annie says, you'll soon be the proud pa of four girls."

"I wouldn't have it any other way. Esther, Lena, and Lola are thrilled to be big sisters, although Lena is confused about how Lola could be a 'big sister' when Lola is—in Lena's words—'just a little girl.'"

John Mark envisioned Lena's puzzled expression. "I can hear her saying that. By the way, thank you for coming."

"When Pa got the telegram, we were concerned, and we're all thankful it wasn't worse. I'll be riding back this afternoon and staying over in Nelsonville with Annie's pa before I continue to Willow Falls. I want to be there the second Doc allows me to see Annie and the baby."

John Mark appreciated the fact that he not only had Pa and Ma for godly examples of married folks, but also Caleb and Annie.

"Poor Charlotte."

"Yes, I figured you would want to call out the posse and go after Cyrus."

"It did cross my mind."

Caleb chuckled. "Annie and I prayed for Charlotte's decision to marry him. Sometimes we're blinded when it comes to others. On another topic, how are you holding up after Russell's death?"

"I had a talk with Pa. He reminded me about revenge and how it's not mine to seek."

"Tough to hear, especially when you lose someone you care about, but the truth. Vengeance is definitely the Lord's. Pa's given me much wise counsel over the years with things I've struggled with. Seems revenge and forgiveness might be some of the most difficult things we encounter."

John Mark was grateful, not only for parents who came alongside of him when he sought godly advice, but also for an older brother. "Russell didn't deserve to die. I can't imagine what his parents and his fiancée are enduring right now. I've mentioned to Hannah that after I heal, perhaps she and I can travel to Bowman where Amaya lives and offer our condolences."

After the noonday meal, Caleb left for Nelsonville. Pa visited next, followed by Reverend Fleming, who'd spent a considerable amount of time with Pa before speaking with John Mark.

The pastor prayed for John Mark then took a seat. "I've given a lot of thought to what you said a while back about there being a lot of need in Poplar Springs. I also spoke at lengths with your pa about it." Reverend Fleming appeared thoughtful. "The missus and I have prayed about it and decided to remain in Poplar Springs only, rather than divide our time between two towns. This will allow us to better serve the abundant needs of the townsfolk here."

"You can always rely on me for whatever you need to accomplish that goal." John Mark thought of Hannah and how the Lord had orchestrated her rescue.

"Thank you. About that, I was wondering if you would be willing to become an elder? Our church is small, but I figured that with you, Mr. Pearson, and a few other men as elders, we might have more hands to do the Lord's work. My wife would like to start a sewing group for women to make clothing items for those in need. Perhaps Hannah would join."

"I'd be honored to be an elder, and I'm certain Hannah would consider the idea of joining the sewing group. She has a heart for others."

Reverend Fleming stroked his beard. "That she does, and I wish we had done more for her. But it awoke us to the fact that there is need here."

"And that's all the more reason to spread hope, and Poplar Springs needs that."

CHAPTER THIRTY-ONE

TIME PASSED QUICKLY, AND two months later, John Mark pinned up the latest wanted posters. Apparently, the arrests of Mayor Roessler and his son; Oslo Dunn, Scowl, Yin, and Harold; and the deaths of Mander and Red Beard hadn't quite squelched the problem of crime in Poplar Springs.

He reached for his coat and opened the door, ready to head home for the day. A blustery wind blew a pile of leaves into a circular swirl in the middle of the road. Winter would be here soon, and with it, the chances of apprehending the lawbreakers would become more difficult.

Just as he was about to walk out into the brisk air, Ambrose bolted toward him from somewhere on the boardwalk. He wrapped his arms around John Mark's waist and buried his face in his coat.

"Ambrose?"

The boy sniffled but said nothing.

John Mark placed his hands on Ambrose's arms and gently attempted to pull him away, but Ambrose tightened his hold. John Mark then patted him on the back, concern overtaking him. A thought crept into his mind and he hoped he wasn't right in his assumption. "Ambrose? Can you tell me what's wrong?"

The lad shook his head and began to sob.

"Is it your grandpa?"

"Yes."

Ambrose's young cries resounded over the whipping of the wind. John Mark tugged him close and allowed him to mourn. How often had he worried about this day?

"I—I—I went to tell Grandpa I was hungry, but he..."

John Mark kneeled to Ambrose's height. The boy stepped back and wiped his nose with the back of his hand. "I went to tell Grandpa I was hungry," he repeated.

"Let's go inside the sheriff's office." John Mark led him inside away from the chilly fall weather. "I have a peppermint stick in my desk. Would you like it?"

Ambrose nodded, but his enthusiasm waned, and rightfully so. The boy was now an orphan for the second time. "Grandpa kept sleeping. He wouldn't wake up even when I asked him to. Then I started singing a song, and he didn't even hear me." Ambrose closed his eyes and began to cry again.

Lord, if there is any way...any way possible that Mr. Miller was only sleeping soundly and that he has not passed, please let it be so.

"Why don't we fetch Doc Thorsen and have him check on your grandpa?"

"All right."

Ambrose wore no coat, so John Mark removed his and wrapped it around Ambrose.

Mr. Miller was a devoted caretaker and loved the boy, but money was tight and even when reminded to wear warm clothes, Ambrose likely didn't always obey.

A half hour later, the doctor confirmed John Mark's fears. Mr. Miller had indeed passed.

"I'm sorry," said Doc Thorsen. He closed his leather bag. "I'll talk to the reverend and we'll round up some men to give Mr. Miller a proper burial."

"Where are they taking Grandpa?" Ambrose asked.

John Mark kneeled beside him and opened his arms. Ambrose flew into them and clasped his arms around John Mark's neck. "I want Grandpa," he wailed.

He knew this day would arrive. Knew it would, understandably, break Ambrose's heart.

John Mark grappled for words to say. "Ambrose…"

But instead of listening, Ambrose pushed himself away from John Mark and curled into a ball on the floor, his head buried in his arms. "Now I got nobody."

Hannah finished mending John Mark's socks and prepared to make supper. A knock on the door sounded and Sheriff Winslow stood on the porch.

"Hello, Mrs. Eliason. I was out this way to check on your pa's old place and thought I'd stop by. First of all, I wanted to thank you for your courage in riding to town that day. You may have saved your husband's life and you for certain assisted us with capturing those men." He handed her Ma's Bible. "Seeing as how the ranch has been sold to another family, I thought I'd make sure there weren't any belongings you might want inside. This looked important."

Hannah gripped her most prized possession. She ran her fingers over the leather of the worn cover before holding it to her chest. "Thank you, Sheriff. This was my ma's."

"Figured as much. I can't stay, but I do want you to know that a nice family from Indiana purchased the house. They have several young'uns and they plan to repair the home and the barn."

Her choked words were muffled in her own ears. "This Bible means a lot to me, and I'm grateful a family will live in the house and create happy memories." She never wanted to return to the place of her childhood and so many terrible remembrances.

"As you know, your pa was found guilty as were the mayor and his men." Sheriff Winslow waited, as if to gauge her response.

While Hannah had forgiven him for his mistreatment, there would be no missing Pa.

"Was he sent to the penitentiary?"

"He and a few of the others, yes. Some received harsher punishments."

No, she wouldn't miss pa and all he'd subjected her to over the years, but Hannah's heart broke some at the thought of his future. If only he'd been a different man. If only he'd surrendered his life to Christ and allowed the redemption to begin. But Pa had never had an interest in the things of the Lord. That thought alone caused a profound despondency deep within her she couldn't explain.

"Mrs. Eliason, are you all right?"

"Yes, sir. Thank you."

"John Mark should be home soon. Please let me know if you think of any other items from your pa's that you might want. The horses, wagon, and anything else of value have been sold to pay some of the debt due the bank."

Hannah again pressed the Bible to her. "This was all I wanted. Besides, I have Russell's horse."

"I know I'm not alone in gratitude that the horse went to a deserving owner again. Thank you for riding into town that day. You're a brave woman, Mrs. Eliason." Sheriff Winslow tipped his hat. "Tell John Mark I said 'hello.'"

After the sheriff left, Hannah sat in the chair and carefully turned the pages of the book that offered her so much hope in her darkest days.

If only Ma had been here to witness God's providence in Hannah's life.

John Mark lifted Ambrose onto the horse, then climbed on behind him. Ambrose's shoulders sank into a bowed heap.

Lord, please help Ambrose. Please give him comfort and please let Hannah be agreeable to my plan.

John Mark rode slowly toward home as he battled gusty winds and the bite in the air from the chilly temperatures. He'd never experienced the sorrow of losing a parent or a grandparent. He thankfully had never known the distress and fear that came with realizing your only home was now gone.

Apprehension clouded his thoughts. There were a host of factors to consider when offering to adopt a child. Would he and Hannah, so new in their marriage, be able to work together to provide a suitable home for Ambrose? Would Ambrose be able to adjust to a new life in their care? Would John Mark be able to provide for a family of three? The burdens weighed heavily on his shoulders, threatening to interfere with the hope he'd experienced about the matter just moments before.

Ambrose's head lolled from side to side. Perhaps he would nod off and catch some shut-eye on the way home. John Mark squinted through the dusty swirls of leaves. Before long the house came into view. Hannah was likely making supper. What would be her reaction? He knew her to be gracious and kind-hearted. But with the losses she'd suffered, would she be able to open her heart to an orphan?

The wind rustled through the trees and John Mark thought he saw a snowflake. Ambrose shivered, even with John Mark's far-too-large coat wrapped around him. The first thing John Mark would do when the mercantile opened tomorrow morning was to purchase Ambrose a new coat. The tattered one he owned was no match for Wyoming winters.

John Mark brought his horse to a halt just in front of the porch. "Ambrose? We're home."

The moment he uttered the words, John Mark thought again about the boy's future. Would this soon be his home? Would another family seek to adopt him? The thought disheartened him, especially in light of his own fondness for the youngster and Hannah's close bond with him.

"Where's Grandpa?" Ambrose asked, his voice groggy from his brief nap.

John Mark lifted him from the horse and tethered it temporarily to the porch post until he could take it to the barn. "Let's go see what Miss Hannah has made us for supper." Ambrose took his outstretched hand and together they battled the wind as they traversed up the steps.

"I brought a guest home for supper," John Mark announced when they'd entered the house.

Hannah pivoted from her place at the stove. "Ambrose! I'm so glad you're here. We're having meatloaf tonight. Why don't you wash up and you can help me set the table."

John Mark embraced Hannah in a hug.

"I missed you today," she said. Several hairs had escaped her braid and framed her face, adding to her beauty.

John Mark leaned toward her and planted a kiss on her waiting lips. "I missed you too." He lowered his voice to a whisper. "There's something I need to tell you about Ambrose."

He saw her attention focus on Ambrose, who lethargically washed his hands and face. "Yes?"

"His grandpa passed."

"Oh!" Hannah covered her mouth with a hand.

They weren't able to discuss the matter further because Ambrose plodded their way. "Hi, Miss Hannah."

She stooped and opened her arms to him. Ambrose ran toward her and nestled his face in her shoulder. "My grandpa died."

"Oh, Ambrose. I'm so sorry." She drew him close and comforted him as if it were the most natural thing to do.

John Mark's chest constricted with emotion. Hannah may never have had a ma herself, but she needn't worry about being a fine one to Ambrose. They had a connection between them, a bond cemented further by the losses they'd both suffered in their lives.

Hannah allowed Ambrose to cry as her heart broke in tandem with his. She knew the pain of losing someone you loved, and although she'd never met her ma, the sorrow due to the void in her life was agonizing.

"I loved him so much." Ambrose's body trembled. "He's not coming back is he, Miss Hannah?" He pulled away and searched her face.

"He's not, but I know he loved you. You brought him so much joy."

Ambrose sniffled as the tears flooded his eyes. "He's in Heaven with Jesus, but I don't know why he can't be here with me." He rested his head on her shoulder again and Hannah prayed for the words to console him.

After several minutes, Ambrose, clearly exhausted from the difficult ordeal, hunched his shoulders and hung his head. "Will you be angry with me if I'm not hungry?"

"Not at all. We can save yours for tomorrow if you'd like."

True to his words, Ambrose ate a meager amount for supper and fell asleep on his bedroll. John Mark took Hannah's hands in his. "Ambrose is an orphan now," he said in a hushed tone. "I've been thinking...what if we adopted him?"

There was no hesitation on Hannah's part as his words mirrored her thoughts. "I'd like that. He needs a home and we already love him."

"That we do." He took a step toward her and wrapped her in his arms. His lips found hers and melted into a tender kiss. John Mark slowly pulled away and his eyes searched hers. "I was hoping you would say 'yes'."

A lingering doubt formed in Hannah's thoughts. "But what if—I'm not sure how to be a ma because I never had one." Could Hannah be the type of mother Lydie was? Or Ina's ma?

"While my own pa set a godly example, I've never before been a pa either, but with the Lord's help, I know we can be the parents Ambrose needs. Besides, Hannah, I've watched you with him. You'll be a fine ma."

John Mark's belief in her made all the difference.

As he had every morning since he'd come to stay with them several weeks ago, Ambrose awoke early. After John Mark blessed the food, Ambrose devoured three pancakes before Hannah had finished her one. "I was so hungry I could have eaten a horse," he declared, barely allowing himself time to chew and swallow his food before taking another bite. "And syrup is my favorite."

"Ambrose," said John Mark, "we'd like to ask you something." He reached over and squeezed Hannah's hand. Her heart thrummed in her chest. They'd decided a week ago that today would be the day, and she'd barely been able to sleep last night thinking about Ambrose's adoption. John Mark suggested they finish the loft as a room for Ambrose, and Hannah had sold the bracelet from Claudelle to cover the expenses. "Miss Hannah and I want to know what you would think about us becoming your ma and pa."

Ambrose's fork stayed suspended in the air. He hurriedly finished the bite he was chewing. "You and Miss Hannah?"

"What would you think of that?"

"I prolly would like it." He turned toward Hannah. "Can we make cookies?"

"Yes, we can."

Ambrose's eyes lit with enthusiasm. "And, Deputy Eliason, can we go fishin'?"

"We sure can, Ambrose."

"And what about Grumbles? Can he live here too?"

Hannah giggled. "Yes, he may, and I think he'll get along quite well with Clarence."

"Oh, he will. He's a friendly sort. And, Miss Hannah, can I call you, 'ma'?"

She choked back the emotion that bubbled to the surface. "Yes, Ambrose, I would like that."

"All right." Ambrose scratched his head. "Do I call you 'Deputy Pa'?"

The three of them laughed and Hannah thanked the Lord for answering another dream of her heart.

That of someday being a mother.

Epilogue

Two Months Later

JOHN MARK ASSISTED HANNAH to the pond, her feet threatening to slip out from beneath her due to the ice skates.

"I'm not sure about this, John Mark," she said.

"I'll be beside you the entire time."

Hannah clutched his arm and cautiously proceeded onto the ice. While the idea of skating seemed so appealing while on dry land, the thought of trying something new gave her pause.

Just ahead of them, Ambrose persevered on his own skates, falling, then standing, then falling again, all the while giggling, his joy contagious. He wore his new brown coat, and with the cowboy hat Lydie and Reverend Solomon had given him, he resembled a miniature John Mark.

"What do you think?" John Mark asked. "Shall we make a tradition of this every year the week before Christmas?"

How could she refuse the glint in his handsome eyes? "Perhaps," she teased. "But next year we may have to ask Ina and Pritchard for some assistance."

"Assistance? Are they adept at ice skating?"

Hannah laughed and steadied herself against John Mark. "I'm not sure they're adept at ice skating, but we may need them to practice caring for children. Just in case they may someday decide to become parents after they marry next spring."

"Pritchard—or shall we say *Mayor Pritchard*—was set on winning Ina's heart and her pa's blessing. I'd say he's won both."

Hannah thought of the woman who had become her dear friend. "I don't think winning Ina's heart was ever a concern."

"No, likely not." John Mark continued to guide her across the ice. "You're doing remarkably well. Are you sure you haven't ice skated before?"

"Not a chance. Although I think once I become accustomed to it, it will become a delightful pastime."

"Then we will want to visit the pond often, not just for our soon-to-be-annual, week-before-Christmas ice skating tradition. But I doubt we'll need Ina and Pritchard's help with Ambrose. He's doing pretty well out here and likely wouldn't want to miss out."

"Yes, but next year the baby will be too little to be joining us."

"The baby?"

Hannah patted her stomach gently as the joy bubbled within her. "Yes, *our* baby. He or she will be far too young for the likes of ice skating."

They stopped skating and John Mark faced her. "Hannah, really?"

"Yes. Doc Thorsen confirmed it yesterday. I was just waiting until the perfect time to tell you you're about to be a pa again."

In a quick movement, John Mark's arms encircled her and he whispered into her hair, "I love you, Hannah Eliason." He kissed the tip of her nose before his lips slowly descended, meeting hers.

As she pondered all the hopes and dreams she'd share with her husband, she thanked the Lord for answered prayers.

AUTHOR'S NOTE

As I penned the last words of this book, I found myself already missing the characters in *Dreams of the Heart*. Creating multi-dimensional characters is exciting for a writer, even when those characters sometimes take on minds of their own, as some of the characters in this book did from time to time.

As was the case with the other two books in this series, I had some tearful moments while penning certain scenes. Would Hannah ever escape from her pa? Would she get her ma's Bible back? Would she and John Mark fall in love? Would Ambrose be all right after the loss of his beloved grandpa? Would Pritchard's dream of courting Ina become a reality?

Hannah had a strong faith in God. While she, for the most part, was isolated and lived in a town with limited church availability, Hannah learned about her Savior in a variety of ways. Most importantly, she read her ma's Bible frequently. She also learned about God

331

in school where reading the Bible was a regular part of the curriculum. Possibly to a lesser degree, she learned about the Lord from her short time with Ramona. While writing this book, I was reminded that nothing and no one can stop the Lord's plans and that He will always find a way to reach those whom He has determined are His from before the beginning of time.

Dreams of the Heart tackled some serious topics. Hannah suffered mental, emotional, and physical abuse at the hands of her father. Unfortunately, abuse was and is not a rare occurrence. Many of the townsfolk turned a blind eye to her plight, and we unfortunately at times see that same apathy today.

Because of the more serious topics, I also wanted to be sure I included plentiful humor via some lighthearted scenes with John Mark and Hannah, appearances by Pritchard and Ina, Frank, Hank, Ambrose, and some interaction between John Mark and his family. Speaking of Ambrose, I've received reader inquiries asking if he and Silas could someday have their own stories. Rest assured, I've added them to my list along with a potential story for Sadie. A short story starring Frederick is currently in the works and will be made available exclusively to newsletter subscribers.

The inspiration for John Mark to rescue the baby bird stems from my own childhood. My sister, cousin, and I would regularly rescue baby robins who fell from their nests. We set up a cardboard box in our laundry room and tended to the birds, even feeding them with a dropper.

One summer our family camped at a campground where the host had a pet pig. She walked him on a leash; hence the inspiration for Grumbles. He was quite well-behaved, and I wondered...what if Little Ambrose had such a pet?

Some highlights during the writing of this book:

- Many of us have heard of famous Old West lawmen such as the Earp brothers (Kansas, Texas, and Arizona), Doc Holliday (Arizona), and Pat Garrett (New Mexico). In my research, I also learned of a Wyoming Territorial sheriff named Christopher Castle who, with his deputies, noted the amount of money an outlaw had in his pocket when arrested. Later, when a fine was assessed, it was that exact amount.

- A fun fact: some of the duties for Old West sheriffs included keeping the peace, collecting taxes, issuing liquor licenses, keeping the streets clear of dead animals, and cleaning up manure. While John Mark did do these other tasks assigned to deputies and sheriffs, for the sake of the story, I gave him the main jobs of doing "rounds," settling disputes, and arresting outlaws.

- Russell's death was inspired by Nate Champion, who was killed during the Johnson County Cattle War in 1892. Russell experienced a similar fate as the real-life Mr. Champion who, after a lengthy shootout, was forced from his home due to fire. When he escaped the burning home, he was shot and killed.

- John Mark carries a Colt Peacemaker revolver. While writing the book, I accidentally typed in "Colt Pacemaker." Glad I caught it, although I'm sure it would have given my editors a laugh.

- Another funny error was when Hannah wonders about whether or not John Mark often frequents the "salon." I'm always grateful when these errors are caught before the book goes to publication!

- John Mark's favorite cookie, the sugar cookie, is believed to have its origins in Nazareth, Pennsylvania, and was named the "Nazareth cookie." Enjoy the following recipe for the cookies mentioned in the book.

Lydie's Famous Sugar Cookies
(AS DEVOURED BY JOHN MARK)

COMBINE THE FOLLOWING:

1/2 C. BUTTER

1 C. SUGAR

1 EGG

1/4 C. MILK

1/2 TSP. VANILLA

2 TSP. BAKING POWDER

2 C. FLOUR

ROLL OUT ON FLOURED COUNTER WITH
ROLLING PIN AND USE COOKIE CUTTERS.

BAKE AT 325 FOR 8-10 MINUTES.

Acknowledgments

To my family. I can never thank you enough for your encouragement, support, and patience as I put words to paper. I'm so grateful for you. Thank you for your patient endurance in living with an author who spends her time predominately in the 1800s (and sometimes forgets to come back to the present).

To my husband. Thank you for helping me brainstorm the shootout scene and offering your expertise on guns.

To my oldest daughter. Thank you for brainstorming with me and for your assistance with the fight scene. I'm so proud of you for all you have accomplished in your own writing endeavors.

To my youngest daughter for your enthusiasm. You make my day when you're reading one of my books and I hear your sweet laugh during the funny parts.

To my mom. You are such an inspiration to me and I thank the Lord that out of all the women who could have been my mom, He chose you.

To my Penny's Peeps Street Team. Thank you for spreading the word about my books. I appreciate your encouragement and support!

To my readers. May God bless and guide you as you grow in your walk with Him.

And, most importantly, thank you to my Lord and Savior, Jesus Christ. It is my deepest desire to glorify You with my writing and help bring others to a knowledge of Your saving grace.

Let the words of my mouth and the meditation of my heart be acceptable in your sight, O Lord, my rock and my redeemer. ~ Psalm 19:14

If you enjoyed this glimpse into the lives of Hannah and John Mark, please consider leaving a review on your social media, Amazon, Goodreads, Barnes and Noble, or BookBub. Reviews are critical to authors, and those stars you give us are such an encouragement.

Coming soon exclusively for newsletter subscribers—the free short story starring Frederick Morton
from *Love's New Beginnings* in the Wyoming Sunrise Series. You can sign up now and I'll let you know when it's
available. Stay tuned!

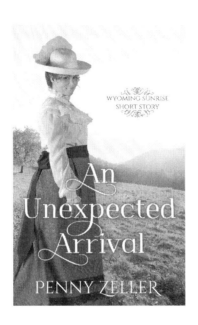

READ A SNEAK PEEK FROM

When Love Comes

WYOMING SUNRISE
BOOK 3

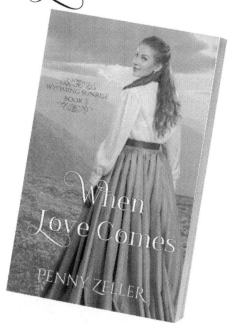

A woman with a broken heart.

A man struggling with the loss of his brother and the subsequent care of his young niece.

And two silly aunts who discover it's never too late for true love.

Coming December 2023

When Love Comes

Sneak Peek

MA WAS RIGHT. SOME time away from Willow Falls would be just the antidote to her broken heart. "After all," Ma surmised, "how can anyone remain melancholy when spending time with the aunts? Just be sure not to eat Aunt Myrtle's baking and you'll be just fine."

Charlotte didn't plan on eating any of Aunt Myrtle's baking as she knew full well her great-aunt's reputation when it came to such matters, but she did wonder if Ma was accurate about the melancholy part.

The couple across the aisle, a handsome duo around Charlotte's age of twenty-two, gazed tenderly into each other's eyes. Charlotte overheard the woman telling another passenger that she and the gentleman were on their honeymoon. Tears welled in Charlotte's eyes and she blinked them back.

Unannounced envy crept in at the most inopportune times. Lest they discover her staring yet again, Charlotte tore her eyes away from the smitten couple and averted her gaze to the book in her lap, rereading the same paragraph for the sixth time. She'd never struggled with covetousness until a despicable man named Cyrus Keller entered her life and exited it, leaving pain and sorrow in his wake.

Her brother, John Mark, would tell her she was dramatic for regaling such thoughts, but the ache still lingered from what she'd eagerly anticipated would be a godly and loving marriage.

Not only had she been foolish to believe Cyrus's affections for her, but she'd also been daft in ignoring the warnings of those closest to her.

Hadn't she always desired to be a wife and mother? To follow in the steps of her own ma, a loving, kind, and giving soul who loved her family only second to the Lord?

A marriage to Cyrus would have filled that longing in her heart. Her former beau, just like a hero in a book, was dapper and charming. However, he lacked the most important characteristics—godliness and integrity.

Now slightly older and hopefully wiser, Charlotte Eliason would never allow herself to fall in love again. If she was to be a spinster, so be it. Not everyone could have a happily ever after reminiscent of the characters in one of her favorite dime store novels.

Ma mentioned that once upon a time Aunt Fern's heart had been broken by a scoundrel named Mr. Wilkins. If Aunt Fern could survive a broken heart, then so could Charlotte. And if it was God's plan for her to be a spinster, then she'd accept her fate, albeit begrudgingly.

Being a spinster wasn't the worst thing in the world, was it? She swallowed the lump in her throat and instead attempted to focus on the adventure that lie ahead.

Charlotte adjusted her posture, prayed for the Lord to set her focus on anything but her fragmented dreams, and determined that very moment that she would set her sights on caring for and assisting Aunt Myrtle and Aunt Fern.

At least the train ride portion was a much smoother and more efficient ride than the first part of her journey by stagecoach had been. Several areas of Wyoming still lacked travel by railway and Willow Falls was one of the towns still without a train depot. Pa had worried that he should perhaps take Charlotte over the mountain to Prune Creek, but Charlotte had asked that she might do this on her own. Ma mentioned something to Pa about her being much like the aunts in that regard, and perhaps, just like the stories she'd heard about them arriving from Minnesota so many years ago for a fresh start, Charlotte would experience a fresh start as well.

Excitement bounded through her as the train entered the Prune Creek depot. Trees on either side of the tracks gave way to a clearing that marked the town that obviously had grown since Charlotte's last visit. She'd only been to Prune Creek twice in her life and both times were years ago with Ma and Pa.

The train slowly came to a stop, its brakes screeching. Charlotte's heart pounded in her chest and she could barely wait a moment longer upon the hard bench seat as the train attempted to stop. She reached for her carpetbag and perused the crowd of people awaiting the passengers. Were Aunt Myrtle and Aunt Fern among them?

Charlotte exited the train, searching the swath of people for her aunts and waiting for the porter to unload the luggage.

Finally, she spied Ma's worn brown trunk and clasped the handle. "Charlotte! Oh, Charlotte!" Two jubilant voices garnered her attention. Aunt Myrtle and Aunt Fern waved at her from the north end of the boardwalk. Charlotte bustled her way through the crowds and toward the aunts.

My, but if they hadn't begun to have a strong resemblance in their older years! Both had completely gray hair, and while Aunt Fern wore spectacles, her round face and pert nose matched that of her sister.

"Best not ever say they resemble each other," Ma told her before she embarked on this trip. *"Even if they do. For you might find yourself sleeping in the chicken coop for such a comment."* Ma and Charlotte had laughed over that, even as Ma insisted it would be detrimental to suggest their likeness.

"Look at you! You've grown into such a lovely young lady," Aunt Myrtle wrapped her arms around Charlotte. "We're so glad you're here."

Aunt Fern gave her a hug next. "Yes, we are. It's been too long since an Eliason was here in Prune Creek. The buggy is thisaway. It's a slight bit too far for us to walk to the Peabody house these days."

"Too far for you, maybe," chided Aunt Myrtle. She fingered her decorative hat. "What do you think about my hat, Charlotte? Mrs. Peabody was about to discard it when I salvaged it."

Since she was taller than Aunt Myrtle, Charlotte could see the top of the hat and the fake bird immersed in a portable flower garden. "It's lovely."

"Well, it is not," declared Aunt Fern. "Who wears a hat with a bird on it?"

Aunt Myrtle lifted her chin, nearly causing the hat to topple from her head. "Women of high society who take a fancy to the latest and most elegant fashions."

"But you're neither."

"Pshaw. Hush, Fern."

They walked down the boardwalk on the way to the buggy. As they passed the barber shop, a balding man with the thickest spectacles Charlotte had ever seen perched in the entryway. "Well, hello, Fern. Would you like a haircut?"

"You know full and well, Mr. Gorman, that I do not need a haircut." Aunt Fern fluffed her gray curls and tossed him a disgusted look. "That vexing man asks me if I would like a haircut every time I walk by the barber shop. Far be it from me to allow someone with magnifying glasses for spectacles to see well enough to fashion my coiffure."

They loaded into the buggy, Charlotte sandwiched between the aunts. The rode along fine until Aunt Myrtle's hat blew off in a gusty breeze. Aunt Myrtle steered the buggy to the side of the road and Charlotte retrieved it.

"Do assist me with this," Aunt Myrtle requested of her sister.

Aunt Fern set it nicely on Aunt Myrtle's head—backwards. She cast a warning glance Charlotte's way and shook her head, finger to mouth to say nothing. Charlotte did her best not to smirk. The hat looked even more hideous backwards as they rode down the street.

"Dear me, there's Clifford." Aunt Myrtle slowed the buggy next to a tall, thin older man carrying a stack of papers. "Hello, Clifford." Was it Charlotte's imagination or did Aunt Myrtle blush when she spoke?

"Well, hello, Myrtle. What brings you out and about on this lovely summer day?"

"Our niece is visiting from Willow Falls. I present to you Miss Charlotte Eliason."

Clifford removed his hat. "Pleasure to meet you." He stared for a few moments up at Aunt Myrtle. "I do declare, Myrtle, that is the most interesting hat I've ever seen."

"Do you like it?"

"Well..." Clifford tilted his head to one side. "Do lean this way, Myrtle."

Aunt Myrtle leaned carefully to the left so as not to tumble from the buggy. Clifford reached up, removed the hat and set it on her head the correct way. "There, now it looks exquisite on you."

"Oh!" Aunt Myrtle's cheeks flamed with red the color of raspberries.

"I best be on my way as I'm headed to the courthouse." Clifford tipped his hat and continued down the street.

Aunt Myrtle glowered at Aunt Fern. "You placed the hat on my head backwards. Such a bothersome sister you are at times."

"I do believe you've set your cap for Clifford."

"Pshaw." But Aunt Myrtle didn't deny it.

Aunt Fern shook her head. "I've always found Clifford to be a kindly gentleman. It's unfortunate he'll soon meet his demise."

Aunt Myrtle's eyes widened. "Whatever do you mean?"

"Once you bake him some huckleberry pie, it will be the end of him."

Charlotte giggled at Aunt Fern's exaggeration. She'd heard the story numerous times from Ma about the huckleberry pie during the aunts' visit to Willow Falls.

"Don't believe a word she says about my baking," said Aunt Myrtle. "You don't win ribbons at the fair for inferior baking skills."

They continued down the main street. "Oh, look, there's the blacksmith shop," said Aunt Fern, pointing to the building on the right.

"The new smithy there is such an extraordinary and upright young man. He's been here all of a few weeks, yet when the wheel of the buggy broke last week, he came to our rescue. Say, Fern, we still haven't invited him for supper like we promised."

The aunts passed a knowing glance and a niggle of suspicion arose in Charlotte. "Are you two planning something?" The aunts were obviously not adept at disguising their schemes. And while the smithy may be an extraordinary and upright man, Charlotte was most certainly not interested in matchmaking ploys. Not after Cyrus.

"Yes."

"No."

"Well, we are planning something," said Aunt Fern. "Planning to have that nice young man over for supper.

He has no family here, poor dear. He lives at the boarding house over on Second Street."

Aunt Myrtle, who Ma warned rarely agreed with her sister on anything—and vice versa—added, "I'm a planner, but Aunt Fern, not so much. She likes to wait until the very last minute. A procrastinator is among us."

They continued to argue all the while traveling the short distance to the Peabody home they'd inherited after the passing of their charges.

And as she watched the passing scenery of her temporary home, Charlotte smiled to herself. Yes, Ma was right. Time with her two feisty aunts would heal her melancholy. And when they invited the smithy to the house, Charlotte would firmly, but kindly, remind them she was of no mindset to fall in love again.

ABOUT THE AUTHOR

Penny Zeller is known for her heartfelt stories of faith and her passion to impact lives for Christ through fiction. While she has had a love for writing since childhood, she began her adult writing career penning articles for national and regional publications on a wide variety of topics. Today, Penny is the author of over a dozen books. She is also a homeschool mom and a fitness instructor.

When Penny is not dreaming up new characters, she enjoys spending time with her husband and two daughters, camping, hiking, canoeing, reading, running, cycling, gardening, and playing volleyball.

She is represented by Tamela Hancock Murray of the Steve Laube Agency and loves to hear from her readers at her website www.pennyzeller.com and her blog, *random thoughts from a day in the life of a wife, mom, and author*, at www.pennyzeller.wordpress.com.

Some memories are best forgotten...

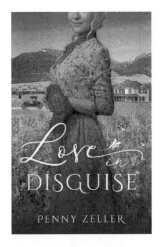

*Who knew concealing one's true identity
could be so disastrous?*

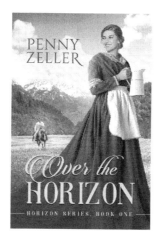

A most unusual proposal...

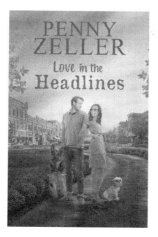

Can paper and paw prints draw
these two nemeses together?

354

Made in the USA
Middletown, DE
28 March 2023

26977193R00217